# THE ABSENT MAN

## A BERMUDA JONES CASEFILE

ROBERT ENRIGHT

*For Sophie,*
*Everything else is.*

# ONE

THE KEYS JINGLED PLAYFULLY in her hands as she tried to navigate them into the front door. Silently cursing herself, Nicole Miller took a few deep breaths before gently slotting the key between the jagged gap. A brisk chill danced across the wind; the cold November was beginning to settle over the city of Glasgow. She stopped before turning it, leaving the lock in place as she contemplated her decision one more time.

It had been a long time since she had invited a man 'up for coffee'. At thirty-one years old, she mentally belittled herself for having nerves when it came to sex.

It was just sex, right?

Her marriage to Duncan had ended over a year before and it had been at least a year prior to that since the last time she had felt the touch of a man.

Had felt wanted.

Behind her was a man almost too good to be true. He had been charming and attentive, a good listener encased in a muscular shell, decorated with dimples, and almost-jet-black eyes.

Her fingers flickered, the decision almost made when

she realised she didn't know much about him. His name was Kevin Parker, and he worked in a bank. That was it. The lack of knowledge began to worry her, and she felt her grip tightening, the urge to call it a night with a quick kiss on the cheek and a rushed goodbye growing in stature.

*No, Nic!* she told herself. *It's time to get back on the horse.*

She sighed, turning the key, and the door to the modest flat opened, the streetlamp sending a warm glow slithering across the wooden floor. She dropped her keys into the bowl that sat neatly on the quaint table that took shelter under a large mirror, the flick of the light switch illuminating the minimalistic ground floor flat.

'This is it,' she offered warmly, slowly taking off her jacket to reveal the dark dress that clung to her slightly chubby physique. She had hated it the moment her best friend, Leanne, had offered it to her, knowing full well she was a size too big.

'Black is slimming,' Leanne had said. Catching a glimpse of herself in the mirror, Nicole decided she was going to stuff the dress down her best friend's throat upon return.

Kevin slowly followed her in, his steps teetering on hesitant as he moved with an eloquence that Nicole found almost intimidating. He had looked out of place at the bar, his embarrassment at attending a speed-dating event matching her own.

It was what had drawn her to him: the fact that he didn't look comfortable in his own skin. His visit to her table was unmemorable, to the point that she couldn't recall how they had spent their five minutes of conversation. When he offered to buy her a drink at the bar, she apologised for not remembering his name.

It was Kevin.

Wasn't it?

'It's not much,' she said, walking to the small cupboard

in the hallway, relieving her feet from the torturous heels she had promised to destroy once alone. 'But I think it's homey enough.'

She entered the front room and turned to her guest, a warm smile across her pretty face, her auburn hair tied back under a flowery clip. He turned, his chiselled face slowly exposing one of his own. She stopped, taking in what she could only describe as his 'traditional' features. He had short, brown hair, neatly brushed into a side parting. His eyebrows were thin and dark and his face was borderline perfect, sat atop a strong body that was wrapped up in a suit which was a tad on the baggy side.

He wouldn't have looked out of place when Wall Street crashed nearly a hundred years ago.

'Coffee?' she remembered, taking his nod as a sign to go and prepare a cafetière, her nerves causing her to tremble as she made her way into the immaculate kitchen. It had been so long, and the thought of this handsome stranger undressing her was sending her into a slight panic.

She flicked the kettle on and dropped the coffee granules into the glass container, carefully selecting what her mother called 'the posh coffee'.

She wanted to impress.

As the water bubbled away and a small cloud of steam began to waft throughout the room, she stared at the metallic door of the fridge. It was littered with crayon drawings, the four-year-olds she taught for a living trying to capture her in their crudely drawn pictures. She loved her job; the young kids at the local school had taken a shine to her.

As had the new year six teacher, however, she decided she needed to, as Leanne so eloquently put it, 'get back on the horse' before she looked for anything more substantial.

The water turned a thick brown as it collided with the coffee beans, the thick liquid rising up the glass jug as if it were being timed. She had no real plan other than to hold his attention for the duration of the drink, and then hopefully he would make the move.

Did she want him to?

Clearing her mind, she marched back into the front room, a smile on her face and a tray of piping-hot coffee in her hands. As she entered, Kevin turned from the mantelpiece that ran along the top of the fireplace with a look of intrigue as he held a photo.

'Is this your family?' His words were calm, floating softly through the tension. In his hand, a photo of Nicole framed by two older, obviously proud parents.

'Aye.' Her Scottish accent forced itself to the surface, causing her to chuckle with embarrassment.

Kevin didn't notice, his dark eyes transfixed on the photo.

'My mum and dad are very nice.'

He nodded. Silent. She placed the tray down and looked up at him hopefully, disappointed that his gaze hadn't wandered in her direction. As he stood staring, a creeping unease slowly began to clutch at Nicole while she poured a coffee.

'Do you have any family?' she asked, desperate to break the silence and to try to steer the evening back on course.

'Not anymore.' His words were heavy as he gently replaced the photo. 'Not for a long time.'

He slowly walked to the sofa and sat down next to her, his movements again astounding her with how rigid he was. She offered him a mug which he accepted with a fake smile, the sadness of his previous statement hanging in the air like a morning fog.

The only sound for the next few minutes was the ticking of the clock above the fireplace and the wind clattering against the window. They sat, exchanging the odd glance that was met with a smile by Nicole. Kevin seemed nervous, unable to maintain eye contact.

He had seemed so charming at the bar, Nicole thought, chalking it up to nerves. While she was growing in confidence for the night to end romantically, she assumed he needed to be guided. That his bravado in the bar was simply an act.

Was he really charming at the bar? She tried to recall. Was she just desperate to remove the feeling of failure that she had pinned to herself, ever since she caught Duncan and his secretary in their old bed?

'You seem distracted,' he stated, very forthright. He placed the cup down. 'I should go.'

'No, wait.' Nicole shot to her feet as quickly as he did, pacing quickly to the front door of her flat to head him off. 'What is wrong?'

He didn't answer, pulling his blazer over his pale yellow shirt, his face stern.

'I need to leave.' He reached for the handle. 'I'm afraid if I stay, you will only get hurt.'

She caught his hand in her own, guiding it and him away from the door, her eyes finally grabbing the attention of his and the magnificent darkness they held.

'Why? Is there someone else?' she muttered feebly, scorning herself for feeling pathetic.

'There is.' His words were straight to the point. 'She was taken from me many years ago. They said I would find her again. I just needed to search for her.'

She gently squeezed his hands as she smiled. 'I'm not afraid of being hurt, and I'm never going to make you compare me to the one you lost.' She gently brushed the back of his hand against her soft, red cheek. 'But maybe, maybe I can help you find something?'

He stared at her, his classically handsome face emotionless. She leaned in, his scent almost as intoxicating as his pupilless eyes. Her hand slid around his waist, reaching for the chain that swung from the door. She latched it, the message very clear. She looked up at him.

'Give me a moment.'

She leant up, her lips pressed against his as she pushed against him. His hands slowly grazed her shapely hips, and she felt her heart start to race.

This was actually going to happen.

She freed herself, quickly walking towards the door to the bedroom, purposely ensuring she wiggled slightly as she walked. It needed to happen now before she changed her mind. Nicole entered and quickly slid out of the tight dress, her body thanking her for freeing it from confinement. Reaching to her hair, she ruffled it up, pulling the rose-covered clip from it and hoping for a more alluring look. Quickly spraying herself with perfume, she applauded herself for having the confidence in wearing her new lacy underwear.

She imagined his strong, powerful arms wrapped around her.

The smell of his body.

The potential to feel wanted again.

She carefully lowered herself onto the bed, adjusting slightly to a more alluring position.

This was it.

It was time to get back on the horse.

'Come in,' she called, oblivious to what truly waited for her on the other side of the door.

---

THE URGE TO leave had been terrific.

As his eyes watched her walk towards the bedroom, he ignored her attempts to allure him with her stride. As she disappeared behind the bedroom door, he slowly bowed his head, gently shaking it.

He would never see her the same again.

That look of innocence.

His neck arched to the side, his eyes locking onto the chain of the door. He could spare her feelings, silently unlatching it and walking away, and the only pain she would feel would be rejection.

Nothing more.

Not like the others.

Not like all the others.

With a judder that betrayed his humanity, Kevin Parker slowly reached a hand towards the chain, the allure of the brisk night air that would greet him growing. He wanted his skin to bathe in the glow of the streetlights.

This one would be spared.

His fingers cut through the air, ready to clasp it, when Nicole's voice broke his trail of thought.

'Come in,' she called.

He froze on the spot.

The words cut through his body, slicing every muscle until it felt like he would collapse. Unfortunately for Nicole, they would only serve as a reminder for his true existence. His real reason for being.

His need to see 'her' again.

The fingers retracted from the door, the idea of a moonlight walk and Nicole's survival slowly collapsing to nothing. His eyes closed as he took a deep breath, turning on his heel, and walking blind towards the door to her bedroom. A mere inch or so from the wooden frame, he stopped, his eyes bursting into life.

The black pupils began to break as if they were leaking into the whites of his eyes and slowly filling them.

Within seconds, both of his eyeballs were entirely jet-black.

He was Kevin Parker no more.

He was the one they had lied to. Had taken everything from. He was not part of their world anymore and could no longer understand their need to interfere.

To take her from him.

On the other side of the door, the young woman lay on the bed, trembling slightly with a cocktail of nerves and anticipation. The thin wooden panel that separated them kept her safe for a few more moments. That was all he would allow.

In one fluid motion, the sole of his foot clattered into the door, flinging it open with a large crack, the hinges powerless to retain order. As the door collided with the wall, he stepped in, confronting the terrified, half-naked woman before him. All of her trust and attraction had vanished instantly as the fear sat her upright.

She opened her mouth to scream.

His hand wrapped around her throat, catching the sound before it could escape. With his fingers tightening, he lifted her clean off the floor, her body swinging like a pendulum in a terrified grandfather clock.

She drew his gaze, and the colour drained from her face. His eyes were jet-black, as if staring into a dark void. The corners of his mouth twisted into a snarl, the gentleman replaced by a feral beast that belonged elsewhere.

Not of this world.

Kevin tilted his head as he stared at her, examining the human before him. Tears raced down her cheeks, each one leaving a small, dark trail of cheap mascara. His gaze fell, his eyes clasping onto her chest, her breasts bulging over a very helpful lace bra.

She began to cough and splutter, trying her best to force words from her mouth. 'Please ... let ... me ... go,' she begged. Urine began trickling down the inside of her leg and gently rapping into a fearful puddle below. Slowly, he began to lower her, drawing her terrified face towards him.

'I must find her.' His words were whispered, tinged in sadness.

'Who?' she mustered, the air struggling through the grip of his powerful fingers. Her eyes begged for her release.

He looked away, his slick, side-parted hair shimmering in the lamplight.

'I am sorry.'

Before she knew what was happening, Nicole found herself soaring towards her mattress, the springs absorbing the impact. His powerful arm still held her down, his fingers pressing her windpipe like a tube of toothpaste. He rose his other hand above her chest as he kneeled beside her.

She stared at him in fear, accepting her fate.

His black eyes conveyed little sympathy.

She felt the searing pain in her chest only briefly, saw a slight splash of blood before everything went black and she left the world.

She would never return.

# TWO

'SHIT! SHIT! SHIT!'

With his breathing struggling to keep up with his feet as he raced to his car, Franklin 'Bermuda' Jones burst through the doors to the third floor of the London car park. Dimly lit with the pitiful glow of the halogen lights, his car seemed further than he remembered.

He needed to get in and get the hell out of there.

As he raced across the concrete, he took a few moments to contemplate how he was spending his Saturday night. While most thirty-four-year-old men were either out drinking or cuddled up with the family for film night, he was racing away from a creature our world could never comprehend.

It was only because of his damned curse that he could see it.

That he could see the Otherside.

Born with a genetic condition known as 'the Knack', Bermuda was gifted the sight of the world that encased our own. Invisible to the naked eye, the inhabitants of the Otherside, known as Others, walked freely throughout his life, yet he was the only one who could see them meandering through the alleyways and dark corners of London.

The only one who watched their world encompass ours.

The only one who knew the truth.

Soon the scepticism had given way to concern, and he had lost everything. His wife had left him, watching with flowing tears as they took him to his padded cell. Certified as insane, it's difficult to tell the world you're not crazy when they have concluded you must be. A crazy person claiming sanity is moot – like an obese person saying they hardly eat a thing.

That was a long time ago. Locked away in that padded cell, cursing the world for their mistake. Losing the respect and love of a woman he would die for and destroying the bond with his beloved daughter.

His Chloe.

As he raced to his car, he thought about her blond hair dancing in the wind, the toothless grin on her six-year-old face as he pushed her on the swing. The slow rebuild of their relationship in the secrecy of carefully planned meetings. Away from the eyes that watched from the shadows.

The eyes of the Otherside.

Working for the Behind the Curtain Organisation (BTCO), the authority that managed the truce between our world and theirs, certainly came with the animosity you would expect. Being the only agent with the ability to physically interact with them painted one hell of a target on your back.

No matter how many cases he solved, how many times he restored the peace, Bermuda knew that the Otherside would come for him. Rich in brutality, it was an existence that had little time for forgiveness or change. The truce, the allowance of refuge for the 'Others' in our world, was based on advances in science and medicine that could change humanity.

They saved our species.

We let theirs live outside the human eye.

Now, as he raced to his car, knowing what was about to burst through the doors behind him, he wondered if burning the truce and locking the goddamn gateway was an option.

'Get in the bloody car!'

Bermuda's voice was rife with panic as he approached the driver's door to his black Honda Civic, the dirt forming erratic patterns across the unclean bonnet. His words were meant for the figure who stood before him. The meek offering of light from the ceiling bounced off the immaculate breast plate of his armour. The dark gold that protected him ended at his broad shoulders, which sprung two powerful, muscular arms, the dark skin exposed.

He stood motionless; fear was a trait that had left him long ago.

His face, a mask of calm, housed the two grey eyes which burnt a pathway to the door with a fierce concentration.

Strapped to his back was the blade that had protected our world for years and had saved Bermuda's life on more occasions than he cared to remember.

Around his wrist, the Retriever – a weapon forged in the other world, which sent many back from whence they came.

Bermuda called to him once more, terror gripping each word as they leapt from his mouth, his handsome face gripped with fear. 'Argyle!'

His partner didn't move.

'Let's get the fuck out of here.'

The floor rumbled as if the car park was experiencing its very own earthquake. Bermuda had one foot in the car, his head peeking over the roof to his partner, who had been raised as a soldier on the Otherside. Exiled in disgrace for reasons Bermuda had never asked, Argyle's slowly lifted his hand over his shoulder. Known as a 'Neither', an Other who had defected to the protection of humanity, Argyle locked his eyes onto the door.

'Get out of here.'

His words were emotionless, an instruction. Argyle's eyes narrowed on the door as his hand gripped the leather-strapped handle of his blade. With a shake of his light-brown-covered head, Bermuda dropped into the driver's seat, slammed the door, and wrenched the key. The engine roared to life, the lights bursting out and casting Argyle in a majestic silhouette: a fallen angel, ready to face the demon on the other side of the door.

With the tyres screeching like a banshee, Bermuda sped through the car park, a small trail of dust following him like a loyal puppy. The car burst through the concrete block, taking a sharp turn onto the spiral ramp that led to the freedom of the street below.

London wrapped around him at speed, his car racing down the ramp as his foot pressed the pedal to the floor, the lights of the capital whipping by in a frenzied blur.

Behind him, he could hear the doors to the third level being thrown from their hinges, the night-piercing howl of the enormous creature that Argyle had stayed to welcome.

He had never seen an Other that big.

That ferocious.

With his steering wheel locked to the left, he circled down the exit ramp before the car smashed through the security barrier, the red-and-white bar shattering and sprinkling the street like hundreds-and-thousands. Bermuda reached for the handbrake, shunting it up, and letting his car spin on the spot, eventually sliding to a halt.

A few pedestrians watched on in shock, one of them quick dialling the police to report a parking violation.

They couldn't hear what Bermuda could.

With the window rolled down, he wished he had a cigarette on the go; the soothing, calming pollution of his lungs would have settled his nerves as he listened to the spine-chilling roar of the behemoth and the clanging of Argyle's sword as he valiantly fought.

No cigarettes anymore. He cursed himself as he raised his electronic cigarette to his lips, the blue light on the end as he inhaled a mocking reminder of his decision to be 'healthy'.

Another roar ripped through the air, unbeknownst to the watching few, all of them perplexed by his decision to break through the barrier and not speed away into the night. He was used to the staring, people judging him or labelling him insane. It happened all the time, but he was a long way past trying to explain.

A long road away from caring.

'Where the hell are my goddamn Tic Tacs?' he muttered to himself, unlatching the glovebox to be met by an avalanche of parking tickets and empty boxes of his beloved mints.

CRASH!

Argyle's armour was the first thing Bermuda noticed, the reflection of light bouncing off it as he hurtled through the brick wall of the third floor. Within seconds, the mighty warrior collided with Bermuda's bonnet, denting the metal as he bounced to the ground.

His face was bloodstained, and a large gash opened across his head that was already willing itself shut, much to Bermuda's continued bemusement. His arms, covered in thick lacerations, pushed against the ground as he pulled himself up.

Bermuda leant out of the window, looking down at his fallen comrade. 'Need a lift?'

The stone-cold stare through the grey eyes told Bermuda the joke, like so many, didn't register. Argyle was the most loyal partner he could ask for. But apart from working for the BTCO, they were worlds apart. Yet combining Argyle's human-like form and his personality, Bermuda couldn't recall a single person who embodied humanity as his partner did.

Who fought for what they thought was right.

Dusting the debris from his body, Argyle strode purposefully to the passenger door, a mighty hand wrenching it open. The watching public pointed in amazement as Bermuda pulled away. To them, they had witnessed a self-denting, self-opening car, driven by a man who talked to the ground.

Suddenly, their attention – as well as that of the two agents in the now banged-up Honda Civic – was drawn to the giant explosion on the third floor of the car park that sat next to Liverpool Street Station. Brick and metal barrier burst from the wall, showering down upon the street below like a heavy rainfall.

A metal post slammed against a car parked nearby.

Two small rocks hammered against a terrified civilian's shoulder.

Then suddenly, the earth shook.

Landing on all fours, hidden from the world, the enormous beast slowly recovered from its three-story plunge. Over fifteen feet tall, with hard, jagged bones jutting from its spine, the beast was like none other Bermuda had seen before. Its dark, grey skin was covered in scales, stretched to the limit from its powerful frame. Small spikes, the crooked bones that ruptured through its skin, burst from its joints.

Its skull was large and dome-like, the top of its head

smooth like a well-sanded table. Its eyes were feral, the pupilless black balls locked on Bermuda. Its giant jaw, snapping like an alligator, revealed a fine selection of razor-sharp teeth.

Embedded in its neck, a latch stone. Forged on the Otherside, it not only granted this beast entrance to our world, it allowed for it to interact too. Three people had been reported missing, with remnants of their bodies found in and around the car park.

Mark Courtney, a father of two and wealthy property developer. Betty Mulligan, a librarian and poster woman for the 'Crazy Cat Lady' community. Thomas Branning, a physics student who walked through the wrong car park while drunk.

All of them were gone, dismembered and digesting slowly within the hideous behemoth before Bermuda.

With a flick of his wrist, Bermuda threw his car into reverse, arching his neck back before slamming his foot down, the Civic launching backwards as the beast slowly moved towards them.

'We seem to be moving away from the creature,' Argyle stated, a slight agitation in his voice.

'Yeah, that's the plan.'

Bermuda reached the end of the road, the concrete merging onto the dual carriageway that cut through the city like an enormous vein. As he approached, he took once last glance back through his windscreen.

The giant beast roared loudly, its powerful lungs shaking the streets and rattling the cars that lined it.

It dropped again to all fours and bounded towards the car, nothing but death in its pathway as it raced towards them, like a dog chasing the postman.

'Hold on!' Bermuda yelled, wrenching the steering wheel and spinning the car completely as it joined the main road, a barrage of horns bursting into the air like an orchestra warming up. Almost clipping the large truck that was hurtling behind them, Bermuda slipped the car into first before it had completed its turn and stamped down the accelerator, the car bursting forward in one fluid movement.

'HAHA!' he exclaimed in excitement, his heart beating ferociously as the adrenaline kicked in. Argyle's lack of enthusiasm quickly ended the excitement.

That, and the giant crash of the truck behind as the giant Other leapt through it, the vehicle exploding into a ball of flames as it emerged onto the dual carriageway, its massive, clawed hands slamming against the pavement as it raced towards them, sending debris hurtling against the buildings that lined the streets.

A light drizzle began to patter against Bermuda's windscreen as he raced through London, his car careering round a corner and onto another main road, scraping the back of a black cab that was then pulverised by the chasing beast.

The bright lights of the city surrounded them like fireflies, buses and cars whipping through the nightlife that dotted the street as Bermuda veered between them, narrowly missing a group of drunken lads. As they turned and yelled abuse as the car dashed by, one of them found himself flying into the nearby wall, courtesy of an invisible monster.

A bus was sent toppling into the front window of Top Shop. Two cars were sent hurtling towards the closed exit of Tottenham Court Road Station.

Bermuda spun a left and hurtled onto the A4 towards West London, the rain now hammering down on his car. Argyle calmly sat next to him, the situation barely registering as a need to panic. Sirens wailed, as a platoon of police cars were now following the path of destruction which they would wrongly lay at Bermuda's door.

Raindrops scattered the road before him as he weaved between the traffic, his foot pressed down and the acceleration rising. Cars whipped past and Bermuda scouted the mirrors, the large creature no longer in the rear-view.

'Where are we going?' Argyle's calm words broke Bermuda's concentration.

'I don't know, buddy. I'm kinda winging it here.' Bermuda pulled the wheel, slipping the Honda Civic around a delivery van, and began to climb the massive concrete flyover that arched its way over Hammersmith. The magnificent bridge brought with it an incredible view, the capital lit up like a world on fire.

'Where is the creature?' Argyle craned his neck, his grey eyes staring through the back window. All he could see was the flashing of lights blurred by the rain.

Bermuda slammed on the brakes.

As if Argyle's word had provoked an introduction, the beast leapt up onto the flyover before them, its legs ripping the metal barriers clean from the edge. Through the broken concrete they could see the Hammersmith Apollo, one of London's most iconic venues, which had emptied. A well-known comedian having decorated its walls with laughter a mere two hours before.

Bermuda stared at the vicious beast, trying his best to recall the last time he had enjoyed anything resembling a normal Saturday evening. His mind wandered to Chloe, his beautiful daughter, as he pushed her on a swing – the moments he was starting to experience. The relationship he was starting to build.

A reason to be doing this.

Behind him, the sirens wailed through the air, the rain bursting with flashes of blue.

The beast waited, goading them to make their move. It snorted through its flared nostrils, its razor-sharp claws screeching across the concrete. The rain battered against its solid scalp.

Bermuda revved his engine.

'Hey Argyle. You have your Retriever, right?'

'Of course.' Argyle patted the metal clasp around his wrist. The Retriever, born of a metal from his own world, was safely secured within, its endless chain coiled and the hook that had caught many an Other lay with it. 'I am required to carry it at all times.'

'Okay, well when I say fire … you fire that thing.'

'Do you have a plan?' Argyle asked, Bermuda letting down the electric window beside him. The cold and rain collided with his armour.

'I have an idea. I wouldn't call it a plan.' Bermuda turned to his partner. 'You're gonna want to put your seat belt on!'

Bermuda flashed him a grin before turning back to the road ahead. The beast had leant forward, ready to spring at any moment. Bermuda took a deep breath and then hammered his foot on the pedal.

The car burst forward, ripping across the flyover towards the giant beast, the rain hurtling down upon them. Police cars chased, their lights adding to the night sky intermittent bursts of blue illuminating the bridge. Argyle leant slightly out the window, the Retriever ready and primed. The rain slapped him in the face like a cold, wet palm.

Twenty feet.

Fifteen feet.

The Other rose up on its back legs, its broad, muscular chest exposed as it let out a roar, a hard, guttural noise that shook the city of London.

Ten feet.

'NOW, ARGYLE!'

Argyle lifted his arm and released. The hook shot

forward, pulling the chain with it as it flew through the night sky and embedded into the meaty neck of the Other, that roared with agony. The hook burst into four as it pierced the skin, hooking round and latching in place. With its arm flailing in agony, the beast swung wildly, its other clawed hand ripping the skin of its neck as it tried to free itself.

Argyle pulled himself back into the car and Bermuda turned the wheel a full lock to the left.

Through the gap in the barrier.

He felt his stomach rise up as the car hurtled off the side of the Hammersmith flyover, the world suddenly feeling like it was in slow motion. Bermuda could feel the ground quickly race up to meet them, and just before it did, everything went black.

The car hit the hard concrete, rolling on impact, with large chunks of metal and shattered glass spraying across the empty pavement. The airbags burst, catching the two travellers as they rattled around like two lone coins in a piggy bank.

The chain of the Retriever tightened, snapping sharply and wrenching the monstrous Other over the edge. With its neck broken, it flopped off of the flyover, its back legs crashing through the roof and side wall of the Hammersmith Apollo, the legendary bricks scattering across the floor like a careless child's building blocks.

The rain continued to batter the crash scene, pedestrians gasping in shock at the damage. Slowly, very slowly, Bermuda began to stir, a thick stream of blood pouring from a gash across his head.

His nose and eyebrow were also streaming blood. His ribs, broken six months previously after he was thrown through a wall, were cracked and swinging loosely.

He could tell his wrist was broken as were the two fingers pointing in the wrong direction.

'Are you okay?'

Argyle's voice covered him like a blanket, safe in the knowledge that his friend was okay. He nodded, wincing in pain at the slightest movement. Argyle patted him gently on the arm with a blood-covered hand. His lacerations would heal at an unworldly rate. Kicking open what was left of the door, the mighty warrior stepped out into the rain, the water washing the blood from his dark skin. His right arm hung loosely, swinging gently from the last few tendons that hadn't been ripped from their socket.

It would heal.

He always healed.

Calm, measured steps took him to the fallen Other, his heart feeling a twinge of sympathy for the death of his own kind. He may not have been as feral or as monstrous as the slain beast, but they were of the same world.

They were brothers in Otherkind.

Slowly murmuring a banishment, Argyle reached forward and wrapped his fingers around the latch stone, the vessel that was keeping the dead within its physical form.

He yanked it from the skin, watching as the Other slowly disintegrated, its life force trailing like a thin plume of smoke into the relic that Argyle held in his hand. He would be deposited back to the Otherside at HQ, for a proper burial.

Argyle bowed his head; the death of another Other hung heavily from his mighty shoulder like a pendant. The rain clattered around him, his blood trickling across the concrete where the slain beast had lain.

It was gone.

*'Don't move!'*

*'Sir, we have him!'*

*'Keep your hands where we can see 'em!'*

Bermuda winced in pain; the shouting of the police

officers that surrounded his car only heightened the throbbing headache. He could feel the whiplash strapped to his neck, the stiffness keeping his head locked in one place.

The world around him was bright and blue, the lights of the police cars flickering like a faulty Christmas tree light. He had once again saved the city, his body was broken, and no one would believe him.

Just another day.

Two officers slowly approached the shattered window beside him, their steps careful and measured. One of them held his torch up, the light annoyingly intruding on Bermuda's vision. With blood splattered across his usually handsome face, Bermuda slowly turned. He had caused a city-wide car chase, untold damage to a number of vehicles and buildings, and had ripped a hole in one of London's oldest theatres.

With his impending arrest moments away, he treated the police to his best, bloodied smile.

'What's the matter, officers? Was I speeding?'

# THREE

BERMUDA'S FOOTSTEPS crunched across the ash, remnants of burnt leaves that now carpeted the street. To either side of him, buildings flickered, alive with the flames that ripped through them.

Every night it was the same; he was beginning to anticipate the next part of his dream before it happened, turning a split second before his name was called.

Everyone he knew was just out of reach, all of them reduced to ash and spirited away in the wind. Their final look was of failure as he watched them die.

An ear-splitting roar echoed in the distance. The giant beast responsible for the destruction of the world was rampaging beyond the smoke. The sky was black.

The only light was that of the fire that burst through every window on the street. The lampposts that stood like pillars rumbled to ash as he passed them.

His ex-wife Angela waited for him. A mere few feet from the woman he had sacrificed everything for, he knew she would crumble as he touched her. He felt his arm reach forward, he watched her reduce to ash.

He knew what was next and willed himself to wake up.

Straining to close his eyes, he wrestled his sub-conscious, trying his best to race back to reality and awake in whatever place he had fallen asleep.

'Daddy.'

Her voice returned him to the apocalyptic street, the world ablaze as the ash danced through the air, twisting with the flaming embers of destruction. He was still there, moments away from watching the Otherside take what was most precious to him.

With tears streaming from his eyes, he turned to face his daughter. Her nightdress was stained with soot and her face was rife with fear. Her eyes, raw from crying, searched her father for any strains of hope.

Suddenly the shadows began to circle, thin, crooked fingers reaching out and wrapping themselves around her limbs.

Bermuda raced towards her, the street stretching as he failed to make up the ground. Each step echoed, drowning out the destruction of the world. All he cared about was his daughter, the need to protect her. As he bounded towards her, she caught his eye one last time, a realisation of the end.

'Help me!'

He leapt, screaming for her as the hands ripped her body in several directions.

---

BERMUDA JOLTED AWAKE, instantly groaning in agony as his body reminded him of his injuries. Above him, a bright light burst through, blinding him slightly as it buzzed from its artificial beam in the ceiling.

'Wakey, wakey.'

The Scottish twang made him wince further, the voice of a disapproving senior. Pushing himself up slowly, he felt the whiplash tighten around his neck like a dog lead, pulling him back to the bed. With a deep breath he pushed himself upwards, battling the stiffness of his spine and the sling that his arm rested in.

His ribs clattered freely, the bones shaking like a box of his favourite mints. Broken. Again.

He was at the BTCO headquarters, a secret underground facility that sat thirty feet below the Shard, one of the premium London tourist spots. The building itself, eighty-nine floors of manmade glass and wonderment, stood just outside London Bridge Station. The sharp, glittering building was glistening in the early winter cold.

Thirty feet below, Bermuda was slowly adjusting himself, his legs swinging gently over the side of the bed. Every movement sent pain rocketing towards his brain. His eyes slowly began to adjust to the glare of the fluorescent tubes that hung from the ceiling, the fuzzy outlines of the three people in the room gradually beginning to find their shape. One of them stood forward, the definition of his face matching the sarcasm of his voice, and Bermuda knew he would have been happier being greeted by a kick in the bollocks.

The Scottish voice belonged to Montgomery Black, head of the Committee, the board of senior officers and agents that oversaw the BTCO. Bermuda had lost count of the times he had felt the wrath of the old man and judging by the sneer that clung to his wrinkled, be-spectacled face, another encounter wasn't far away.

'What does the BTCO stand for?' Black locked his hands together at the base of his spine, slowly turning away from Bermuda with a straight back and a disregard for pleasantries.

'I'm okay, by the way.' Bermuda flashed a glance to one of the other figures. 'Aren't I?'

Taking a few steps forward was Vincent, the most

senior Neither working for the BTCO. His greyish skin clung tightly to his bones, his eyes a dark black, his nose thin and pointed. Like Argyle, Vincent had defected to our world, dedicating over half a century to building a workable truce between the Earth and the Otherside. Respected on both sides of the divide, Vincent was an archive of knowledge and expertise, working very closely with the other man in the room.

Lord Felix Ottoway III. The director of the BTCO.

Rapidly approaching his eighty-second birthday, he watched Bermuda with the kindness in his eyes he always had. He'd spent over sixty years in the agency, the clock ticking as the cancer continued to grip to his lungs, daring him to take his final breath.

Vincent's voice was barely a whisper.

'You have suffered a broken collarbone, broken fingers, and a broken wrist. You have a severe bout of whiplash and your ribs have been – how shall I put it? – re-shattered.'

Bermuda winced as he pressed a finger into his side, only to be greeted by a searing pain.

'Other than that, no lasting damage.'

Bermuda nodded before turning to Black, who still wouldn't look at him.

'See? I'm fine. Almost died in the line of duty, but thanks for checking.'

'What does the BTCO stand for?' Black's deep voice echoed through the basic room, reverberating off the empty walls.

On a small, white table to the side, Bermuda's possessions lay messily, his clothes balled up on the floor below. Blood had dripped from the gash above his eyebrows onto the BTCO-issued white T-shirt. His toned arms hung from the sleeves, covered in the scrawling ink of the tattoos that covered his whole upper body. Incantations to symbols, all of which had been in a hope of warding off the onslaught of the Otherside. As he shifted uncomfortably, the pain bouncing around his body like a pinball machine, he couldn't help but think they weren't working.

'Behind The Curtain Organisation,' Bermuda droned, bored with the question already.

Black snapped round to face him. 'Don't be facetious.'

'You asked.' Bermuda rolled his eyes. He slowly patted his thighs, realising he wasn't wearing his jeans, and immediately grateful they had left his boxer shorts on.

'But what does the organisation stand for?' Black's voice seemed incapable of compassion.

Bermuda spotted his electric cigarette lying sloppily amongst his possessions on the side. He sighed. 'Two worlds. One peace.'

'Exactly. We are here to maintain the harmony that exists between our worlds. A truce that has stood the test of centuries, two worlds working towards a common goal. A peaceful existence.'

'With all due respect, that giant hell-dog tried to rip me to pieces and didn't seem to give a damn about what it had to do to get to me. So, you can cram that peaceful existence up your arse.'

'Jones!' Ottoway's voice snapped like an outraged headmaster's.

Black's eyes narrowed with fury at the disrespectful agent who slowly pushed himself to his feet. Managing a few wobbles, he slowly made his way across the room, the pain riding his spinal cord like a rollercoaster. Lifting his electric cigarette to his mouth, he took a puff, exhaling loudly as the cherry-flavoured smoke clouded around the room.

'What on earth are you smoking?' Vincent coughed, his long-fingered hand balled in a fist.

'This?' Bermuda waved his e-cig lazily. 'It's my electric cigarette.'

'Electric? You humans will smoke anything.'

Before an amused Bermuda could respond, Ottoway cut back in. His wrinkled face was calm, betrayed by the sternness of his voice.

'We appreciate you apprehending the feral Other last night. However, there is a chain of command that has provided the backbone of this organisation for years – long before either one of us was even a twinkle in our father's eye.'

Bermuda rolled his eyes, angered by the reminder of his deadbeat father.

'Let us not forget our manners. In other words—'

'In other words, watch your mouth,' Black cut in, his eyes burning a hole through Bermuda, who was slowly easing himself into his jeans. 'I am growing tired of your complete disregard to your duty.'

Wincing through the pain barrier as he slowly buttoned his jeans, Bermuda turned to the antagonistic senior.

'Please enlighten me.' He took a drag on his e-cig, an impressive cloud of smoke carrying his words. 'Did I not just stop that thing? Where is Argyle? He can vouch for—'

'Argyle is resting,' Vincent cut in, his words curt and to the point.

'Well anyways, this world should be thanking me. Not sending in Chuckles over here to yell at me while my head is ringing.'

'The world isn't ready for the truth.' Black spoke, not looking at Bermuda nor acknowledging the insult. 'This world lives in a blissful naivety that we maintain through our diligent work and our honour of the truce. The Otherside has been responsible for some of the greatest scientific breakthroughs mankind has laid claim to. With their help, Vincent is close to synthesising a cancer suppression.'

Ottoway shifted uncomfortably as Black continued.

'The world needs us to keep the gate open and I WILL NOT allow your incessant disregard to threaten the progression of humanity.'

Bermuda sighed as he took a seat on the edge of the bed again, his own shirt resting in his hands. Pain slowly slithered around his body like a serpent.

'I was doing my damn job,' Bermuda muttered, slowly peeling off the bloodstained white T-shirt, revealing his toned, ink-covered body. Perfectly scribed words scrawled across his abs, the only blemish the three large scars that ran along his chest, a memento from a behemoth Other who introduced him to the roof of the *Cutty Sark* six months prior.

Black continued, his rage drawing forth a large vein on his forehead and heavier twang to his Scottish accent. 'Your job is to be covert. Not destroy half the city. There is video footage of cars flying through buses already on the Internet.' Black shook his head. 'For Christ's sake, you destroyed half of the Apollo!'

'Technically, I didn't. The giant killing machine … that destroyed the building.'

'The *Cutty Sark*? Do you remember blowing two holes in that ship?'

'Again, that was more a "they hit me through the ship" kind of thing.' Bermuda pulled his Tic Tacs out of his jeans pocket, popping a couple into his mouth. His mind shot back to that horrifying night on the famous ship, the giant monster that slammed him through the roof, scarring his chest and almost devouring him. At that moment, he remembered just how grateful he was to have Argyle, the one person who realised just what saving the world really took.

'You blew out one side of Big Ben!' Black, heavily animated, had begun to pace.

Vincent approached Bermuda with a sling, carefully helping him into position to reset his collar bone.

'While saving the world,' Bermuda retorted, looking at the two senior figures before him. 'You're welcome, by the way.'

'At what cost?' Black's words hit Bermuda like a sucker punch.

The cost had been huge, and Bermuda cursed himself for the daily blame game he played with himself. Hugo LaPone, as handsome as he was irritating, was the envious agent who had lost his life that night. When the Otherside's worst terrorist, Barnaby, was merely minutes away from ending the world, Hugo had met his demise. Not a day went by that Bermuda didn't blame himself, trying to absolve his guilt in pint after pint of Doom Bar.

Black's compassion was as empty as those pint glasses. 'Then there was the Hamley's incident.'

'Hamley's?' Ottoway questioned, a thick grey eyebrow raised at the mention of the famous toy store.

'An Other threw him through the front window of the store after he drunkenly challenged it to a fistfight.' Black sneered, and both senior figures and the ancient Other turned and looked at Bermuda, a cloud of cherry fumes surrounding him.

'Okay, that one was my bad.'

Ottoway shook his head, turning on his heel and slowly walking through the door, disappointment following him like a tail. Bermuda cursed himself, surprised at how genuine his anger was to have let down the one person who believed in him.

Black stepped back into his eye line, his eyes glaring behind his glasses. 'You are nothing more than a liability. Ottoway, he believes you are important. That is why he assigned you Argyle and why he has destroyed his own reputation to keep you in the field.'

Bermuda looked up, his eyebrows raised with surprise.

'You claimed you could be the balance, Bermuda. Yet you can't even keep yourself in line.'

'That's enough.' Vincent spoke up, gliding from the corner of the room, his long, grey fingers interlocked in front of him, the black gown he always wore giving him the grandeur of a wizard.

Black's face contorted into a snarl. 'I will tell you when it's enough.'

'He is my patient, and he needs to rest.' Vincent flashed a reassuring look at Bermuda. 'Besides, you need him ready to leave by tomorrow.'

'Wait. Leave?' Bermuda shot glances at both men as a sinister smile slowly took control of Black's face.

'Yes. We have a new case for you.'

Bermuda took a long, hard puff on his e-cig, the liquid bubbling loudly before an avalanche of thick white smoke snaked from his mouth. 'Fan-fucking-tastic.'

'Aye. Vincent will fill you in. But wrap up warm – Glasgow gets quite chilly this time of year.' Black said with a wry smile. The reaction was as expected.

'Glasgow? What the fuck?'

Bermuda spun round, searching Vincent's face for any signs of help. There were none – just the cold, recognisable stare of something not of this world.

'There has been a report of a murder. A young woman, found on her bed with a hole in her chest. Her heart has been removed and is missing. Once you have rested, I will take you to the Oracles to extract what I can.'

Bermuda shook his head in anger, a trip to the information hub of the BTCO doing little to appease him. Black, taking a sickening pleasure in Bermuda's angst, stepped forward.

Bermuda angrily addressed him. 'Wait, what happened

to the agent covering Scotland? Johnson or Jensen, whatever his name is.'

'He is on vacation,' Black stated, his words cutting and unsympathetic.

'Wait, since when the hell did we start getting vacation?'

'When you stop destroying London landmarks. Besides, they specifically asked for you,' Black retorted, enjoying his victory over the troublesome agent. 'Give my regards to the motherland.'

'Give my regards to your wife.' Bermuda winked back, staring directly into the eyes of his adversary. Black was a powerful man and Bermuda knew drawing his ire was a mistake. But considering how badly his curse had destroyed key parts of his life, he wasn't going to let an old man with outdated ideals belittle him for using it to save people. He was starting to accept it, slowly embracing the life he was forced to lead.

Black chuckled to himself before turning and making his exit.

Bermuda called out one last time. 'What time is my flight?'

Black stopped, turning his head slightly, his wrinkles doubling as he smiled, his thick Scottish accent escaping through his rotten false teeth. 'You can get the train.'

The door slammed, shaking the room and encouraging Bermuda's headache to worsen. Bermuda flashed a glance towards Vincent before catching a glimpse of his battered and bruised face.

'Terrific.' He sighed, wondering how life was going to take an even bigger shit in his cereal.

# FOUR

ARGYLE SAT in his designated room within the BTCO headquarters, the blank white walls surrounding him. Above him, a halogen bulb hummed gently, basking his minimal possessions in its manmade glow. His bed was well-made, the white sheet and pillow untouched and evident of a sleepless night.

To the left, a small white desk was dominated by a metal stand on which his mighty blade rested – the same blade that had killed Barnaby, saving the world on that rain-soaked evening atop Big Ben.

The same sword that had saved Bermuda's life countless times.

He stood, his powerful body motionless as he stared at his armour hanging from its designated hooks on the wall. The lacerations across his dark skin had closed, his alien genetics healing him within hours. The arm which had been wrenched from its socket, now rested comfortably over the other as he crossed them.

The Retriever lay beside the sword, ready to be launched at a moment's notice.

All Argyle could think of was his partner. Was he okay? Their plummet from the bridge had been a momentous one, the car crushing like a Coke can on impact. He had heard him breathing and even heard a trademark quip to the officers that surrounded the car.

But now he was alone, trapped in a room with superiors that wanted him gone. Mr Black had made his feelings for Bermuda clear and it was only the honourable Ottoway who kept him at arm's length.

Soon Ottoway would be gone, his health declining by the day. Then, Bermuda would need more than Argyle's sword to protect him.

He shook his head; letting Bermuda be ostracised by Black as a power play was not going to happen. Bermuda had given something to Argyle that no creature, on this side or the other, ever had.

Friendship.

Bermuda had not only welcomed Argyle into his life, he saw him as the only positive of the gift he was slowly starting to accept. And despite his constant attempts at humour – which were never funny, Argyle found endearing – Bermuda was the most honourable of all the humans Argyle had met. He had walked two worlds, and no other inhabitant possessed the strength or integrity of Bermuda.

Even if he didn't know it himself.

He slowly opened his grey, pupilless eyes, and they latched onto the shimmering blade before him. With a powerful hand, he snatched it from its resting place, slicing it through the air as he began another bout of training.

With every cut of the air before him, Argyle hoped that his partner would be okay.

BERMUDA SHUFFLED UNCOMFORTABLY DOWN the corridor, his footsteps irregular as he struggled to keep up with Vincent, the regal Neither gliding before him. His movements were so smooth, Bermuda questioned whether he had feet under the long, dark gown he wore. The glow of the lights cut through his brain like a razorblade, the effects of colliding with his steering wheel hitting him with a painful reminder.

His arm was locked in place, the sling tight enough to keep his shattered wrist and collarbone in place. Blood stained his white T-shirt, wrapped around a body that rattled with every step, the ribs celebrating their independence from the rest of his skeleton.

They would heal.

He always healed.

They passed a few faceless men in suits, people Bermuda had never spoken to nor wanted to, as they rounded a corner, marching passed a few cells which housed illegal Others ready to be transferred back to their world. The procedures and paperwork were not something Bermuda concerned himself with, letting those with more sense sit behind the desks.

They turned another corner and a few women in white coats stopped and stared, analysing the injuries that Bermuda wore on his body like medals. The entire organisation knew who he was, the famous Bermuda Jones.

The one who could walk in both worlds.

While he knew their admiration would make his flirting easier, the searing pain that encased his body demanded more attention than a potential romance. Also, her face jumped back into his mind, reminding him of a different pain that exploded in his chest.

Sophie Summers.

The most beautiful woman to have ever crossed

Bermuda's path, she was so close to falling for him as he had for her. Maybe she had. However, she came face to face with the most dangerous force the Otherside had ever created and was a Bermuda's-width away from being lost to their world. Brought together by her friend's disappearance six months ago, she had deemed Bermuda's life too dangerous.

Another wonderful plus of having the 'Knack'.

He had checked up on her from time to time, his 'detective' skills going no further than the occasional search on Google or quick online stalk of her Facebook profile. Her career was going from strength to strength, her dazzling looks propelling her modelling career to a high street fashion brand. Every time he saw her dark eyes, the playful tilt on the edge of her smile, his heart broke slightly.

This world would never allow it.

Neither would the Otherside.

Walking two worlds had never been lonelier. A large scraping of metal shook Bermuda from his self-pity. The huge iron doors to the Archive slowly opened, the light from within spilling out like an overstuffed wardrobe. As Vincent stood awaiting his entrance, Bermuda admired the intricate markings across the iron, the patterns all meaning something in a language he would never comprehend. Sometimes he marvelled at how his life had turned out.

A lot of the time he cursed it. But being able to see his daughter again was starting to change that.

It was giving him a reason.

The Archive was the link to the Otherside, a vast library that documented the rich tapestry of the truce. Every agreement, every significant event was locked away in there somewhere; the rows of leather-bound books overwhelmed Bermuda. Within each one were thousands of pages with words written in criss-cross patterns that not even the cleverest codebreaker could decipher.

The Otherside was a mystery.

Even after the hundreds of years, our world had only scratched the surface of theirs, an untapped potential that maintained the truce. The advances and changes that humanity could gain from this world outweighed the danger of letting their kind across – at least in the eyes of the higher-ups, the patronising suits who sat safely behind their desks while Bermuda took a nosedive off the Hammersmith flyover.

'This way.'

Vincent's voice was rich, full of calm as he led the way through the rows of desks, a select few occupied by those with Level One clearance. Bermuda was pretty sure he was Level Not in a Million Years clearance; however, with Vincent by his side, the sneering glances dissipated quickly.

As Bermuda's footsteps echoed off the high, arched walls, he wondered where within the books was Barnaby. Just thinking of the name drew a shiver down his spine as if the creature himself had run a finger down it. Barnaby had come within moments of ending the world, his desire and drive to vanquish humanity as terrifying as the jet-black eyes that had adorned his scarred face.

Bermuda had stopped him. Just.

The ramifications of that night were still ongoing: the rebuild of the destroyed face of Big Ben, the yearning for Sophie, who had walked away from him that night. And of course the death of Hugo LaPone, which was still being laid at his door. Despite it all, the heartbreak and the heavy conscience, Bermuda had saved the world.

'Wait here,' Vincent stated, gliding beyond the final row of books and between a maze of metal filing cabinets. As he disappeared into the glow of the room ahead,

Bermuda couldn't help take a few steps forward to the end of the walkway. The large humming of computers echoed off the walls, the bright lights over several screens that surrounded four pods, each one with wires scattered everywhere like a bowl of spaghetti. Within the pods were four, pale blue Neithers, reclined back on their chairs. Their smooth, naked bodies gave off the same gleam as the marble on which Bermuda stood. The wires linking each Neither to a machine, a hard-line directly into the Otherside. Their ability was not to link to the Otherside, but to the Others themselves, their connection allowing the BTCO to monitor all activity, with their constant surveillance working out the likely percentage of Other involvement.

It's how the BTCO assigned their cases.

They were, without a doubt, the heartbeat of the entire organisation.

Bermuda watched in awe as one of the Oracles started the shake, the lights on the screen flickered, lines dashing across as if a coded message was arriving. Before Bermuda could even understand the situation, the robed arm of Vincent guided his gaze away.

'Leave them. They may seem docile, but I discourage unfamiliar presence in this chamber.'

'You don't have to tell me twice,' Bermuda retorted, slightly unnerved at how little he knew of the world he was entrusted to investigate.

Vincent led him back through the labyrinth of cabinets, each one housing years of history. As they emerged back into the open area, Vincent slapped a manila folder down on the nearby desk. Bermuda looked at it before looking back to the gangly Neither with a curious eye.

'Your case.'

'Well I gathered it wasn't a pay rise.' Bermuda rattled

some Tic Tacs free with his good arm, the clattering mints drawing a few scowls from the quiet obsessed.

'A young lady has been found dead in Glasgow. No signs of forced entry except a bedroom door that was nearly launched off its hinges, and her body, which was thrust onto the bed.'

'You sure this is a case for me?' Bermuda asked, the bruising on his face a clearer colour than hours earlier.

'She was found with her heart removed. No evidence of weaponry or surgical tools.' Vincent's pupilless eyes rested on him. 'It was taken cleanly with the murderer's bare hands.'

Bermuda whistled, reaching for the folder with his unstrapped arm and flicking it open. A measly couple of pages comprised the details of the case. He raised an eyebrow, heavy with stitches.

'Not much to go on, is there?' he said, not looking up. 'How do we know it's for us?'

'Three found significant probability that a human could not have carried out such an act.'

Bermuda shuffled uncomfortably at the Oracles being referred to by number.

Vincent cleared his throat. 'And you have been asked for, by name.'

Bermuda turned back to his superior, confusion wrestling with agony for control of his face. 'I have zero connection to Glasgow.'

'An old BTCO officer, Tobias Hendry. He was formerly in charge of the old gateway which was situated on the outskirts of Glasgow. Since its decommission he acts as an informant, if you will. He's human.'

'He's Scottish.'

'With our other agent away, he has requested your presence.' Vincent clasped his hands together, the sleeves of his robe hanging low like a wizard. 'You may not know this, Bermuda, but your reputation precedes you.'

'Woopie-fuckin-do,' Bermuda muttered. The idea of a winter in Glasgow wasn't exactly appealing. He turned the page over, examining the photo of a young lady lying in her underwear, her curved body splattered in blood.

Someone had taken her heart.

Why?

He winced, shuffling uncomfortably as a searing reminder of his car crash shot through his ribs. He tried to readjust, the sling strapping his wrist and collarbone in place acting like a straitjacket – a memory he was all too happy not to revisit.

'I am sure you will be healed by tomorrow,' Vincent suggested, his voice quiet and warm.

'What do you mean?' Bermuda quickly spun, concerned.

Vincent stared at him until he released a deep sigh, aware that the secret was strictly between them.

'It's getting worse.'

'Worse?' Vincent questioned. If he'd had eyebrows, Bermuda was sure one would have been risen.

As the only human to have crossed to the Otherside and returned, Bermuda knew he was unique. He was admired, envied, and feared in equal measure. While the BTCO proudly proclaimed him as 'the balance' between two worlds, the Otherside held him in less regard. Having been responsible for the deaths of some of them, Bermuda knew he was a marked man.

He also knew that no one knew of the side effects.

Ever since he had returned, he could feel a call from the Otherside, a delicate whisper dancing on the wind that whipped by. Whenever he came into contact with something from that world, he could feel its pull, trying its best to reclaim what they felt was rightfully theirs. Although he hadn't been blessed with the strength or speed of Argyle, he had noticed that his body had begun rebuilding itself at an unearthly rate.

He healed like an Other.

While his face resembled a dropped pizza and his body had been crumpled like an empty Coke can, he knew it would be fine within a matter of days. Bones began to fall in to place quickly. Scars faded fast.

Bermuda was keen to keep it secret, not wanting the BTCO to look too far into it. It hurt him to keep it from Argyle. Although his partner was the only being in the two worlds he could trust, he didn't want people to see him as even more peculiar. Vincent knew – his wise eyes had cottoned on pretty fast – but it remained between the two of them.

A silent promise.

'Yes, worse,' Bermuda stated firmly, returning to the conversation. 'I'm healing faster than Argyle.'

'Not quite, but this is incredible. Remarkable.'

'Do you know what the usual recovery time of a broken collarbone is? About six weeks, eight at the most.' Bermuda's words were steeped in disappointment. 'I can already feel it fusing, and it's been a day.'

'That's because you're one of us now.'

The deep voice boomed through the archive, leaping from the walls and exploding around them. Bermuda spun on his heel. The clomping footsteps and voice had emanated from the giant, hulking figure of Denham. His face, world weary and framed by an eyepatch, wore a wry smile, the caramel-coloured skin creasing at the corners of his mouth. Semi-retired from field duty, Denham was in charge of new recruits, his no-nonsense approach scaring the fear out of the newly 'Knack'-aware before they entered the 'real' world.

Standing as tall as Argyle but with a severe bulk that

would stand out in professional wrestling, the mighty Neither carried a black bag in his hand, swinging from his fingers like a yo-yo. Bermuda shot a glance back to Vincent, who remained motionless.

'How does he know?' Bermuda exclaimed, his pitch rising, and a few other inhabitants of the Archive slowly made their way to the door, not wanting to intrude.

Denham slammed the bag down next to the manila folder and exhaled. 'What, that you are like us now? Vinnie told me.' He motioned towards his superior with his thumb. 'It's good, we have more in common now.'

'I am not like you,' Bermuda retorted, his anger slowly boiling.

'I'm afraid you are,' Vincent calmly interjected, his words a comforting buffer between the two beings before him. 'Denham has promised the utmost discretion.'

Bermuda looked back and forth between the two Neithers, both of them as commanding as they were different – a shining example of how bizarre the Otherside was, how little made sense, and how dangerous it could be. Denham's reputation as a soldier was unquestionable, as was his loyalty and ferocity. Bermuda sighed, relenting.

'It ain't so bad,' Denham offered. 'You could still be pissing in your pants like Thorpe.'

'How is he getting on?' Bermuda asked.

Bobby Thorpe was the latest recruit that Denham was breaking in. The poor man was going through a torturous introduction to BTCO life that Bermuda knew only too well.

'Well let's just say he's gone through more pairs of underpants than Mick Jagger!'

Bermuda burst out laughing, his ribs chattering like teeth in the cold. Hearing Denham reference pop culture was surreal. But then standing in an underground vault talking to two creatures from another world about a secret murderer in Scotland made surreal seem like a false concept.

Denham reached out one of his mighty hands, the fingers clasping the zip of the bag. It opened with a mighty yawn and he reached in, pulling out a thick, bunched-up roll of grey material.

'For you.' He smirked in Bermuda's confused direction.

'What's that?'

Vincent stepped forward. 'I asked Denham to create some clothing for you. Obviously, due to his seniority, he had a right to know the reason why.'

A large slap echoed through the Archive and sent pain racing through Bermuda's body as Denham's hand clattered against his back.

'You're welcome, buddy.' Denham's words were softer than his back pat. 'Hopefully the next time you come up against an Exceptional, this will keep you safe.'

'A what now?'

'An Exceptional,' Denham replied, confusion dripping from his words.

Bermuda arched a stitched eyebrow.

'You didn't tell him?'

Bermuda turned slowly, his shattered body creaking like a rusty door.

Vincent sighed.

'Tell me what?' Bermuda demanded, his one good hand fumbling in his pocket for his e-cig.

'It is not something to tell.' Vincent began gliding towards the darkened corner of the Archive, beyond the Oracles and the links between worlds that Bermuda would never comprehend. The Neither looked back, his eyes almost sparkling with excitement. 'It is something to show.'

Bermuda shuffled after him with slow, painful steps, his dislocated shoulder demanding attention. A cloud of berry-flavoured vapour drifted into the air. 'Show me what?'

Denham eagerly marched past Bermuda, bursting through the cloud of synthetic smoke like a game show contestant. His war-worn face uplifted in a wry smile as he arched his large skull back, his one good eye twinkling like a lone star. 'Your legacy.'

# FIVE

THE SHADOWS CREPT over the stone walls like paint dripping down the old, crumbled brick work. The hill was set on the outskirts of the town, a world unfamiliar to him. These people were not the ones he had encountered before; the last time he was free to walk the earth.

Stone slats rose from the surrounding grounds like jagged teeth. On them, the names of the deceased, a needless tribute to a worthless life. They were all worthless, each one of them nothing more than a maggot, slowly eating its way through the corpse they called life.

All of them except her.

He could still see her face, her hazel eyes twinkling as they danced in the moonlight, its beauty only matched by hers. Her dark, brown skin as smooth as silk, the moonbeams shimmering off it like a sunrise on a lake. He closed his jet-black eyes, taking a long, controlled breath, his memories dancing through his mind in sync with their bodies.

She was gone.

There was always that creeping, nagging doubt that he would never see her again. That her beauty had been lost over time, and his search had been for nothing. All that time wasted in the dark.

The chains that held him to the walls.

The voice that taunted him.

He shook it from his memory, allowing the same moon that illuminated his great love to bathe the Necropolis in its glory. Each footstep crunched on the dried leaves, their fight for survival long since abandoned. The sleet slapped against his face, the skin – still the same as it had been back then – ignoring the cold that accompanied it.

With each step, he felt the raindrops falling from his body, the thick, red drops of blood that fell through his fingers.

This was what was requested.

This would bring her back.

The iconic graveyard that sat just on the outskirts of Glasgow was steeped in tradition. Over five thousand people lay beneath, all of them consigned to the earth upon their expiration, bodies amassing the collection for nearly two hundred years. The hill, surrounded by old, brick walls, was awash with stones and monuments, all of them lovingly chosen by those who were left behind.

The Necropolis was a place of pain.

Thirty-seven acres of death.

As he meandered through the tombstones, his hand tightened its grip. The woman had been accommodating, a friendly soul who was unfortunate enough to be his chosen one for the evening. It was she who'd made the motion to leave, inviting him home with a slightly pathetic desperation.

Now, as her blood splattered the ground, he held her heart in his hand. His cold fingers had ripped right through her skin, shattering the ribs and breastbone before wrapping around it, the beating reaching a crescendo as he pulled it from her body. It had stopped in unison with the life fading from her eyes.

He would remember her face.

He had remembered them all. All these years.

But this would lead him to her one more time as instructed. With each new face he struggled to place hers. The contours of her shapely cheekbones now rested undefined, the outline of her body was skewed, like the thread of a frayed knot.

He was losing her.

His shoes crunched off the dead leaves and clapped against the stone path, the mighty tombs that belonged to people of historical importance looming over him like a tidal wave of concrete. He wasn't bothered with their names, or the need to celebrate their life with such a creation.

All he knew was this was where he would deliver the heart. This was where he remembered.

He took a few more steps towards the door of the small, crumbling shelter, the carved pillars cracked and faded. The rain hammered against the stone, rendering the dull building an even darker shade of depressing.

It reminded him of a place in time, a memory that was dancing on the outskirts of his mind, somewhere he couldn't place. He remembered nothing of life before her. All he knew was his name and how he loved her. How he would have run through every door imaginable just to be by her side.

Now she was gone. Taken from him so long ago.

With a solemn bow of his head, he lowered himself to one knee, the wet concrete soaking his trouser leg. He reached out with his free hand, his fingers slowly running down the damp wood of the door. The tomb stood still amongst the powerful rain, a symbol of eternal loneliness

That's what he had been sentenced to.

With great care, he placed the static heart on the ground, the rain washing the last of the blood from the organ and sweeping it down the steps. He slowly rose, looking around the cemetery with his dark eyes before running a hand through his dripping hair.

As requested, he had brought them what they had asked for.

He would return to the outskirts of this world, hoping that today was they day they would return her to him.

---

AS THEY WALKED past the Oracles, Bermuda watched One begin to jolt, its machine ramping up the beeps as it pumped information from their world to ours. He shook his head in disbelief at how, even if he could describe the finest details, he would be locked up again just for speaking of it. Its eyes, a pale cream with no pupil, stared straight upwards, as if they had rolled back into its skull.

The other three lay perfectly still.

The only sound was the beeping of their machines. Did they even know he was watching?

'Hey!'

Denham's voice echoed through the archive, stirring Bermuda back into the bizarre reality of his life. The mighty Neither beckoned him over, which he obliged quickly. Looking back over his shoulder, Bermuda noted that the Oracles hadn't even flinched. He exhaled, and a slight creep danced up his spine.

'Don't stare at the Oracles,' Denham ordered as Bermuda joined him. His hands clutched the grey gift tightly. 'It's rude.'

'Do they even know I'm there?'

'They know everything.' Denham's words were final, his mighty arms folded across his powerful chest, the black

'BTCO' T-shirt stretched to near breaking point. With his one good eye, he returned his gaze to Vincent, who slowly lowered a large book onto the secluded desk between them.

Bermuda glanced at the two senior Neithers, his eyebrows raised. 'Is it story time?'

'This, Jones, is your legacy.' Vincent spoke, ignoring the quip. 'After what happened six months ago, we have taken extra steps to ensure that the fate of the world doesn't rest upon just your shoulders. Do you know how?'

Bermuda looked up at Vincent, meeting his grey eyes and slowly nodding. 'By reading?'

Denham sighed, rubbing the bridge of his nose with frustrated fingers. Vincent projected a warm smile, his patience higher than that of his fellow Neither.

'By making sure we are prepared. We knew of Barnaby and were following up reports of his escape. While you were adamant of the incoming danger, we were unprepared. An Other as dangerous as he should not have been left in your capable hands. You were, as much as Mr Black hates to admit it, very much right on that one.'

'Well if Monty wants to thank me for being so inspirational, he knows where to find me.'

'Quite,' Vincent continued, slowly opening the mighty book. Again, as with all the documentation from the Otherside, the letters were indecipherable, dancing across the pages in a criss-cross pattern. 'This is the Tome, a new record that I alone have access to. A new brand of Other has been agreed, a way to monitor those who pose a serious threat to our world. We are no longer going to use a grading system, merely the new term.'

'Exceptionals,' Bermuda interjected, his lips tightening as he scrutinised the idea. 'I like it.'

'So far, we have only two on record, one of whom has been vanquished by yourself and Argyle.'

'Even I have to admit Argyle did the worlds a favour

killing that piece of shit,' Denham added, his face betraying the praise for Argyle, a hatred that had Bermuda never understood.

'With this Tome, we can help create a better balance between the worlds, keeping them safe and secure.' Vincent nodded at Bermuda warmly. 'Two worlds, one peace.'

'Yeah, yeah.' Bermuda waved off the BTCO creed, taking a large puff on his e-cig. The fruity plume of smoke surrounded the three of them as his eyes lit up. 'Who else is in the book?'

'You will only be informed of Exceptionals should it pertain to your case.'

'So, whatever's happening in Glasgow doesn't involve an Exceptional?'

'Not as far as we have been informed.'

'Then who is it?' Bermuda asked cheekily. 'Is it you? Is it Denham?'

'You will be informed of Exceptionals—' Vincent began to repeat.

Bermuda cut him off. 'Is it me?'

'Enough,' Denham interrupted, the frustration rife across his wrinkled face, the frown arching over his eyepatch. 'No one knows but Vincent, so leave it be.'

'Sorry.' Bermuda held his hand up, his other resting in the sling that was becoming less necessary by the minute. He scowled at the changes his body was going through, the effect of the Otherside.

He had always felt different.

Now he didn't even feel human.

It was bad enough that Vincent had figured out that he was developing an Other's ability to heal, but now Denham knew, he began to feel even more like a freak.

As if he could read Bermuda's mind, Vincent slowly closed the thick, leather cover of the Tome, locking away

Bermuda's legacy for the day. His words were slathered in warmth. 'Denham has a gift for you.'

Bermuda raised his stitched eyebrow in surprise, turning to the hulking recruiter, a fiendish grin across his face. With an arm thicker than Bermuda's torso, he reached for the dark, grey blanket that clung tightly to its contents that he had removed from the bag earlier.

'Think of it as a get well soon gift.'

Bermuda scoffed at the remark, slowly unravelling the grey material with one hand. As it fell to the floor, Denham unfolded and flapped open a brand-new coat, the thick, dark grey material crisp and pressed.

Bermuda let out a whistle of admiration. 'Now that's a nice-looking coat.' He beamed at Denham. 'Didn't know you were secret haberdasher.'

'Sword, needle … it's all the same.'

Bermuda chuckled at the boast, knowing full well that Denham was one of the most fearsome soldiers that belonged to the Over Watch, a sort of army of knights that policed the Otherside. Argyle was also a former soldier that much Bermuda knew; however, he never spoke of what Bermuda could tell were harrowing experiences.

'Well thanks. Speaking of swords when can I have mine back?' Bermuda asked, his frustration apparent.

'You do not possess a sword,' Vincent responded curtly. 'You were entrusted with a tomahawk of great value and rarity and Mr Black feels that until you prove yourself responsible—'

'Whatever,' Bermuda cut him off, shaking his head at the suspension of his weapon privileges. Besides, he still had Argyle, and, as he admired it, a new coat.

'It is for your protection,' Vincent informed, pointing to the inside of the jacket with a long, bony finger. 'The inside is lined with Argiln, the very same material that we build our armour from.'

'Hmmm,' Bermuda murmured, remembering the material shattering when he was slammed through a wall by Barnaby all those months ago.

'It's re-enforced,' Vincent reassured him. 'Denham has done an exemplary job in fitting it between the lining of the jacket, ensuring that your actual body will have no physical contact with it.'

'So that way, you won't keep turning into one of us.'

Bermuda flashed Denham a stern glance, his anger outweighing his fear. He relaxed upon seeing his colleague's pearly white smile. 'Thanks. I appreciate it.'

'Maybe it will do what Argyle seems incapable of and keep you safe.' Denham spoke, refolding the grey blanket over his rippling forearm.

'Argyle has saved my life more times than I can count. Show some damn respect.'

Denham's one, pupilless grey eye glared at Bermuda, his hatred for Argyle a mystery that seemed to be held by the entirety of the Otherside.

Vincent, once again, cut through the tension with a measure of calm. 'Thank you, Denham. That will be all.'

With a cocky salute, Denham turned and headed back towards the mighty iron doors of the Archive, his booming voice bouncing off the walls like a ping-pong ball. 'Let me know if there are any problems with the coat.'

Bermuda and Vincent stood in silence, listening to the regimented stride of Denham echoing off the marble floor of the Archive. With a mighty clang of metal, the large doors slammed behind him, leaving Bermuda stood by the desk, his hands clutching the protective coat in question.

'It's not black!' he muttered, quietly enough that no one could hear the ridiculous complaint. The BTCO had just offered even more protection, yet he couldn't see beyond the gesture.

They were sending him to Glasgow.

A wild goose chase over a bizarre murder.

With a shake of his Tic Tac box, Bermuda made his way to the door, the manila folder and a new Otherside-infused jacket under his arm and a scowl on his face that would scare Satan himself.

'Where are you going, Jones?' Vincent called after him, his voice dancing carefully between a whisper and a murmur. 'You are needed there as soon as possible.'

Without looking back, Bermuda responded, his voice almost as broken as his body. 'I need to make a call'

The iron door slammed behind him, locking away the heartbeat of the BTCO once again.

## SIX

BERMUDA'S FOREHEAD pressed against the large, clear windows that lined the Virgin Train, the Midlands whipping by his window at breakneck speed. The train, a Pendalino, was designed to take corners at an angle, the entire carriage feeling like it was sliding off the tracks.

Every time it made Bermuda feel a little sick.

He exhaled loudly, a few gentlemen scowling in his direction across the aisle. Sat around a dingy plastic table, their fingers clicked over laptop keyboards while they spouted nonsense about 'blue-sky thinking' and 'deep-diving analysis'. Bermuda looked at their suits, the ties clasped around their necks. Turn them the other way around and they became nooses.

He looked down at himself. His grey T-shirt clung to his well-toned frame, his heavily tattooed forearms bore the words of incantations wrapped around mystic symbols. He couldn't explain what they meant, just that Argyle had advised him on what would keep the monsters at bay.

The religious held up crucifixes to keep the devil from the door.

He just had them burnt into his skin.

The chair in front of him shook slightly, the portly gentleman grunting as he slept. Bermuda's drink, a warm can of Carlsberg sold at an extortionate price on board, shook on the flimsy table that hung from the back of it. He let another sigh, trying his best to relive the words of encouragement Ottoway had given him, trying to recreate the sense of purpose he felt then.

He was the balance. Humanity's best hope of maintaining the truce and marshalling the merging of the two worlds. He had power beyond any human. He could see the truth, what existed behind the curtain and what the naïve could only comprehend as a fairy tale.

He was, in effect, the most powerful human being on the planet.

The balance.

Now that was a job that came with pressure.

Bermuda took a swig of warm alcohol, coughing a small choke as the warm liquor sloshed the back of his throat. As it swirled down to the pit of his stomach, it rubbed shoulders with the fresh batch of guilt that he'd cooked up before his train had departed.

He closed his eyes and thought back to earlier that afternoon.

---

BERMUDA SAT on the uncomfortable plastic chair, gently testing the swivel feature as he waited. The photo booth was cramped, the walls lit up like light boards, the screen ahead repeating an advert of a young girl taking her passport picture incorrectly. The curtain had been pulled to, shutting out the busy world of Euston Station.

He had called Angela as he had left the Shard, the November lunchtime hammering a cold shower over the landmark heavy skyline of London. It had been years since he had said goodbye to her, her eyes heavy with tears as they carted him off to his cell, the world agreeing with her that he was mentally unstable.

Unfit to be a husband.

Too dangerous to be a father.

As the years had passed, she had stayed on the fringes of his life, communicating with his sister Charlotte and ensuring he was updated as Chloe grew up idolising her stepfather. Ian was a good man, a great husband, and a wonderful father figure. He had even been polite the few times Bermuda had called, even humoured him when he spoke of the monsters in the shadow.

An all-round nice guy.

A real son of a bitch!

Despite his seething envy, he couldn't hate the man, especially after everything he did for his daughter. Bermuda had a suspicion that Ian had encouraged the recent bridge that Angela was building with him, a slow pathway back to having a relationship with his daughter.

She was even adhering to his requests that he meet Chloe in secluded locations, the small photo booth outside the security barriers being the latest meeting place. His Converse trainers rested on his overnight bag, a few shirts and underwear crammed in for an undetermined stay in the freezing North. That wasn't the problem.

The problem was the guilt.

Sure enough, two sets of feet appeared on the other side of the curtain, one of them considerably smaller than the other. Before he could move, his heart melted as the blue-eyed, blond-haired face of his daughter poked through the curtain, a gap in her smile where the Tooth Fairy had visited.

'Hi, Daddy!' Her voice was trimmed with excitement.

'Hey, Kitten.'

She smiled again, scrambling into the booth, her little feet trampling over his belongings.

'How you doing?'

'I'm fine.'

'Yeah? You behaving?'

She nodded, her piercing eyes darting around the booth, the bright lights dazzling her.

'How's school?'

'It's okay.' She looked up at him, her eyes rendering him powerless. 'Mummy said you can't come to my birthday?'

There it was: the guilt, bubbling up inside his stomach and uppercutting his heart. He tried to maintain his composure, refusing to divert his gaze from hers. The puppy dog eyes made his heart wince again.

'I have to go away, Kitten.' He stroked her hair from her eyes, the corners slowly building up with tears. 'But I'll tell you what. When I get back, we will go and have the biggest bowl of ice cream EVER!'

'Really?' The hope clawed at his chest, her love-filled words yanking on his heartstrings like an acoustic guitar.

'I promise.' He extended his little finger, which she hooked onto with her own. 'And I will call you first thing on your birthday and sing you a brand-new birthday song!'

She smiled at him before reaching up and wrapping her arms around his neck. He held her close to him, embracing the fruity smell of her blond hair, the fluffy trim of her coat hood tickling his nose.

'You be good for your mum, okay?'

Chloe nodded and then slowly backed out of the booth, her gloved hand wrapping around her mother's.

Bermuda stood and followed, stepping out onto the busy concourse and into the disappointed glare of his ex-wife. 'Hi, Ange.' He spoke carefully. 'You look pissed.'

'Language!' Angela scorned him, tutting as he mimicked being scared, to his daughter's amusement.

'I'm sorry.'

'You really can't make it?' Her voice was heavy, tired of having to question him. 'It's her birthday, for Christ's sake!'

'You think I want to miss it? And if I did, do you really think I'd go to fucking Glasgow?' He immediately held his hand up in apology.

Angela rolled her eyes.

'It's my job.'

'Well I'm glad that your job is very important.'

'Hey, that's not fair!' he replied, his voice betraying his sternness.

'Fair?' she angrily whispered, leaning away from their daughter's earshot. 'What's not fair is you spending the last six months getting her hopes up and then bailing when it's time for you to act like her dad!'

Before Bermuda could respond, Angela tightened her grip of Chloe's hands and used her other to wipe the tear that Bermuda's curse had caused.

It was getting hard to keep the positivity up.

The curse was becoming a curse again.

'Ange, I'm sorry,' he meekly offered, his vision blurring at the edges as the tears seeped in. He couldn't even look at his daughter.

Just as the only two women he loved were about to disappear into the relentless stream of commuters, Angela turned to him. The mother of his most treasured possession. The woman he had vowed to spend his life with.

'I'm sorry, too.'

With his heart breaking once more, Bermuda watched them vanish in the crowd, whisked away by the continuous rush of London. The shrill call of a whistle cut through the air, drawing his attention to the platform. With a deep sigh and a lifetime of regret, he slowly made his way to his seat, grimacing at the journey ahead.

---

THE TRAIN ROLLED TO A STOP, jolting slightly and guiding Bermuda to a face-first collision with the window. Muttering under his breath, he slowly eased himself out of his chair, amazed as he reached for his bag with an arm that earlier in the day was supported by a sling.

He was healing.

Rapidly.

Concern etched its way across his face, the idea of merging fully with the Otherside enough to make his stomach flip. He had been to that world once, the swirling smoke that engulfed the land. The blood-red eyes that had stalked him. Since that moment, he had been threatened countless times, the words of another world promising to tear him apart.

One day they would claim him.

Just not yet.

He followed the businessmen off the carriage, stepping onto the freezing cold platform at Glasgow, the glass ceiling hoovering up the moonlight before throwing it onto the concourse below. It was just after eight o'clock in the evening; the world was at home, sitting on sofas eating TV dinners or spending some quality time with the family. The boring, mundane repetition of life.

As Bermuda slowly made his way towards the ticket barriers, he yearned for that existence, to have no other worry other than what Sophie was cooking for dinner. He shook her from his mind, not wanting to re-tread the pain of the 'one who got away'. Well, more like the 'one who ran away'. With a deep sigh, he posted his ticket through the machine and reluctantly stepped through.

God, it was cold.

Even in the brightly lit station, with its row of coffee shops and fast food stands all ablaze with activity, Bermuda felt a chill, as if an ice cube had been dropped into the crack of his arse. He arched his neck up, his eyes scanning the large clock that hung from the centre of the glass arched roof.

An Other clung to it, its long fingers stretched across it like wild roots. Its body was slim and shiny, and a small indented pattern ran across it. Its face bore sharp teeth and completely grey eyes. Its head slowly moved back and forth like a typewriter carriage.

It was hunting.

Bermuda dropped his overnight bag, its contents a mishmash of unfolded shirts, underwear, and toiletries. He stared at the Other, waiting patiently before its shimmering face turned, their eyes meeting for the first time. Its eyes narrowed as it hunched its shoulders, coiling itself like a spring.

It drew back its lips, razor-sharp teeth zigzagging across one another like the head of a broom.

Bermuda could sense its hatred.

'He is not of our concern.'

Argyle's words were calm as he approached Bermuda, his ability to meet him at any location no longer surprising Bermuda.

'I know.' Bermuda spoke, his stare maintained. 'I just want it to know I'm watching.'

The creature continued its stare, its sharp, jagged fingers screeching across the clock face. Saliva dropped from its vicious snarl, the teeth that may very well have ripped flesh from bone.

Bermuda crossed his arms.

The creature snarled.

Sure enough, it broke the stare, its misshapen skull

whipping back and forth before it scuttled around the clock and shimmied across the glass roof and away towards the welcoming darkness of the shadow. With a sense of victory, Bermuda picked up his bag and smiled at his partner.

'See? I win.'

Argyle shook his head as he watched his partner stroll towards the exit. 'Your sense of victory is very strange.'

Bermuda continued walking, carefully dodging the frustrated commuters who dominated the concourse, all angrily checking their watches and muttering as 'delayed' appeared next to more and more trains on the timetable.

'Well to be honest, mate, I was in a pretty bad car accident, I'm missing my little girl's birthday to come and catch what we believe to be an Other-worldly murderer, and to top it all off, I'm in fucking Glasgow.'

A few commuters scowled at the bizarre man, cursing their town to himself.

'So I am looking for victories wherever I can.'

'You seem displeased to be here,' Argyle stated as the two of them strode through the large automatic glass doors of the station to be hit by a wall of cold.

Bermuda almost stopped in his tracks, the freezing wind hitting him harder than any creature from another world could. It ripped through his skin, shattered his bones, and froze his marrow.

'JESUS!' he exclaimed, frantically pulling his armoured coat together and latching the buttons. He fitfully rifled though the pockets, slipping his hands into his black gloves before attaching his beanie hat to his head. The tip of it was longer, flopping over to the side like a gnome's hat.

Bermuda had been called worse.

Shaking violently and struggling to stop his teeth from chattering, he turned to Argyle as a slap of drizzle drifted through on the wind and caught him on the cheek.

Argyle stood unhindered. His armour covered his chest, but his arms were naked, the moisture of the night sky causing them to shimmer in the moonlight. He peered back at his partner, his grey eyes offering nothing but innocence.

'Are you cold?' His words were caring.

'Just a little, Big Guy,' Bermuda responded, his hands stuffed in his pockets and his shoulders hunched. He bobbed on the spot, his body clutching at every straw for warmth.

'We should head to the crime scene. You are to liaise with a DC Sam McAllister.' Argyle looked down the street, the wide roads lined by tall, gothic-looking buildings, the ground floors all turned into the usual high street stores. People sprawled across the street, crossing paths as if the words of the Tome had come alive.

'Will he even be there?' Bermuda questioned, raising his arm to hail a cab. One flashed its headlights.

'We shall see.'

'That sounds very positive.' Bermuda knew his sarcasm was lost on Argyle, but he smiled as the cab pulled up to the curb. He opened the door, tossing his bag onto the back seat. As the wind cut through him once more, he slowly turned back to Argyle. 'Race you there?'

Argyle grunted, standing motionlessly as Bermuda closed the door behind him.

The cab pulled away, heading towards the looming, ice cold city of Glasgow as the hunt for the murderer began.

# SEVEN

IT WASN'T ENOUGH.

That had become clear to him when she hadn't returned. He had done as asked, delivered another heart, and yet they still hadn't been appeased. He had walked away, leaving the heart at the door as instructed and making the lonely walk back to the darkness.

Now, as he sat across the bar and watched the young women chatting enthusiastically as one of them showed off a pathetic new piece of jewellery, he knew they needed more.

They would require another.

He looked down at his fingers, the wrinkled knuckles stretched as he clasped his glass. The burning scotch that filled it would have little effect.

The barmaid had called it 'classy' when he had ordered it, more out of habit than desire. It was for appearances. The world saw him as one of their own and he would not pull back the veil just yet. There was no need.

There was no her.

He lifted the glass and relieved it of its contents, the liquid burning the back of his throat and disintegrating before it reached his stomach. The thumping noise from the speaker above was foolishly labelled music, a disgrace to the wonders he had heard when she was in his arms.

Where were the trumpets? The strings?

The sense of class?

He shuddered, looking at the scantily clad women that adorned the high seats, all of them leaning over cocktails with their bodies on show. Like a low-rent meat market. Beyond them, leering men looked on, all of them nothing more than cheap aftershave and misplaced machismo. Nothing like how men used to be.

How he used to be.

As he gently gestured for a refill to the waitress, a dark feeling crept into his mind, like a leak slowly filling up a bucket. What did he used to be? He had always been him. That nagging doubt, this vague recollection of dust and stone flickered and disappeared as quickly as a lightning bolt.

He was Kevin Parker.

A man who was doing what he could to bring back the one he loved. The one they had lied to. His concentration was broken when a napkin, shortly followed by a scotch, was placed in front of him by the waitress, her smile as fake as her tan.

'Thank you,' he uttered politely, a gentleman's smile her tip. He reached for his wallet.

'No need.' She spoke through chewing gum. 'It's already been paid for.'

She directed his gaze to a smiling woman sat by the bar who looked over with interest. She was pretty, petite but not in a worrying way. Her auburn hair was pulled neatly into a bob, her large, blue eyes were framed with a gentle purple shadow. She wore a tight-fitting pair of jeans and a rose-patterned top.

He smiled, gently easing himself up off the chair and

falling into the role of the grateful stranger. All he would have to do is be polite, compliment her a few times, and pretend to care what she said.

It was almost too easy.

He noticed her straightening her top and shuffling anxiously on her stool. He had to ignore the sharp prod of guilt that accompanied each step.

She didn't deserve this.

But then again, neither had the one they took from him.

The young lady turned slightly, noticing his hesitation. 'I don't bite,' she offered playfully, her smile revealing cute dimples.

'Of course not.' Kevin stumbled, looking towards the exit.

'It was just a drink. You don't have to stay.'

'No, it's not that.' He offered her a weak smile before looking to the door again.

'Are you married?'

'No.'

'Is there another woman?'

'Why do you ask?' His voice instantly hardened, and his back stiffened as well.

'You keep looking at the door as if someone is going to burst in and catch you.'

His shoulders relaxed, and he chuckled, taking a sip of the drink she had bought him. She frowned, her delicately plucked eyebrows pulling her face inward.

'There is no one.' He took another sip. 'Not anymore.'

'Then have a seat …' she gestured to him.

'Kevin.'

'Katie.' She extended a small, open hand. 'Nice to meet you, Kevin.'

'Nice to meet you too, Miss …' he raised his eyebrows, his smooth, chiselled face more welcoming.

'Oh, Steingold. Miss Steingold. But like I said, Katie.'
'Katie it is.'

She chuckled, looking slightly baffled by the strange behaviour of the handsome stranger. He was well-groomed and seemed to be in good shape. His suit, while custom made, seemed slightly too big for him.

'You seem different,' she stated abruptly.

'Different?' he questioned, finishing his drink and motioning for another. 'You don't know me.'

'I mean different to all the other men in here. You actually seem like the type of person who can hold a conversation. Who is actually out for a drink, as opposed to a walking hard-on who is looking to get coked up and hope to avoid an STD.' Her accent became stronger the more she ranted, the Glaswegian girl escaping slightly.

'I don't see the point in the drugs they take or the behaviour they embody. There is a decorum lacking in today's society and I refuse to condone or partake.'

She giggled slightly, sipping her gin until the straw roared against the bottom of her glass. The barman placed a fresh drink before them both. Kevin handed over a note, waving away the notion of being handed back change.

'That's a very generous tip,' Katie exclaimed. 'I wish you'd came into my shop.'

'You will have to tell me where it is, so I can experience your hospitality.'

'Hehe. You do talk funny, you know that?'

'I merely speak properly.' His words were smooth, his voice soft.

She took a sip of her drink before flicking her hair back, hoping he picked up on the body language. He remained stoic, and the difficulty she had reading him was becoming slightly arousing. She composed herself, sipping her drink before peering into his unflinching gaze.

'You must have stolen a heart or two in your time,

huh?' She leaned slightly towards him as he grinned a perfect set of teeth.

'You have no idea.'

His whispered response was lost on her as their lips pressed together. The thumping music slowly vanished and he could feel her heart racing.

Her heart.

With an excitement in her eyes, she left her chair, leading him by the hand towards the door. As they slithered through the dance floor, evading the drunken and the desperate, he gazed upon her one more time.

She would be dead by sunrise.

Hopefully this would be the last one.

---

'MCALLISTER HAS ALREADY LEFT for the evening.'

The thick Scottish accent belonged to PC Billy Ferguson, a large, heavyset Scotsman with a thick ginger beard. He looked like he had leapt straight off a box of porridge. Bermuda sighed, the freezing wind jabbing at him with frozen fingers. The door to the flat was closed, police tape criss-crossed from the frame like a morbid gift. Ferguson had been sat in his car, heaters blazing as he watched the premises.

'I need to see the crime scene.'

'You press?'

'No.' Bermuda scoffed. 'Even I'm not that much of a dick.'

'You ain't from round here, lad. You from London?'

'For my sins.' Bermuda clenched his fists, willing his hands back to life. The cold clung onto them, claiming them as its own.

'What's it like being a big southern softy in this weather?' Ferguson smirked, his toothless grin a testament to a few scrapes. Bermuda got the impression he was not the sort of police officer who sought peaceful resolution.

'It has its perks.' Bermuda smirked. 'Education, good looks, decent pay. What's it like being Scottish?'

Ferguson's brow furrowed, his thick ginger eyebrows almost covering his beady eyes. His police-issue raincoat was zipped up to the neck, the collar consumed by his mighty beard.

'You wanna watch that mouth of yours.' He shook his head, stepping past Bermuda and onto the two steps that led to the front door. 'But you are not getting in this flat without a warrant or McAllister present.'

'But I'm the specialist they were sending.'

'You could be Angelina Fucking Jolie, I still can't let you in.' He broadened his shoulders, his imposing frame almost filling the doorway. 'Now run along, before I lose my temper.'

Bermuda muttered under his breath, and a fresh army of raindrops clattered against him as the Glasgow night took a turn for the worse. Ferguson crossed his arms, the thick forearms resting on the slight paunch of his stomach. The rain covered everything in a beautiful shimmer.

The bitter cold almost froze it solid.

After a few moments of glaring, Bermuda slowly turned on the heel of his Converse and headed back down the small path, passing the metal gate and running a hand through his drenched hair. His entire body shook, the slight remnants of his injuries struggling to be heard over the numbing temperature. He almost chuckled – the thought of hurtling off of Hammersmith flyover made him remember how goddamn absurd his life was.

'We need to get into the residence.'

Argyle's words were calm yet firm, the voice of a soldier. Bermuda nodded, slapping two Tic Tacs into his mouth and hoping they didn't freeze. The water bounced off of Argyles chest plate, the droplets exploding like fireworks on impact.

'Well, Bonnie McHaggis over there won't let us in.' Bermuda patted Argyle's exposed arm, the cold bouncing off his skin. 'Let's go before my testicles are lost forever.'

Bermuda took a few steps before turning back. Argyle stood staring at the burly police officer, whose glare was locked onto Bermuda like a missile.

'But we need to get into that residence.'

'Well next time, Argyle, make sure the person we need is actually here,' Bermuda replied, frustration wriggling free through his words. 'Or move that deep-fat-fried dickhead out of the way.'

'I cannot harm humans. You know my job is to protect you, not instigate violence.'

Bermuda smiled. Even in the freezing cold downpour of a Glasgow night, Argyle never wavered.

'I know, Big Guy. Let's head back.'

Bermuda turned again, scolding the notion of a soulless Premier Inn bedroom, the same linen and layout in every room. The same plastic meals and tepid showers.

It had a bar though. Although he was pretty sure it wouldn't have Doom Bar.

'Did he threaten you?'

Argyle's question was laced with innocence.

'Who? PC Scotsman?' Bermuda pointed sloppily with his thumb towards the law-abiding blockade. 'No.'

'Oh that's a shame.' Argyle turned, his face expressionless. 'If he had, I would be forced to act.'

Bermuda frowned in confusion for merely a second before realisation kicked in, taking the form of a sly grin across his handsome face. 'Argyle. You fiend.'

'Did he?' Ever the soldier, he turned his attention back to PC Ferguson, who rubbed his leather-clad hands together for warmth.

'Yes he did,' Bermuda lied. 'He threatened me constantly.'

Argyle nodded, his powerful footsteps silent as he crunched through the puddles, the heavy downpour adding to his majesty. The rain clattered against his mighty frame, the streetlights making them glisten. The metal band that housed the Retriever dripped freezing droplets. His massive sword swung from his back, the blade slippery and bright.

He looked every bit the soldier.

Ferguson glared towards Bermuda, who was staring at him. Before he could confront the annoying Londoner, he suddenly felt himself hunching forward, his body uncontrollably folding onto itself.

'Help me!' he bellowed, his voice struggling over the orchestra of the rain. 'Someone!'

Slowly, he found himself staring at his knees, his entire body hunched forward as much as possible. He swung his arms aimlessly, each swing whipping through the freezing air and colliding only with raindrops. Bermuda took a few steps towards the gate, stepping to the side to avoid the wild fists.

Bermuda chuckled. He had watched as Argyle had approached, and with one swift movement grabbed the back of Ferguson's stab-proof vest. With effortless force, he had pushed Ferguson forward, arching his back and bunching him into a ball towards the wet pavement. His swings and cries for help were in vain.

Argyle slowly lowered his captive to the ground until his knees were firmly planted on the cold concrete, his head resting against them.

'Keep him quiet, mate,' Bermuda instructed as he pushed open the front door to the building and ducked under the yellow and black tape.

Argyle obliged, reaching down with his other mighty

hand and clasping it tightly over Ferguson's mouth. A passer-by stopped for a second on the street, observing the bizarre policeman hunched over in the rain.

He couldn't see the hulking warrior who held him in place.

He hadn't seen the BTCO agent who had snuck through the front door, either.

---

ONCE INSIDE, Bermuda took his wet hat off, his hair slicked against his forehead. Drops from the drizzle snaked down his face before suicide diving towards the ground. The modest flat was homely, a 'woman's touch' clearly evident. On the delicate dining table sat two cups, one full of coffee, the other, lipstick heavy, was almost empty. The cafetière was clogged with slowly solidifying coffee, and the thought made Bermuda gag.

There were worse things in this flat than stale coffee.

He looked at the sofa, the cushions askew, their random scattering out of place in the neatness of the home. They had both been in here, their night winding down to what she must have believed would be a happy ending. They had established a trust, no matter how fresh, and that was duly betrayed.

A fatal consequence.

Slowly shaking his head, he looked around the room, the TV straight and well-polished. The photos that lined the unit, and the fireplace were also straight, all of them showing a pretty woman with a smile across her face.

Nicole Miller was a recently divorced schoolteacher. That was all he had to go on. She was a few years younger than Bermuda, and she had no history of trouble. No potential enemies. A scumbag ex-husband, but no one who would want to hurt her.

To kill her.

He sighed, the feeling in his numb fingers slowly returning as he pulled his e-cig from his pocket. A sudden clatter, like someone spilling dry rice on a metal floor, caused him to startle, the rain raising its ferocity as it lashed the streets outside. He thought of Argyle and how long he could hold that officer down before a passer-by intervened or his fellow officers noticed his silence.

He needed to hurry.

With careful steps, not wanting to contaminate the scene, Bermuda edged through the front room, a small flash of blue and then fruit-flavoured smoke as he drew on his e-cig. Through the door to the hallway, he noticed the kitchen, the streetlight outside illuminating the modest appliances. The silver fridge glistened, the random, colourful scribblings of toddlers displayed proudly.

To the left of the kitchen was the bathroom. To the right was a hole where the bedroom door had been. The wooden frame was fractured, shards of wood sprinkled the floor like a bed of hay, and the hinges where wrenched beyond repair. Through the darkened doorway, he could see a remnant of the door, broken and shattered from a collision that was too strong to be human. He could imagine her fear.

She was found on the bed in her underwear, undoubtedly waiting for him to enter. She must have been terrified.

Bermuda took a deep breath and walked into the room, staring ahead at the broken door panels that were scattered across a dressing table, a few more roughly resting against the wardrobe.

He slowly turned to look at the bed.

Nicole was no longer there, the coroner respectfully having moved the young lady to be cleaned up. Her family would still need to identify her body, but there was no confusion as to the cause of death.

The blood that still adorned the walls and doused the bedsheets confirmed what Bermuda had been told.

Nicole Miller's heart was ripped from her chest.

There was no weapon. No signs of cuts or restraints. Just a handprint on her throat and a hole in her body. A hand had ripped through flesh, bone, and muscle to wrench her life from its cage.

Something had brutally killed her.

Bermuda took a moment, the gentle rattling of rain against the window echoing loudly as he imagined the scene, the beastly Other leering over the scantily clad woman before ending her life.

Before committing the biggest crime an Other could.

Killing a human.

Punishable by deportation, and then, ultimately death.

Slowly, Bermuda's fingers began to curl, squeezing into a fist as his rage began to bubble. He thought of her family, the pictures of proud parents stood beside her that mounted the fireplace. A father, just like he was, would now be mourning his daughter, having to plan a funeral he could never have comprehended. With a silent nod of the head, Bermuda promised Nicole's family he would find her killer.

Her family.

Suddenly, his head snapped back to the front room, and he dashed through the hallway. As he did, he could hear the crackle of a police radio through the rain-covered window. They wouldn't receive a response, which meant another officer would be sent. He listened carefully.

'*ETA three minutes.*'

With the final grains of sand in his hourglass losing their battle with gravity, Bermuda took out his e-cig and flashed the light over the mantelpiece that adorned the fireplace. Everything was meticulously straight.

Except one photo.

It was of Nicole, her face a picture of happiness as her parents framed her, their pride leaping from the photo. She wore a dark gown and a square hat, the family celebrating her graduation. The start of a long and happy life.

A life snatched away.

The frame had been placed back on the ledge, almost straight. But as the light from outside shone through, Bermuda looked carefully down the line of the shelf. It was off. It had been placed back without care. Carefully reaching into his pocket, Bermuda pulled out a small leather pouch, another toy from the BTCO. Unlike with his tomahawk, Bermuda was at least entrusted with some tools of the trade.

He unclipped the pouch and pulled out a thin white sheet with a pair of tweezers. It looked like a sheet of paper made of smoke, the material so thin you could see straight through. Durable but extremely malleable, the element known as 'mundra' was sourced from the Otherside and combined with flour, which Bermuda found incredibly strange.

Slowly, he draped the mundra over the frame before pressing it against the frame firmly with the flat side of the utensil. The material would clasp on, then when removed, would reveal any relevant markings.

A fingerprint.

Bermuda counted back from thirty, his eyes darting round the room as he heard the faint wailing of a siren shrieking in the wet Glasgow night.

Time to go.

He carefully loosened the edges before pulling the mundra off the frame. With his other hand he fished a clear plastic bag from the pouch and stuffed the sheet in. Whatever was on the frame, he would know as soon as he located the BTCO office in Glasgow.

The siren grew louder, its screams arching through the

rain. Bermuda slipped back through the door; Argyle was still crouched down, his hands firmly planted on Officer Ferguson, who had long since given up the fight. He lay still, completely drenched, as a few civilians took a few steps back.

Bermuda flashed his BTCO badge.

'Argyle.' He spoke through gritted teeth. 'Let's go, now.'

Bermuda walked briskly through the gate. The onlookers' confusion was buying him a few seconds before questions would be asked. Argyle released Ferguson, who slowly began to wriggle. He slowly pushed himself to his knees, his beard littered with gravel.

One of the passers-by offered him a hand up.

A police car screeched around the corner.

Bermuda and Argyle had disappeared into the wet of the night.

# EIGHT

THEY HAD BEEN WATCHING from the moment he had arrived.

From the moment he had stepped through the doors of Glasgow Central Train Station, they had followed. Clinging to the shadows, they had moved in unison, two to the street of occupation, two to the street ahead, and two to the street behind. They had slithered between buildings, cloaked in darkness.

He was as they had been told.

Partnered with a creature of incredible power, they were wise to stay to the edges. To only follow. Now, as the one they called Bermuda emerged from the house, Argyle released the human he had pinned to the wet ground.

They ran.

Stood in the shadows, the soldier slowly raised a gloved hand, pulling down the hood that adorned its skull.

Its mask was sheer white.

No grooves, no markings. Nothing that would identify as a facial feature. Just a smooth crescent of white that curved to the neck. Below hung its cloak, draped over powerful, armour-clad shoulders. The rest of its imposing frame merged with the darkness, camouflaged to the night and undetectable to the human eye.

As Bermuda and Argyle raced towards the horizon, the soldier peered across the street, beyond the crowds of vile humans being lashed by the downpour of an unforgiving storm. Beyond the powerful, fuel-consuming cars that destroyed the planet.

An alley cut a line between two houses, the light from the street lamp trying its best to invade the opening. In the shadows, another white face emerged, another watcher.

One of the Legion.

Knowing more would be lining the streets, they would continue to monitor, watch, as they slowly learnt what he could do. Their leader had informed them that the target could walk in both worlds, that he possessed power far greater than he knew.

His partner would die for him, their loyalty born of their mutual rejection of the worlds they inhabited. He was a threat, a mistake of their world that this one crudely called 'the Otherside'. Those humans, the ones who could see them, would soon fear them again.

They were the Legion.

They were one of many.

As their targets vanished from sight, the two soldiers took a few steps back, enveloped by the shadows. Their watch was over, and together they would report back to Mandrake, their general.

He was the one who had found them.

The one who had made them the Legion.

They had all shared the same journey. All of them had been created in the dark fields of the Otherside, some of them lucky to survive the frozen times. As the elements, wild inhabitants, and time passed through their settlement, they had whittled the group down to the remaining few.

Once they had outgrown their creators, they killed them, feasting on them for sustenance.

More humanoid than the wild creatures that stalked their world, the eight of them pilgrimaged to the historic land of Healund, where civilisation had been formed by the more controlled of their species. All eight of them were over seven-foot tall, their shoulders broad and their eyes a pure black. Their skin, thick and grey, wrapped around skeletons that had arms slightly too long and protruded sharp, jagged bones from their shoulders.

Six fingers hung from meaty hands, all of them tipped with razor-esque talons.

Most striking of all was they had no mouth – just a small, vertical strip that ran from their eyes to chin that could syphon nourishment when the skin was broken.

Feeding was a rarity then.

They had survived together for three light passings, one of them nearly being feasted upon by a wild beast which was slain and consumed. They communicated through grunts and signals, eventually establishing a bond.

They became a family.

Eventually they hit the walls of Healund, their imposing formation causing a panic amongst its habitants.

They eventually were brought to Mandrake, who formed what would become the Legion. They were teamed with the greatest warrior their world possessed until his betrayal had seen him banished.

They would become the most feared rumour within the Otherside.

A death squad.

The Legion.

And as Bermuda and Argyle ran through the freezing, wet Glasgow night, they had no idea that they were being watched.

AS THE BRIGHT sign of Premier Inn came into view, Bermuda decided to stop jogging. His lungs ached, still paying him back for years of nicotine abuse, his decision to quit off the back of having to run up the steps of Big Ben six months earlier.

But that was for a true reason.

He scolded himself, annoyed that he had allowed his mind to flicker back to the beautiful face of Sophie Summers, the woman he was sure could have loved him if his life didn't involve hidden monsters and problem drinking. The rain had calmed, reducing itself to a light drizzle, and after running over two miles, he found its coldness refreshing.

Argyle came to a stop beside him, the water shimmering off his magnificent armour. He stood proudly, the run having no effect on him at all. 'I believe we have placed ourselves a sufficient distance from the scene.'

Bermuda nodded, still trying to catch his breath, stretching his legs out to avoid the inevitable cramp.

'As an agent, you should train your body to tolerate such abuse.'

'I do.' Bermuda smirked. 'You've seen me drink.'

They began walking, Bermuda's adequate room awaiting.

'Ah, the alcohol.'

'You're telling me, back in your world, you didn't have tipple?'

'Tipple?' Argyle's voice oozed confusion.

'Yeah, you know, a drink of choice?' Bermuda puffed his e-cig. 'I have visions of you slamming steins of mead before laying a bar wench.'

Argyle stared blankly ahead, allowing the silence to

hang between them. Eventually, as the door to the hotel became visible, he spoke.

'My time spent in my world was not filled with laughter. It was darkness, which led to nothing but bloodshed and death.' He turned and looked at a shocked Bermuda. 'Here, on this world, I feel at peace.'

Argyle walked on, his eyes conveying no emotion, but Bermuda respectfully nodded. As powerful as his partner was, he knew there was a softer side to Argyle, a strange sense of humanity trying its best to surface.

They marched forward, their footsteps slapping wet pavement as the drizzle surrounded them. A few taxis shot up the wide street which was lined by large, gothic-looking buildings that arched over the pavement like the branches of a cliché horror tree. The magnificent buildings glistened in the wet moonlight, wrapping around the busy city like an impenetrable wall.

As Bermuda reached the steps of his hotel, he heard a loud yell. A clearly drunk homeless man on the other side of the road was yelling profanities at a group of teenagers, all of them chuckling as they mocked. Their thick Glaswegian accents were lost on Bermuda, who shook his head and left them to it.

Somehow, Argyle found peace on this world.

A few hours later, Bermuda had found his, the last of the thick, cool liquid hitting the back of his throat as he brought his pint glass back to the bar. It rattled slightly, garnering a disgruntled scowl from the bartender who wanted to be anywhere but there.

Bermuda could relate.

He had entered his hotel room that night and unpacked his stuff, the anger at McAllister's absence gnawing at him like a termite. McAllister knew he would be arriving, therefore he should have waited and briefed him of the scene and next steps. Now he was sure that the unfortunate PC who had experienced Argyle's handiwork would put in a complaint, which somehow would filter back to Montgomery Black back in London.

That was a phone call he was looking forward to as much as a prostate exam.

Bermuda motioned to the barman for another Doom Bar, tapping his empty glass and wearily trying to recount the number preceding it. It didn't matter. He wasn't drinking for joy or sadness. He was drinking out of boredom.

As the screens above the bar replayed a hard-looking tackle on a pre-taped rugby game, Bermuda woozily peered around the establishment. The bar was dimly lit, a few bright beams across the far walls illuminated booths, all filled with chirpy groups of friends – a few of the lads knocking back shots to the cheers, another bunch of girls, all white teeth and fake tans, were posing for the perfect selfie.

A few old Scotsmen sat on opposite sides of the bar, propping up the walls like pillars built into the pub itself, and would occupy their seats until the day they died. They were more than just locals; they were inhabitants. Life outside on the freezing streets of Glasgow held nothing for them anymore.

As he wondered about the families they had lost, his mind flashed to Chloe, his beautiful daughter and the relationship he was still clinging to. In the six months since he'd welcomed her slowly back into his life, he had begun to accept his gift. His ability to help save two worlds meant he could keep hers safe and keep the horrors of the Otherside at bay. He had embraced his position, even impressing Argyle with his few attempts at exercise and his refusal to smoke.

But missing her birthday because a goddamn Other

couldn't unhook a bra properly sent his newfound positivity straight into a brick wall.

The barman sat Bermuda's drink in front of him, the thick froth sliding down the glass like a white snake. He handed the barman a note, waving away the change and quickly sipping the ale in a hope to remove the onset of depression and replace it with the numbness of a sweet inebriation.

He may have been in freezing Scotland. He may have had no clue what the hell had happened to that poor girl. He may have been missing his daughter's birthday.

But goddamn it, Bermuda was going to have a drink!

'Mine's a G'n'T.'

The soft voice was laced with a thick Glaswegian accent and Bermuda groggily turned to his left. The woman smiled; her brown hair was messy and her eyes, a deep green, were vacant. She swayed next to him, her athletic body wrapped in a tight red dress. She definitely looked after herself, but her body seemed more practical than perfection.

Bermuda was looking at her legs when a finger, adorned by a peach nail, beckoned him up.

'Hey. No looking till you buy me a drink.'

She was smashed. But hey, so was he. Bermuda ordered her a gin and tonic, with the bartender making it clear he wasn't going to serve them beyond that drink. The lady retorted with a middle finger and then chuckled to herself, her concentration spinning as much as the room was. She rested her hand on Bermuda's shoulder, steadying herself before knocking back the clear drink in one. The ice rattled as she slammed it back in the bar.

'So, you gonna take me back to yours or what?'

The question took Bermuda by surprise and he spluttered his drink, the dark brown ale splattering over his lap.

He laughed as he turned to her, the sternness of her face telling him it wasn't a joke. He took another sip.

'I don't even know your name,' he offered. He took another sip.

'Does that matter?'

Bermuda looked straight ahead, weighing up the situation in his head. Every sensible part of his brain was being slowly silenced as well as the eradication of his self-respect. He shrugged and downed the rest of his pint. 'Let's go.'

---

THEY STUMBLED through the door of his hotel room, with the lady staggering forward, laughing wildly as he fumbled with the door. A few of his clothes were draped across the well-made, adequate bed of the Premier Inn. She managed to make it to the dresser, beckoning Bermuda to her as he tried to wrestle control of the alcohol. She unbuckled his belt, and before he could move, she had him in her hand, guiding him to the bed where their clothes messily came off. With considerable effort, their lips locked, their naked bodies writhed over each other, and soon she was sat atop him. As they bounced on the bed with zero rhythm, Bermuda took stock of her body. Her slim figure showed a few scars, especially across the tops of her arms and legs.

He ran a finger over them, her hand instantly shooting down and guiding him back to her body. She pushed down harder on him, a rage almost taking over her as she panted, her eyes closed, and teeth gritted. Bermuda reached up and held her shoulder, his quizzical fingers again finding the scars, this time that criss-crossed her bicep. She angrily slapped his chest.

'Fuck off!'

In a moment she was off him, trying to roll to the side,

but her momentum soon sent her naked and sprawling to the floor.

Bermuda chuckled, fumbling for a lamp and quickly casting a small glow over her crumpled, naked body. 'Need a hand?'

She reached up and slapped his face, her eyes watering with sheer venom. He shook it off, perplexed by the fury that resided in her. She marched around the room, collecting her discarded clothes and purse and slipping herself back into her underwear.

'Look, let's just calm down. Here, have some water.'

Bermuda hand-poured some water into a glass and offered it, his voice calm as he tried to recover the situation. It had been a while since he had had sex, and this wasn't exactly the 'big finish' he had in mind.

The woman grabbed the glass and threw the water at him. Then the glass itself. It cannoned off his elbow, causing him to swear in pain.

'Fuck you, you prick.'

Her vicious words followed her like a trail of smoke as she slammed the door behind her. Bermuda stood, holding his fast-bruising elbow, naked and despondent. The moment had gone, and he woozily collapsed on the bed, wondering when he had become so terrible at sex.

He was asleep within seconds.

# NINE

THE MORNING SUN cut through the curtains, an unwelcome wave of brightness that caused Bermuda to stir. He moaned loudly, his hangover colliding off the sides of his skull like a cruel game of Pong. He slowly pushed himself to a seated position, the world swirling around and slowly coming into focus. The cheap, minimalistic furniture of the Premier Inn slid back into its correct position. The on-brand purple curtains stopped swaying and provided an inadequate shield to the outside world.

He felt like shit.

Bermuda took a deep breath, the memories of the night before returning to him in pieces, a jigsaw that had been placed in a blender. A few pieces fit. He recalled the freezing cold and breaking into a crime scene. There was definitely alcohol, the temptation of vomiting, and the brain-piercing headache was testament to that.

The woman.

Bermuda lifted the sheets, greeted by his naked body. The woman who he could vaguely remember, but whose name escaped him. Did he even ask for it? Did she want him to know? He fell back on his pillow, trying his level best to remember her face. An image of her naked body writhing on top of him appeared then vanished, an echo of a memory.

She had fallen. He had laughed.

With a deep sigh, he chalked it up as just another unsuccessful night, a never-ending cycle of sexual failure. He also scolded himself for thinking of Sophie as if his drunken escapade amounted to an act of betrayal. What they had had was tender. They had shared one night where it was more than sexual attraction.

It had been real.

Slowly, he hauled himself out of bed, his legs feebly shaking as he held himself up via the wall. The room was a mess, his clothes strewn over the floor, his case turned upside down. A glass, slightly cracked, lay on the floor.

Had she thrown it at him?

His feet slapped against the fake tiles of the bathroom floor and he turned the taps. Splashing water against his stubbled face, he slowly raised his eyes, which were bloodshot and heavy with sleep, to the mirror. He looked a mess. His hair, usually pushed to the side, had burst like a firework over his skull.

His body, chiselled and muscular, was covered in ink, all the random scrawlings, incantations, and symbols that, through the years, had kept him safe from the world that framed his own. Three brutal scars burnt through them all, a painful reminder of how close they had come to claiming him.

Bermuda stepped into the shower cubicle, the jet shower shooting out a hot stream of water that collided with his body, the warmth enveloping his body and washing away the sins of the night before. He stood for an eternity, allowing the drops to slap against him, the freshness wiping away the self-hatred and the drink-induced idiocy.

Maybe Argyle was right. Maybe he should quit?

As he scrubbed the soap across his chest, Bermuda's mind fell back to a time before, when he was living the life he had always wanted.

Angela, his then wife, joining him in the shower before work.

Their daughter, asleep and loved.

Now it was just monsters and failed one-night stands.

With another heavy sigh, he turned the tap, the shower powering down, steam rising from his body like a hot pan. He stepped out of the cubicle and nearly fell to the floor.

'ARGYLE!'

Stood in the bathroom doorway, arms folded and with nobility oozing from him, was Argyle. He raised an eyebrow.

'Is there something wrong?' Never had he been more genuine.

'Yes.' Bermuda scrambled for a towel. 'I'm naked, for fuck's sake.'

'Are you ashamed of your body?'

'No.'

'Then what? Your genitalia? You humans have such a bizarre fixation with your anatomy.'

'No ... it's just ... weird!' Bermuda pulled the towel tight, the absorbent material affixed like a sarong. 'I don't peep on you when you ... do you even shower?'

'My genetic makeup runs a self-sacrificing cycle where my stained or soiled genes are eradicated before they can come to pass, rendering my body completely clean, strong, and at optimum condition.' He then looked at Bermuda, his grey eyes full of innocence. 'Does this trouble you?'

'No, it just makes you even stranger.'

Bermuda pulled his toothbrush to his mouth and began to scrub his teeth, the sour taste of ale being rubbed clean from existence. Hopefully the rest of the failed sexual episode would join it. As his mouth foamed with toothpaste, he looked at his partner in the mirror.

'Hang on.' He spat. 'Why are you here?'

'There has been another murder.'

'I never pegged you as a Taggart fan,' Bermuda replied, searching Argyle's face for any recognition of the reference. None.

'We need to get to the crime scene. Detective McAllister has asked for the specialist, which I understand is you.'

'Oh, McAllister has actually shown up this time, has he? Well let me put on my Sunday fucking best.'

'It's Monday.'

'I was joking!'

'Oh.' Argyle stopped in thought for a moment and then looked stone-faced. 'Very amusing.'

Bermuda shook his head and spat the rest of the toothpaste down the sink before reaching for his mouthwash.

After freshening up, he slowly plodded back to the main room, demanding Argyle turn around while he slipped into a pair of jeans, and a denim shirt with a long sleeved T-shirt underneath for warmth.

On went the coat, the thin lining of Argiln undetectable in the weight. He wrapped a thick woollen scarf around his neck and finished it off with some gloves and a wool beanie hat.

'Let's rock and roll.' He puffed out his cheeks, the hangover latching to him like an overstuffed backpack, trying to haul him to the floor. They would walk out into the horrendous downpour and freezing wind and find a coffee. Then, hopefully, he could start feeling normal again and put his hangover and the horrors of his sex life behind him.

For good.

SAT in the back of the cab, Bermuda looked out at the ancient city of Glasgow. The tall, stone buildings lined the streets, their roofs arching over like demonic fingers, and their gothic aesthetic was as authentic as it was beautiful. Begrudgingly, he had to admit that the town held an aura, a sense of grandeur that a lot of cities, London included, couldn't match. As the rain fell against the beautiful city, it shimmered.

He sipped his coffee, the caffeine hug wrapping its arms around him and fighting away the hangover. He needed to concentrate, forget the crazy, nameless woman from the night before, and focus.

Another woman had been found dead, her heart removed.

This was the work of an Other. He could feel it.

Somewhere in the dark shadows of this city was the killer, a creature from a different world that was brutally slaying these women. Why or how, Bermuda didn't know. But just as he had promised the parents in the photo of the first victim, he was going to find out.

The cab turned onto the road and immediately stopped. At both ends were police cars, a thin layer of police tape draped from tree to lamp post. Bermuda paid, not bothering for a receipt as he stepped out into the rain. A few more cars were dotted down the street, an ambulance and the white tent.

SOCOs were on the scene which meant Bermuda was pretty sure he would get nowhere near the crime scene. As cool as it could be to say you worked for a specialist arm of law enforcement, it sucked when no one cared or believed you. As he scanned the crime scene, Argyle emerged next to him, his arrival as prompt and mysterious as always.

'We need to examine the rooms.' Bermuda spoke,

turning to his partner. 'Shall we try to do it without you needing to flip a car or manhandle a policeman?'

'I merely follow your orders.' Argyle nodded to the nearest police officer. 'He wears a uniform. I do believe if you-'

'Argyle, I'm not wearing a uniform.'

'I wear my armour.'

'Yeah, and you look like an extra in a Thor movie.' Bermuda looked at the police officer, engaging eye contact.

The officer, a young man with a warm smile, beckoned him over. He wore thin, plastic wraps around his uniform to counter the rain. His accent was lighter than most. 'Can I help you, sir?'

'Yes, my name is Agent Jones. I believe DC Sam McAllister is waiting for me.' He flashed his badge, resigned to defeat.

'Aye. Get on in there and get dry.' The officer lifted the tape and smiled, motioning for Bermuda to cross.

Surprised and chuffed, Bermuda strolled through, making his way past a few other officers. The street was traditional suburbs, the pavement lined with cars and driveways, neat front gardens that, in the harshness of winter, were void of any life. Bermuda carefully approached the house, the white overalls of the Scene of Crime Officers were damp with rainwater as they scurried between the residence and their base tent. Behind him, Argyle manoeuvred between people, careful not to collide with them. He, like others of his kind, wore a latch stone, allowing them to interact with our world. The last thing they needed was someone colliding with an invisible brick wall.

Bermuda approached the tent, flashed his badge, and to his surprise, was given a white suit and gloves. He changed quickly; the novelty of being respected was more than welcome.

After a terrible night, this day was going pretty well.

He made his way into the house which had been split into two flats. The door to the left led upstairs to another front door, which had been taped off. He took the door to the right, following the sound of police officers chatting, their voices muffled behind their white masks.

The flat, similar to the one belonging to Nicole Miller, was decorated neatly. Pictures of fun memories and cherished moments hung from specially selected frames. The front room furniture was neat and tidy, a woman's touch evident. Bermuda's heart clenched slightly at the picture of proud parents and their daughter at her graduation. She was pretty, her brown hair framing her face. Her parents towered over her.

'Are you the specialist? Agent Jones?' One of the SOCOs' voices broke his concentration.

'Yep. That's me.'

'The gaffer wants a word.' He pointed to the figure in the white overalls in the kitchen, hands on hips. He was a very slender man.

'Detective McAllister?' Bermuda asked, pointing to the person in the other room.

'Yeah. Careful though,' the young officer warned. 'She's pretty pissed off.'

'She?' Bermuda murmured to himself as he stepped through the doorway to the tidy hallway, allowing a few more SOCOs passed before emerging into the tiny kitchen. Every piece of cutlery and pan was in its predetermined place. A well-maintained kitchen. The complete opposite to the nuclear wasteland that resembled his own.

'Detective McAllister?' Bermuda asked, his voice twitching nervously.

She turned and both of them gasped, her eyes narrowing with anger. A few seconds felt like an eternity.

He was looking at the woman from his hotel room.

'What the fuck are you doing here?' She spoke through gritted teeth, her anger seeping through on each word, her accent thick and intimidating.

'I'm Agent Jones.' Bermuda cursed his luck, yet again.

'You're kidding me.'

'No. And you? Sam?'

'Samantha.'

'Well I get that now.' Bermuda looked around, making sure there was no one in earshot. 'Look, about last night.'

'Forget it. A woman has died, and I'd rather think about the cavernous hole where her chest used to be than about your hands on my body.'

'And there I was thinking we had something,' Bermuda responded, his words dripping with sarcasm.

'Can we just focus on the murder?' McAllister spoke with authority; her eyes, bloodshot, told Bermuda she was battling her own hangover. They would thrash it out, he knew that much.

Just not here.

'Let me guess. Same as Nicole,' Bermuda offered.

'Aye. Single woman. Twenty-eight years of age. Lived alone. Regular social life, on the usual dating scene. Tinder. Bumble. The lot.'

'Are they drugs?' Bermuda asked.

McAllister growled at him.

'I'm literally adding to the tension aren't I?'

'I think it would be best if you didn't say anything.'

Bermuda bit his tongue not to liken it to last night, just nodding and following her through the hall to another door.

'Are you squeamish?' she asked, her eyes dead and her tone uncaring.

'I need to see her.'

McAllister shrugged and pushed open the door. Bermuda stepped in and instantly looked away. At Nicole's flat it had been different – the darkness had surrounded him, the broken door lay in shards in the corner, and the bed was splattered in blood. It was haunting, but it was all past tense. It had all happened, and he had arrived at the end.

This was in the midst of it.

On the bed, Katie Steingold lay motionless, her eyes closed, her head slightly leant to the side. Her rose-patterned top was ripped open, a gaping hole in her chest. Her ribs were shattered or bent in, and one of her lungs lay flat and punctured. Her spine was shunted to the side, an agonising death.

Her heart was clearly missing, the veins leading to it resting on her stomach like an overgrown weed.

She had been brutally murdered.

Seeing the body, Bermuda could feel a tear slowly forming in the corner of his eye. His fist slowly starting to clench. He had made peace with the Otherside, despite its efforts to kill him and those he cared about. He understood the need for the truce; despite his attitude, he agreed with the need for balance.

This was different.

This was a brutal killing of innocent women.

McAllister entered the room, her anger obvious and worn with pride.

'The bastard removed her heart, same as before. No fingerprints, no signs of struggle. No semen. Nothing. No leads to our man.'

'If it is a man,' Bermuda muttered, louder than he intended.

McAllister shifted on her feet. Her default stance was threatening. 'You think this was done by a woman?'

'No, I don't,' Bermuda said, scanning the lifeless, heartless body before him. 'I think it was something else.'

Before McAllister could respond, her radio crackled

into life, the rasping of the machine under her overalls. A seasoned pro, she grasped the button without looking.

*'Ma'am, we've found it.'*

She sighed, looking back at the dead body of Katie Steingold and aching to put it right. She looked at Bermuda, disgust at the night before battling her need to have someone by her side through this.

'Let me guess. The Necropolis.'

The voice on the radio confirmed it and she angrily slammed her fist against the wall of the room before storming out, barking out orders to the team that another team was needed at the Necropolis.

She turned back to Bermuda, eyeing him up and down, not even hiding her disdain. 'I guess you'll be wanting to come along.'

'What's at the Necropolis?' he asked as they burst through the front door of the apartment, removing their overalls and allowing the cold, harsh rain to attack their clothes.

'Her heart,' McAllister replied coldly.

'Huh?' Bermuda patted his coat for his e-cig. 'How do you know that?'

She turned and scowled at him through the cloud of smoke he produced. 'Because it's the same place he delivered the last one.'

She motioned to some of her officers to get going, their cars revving to life as they left in a whirlwind of flashing blue lights and screaming sirens. Argyle, who had stood calmly to the side of the tent, approached Bermuda, his armour glistening in the wetness of the Scottish morning.

'Where are we departing to?' he asked, adjusting the Retriever that lay on his wrist.

'The Necropolis.' Bermuda turned to McAllister, who was one part angrily beckoning him to get in the car, one part curious as to who he was talking to. 'Stay here and keep an eye on things.'

'Why? What's going on?' Argyle asked, watching Bermuda race across the wet crime scene to the detective's car.

Bermuda yelled back before he opened the door. 'I have no fucking idea.'

# TEN

HE HAD DELIVERED IT. Just like the others.

Every time he felt his hand in the warmth of their chest, he imagined her face. Although the light of this person had died, it would illuminate his path. His steps were calm and measured, meandering through the random tombstones, needless memorials to those who had long since passed.

What did they care?

Humanity had always been an odd concept even though he himself was human. He had the memories, a life spent beside her, his beautiful world that was taken from him. He remembered their love but dare not think her name.

Was there more?

Was there another place in his heart, filled with warmth for another creature, one he did not meet nor recall? He shook the notion, allowing the freezing rain to collide with his skin, the sensation of the chill dancing across his skin.

His human skin.

His hands dripped blood, the last remnants of Katie

Steingold. She would be discovered soon enough, eyes wide in fear, her chest a cavernous hole of broken bones and ripped muscles. He had tried to make it quick, hoping she felt as little as possible. Her sacrifice, while final, needn't have been excruciating.

The Necropolis was filled with death; Kevin could sense it in the air as he headed to the exit, his ill-fitted suit flapping in the wind, his tie waving proudly like a flag. He had left the heart in the same place, by the door to the tomb, and made haste to the shadows.

Surely this would be enough?

They said they would return her soon.

As he began to question his deal, he thought back to their first meeting. He remembered his arms held high, metal clasps around his wrists that latched him to the heavy chains bolted to the stone wall. His body, naked and beaten, was being left to rot.

A human body needs care.

The man who had approached him seemed familiar, as if they had met some place in time, in an era that didn't exist, in a world that didn't match.

He had told him he could see her again.

All they needed Kevin to do was bring them the heart of the woman. That was the mission.

That was all it would take.

As the final drops of Katie's blood left his fingertips, he stopped. The Necropolis, a beautiful monument of death, bled behind him like a sinister watercolour painting. Kevin Parker lowered his gaze to his hands, stretching his fingers and staring at his palms.

They had held her so tightly. She had loved him, as he had her, and he remembered twirling her on the dance floor, their fingers interlocking as they made love. His hand resting on her stomach.

The hands that they had wrenched from her, the image

of the dark figures pulling her down the corridor from him, his chilling screams of anguish echoing like a howling wind.

The hands that he would murder those responsible with.

The very hands he was using to kill these women.

For a brief instance, a twinge of guilt passed through him; the thought of removing a love from a life as he had felt was not an easy task. However, he needed her back. He had spent so long in the dark, rotting away to a pointless end.

The man had saved him.

Offered him a purpose.

He recalled the promise, to deliver every heart for hers. That was all. That was the bargain. With the sense that he would soon hold her again, smell her scent and feel even a shred of meaning, it was worth it.

Shaking off any notions of guilt, Kevin Parker stood straight, allowing the freshness of the morning to collide with him. The sun would soon rise and the heart would be found, as always, by the old groundsman, with his pitiful existence of watching over the dead.

The police would arrive, hopefully after they had found and respectfully tended to the body of Katie Steingold.

An integral sacrifice.

Her death, unlike her life, would have a meaning.

That meaning would soon be upon him.

As the wet leaves danced across the graves of the departed, Kevin Parker walked through the cold metal gate of the Necropolis, taking one moment to pause and turn back.

His handsome, chiselled face was splattered with raindrops.

His hands now blood-free.

The heart lay on the cold concrete, blood pooling slowly around it.

She would be with him soon.

He strode up the street and to the shadows, allowing the darkness to take him.

---

THE RAIN HAD UPGRADED from a cold drizzle to a freezing shower, relentlessly assaulting the tombstones that shot from the ground like blunt stone spikes. A scattering of police cars at the entrances to the graveyard were blocking the civilians from entering. A team of white-clad SOCOs scurried around the tomb where the heart had been found; the organ itself had been removed with expert precision.

Bermuda stood, hands on his hips, surveying the scene, two Tic Tacs sloshing around his mouth like a washing machine. He was soaked through, a chill terrorising his body as he tried to focus.

Why here?

His eyes scanned the officers as they went about their duties, fighting a losing battle to recover any evidence on a crime scene that the rain had long since destroyed. The officers standing guard were wrapped in see-through plastic to protect their uniforms. The only thing more miserable than the weather were looks on the officers' faces.

McAllister's suit, a darker shade of grey, clung to her athletic frame; her brown hair had given up its fight with the elements a long time ago. Her green eyes, as fierce as they were striking, burnt holes through whoever was delivering her the inevitable news that they had recovered nothing of any help. She shook her head, sighing deeply as the officer shrugged and took his exit.

Bermuda squinted as the droplets attacked his eyeballs, trying to cast his gaze upon the tomb itself. The building was a miserable, dull, stone creation, long since abandoned. There was zero religious or historic significance to it, yet it was the second heart in two days to be delivered to its front door. Anymore and Deliveroo would be trying to get in on the action.

Chuckling at his own joke, Bermuda puffed his e-cigarette and squatted down by the wall where the heart was found resting, the bloodstains replaced by torrential rain. Slowly, Bermuda reached out his hand to the wall, gliding it carefully over the coarse stone, searching for anything that told him the BTCO was right.

That this murder was because of the Otherside.

McAllister turned, looking for the 'specialist' who had been nothing more than a smart-arse on the scene and a disappointment in the bedroom. She marched through the rain, nodding her gratitude to the SOCOs who greeted her with a respectful, 'Ma'am'. She stopped, her eyebrows raising in confusion as she saw him, hunched down by the discovery point, running his hand over the wall.

Suddenly he stopped, shuddering as if someone had dropped an ice cube down the back of his shirt.

She approached, infuriated and intrigued in equal measure.

'What the hell are you doing?' she demanded as he turned up, his face taut with what she perceived as fear.

'I'm just doing my job.'

'Please explain to me how you contaminating my crime scene is in any way helping?'

'Contaminating? With all this rain?' He held his arms out to hammer home his point. 'There is no crime scene.'

'Two women are dead!' McAllister snapped, taking a step forward.

'And I'm your best chance at catching the creature responsible for it.'

'Creature?' She raised her eyebrows. 'You mean the person?'

Bermuda hesitated, taking a step back from the inevitable collision, and despite Argyle's best efforts, he was pretty sure that McAllister would floor him in seconds. He took a puff on his e-cig and let the rain wash across his face.

'Well?' McAllister angrily asked.

'Look, there is the possibility that there is something going on here beyond the usual human-on-human violence.' He took another puff, knowing how absurd he sounded. 'That's where I come in.'

'Sorry, but this doesn't make much sense. I was told by Detective Inspector Strachan that a *specialist* named Agent Jones was being assigned to work the case with me. Then you turn up, looking like a man clinging desperately to his teen years, and all you have done so far is get in the goddamn way!'

'Because you are all doing such a sterling job without me, eh?' Bermuda snapped back, regretting it instantly.

'I will find this killer and I will make him or her pay. What squad are you even with?'

'I'm an agent with a government agency. That's all I'm at liberty to say,' Bermuda lied, doing his best to channel his inner Fox Mulder.

'Well this is MY case. So do me a favour: keep your mouth shut and your hands in your fucking pockets.'

Before Bermuda and McAllister could pour more fuel on the fire, a young, pretty police officer approached, strands of ginger hair creeping from underneath the front of her police hat like spider's legs.

'Ma'am, we may have a witness.' She was slightly out

of breath, her enthusiasm catching up with her. 'The groundsman.'

'Did he see anything?' McAllister asked, turning her back on Bermuda and their argument.

'Not really, but he has asked to speak to the agent in charge.'

'Agent?' McAllister raised her eyebrows. 'Tell him that Detective McAllister will be with him momentarily.'

'Sorry, Ma'am, but he asked for him by name.'

'Who?'

'Bermuda. Bermuda Jones.'

McAllister connected the dots, turning to Bermuda, who slowly stepped forward, ignoring every part of himself that wanted to rub it in her face. He greeted the young PC with his best smile, receiving one in turn that alluded to more if he pursued it. However, with the rain lashing against him and the death toll likely to rise, Bermuda put his libido at the bottom of the priority list.

'Where is he?' Bermuda asked, trying to sound authoritative.

'He said to meet him in the tomb itself, says he doesn't like standing out in the rain for too long.'

'Thank you, Officer …' Bermuda lingered.

'Officer Stokes, sir.' She beamed.

'Don't call him sir,' McAllister interjected, stepping between the two and scowling at Bermuda. 'I'm coming with you.'

'No, he asked for me.'

'Like I said, I'm coming with you.'

'I know you don't like me and you don't know why I'm here. But like you said, there are two women dead in two days. It doesn't take a genius to work out that there will probably be three in three by tomorrow. Right now, I have the faintest of leads that this might be in my area of expertise, and I can either spend the next thirty minutes failing to convince you that what I do is real. Or ... you let me speak to Tobias Hendry in there and maybe, just maybe, we find out what the hell is going on.'

The two stared at each other, any lingering lust from the failed night of passion having evaporated.

McAllister looked him up and down one more time, disgust across her face. 'Who the hell is Tobias Hendry?'

Bermuda turned to the young officer who took a second before she realised she was being silently asked.

'The groundskeeper is called Tobias Hendry, Ma'am.' She turned to Bermuda. 'How did you know that? I didn't mention a name.'

He answered her, but looked at a baffled McAllister. 'Because I'm not here by accident.'

McAllister snarled in silence as Bermuda turned and trudged through the mud towards the grotty, cracked stone of the tomb, the elements lashing against the Glasgow Police Service. She dismissed PC Stokes, who scurried back towards her post, a fine officer who McAllister had high hopes for.

She took a few steps and then sighed deeply, the previous night's hangover and lack of sleep hanging as heavy as her drenched clothes. The absurdly named 'Bermuda' Jones was already becoming an irritating problem that she was sure would do nothing but hinder the case. Government agencies were renowned for having their own agenda, and she didn't trust him one bit.

She leant against a nearby tombstone, her eyes locked on the tomb that Bermuda had just entered, fighting back the urge to throw up. She would persevere, make it through this crime scene, and then report back to DI Strachan, determined to know what the hell Bermuda Jones was there for.

What did he mean by 'what he did was real'?

Why was he sceptical that it was a human?

Infuriated by her lack of answers, McAllister stood on the spot, waiting for Bermuda to return, unaware of the hooded figures that were lurking in the shadows of the Necropolis, all of them staring at the same building she was.

# ELEVEN

MOMENTS after his partner had departed for the Necropolis with the brash McAllister, Argyle stood and watched the humans work. He marvelled at the fluidity of their actions, appreciating the skill and dedication they had to their craft. All of them were there to help, to try to uncover what had happened to the poor female who had suffered such a brutal slaying.

The rain was cold, yet fell to nothing against him as he slowly stepped amongst the scurrying hotbed of activity, careful not to cause a surprising, invisible blockade. It hadn't been too long ago, during their pursuit of the terrorist Barnaby, that Argyle had collided with a small child by the surrounding grounds of the *Cutty Sark*. While lifting her into the air and causing widespread panic was misguided, he was thrilled to have seen those Morris dancers.

In a way, the white overall-clad officers at work reminded him of those majestic men – years of knowledge and practice resulting in a clockwork operation. A selection were dusting for prints while others were placing potential clues in see-through bags. Senior ranking officers were marking them down on clipboards while the medics had come and removed the body in a dignified manner.

The poor woman had had her heart pulled from her chest, which had distressed Bermuda immensely. Perhaps, Argyle mused, it was because of Bermuda's love for his daughter, and how she was a similar species to the recently deceased. That relationship, which he viewed from afar, was another reason his loyalty to Bermuda was unquestionable.

Despite all the wisecracks and the negativity, Bermuda cared. He had precious things tying him to the world, and Argyle had seen first-hand that when something came along that threatened it, Bermuda would give everything to protect it.

Mr Black at the BTCO called him an irritant.

Sir Ottoway called him 'the balance'.

Argyle saw him as a hero.

Stepping through the house, Argyle looked at the belongings of the young girl, trinkets that lined her living room that she had at some point felt a connection to. The symmetry was impressive, each item clearly purchased with a designated spot in mind. A shelf sat above the sofa, with moments of her life captured that had been worth framing.

As Argyle continued to slide through the crime scene, he made his way to the bloodstained room, the walls and bedsheets still thick with her blood. A few officers were dusting a corner table, their brushes sweeping around the splatter. Her wardrobe was open, revealing rails of pretty clothes that would soon be moved on. Rain clattered against the window and Argyle directed his grey eyes to the road below.

That was when he saw the cloaked figure.

Stood in the alleyway opposite, it was too tall to be human. Its powerful figure was cloaked in a long, black robe, the hood flipped over a shadow-covered face.

The face was a perfect, featureless white.

Argyle quickly wormed back through the flat, accidentally colliding with a young officer, sending her sprawling into the wall. As her colleagues gasped in shock, he burst through the door, the rain beating against him as he stared across the street.

The hooded figure was gone.

With careful steps, Argyle walked across the road, a car narrowly missing him. His hand reached over his shoulder, his mighty fingers grasping the handle of the blade that clung to his spine. He approached the alley, his mind flickering back to a time when his partner entered one similar while he lifted a car and confused a crowd of people.

Now, cold rain clattered against the walls, the shadows thick and dark. Careful step after careful step, Argyle walked further into the dark.

Something scurried nearby. A rat.

An empty packet of crisps fluttered down and beyond him.

He heard a noise behind him and turned.

There he was.

The cloaked figure.

Beyond the crime scene he had just ventured from, between the two buildings, the figure stood, intimidating with its stillness. A few police officers walked past, none of them aware of the ensuing stare down of another world. The figure, shrouded in darkness, stood deathly still, and Argyle took a few steps back towards the entrance of the alleyway.

A footstep behind him.

He spun on his heels, and at the other end of the alleyway a cloaked figured loomed. Drawing his sword instantly, Argyle stepped back, ready to attack. He glanced back across the street to the original figure, but it was gone. He turned back to the alley ahead.

The figure was gone.

Neither of them were anywhere to be seen and Argyle, with a calmness that defied the situation, slowly sheathed his sword, glancing with worry in both directions. After a few moments, and secure in the knowledge they had gone, Argyle stomped from the alleyway, making his way towards a place called the Necropolis.

---

EVERY ONE OF Bermuda's footsteps echoed as he stepped through the large door to the tomb, a faint splash as a hidden drip continued its eternal plunge. The room smelt damp, the blistering storms outside rotting away at the ancient brick, the moisture bursting out in a foul odour. He was surprised how large it was inside; the spacious room was cordoned off in certain places, a few numbered boards marking potential points of interest.

As he entered, a couple of SOCOs nodded respectfully and exited, a sign of respect that was usually absent. Looking around at the dank, grey room, Bermuda drew on his e-cigarette, a cloud of strawberry-infused smoke wafting towards the brick ceiling. The only light was struggling to get through the doorway behind him.

'Mr Jones?' A voice creaked from the corner like an eerie rocking chair.

'The one and only,' Bermuda responded.

'Jones is a terribly common name.' The voice was posh, a surprising English accent hidden away in the dark corners of Scotland's most famous graveyards. The man slowly trundled from the darkness of the side room, emerging into the struggling light. He was old – easily eighty years old, with skin that hung from his bones in a worryingly unnatural way. Bermuda could see the struggle he had walking. Years of working the grounds had broken the man's body.

He didn't look human at all.

The old man sniffed; the lingering aroma of Bermuda's cigarette clung to the airless room.

'What on earth is that smell?'

'Strawberry.'

'Never mind.' He extended a bony hand, the skin tightly wrapped around the knuckles twisted and wrinkled. 'May I call you Bermuda?'

'You may.' Bermuda smiled. 'Can I call you Toby?'

'Tobias.' He grinned, shocking Bermuda with immaculate teeth. 'I am glad you have come. Is your partner not with you?'

'Argyle? He is doing his own investigating. Figured I could handle you on my own.'

The old man chuckled. 'I still have some fight in these old bones. They haven't put me out to pastures just yet.'

'You are a friend of Montgomery Black?'

'Ah yes, Mr Black.'

'What's that like? You know, knowing him on any level where he is not a complete dick-head?'

Tobias frowned, slowly moving towards the doorway, the rain hurtling itself over the threshold.

'Montgomery Black was one of the finest agents the BTCO had ever had. He was the one who established a gateway here in the Necropolis many years ago. Before you were even born.'

'What happened to it?' Bermuda asked, realising he should be taking notes, patting his jacket for his pad. 'Why did the gateway close?'

'Oh, it was a long time ago. An unfortunate death of a young woman.' Tobias shook his head with regret. 'They decided to reduce the number of gateways, rendering

London the only port for this side of Europe. Those were dark days.'

Bermuda scratched words onto his pad, trying his best to remove the image of Montgomery Black wandering around 1950s Glasgow like Magnum PI, moustache and all. He chuckled out loud, drawing a confused look from his elder.

'I was offered the chance to move on or go to London. But this is my home. I offered to stay stationed here in Glasgow, at the office in town. Then, as age crept up on me and stole my wife, I came here. The dead are silent, but they never leave you. Here, I am never on my own.'

A jolt of sympathy ran through Bermuda for the old man, who had found peace and acceptance where everyone else found the afterlife. As he scribbled notes down, he cast an eye at him, again perturbed by the way his skin hung from him.

Age had not been kind.

'Why did you ask for me?' Bermuda asked, breaking the silence.

'Because Agent Jenson is currently in the Bahamas.'

'Lucky bastard!' Bermuda muttered, angered by the notion that other agents received annual leave. 'But why did you request me?'

'Ah, I see.' Tobias lowered himself onto a small stone border that framed the wall. It felt like an eternity as he lowered himself. 'We needed someone here quick and someone who would see the job through. Now despite what Black thinks of you on a personal level, he does speak highly of your work. He says that you and Argyle are quite the team.'

'Well, we're no Magnum & Higgins.'

The blank stare told Bermuda that the joke was very private. He nodded, indicating for Tobias to continue.

'There is something wrong here. Something dark that

has been let out over this city.' Tobias stared out over the Necropolis, the beauty of the grounds encased in a wet curtain. 'This creature is not of our world, Bermuda, but I am not sure it is completely of theirs.'

'What, like a Hovis situation?' Bermuda asked,

Tobias's confused glare encouraged clarification.

'You know, a best-of-both kind of deal.'

'Or the worst?' Tobias questioned, his sombre words drifting out of the door to the tomb.

Bermuda frowned, the feeling that something wasn't quite right was settling uncomfortably on him like an ill-fitting shirt. An unnerving silence sat between them.

'Why does he take the hearts?' Bermuda broke the tension with a forceful tone.

'The hearts? I don't know. Trophies?'

Bermuda shook his head, drawing his mouth into a thin line. 'I don't think so. Usually a killer would take a different trophy per person. This is more of a collection as if they have been requested. These women are not linked in any way, and both of them have been found in their bedrooms. What does that tell you?'

'I'm sorry, my mind is not as fast as it used to be,' Tobias offered in his posh, old charm.

Bermuda continued. 'It tells you that they trusted the killer. Now both women are heterosexual, so to be found partially clothed but with no signs of sexual trauma would indicate that they wanted our killer in the room with them. My theory, he is seducing these women so he can get them to a place where they let their guard down and no one sees What's about to happen.' Bermuda looked at Tobias, who could only manage a strangely perfect smile. 'It makes me think he looks human.'

'It's not uncommon for an Other to look human,' Tobias replied. 'I hear Argyle looks human.'

Bermuda shrugged. 'Humanish. But he is too big, too powerful, and way too kind to be a human.'

'I think it would be beneficial for me to meet with him as well.'

'He's kind of the brawn of the duo.' Bermuda took a moment, tossing something over in his mind. 'And probably the brain too.'

'Either way, I would like to meet him. Soon.'

Bermuda nodded, scribbling 'Argyle?' into his book before flicking it shut.

'So our suspect is a handsome, charming man? Won't be too hard to find in this hellhole.'

Tobias chuckled, slowly easing himself back to his feet and waving away Bermuda's offer of assistance. 'Find him. Before more women die.'

He patted Bermuda on the back with a shocking amount of strength before slowly hobbling back into the depths of the tomb. Bermuda watched him, again surprised how age had really taken its toll. The crippled limp, the saggy skin. It was an unfortunate portrayal of the fool that time makes of us all. Bermuda went to step into the rain but stopped at the threshold, peering back as Tobias almost stepped into the dark.

'Why bring the hearts here?' Bermuda motioned to the tomb.

Tobias turned, flashing his pearly white grin one last time. 'Because this is a chamber of death on the land of the dead. A heart is the human essence of life.'

'So what, he's offering it?'

'Perhaps.' Tobias stepped into the darkness.

'Why?' Bermuda called out. 'What is he bargaining for?'

Silence for a few moments before the creaky voice cackled out one more time. 'You're the detective. You tell me.'

On that unhelpful note, Bermuda stepped back out into the crime scene. A few mourners stood by the cordon, watching with the usual fascination that the public have when they think *CSI* is happening live in front of them. A young policeman was ushering them on, his uniform soaked through. Bermuda trudged across the grass, slamming two Tic Tacs into his mouth as a furious McAllister approached him, her hair plastered to her head and her minimalistic makeup slightly smudged. He could smell the alcohol on her, mixed with cigarette smoke and Chanel perfume.

'What did he say?' she demanded, marching alongside him as he walked to her car.

'Not much. But it's clear that this won't stop until we find him.'

'So you DO think it's a man that has done this.' She smirked, triumphant.

Bermuda turned to her, the wind hurling rain into his eyes. 'No.' He offered her a smile. 'I think it's something that we should be worried about.'

'Like what?'

'Like you know when you're a kid and you thought places like this were the scariest in the world? Yeah, that kind of scary, but with people dying.'

He patted her on the arm and stuffed his hands into the pockets of his new coat, the lining soft against his wet hands.

McAllister frowned, the lines across her forehead rising to the challenge. 'Where the hell are you going?' she called after him as she stood by the door of her car.

'I gotta get to work,' he yelled, marching onwards.

She tutted and dropped into the front seat of the car, the engine roaring to life as she pulled away. Bermuda trudged through the muddy ground, respectfully dipping between the graves instead of over them. The trees that lined the paths were derelict, their leaves long since committed to the earth. Their branches poked up towards the sky like jagged, naked fingers. As Bermuda stepped off the final step and out through the gate, he was met by Argyle who, for the first time since Bermuda could remember, didn't look the picture of calm.

'You okay, Big Guy?' Bermuda asked, puffing his e-cig and smiling at his partner.

'Yes.' The response was stone-cold. Argyle's eyes darted around the large Necropolis, almost sure that hooded figures were amongst the shadows. 'I just feel that not everything is at it seems.'

'Oh believe me, buddy…' Bermuda started walking back towards the city centre. 'I couldn't agree more.'

As the two crossed the road and headed back towards town, the hooded figures watched from the Necropolis, calm and motionless. They watched as the two agents of the BTCO slowly disappeared from their eye line. Soon they were gone.

Silently, the watchers fell back into the shadows.

They were here.

Where they needed them to be.

# TWELVE

IT WAS BECOMING RELENTLESS.

They had told him that if he brought them the hearts, she would be returned. The only person or thing he had cared about in his life, a life he was certain had only existed on this earth. There were faded memories – dark skies and cold, stone floors. Bloodied corpses lying in rotten fields. Something scuttling across a broken, grey-bricked wall.

They came in flashes, horrible images flickering like a snapshot, as if cut into one tile on a roll of film.

All he could see beyond them was her.

Her smooth, dark skin. He remembered running his fingers down her arm, the tips gliding as if he was testing a varnished table top. The smell, fresh and sweet, and her smile a small line filled with white pearls.

The personification of perfection.

Kevin Parker tried to recall where he was. He had been to a young lady's house, her name a sadly forgettable detail but her heart a crucial souvenir. He had removed it with his bare hand, the warmth of her bodily fluids washing over his fingers as they plunged through her muscles.

The shards of ribs ripped at his flesh, which soon stitched itself back together.

Life had left her quickly and painlessly.

He had delivered the heart.

She had not been returned.

*'Where are you, Kevin?'*

He chanted over and over to himself, staring at the dark walls of the room he sat in. It took a few moments before the clarity arrived, the lines of the floorboards slowly forming in the darkness. He was where he sat during the day. An abandoned factory that sat dormant on the outskirts of the town.

He recalled it was called Glasgow.

There was no rhyme or reason to his being there, nothing that he could link to in the chasm of his mind. There were just empty pockets of knowledge as if he should know more than he did.

He only knew of her.

How they had taken her from him.

They would not release her until they had what they wanted. He could feel the dried blood of Katie Steingold under the nails he was sure were his own. The final beat of her heart against the dry palm of his hand. It was worth it. As long as it brought him closer to her, then he would rip every heart from every chest.

He sat in silence for an eternity.

It reminded him of another time, chained to the floor and unable to move. Unable to grieve.

That voice, tinged with a hatred that mocked him from the darkness, accusing him of her death.

That it was his fault.

That same voice which reached out to him recently, demanding he bring the hearts to the stone house and then leave.

One a night.

Every heart until hers could be returned.

This was his life now. He existed purely to end existence. It was a cruel plight, but one which would enable him to see her again.

To be with her.

Be himself.

As the shadows of the room slowly disintegrated as the sun burst through the jagged holes that littered the ceiling, Kevin pulled his legs in close to his body, protecting himself. Rain dripped through, and he soon smelt the damp wood beneath him.

They would find her body.

They would find her heart.

But they would never know why.

He struggled into the darkest corner of the desolate room, curled into a small ball, and tried to rest his eyes.

All he could see was her.

Her, and the cavernous voids he had left in the chests of the innocent women.

He slept.

---

BERMUDA AND ARGYLE slithered through the busy streets of Glasgow, the locals all wrapped up in thick woollen hats. The rain was subsiding, replaced by a bitterly cold wind that ran rampant between the gothic buildings. The shops were busy, the usual hustle and bustle of a town centre. Argyle watched with a calm awe at the consumerist nature, with lines of people following each other into River Island while people marched out of Boots with bags hanging from their gloved hands.

Humanity was bizarre, he told himself.

Bermuda stopped walking, gazing down at his phone

with a raised eyebrow. He whipped his head in different directions, clearly lost.

'Are you lost?' Argyle stated the obvious.

'I'm afraid I am, Big Guy.' Bermuda turned to the left, approaching a derelict building, the doors boarded up, papered with faded fliers and *keep out* signs. He frowned. 'This is meant to be it.'

Argyle stepped forward. The wooden panels were soggy, drenched by the elements. To the side of the building was a metal post box, overstuffed with pizza fliers from poor delivery drivers who never got the message. 'This is the BTCO office.'

'It was.' Bermuda gestured to the rotten boards. 'Seems they closed more than just the gate.'

Argyle looked at his disappointed partner before extending one of his powerful arms. He spread his hand and placed it on the face of the mailbox, a small red light flashing underneath Farmhouse Pizzas smiling mascot. Bermuda watched, his jaw dropping as once the light finished, a thin black line filtered down from the top of the board in front of him, carving a small cut through the wood. It filtered down and then split, following a predetermined line that began to slice a doorway into the panel. Slowly it came to a finish and Argyle, without a word, pushed it open, beckoning his partner through in one of his usual acts of chivalry.

'I really need to stop letting myself be surprised,' Bermuda muttered as he stepped through. Once Argyle followed, the board healed up, removing the entrance and shunning the world from one that existed in secret.

The Otherside.

Bermuda ascended down a flight of stone steps; old, broken concrete lined the walls of the tunnel. Behind him, Argyle stooped low, his seven-foot frame encased by the darkness. Suddenly, a blue light burst momentarily, followed by the sweet smell of Bermuda's e-cig.

'So they can afford a fancy handprint thingy-ma-jig for a doorbell, but they can't get a goddamn lamp for the hallway?' Bermuda muttered.

'The darkness has no bearing on our eyes.'

'Your eyes, maybe,' Bermuda continued, taking each step carefully as the large, double metal door loomed ahead. 'But we are not the same, are we?'

'That is true. Yet we have loyalty.' Argyle stated. 'That means we are equal.'

Bermuda stopped and peered into the darkness at Argyle, who proudly stood to attention. Bermuda cracked a smile.

'Can I have a hug?' He opened his arms.

'We do not require a physical interaction.' Argyle stepped past Bermuda, who was smirking.

'Just a quick one.' He followed his partner down the final remaining steps. 'Like a quick squeeze.'

'We have a murderer to find,' Argyle stated, ignoring his partner's attempts at irritation. He stomped towards the metal doors, stopping a few feet from the handle.

'So let me get this straight,' Bermuda began, following his partner through the darkness. 'You can say things about how our loyalty makes us equal. You would willingly lay your life on the line for me, yet you won't give me a hug?'

Bermuda arrived next to his partner, smirking as he gazed up to his stern face. Instantly he regretted it as, like on so many occasions, Argyle was showing emotion that didn't exist on the Otherside.

Emotion that barely existed on our side.

After a few awkward moments, Argyle's calm, authoritative voice sliced through the tension. 'Why don't you request one from McAllister? You have already laid with her.'

'Not going to happen.' Bermuda shook his head, patting his pocket for Tic Tacs. 'I've disappointed her professionally and sexually within the space of twenty-four hours. Even for me that's bad.'

'You lack respect.'

'For her? No. She is just very volatile,' Bermuda said, waiting for Argyle to open the door.

'For yourself.'

'Ouch.' Bermuda chuckled to himself. Argyle shocked him at times, with an insightful view on the world – and him personally – which would probably cost thousands in therapy bills. 'Let's just crack on, shall we? This crazed, murderous, heart-stealing creature isn't going to stop itself.'

Argyle reached out and grasped the metal handle with his mighty fist, the golden bracelet that held the Retriever glistening as light escaped through the crack in the door. He hauled it back, opening the secret BTCO Glasgow Office to Bermuda. Compared to the Shard, it was incredibly small, with old, wooden desks pressed against each other, separated by flimsy plastic dividers. A few basic, lifeless PCs sat atop them, a thin layer of dust over everything. A few neon lights hummed above, one of them flickering intermittently.

Bermuda let out a whistle.

'You sure this place is open?' Bermuda asked as his partner strode between the desks.

Right on cue, a PC chair whizzed by, the wheels screaming for WD40. Atop it sat a plump, middle-aged lady with a ginger bob, thick-rimmed glasses, and teeth a little too big for her mouth. Her eyes were wide with adoration.

Her accent was more Scottish than a bagpipe-playing haggis.

'Bermuda Jones! This is such an honour.' She rose from her chair, her stumpy legs poking out beneath her neatly ironed skirt. She wore a green, knitted jumper with a floral shirt beneath it. 'Welcome to our office.'

'Thanks … err …'

'Kelly. Kelly McDonald.' She curtseyed in front of the uncomfortable agent.

'Thanks. I'm Bermuda …'

'Jones. The legendary agent who has been to the Otherside, stopped Barnaby from unleashing hell on earth, and is widely considered the best agent in the organisation.' She beamed as she sat back down. 'Your legend precedes you.'

'Right.' Bermuda looked over to Argyle, who was carefully studying pictures that symmetrically lined the walls, all of them of pompous-looking men – undoubtedly former agents. 'Do you have a lab here?'

'We do,' Kelly squealed, zipping off on her chair behind a stack of files that lined a desk hidden behind a filing cabinet.

Bermuda waited for a few moments for her return, but nothing. Gently massaging his temples, he stepped across, peering over the cabinet. 'Could I use it?'

'Malcolm is out at the moment. But you are welcome to stay.' She flashed him a grin, one that he was sure greeted a plethora of cats when she got home at night.

'Malcolm is the techie?' he asked, studying the mountains of paperwork on her desk, oblivious to the red tape that surrounded his work. Being out in the field, he realised he took it all for granted. Someone probably had to process the countless bills he had racked up. No wonder Montgomery Black hated him. Still, as Kelly clattered her fingers aggressively on the keyboard, he wondered which form was the annual leave request of the agent who should have been there.

'Malcolm does all the Other-worldly stuff,' she explained, slurping a large mouthful from her coffee cup.

Her glasses wobbled on the end of her button nose, littered with freckles. 'His Knack is stronger than mine.'

'You have the Knack?' Bermuda asked with genuine intrigue.

'Barely. I mean, I can see your partner but I don't really know what he looks like.' She wildly motioned in Argyle's general direction, beyond the cabinet. 'No, my strength lays in looking after the office and keeping things in order around here.'

Bermuda glanced to the shelving unit above her, with a hazardous pile of folders stacked worryingly, all of them with protruding sheets. The dust was thick and in blatant contrary to her claims.

'So when will Malcolm be back?' he asked politely.

Kelly stopped her vigorous tapping and clicked into a calendar on her screen. Bermuda scanned over the office, noting Argyle had ventured beyond his vision. Before he could look any further, Kelly's disappointed tutting brought him back to her.

'I'm afraid he is out at a conference today.' She snorted to herself. 'I did think it was pretty lonely today.'

'Today?' Bermuda mocked, scolding himself for letting her irritate him. 'Could I possibly leave something with for him? It's important.'

'Oooo … is it case work?' she clenched her fists, shaking with excitement like a toddler being handed the keys to a toy store.

'I would love to be here purely socially, but yes, Argyle and I are working a case and I need Malcolm to run a print on this.' He handed her the envelope which housed the mundra print he had obtained at Nicole Miller's flat. At that moment he took stock. He was stood in a secret office of an organisation dealing with paranormal crime while handing over evidence printed on a material that couldn't be seen by normal humans.

This was why he couldn't be at his daughter's birthday.

Slowly, the usual anger and resentment began to seep in over the corners of his mind. The booming voice of Argyle shook him back to reality.

'That print will take at least a day to process. We should return either to the latest scene or the tomb once again.'

Bermuda nodded in agreement, turning back to the eagerly smiling secretary. 'Can you put that to the top of his list?'

She nodded enthusiastically. Bermuda offered her a warm smile and nodded to Argyle to head towards the door. She called after them.

'If you are heading back to the Necropolis, tell Toby we all said hi. It's been a while since we have seen him.'

Bermuda stopped and turned on his heel, his brow furrowed. 'Is Toby still a BTCO employee? I kinda figured he worked at the Necropolis now.'

'Oh, he does. He's the groundsman. He used to be employed by us when the gateway was there. However, when they closed it down, he didn't want to leave. It's sad, really. Must be lonely.'

Her words trailed off sadly in understanding.

'You ever think there was something a bit odd about him?' Bermuda asked, revisiting his conversation with the ancient groundsman, how something didn't sit right.

'What do you mean?' Kelly asked, her green eyes wide and innocent.

'I don't know. I mean, he looked a little a funny.'

'Well he's no Tom Selleck, let's put it that way,' she replied, raising her eyebrows suggestively.

Bermuda smiled inwardly, especially after his *Magnum PI* reference had fallen on Toby's deaf ears.

Argyle stood patiently by the door.

'Okay. Well, thank you for everything,' he offered as he again turned to leave.

'Although I am surprised that Toby didn't mention the others,' Kelly said, her eyes locked on her screen as her fingers tap danced across the lettered keys before her. 'If you saw him earlier.'

'Others?' Bermuda asked, his voice rife with confusion. 'Like Argyle?'

'No. The other girls. Years ago.'

Bermuda looked blankly at her. 'What other girls?'

Kelly looked at Bermuda and the blurry outline of his dominant partner. She sighed, locking her computer and pushing herself up off of her seat. 'Follow me.'

# THIRTEEN

KELLY LED BERMUDA TO A CUBICLE, and a crummy computer on a wobbly desk that was sprinkled with dust. She booted up the ancient machine, the insides churning against each other like a car trying to get out of gear. He stood back, awaiting the explosion.

Microsoft XP unsurprisingly flashed upon the thick, white-rimmed screen. Bermuda shook his head in amazement. At HQ, they had automatic doors and Oracles plugged into state-of-the-art computers. They had tomahawks forged on the Otherside and an ancient gateway which Bermuda constantly referred to as Stargate.

Here, they didn't even have a supported OS.

Kelly clicked away on the keyboard without even a hint of realisation, her gentle humming strangely soothing. Bermuda felt an odd emotion.

Jealousy.

She was content – clearly happy with her role and what the world had given her. She had been pushed to the side with all the other freaks and weirdos that compromised the BTCO's roster, but she took pride in it. She thought she had everything she needed.

His heart ached for Chloe.

For Sophie Summers.

For a cigarette.

He shook the incessant craving away, his fingers rapidly diving into his pockets to retrieve his e-cig while his mind tried to lock away Sophie's beautiful face. After a few puffs, Kelly flashed him a smile.

'Here you are. I have just logged you into the Nexus.' She pushed herself up out of the chair, gently bumping into Argyle. He instantly moved.

Bermuda thanked her and took a seat, stretching his fingers until they clicked. The Nexus was a series of interlinking servers that channelled straight into the Archive. The Oracles, while linked to their computers, were linked to the Otherside, their knowledge of anything relating to their kind filtering through and being applied to the goings-on in the world. Should a child go missing, or a strange, heart-shaped hole appear in the chest of a young woman, they would calculate the possibility of Other activity and assign the case.

They watched both worlds.

The Nexus was a hard link straight into that data, a constantly updating, living server with knowledge bursting from the seams like an overstuffed mattress. Here, Bermuda could search anything, and the four naked, pale captives back in that wondrous library would filter through and send him what he needed.

Their own personal Wikipedia.

Just slightly more reliable.

His fingers clattered the keys, typing in the keywords of 'heart' and 'stolen'. The office was cold, the outside freeze slowly filtering through the old walls that ached for a repaint. Behind him, Argyle stood protectively, arms crossed and his eyes locked on the screen. Human technology fascinated him.

All he knew was the sword.

The Oracles went to work, the screen resolution flickering like a satellite battling for reception. Their connection wasn't the fastest, but he started to see the icons of articles appearing on his screen.

He clicked the first one, dated 18 September 1982, and began reading it out loud.

'Police refused to rule out a ritual killing, as a young woman was found murdered in her house yesterday afternoon. The woman, who will remain nameless, was found by her husband with her heart missing. Police chief … yadda yadda …'

Bermuda clicked the next one.

'Hunt for Heart Snatcher intensified when a third woman was found within the last week with her internal organ removed. Police are asking for anyone to come forward with knowledge.'

He clicked through a few more, the articles all dated from the early eighties. After a few moments, he turned and looked up into the grey eyes of Argyle, who had been watching in amazement.

'We need to speak to Toby – see what happened all those years ago.'

Argyle nodded in agreement and turned, almost squashing Kelly, who stood shyly behind him. 'Can I help you, Ma'am?' he asked, his tone formal.

'I was just watching him work. It's a real honour.'

Bermuda disconnected, the computer shaking as it severed its ties with the all-powerful Neithers. Embarrassed, he pushed himself up. 'It really shouldn't be.'

'But it is. You're a legend.'

'I'm not.' Frustration grew in his voice as he slid his arms into his armoured coat, the material still damp from the weather, which was ready to welcome him again.

'You are. You stopped Barnaby,' she exclaimed excitedly. 'You're a hero!'

'I'm not a goddamned hero!' Bermuda snapped, causing Kelly to gasp. 'A fellow agent died that night, because I goaded him again and again. I'm sorry but I don't deserve whatever it is they tell you, okay?'

Kelly stood, tight-lipped, looking straight at the ground.

Bermuda looked at a disapproving Argyle and sighed. 'Look, Kelly. I'm sorry,' he offered. 'I appreciate it, I really do. But when we are a team, there is no space for a hero. And we are a team, right?'

She smiled, eventually nodding and thanking him with her eyes.

He nodded and headed for the door, his mighty, armour-clad compadre in close pursuit. The metal door clattered behind them and Bermuda felt a calm wash over him like a cooling breeze, the need for some fresh air and a pale ale beginning to overwhelm.

They ascended the stairs in the dark, in silence for the majority. As they neared the reappearing door in the soggy cardboard that awaited them at the top of the stairs, Argyle broke the silence that flittered between their strides.

'I believe you to be a hero.'

They stood as the daylight filtered through the slices that began to appear in the cardboard panel, the mystery of the Otherside slowly peeling it back and opening a doorway for them. As a show of appreciation Bermuda slapped his partner on the back, and the two of them set out into the rain with no clue how to stop the murderous rampage.

THE POLICE PRESENCE had all but evaporated by the time they returned to the residence of Katie Steingold. A panda car was parked a few cars down, a few strips of police tape criss-crossed the door like a disturbing Christmas gift. The bitter chill in the air danced along the wind, sending a shiver down Bermuda's spine and causing him to lift the coffee to his lips. The warm caffeine trickled down his throat, sloshing into his stomach and becoming one with his many other vices.

He clenched his teeth, hissing slightly at the freezing gust that snapped at him. Argyle had met him at the scene as usual, perplexing Bermuda with his speed of travel. With a careful eye, Argyle glanced to the alleyway to the side of the house, the hooded figure he had seen long since gone. He checked the alley behind them – again there was nothing.

They had been there.

He was sure they were being followed, but he didn't want to alarm his partner.

Not unless he had to.

Bermuda pulled him back to the freezing late afternoon in 'bonny' Scotland.

'Why the hearts?' Bermuda questioned, to himself more than Argyle.

'Hearts are the life force of you humans,' Argyle offered, both men staring at the flat. 'The easiest way to kill you is to remove it.'

Bermuda shook his head, taking another sip from the red corrugated Costa cup. 'No, that's not it. If he wanted her dead, he could have choked her or snapped her neck. He's strong – strong enough to punch a hole through a rib cage.'

Bermuda took a few steps towards the gate, the metal creaking as he pulled it to the side. A gentle rain clattered against the stone steps as he ascended to the front door, his eyes fixed on the unwelcoming tape.

*Do Not Cross.*

Bermuda crossed.

He pushed the blue front door gently, the warmth of the house beckoning him inside. With a cautious step he crossed the threshold, slowly wandering through the quaint hallway. To his right was the homely living room where he could imagine the young lady cuddled up in a blanket, binge-watching Netflix and relaxing in the wonderful life she had made for herself.

A life that had been taken.

Snatched from her chest in front of her own eyes.

He shuddered, a bolt of anger rode through his body, and his knuckles clicked as his fists clenched. To the left was the kitchen where he had met McAllister. Well, where he had been introduced to her, merely a few hours after their drunken liaison had turned into a myriad of expletives and hurled objects.

Another wonderful night in the life of Bermuda Jones.

Slowly he gazed around the kitchen. A row of brightly coloured mugs hung from a specially designed rack. A matching kettle and toaster sat proudly next to it. The cleanliness alone was alien to Bermuda, but the regiment and order of it was baffling. No matter how hard he tried, his kitchen always looked like someone had let off a bomb in a coffee shop.

He reappeared into the hallway, noting that Argyle was stood in the front room, arms folded and surveying everything. It reassured him.

He wasn't alone.

With slow, soundless steps, Bermuda climbed the stairs, his mud-spattered Converse squelching slightly from the rain. The landing was small but proudly displayed a photo frame branching out to hold multiple photos – family, friends, and memories all pinned to one wall. All belonging to a person who would no longer remember them. To the right, the bedroom was shut tight, another cross of brightly coloured police tape tacked to the frame.

Bermuda ducked under and pushed open the door.

Thankfully Katie had been moved, her body respectfully taken to a police morgue for an autopsy from a leading forensic pathologist – although Bermuda was sure the gaping hole in her chest was an answer enough. Slowly he entered the room, careful not to touch too much, even after forensics had dusted every nook and cranny.

They would find nothing.

Hopefully Malcolm wouldn't take too long with that print. An image of Kelly spinning on her chair while her mystery technician readjusted his telescope gave him a brief moment of joy. A smirk almost came across his face.

The bloodstained bed and walls before him brought him back to reality with a bump. And what a reality it was. This other-worldly creature was preying on the women of Glasgow, wrenching out their still-beating hearts in their own homes.

They must have known him.

Or at the very least trusted him.

Bermuda drew his lips tight, his brow furrowing with frustration at the helplessness. This man could strike at any moment at any woman in the city. He had been assigned to stop him, but all he could do was wait for a technician he had never met to provide a print he might not be able to match.

Perhaps Vincent had a book back at the HQ that had everyone's finger prints, an Argos-esque solution to their identification problems. It could sit proudly next to the tome, where their two known Exceptionals were documented.

Perhaps this was the other Exceptional?

Bermuda hoped against hope that wasn't the case. The one Exceptional he knew about was Barnaby, and he came a doorway away from ending the world as he knew it.

If this creature – this heart-stealing Absent Man – was even a tenth of what Barnaby stood for, then everyone was in trouble.

Bermuda almost jumped out of his skin as his thoughts were pierced by an unfriendly tone drenched in a thick Scottish accent.

'What the fuck are you doing here?'

He spun. The angry, snarling face of DS Sam McAllister glared at him as she stood in the doorway, her fists clenched and pressed against her hips. Her suit hung tightly to her skinny frame, and her hair was wet and messy.

Bermuda sighed. 'I dunno,' he offered, his hands out in a pathetic shrug. 'Maybe there was something we had missed.'

'Oh, good point. My team of expertly trained SOCOs have already swept this house like Cinderella's, but the super-agent may just find something they didn't.'

Bermuda forced a smile, refusing to rise to the goad.

She glared at him with disgust, stepping to the side as a clear indication for him to leave. He held his hands up in surrender, trying to edge past her in an overly elaborate way which she found as annoying as he did amusing. As Bermuda ducked under the tape, he wondered if antagonising the lead detective was a smart move.

Sleeping with her certainly wasn't.

Just as Bermuda was about to embark on a revolutionary journey into his poor life decisions, McAllister emerged into the hall, slamming the bedroom door shut. She descended the stairs at pace, ushering Bermuda towards the front door and effectively frog-marching him from the property. As he passed the living room, he locked eyes with an apologetic-looking Argyle. Bermuda scowled at his partner as he was hurried through the door and into the unforgiving elements. As the wind clattered against him and dampened the side of his face, he turned to the furious McAllister.

'Look … we completely got off on the wrong foot.'

'We don't need to address it. We were drunk. It was shite. End of discussion.'

'Thanks.' Bermuda swallowed his pride. 'But if we are going to work together, we should at least find some sort of common ground.'

Taken aback by his level of maturity, Bermuda instantly wondered if Montgomery Black had assigned him for this entire reason: for Bermuda to mature, become the agent they all knew he could be. As his trail of thought started to venture to whether 'Monty' in fact wore a wig, Bermuda realised his thoughts of maturity were slightly premature.

'We are not working together,' McAllister stated, not even looking at him. Her eyes gazed beyond the parked cars to the road. 'You have been sent here by a department we have never heard of. I have zero intention of seeing you again after today.'

Argyle eased his way under the police tape, his mighty frame gently grazing one of the strips, ripping it from the doorframe. McAllister, damp and frustrated, let out a sigh and reached for it.

'With all due respect, that isn't your call to make,' Bermuda insisted, refusing to raise his voice and, in doing so, the tension.

A car slowly pulled up and stopped in the road opposite the house. McAllister reset the police tape and ensured the door was locked. She turned, facing Bermuda and admitting to herself that he wasn't the worst-looking one-night stand she had had.

Just the most irritating.

She barged past him. 'I know it's not.' She nodded to the car ahead. 'It's Strachan's.'

DI Nick Strachan was McAllister's superior and who Bermuda assumed had been handed the order by the BTCO. It couldn't have been easy for Strachan. Spending your whole life working up a chain of command, dedicating yourself to your profession, and then being dictated to by an organisation that you realised you weren't 'important' enough to have heard of. Bermuda expected what he always expected when he met senior people within the many police services he had pissed off.

Pure resentment.

Bermuda had managed to read the file Vincent had given him on his arduous train ride and got the impression that Nick Strachan wasn't thrilled at their involvement. In fact, the file quoted him saying they were a 'Saturday morning cartoon!'

With a sigh, he watched as McAllister strode through the drizzle, turning from the gate and heading towards her own car parked further down the street. Slowly, footsteps approached, and Argyle blocked some of the water from attacking Bermuda.

'You had one job, Argyle.' Bermuda spoke, staring ahead at the car.

'I apologise,' Argyle instantly replied, conflicted to tell his partner why he had been distracted.

Bermuda chuckled and looked up at his partner. 'Meh … on the law of averages, I'd say you are owed a fuck-up now and then.' He flashed his partner a smile. 'Right … now for a bollocking.'

With a surprising spring in his step, Bermuda bounced down the path, through the gate, and towards the black BMW car that waited. The rain clattered the roof and Argyle watched as his partner flung the door open and lowered his drenched body into the warmth of the vehicle. He solemnly lowered his head and vacated the premises also, sure as he could be that he had seen the cloaked figure again.

As Argyle waited in his noble, invisible silence, the peering eyes of the hooded stalkers pierced their white masks and locked onto him and the car that contained his partner.

From deep within the shadows, eight of them lined the streets, stalking them both.

With both Argyle and Bermuda surrounded, they watched.

# FOURTEEN

THE BMW WELCOMED Bermuda with a warm hug, the white leather seats that lined the back compartment of the car shiny and clean. He almost felt guilty as he slid in, his drenched, secretly armoured coat sliding all over the leather. But he then remembered that they would probably charge the cleaning of it to the taxpayer and regretted not stepping in dog shit on the way in.

The heater was in, warm air pumping through the vents and laying siege to the cold that had invaded his body. He felt the numbness leave his fingers, listening to the bones crack as he stretched them.

'It's cold out, isn't it?'

Bermuda jumped suddenly, oblivious to the small, portly, middle-aged woman who was sat in the back of the car with him, her uniform immaculate. Small spectacles rested on the end of her nose, which she gazed over like a put-upon teacher. In her hand was a notebook, biro scrawlings that would take days to decipher. Her brown hair, streaked with grey, was tied up in a neat bun. In his excitement of warmth, Bermuda had completely forgotten to introduce himself.

'I'm Agent Jones,' he offered, extended a hand that was completely ignored as she scribbled notes down.

'Yes, we know.' She didn't look up. At the word *we*, she nodded to the front of the car. A burly officer sat, hands clasped to the steering wheel, his knuckled worn from years of never losing a confrontation. Chances were, Bermuda thought, his record wasn't in danger.

They sat in silence for a few moments, the introductions clearly over. The rain rattled against the car window as if someone was showering it with rice. The police radio cackled, but the driver turned it down before the orders came in.

'So, can we go see Strachan now?' Bermuda asked. 'I hear he is a pain in the arse so I'd rather get my spanking over and done with as soon as possible.'

The woman sighed, clicking her pen closed and placing it on the pad. She turned, her green eyes peering over her spectacles and fixing Bermuda with a condescending look.

'I am Detective Inspector Nic Strachan.' Her voice was flat and uncaring.

Nic. Not Nick.

Bermuda shook his head in disbelief, especially after mistaking McAllister for a man. Just as he was starting to lose faith in naming conventions, Strachan broke his thought pattern.

'We didn't ask for you to be here, Mr Jones. In fact, I thought you would be nothing more than a hindrance.'

'Thank you for your vote of confidence, Ma'am.' Again, Bermuda questioned his life decisions.

Strachan ignored it. 'Quite. I told the senior officers who told me of your impending arrival that you were not needed, and as I had never heard of this BCTO—'

'BTCO,' Bermuda corrected, shocked by his loyalty to the organisation.

'Whatever. I said you were a mock detective and would

do more harm than good. Now I have given you access to the crime scenes because I, for one, don't want to tarnish how hard I and my team have worked to get to the position we are in. However, you are becoming a nuisance, and one that I will not tolerate.'

Bermuda checked the outside, sure he would be meeting the weather again soon. The rain had picked up, clattering the surrounding cars with a wild fury.

'Are you listening to me, Mr Jones?'

'Yup,' he replied nonchalantly.

'Good. So we are understood, I expect you to return to your hotel, enjoy our fine city for a few days, and then head back to London. We will take it from here.' Strachan straightened her skirt and then lifted her pad, the biro clicking into action. Her resuming of her task indicated the conversation was over.

Bermuda clicked the door handle and then ignored the part of his mind begging for an easy life. 'Actually, we are not understood.'

He firmly shut the door. The large officer swivelled in place and Strachan held up a hand, effectively telling her attack dog to heel.

'No?'

'No. You see, I don't give a fuck if you want me here or not. Do you think I want to be stuck in a shit hotel in this shit-hole city? I'm here because what is going on, neither you nor your hard-working team could possibly grasp. If they thought you were capable they wouldn't have sent for me.'

'I will NOT be spoken to like this,' Strachan yelled, clicking her chubby fingers.

The brutish driver flew his door open, the rain hitting the inside of the car and echoing like chattering teeth. With his heavy footsteps, Bermuda expected to be hauled from the car within a few moments.

Three …
Two …
One …

Just as they heard the door handle click, they heard a grunt of pain and the sound of a body collapsing to the ground. Both looked concerned and Bermuda turned back to an irate Strachan.

'Get the fuck out of my car,' she demanded, her language defying her previously calm demeanour.

'With pleasure.' Bermuda pushed the door open, the metal panel bumping against what he assumed was the body of her hulking minion.

Before he stepped out into the wonders of the Scottish wintertime, he turned back.

'I will solve this case. With or without your help.'

'You will receive no help from the Glasgow Police Service,' she said sternly while running a wiping cloth over her glasses.

Bermuda offered her his most charming smile. 'No change there, then.'

Strachan's eyes lit up with anger and Bermuda waved as he pushed himself out of the car. His Converse trainers splashed against the ground, the water soaking through to his socks. He slammed the door shut and looked at the large officer before him, hunched over on his knees and wheezing heavily.

The wind had been driven cleanly from him.

The officer groaned in agony. The sudden influx of stomach cramps had been instant and disabling, bringing his huge frame to its knees. It was like he had been hit with a sledgehammer, the cramps crushing his gut in one go.

Bermuda observed for a few moments with zero inclination to help. He looked to his right, where Argyle was stood, gently shaking his hand as if to shake out the pain.

Bermuda smiled warmly against the cold rain.

Argyle had clearly clobbered the officer straight in the stomach. Knowing the sheer power and accuracy of his partner, Bermuda felt just a twinge of sympathy for the victim, but turned back to his partner.

'I am shameful,' Argyle uttered, his voice sad and honest. 'I have struck a man of nobility.'

'Believe me, Big Guy,' Bermuda said, patting his friend on the arm and ushering them to walk away, 'there is nothing noble about that man.'

Argyle spun his head back as they walked, watching as the large lawman was hauling himself up, fingers grasping the wet vehicle. The woman inside had made no effort to help.

'Are you not mad that I struck a man of law?'

'Mad?' Bermuda chuckled, spinning his e-cig in his hand like a drumstick. 'I'm bloody ecstatic.'

The two walked down another rain-soaked road of Glasgow, identical to all the others. Bermuda summarised in his head how they were no closer to catching the killer and he had now effectively burnt the miniscule bridge with the police. Word would reach the BTCO, Montgomery Black would be furious, and the fingerprint they had left with the mystery technician would probably lead to nothing.

Just another day in the life of Bermuda Jones.

However, after Argyle's intervention a smile cracked across his face. The two walked through the suburban streets, soaked through. Bermuda admired the houses, all of them set back slightly from the pavement, guarded by small courtyards. Inside each house lived a family, a story of how they came to be in the lives they now lived.

Within the shadows of the city, some creature was looking to snatch that life from them.

A feeling of helplessness covered Bermuda, and he

looked away from his partner, hoping Argyle didn't notice. He did. Of course he did, Bermuda thought.

Argyle noticed everything.

Well, except DC McAllister when she was on the warpath.

As the rain slapped against his skin, Bermuda's mind raced back to the previous night. Flashes of McAllister's naked body came and went, their sexual adventure coming to an abrupt and volatile end. She was an angry woman, there was no denying that, and Bermuda was sure there was more to it than just their failed intercourse.

He knew a self-hater when he saw one.

It takes one to know one.

They carried on down a few more streets before they came upon Partick Station, one of the fifteen stops on the Glasgow Subway, an underground metro train service that had wrapped itself around the city for well over a century. The station was the first above the River Clyde, the track looping round and travelling clockwise around the city. The route, a bright orange loop printed on a map, was nicknamed 'the Clockwork Orange'.

The owners of the train company were obviously keen to move away from that nickname.

Bermuda carefully descended the steps, turning back to find that Argyle had left him to it. As bemusing as it was, Bermuda had grown accustomed to Argyle's travel arrangements.

He didn't understand them. But he was beyond questioning them.

As he approached the platform, he shuffled quickly to the train that was waiting impatiently, the shrill beeps indicating its imminent departure. With a quick dash, he slipped through the doors as they closed. Feeling pleased with himself, he dropped into one of the seats that lined the train, forcing the grumpy commuters to face each other.

Bermuda spent most of his time in London. He was well-versed in the unwritten law that 'a commuter shall not look another in the eye, let alone speak to them'. He slid the soaked beanie hat from his head, his hair bursting out in every direction, gasping for air. He wrung the hat out like a flannel, watching the rainwater clatter to the sticky floor of the metal tube.

He closed his eyes and tipped his head back, the top of his skull gently bumping off the glass window.

He needed something.

Anything.

A clue. A lead.

A pint of Doom Bar.

As he contemplated indulging his thirst, he felt a twinge of guilt. Not just for the heartless women, but for their families. Fathers who had lost their daughters. Knowing his beautiful Chloe was safe and sound, he couldn't imagine what losing her would be like.

To see her ripped from him by the shadows of another world.

He sat upright, his eyes blinking wildly as he realised he had nodded off. A flash of the recurring dream, the nightmare of losing those he loved, had jolted him like a cattle prod.

He rubbed his hand on his stubbled jaw and caught a glimpse of himself in the window, the reflection set against the blackness of the tunnel. He looked older. His skin, pale and tight, sat across a face that used to turn many a head. Bags hung from his eyes.

He didn't need a beer. He needed a coffee.

And to catch the goddamn heart-stealing bastard.

The train whizzed around the tracks, eventually alighting at St Enoch, right in the city centre. Bermuda departed and stomped up the steps of the station, ignoring the whipping chill of the evening and the bursting brightness from the streetlights that greeted him. Darkness had fallen, his eleven-minute train journey had felt longer, the night sky stealing the sun as easily as this killer had stolen those hearts. He stuffed both hands in his pockets, one of them to retrieve his phone.

The other for his Tic Tacs.

As two mints sloshed their way around his mouth, he held the phone to his ear, impatiently tapping his foot in a shallow puddle. After a few more rings, the phone clicked off.

The BTCO Glasgow Office had closed for the evening.

He stared at the screen, droplets of water splattered randomly against the glass as he contemplated calling the London office. Montgomery Black would have certainly have received Strachan's complaint. On reflection, Bermuda decided having his arse verbally kicked wasn't good for his increasingly downbeat mood.

He contemplated calling Chloe. The thought of his daughter's voice warmed his body, defying the freezing cold of the winter's evening.

Angela would answer the phone. Again, he decided that a verbal arse-kicking wasn't the solution.

He thought about calling Sophie Summers.

Instantly, with his heart aching, he scorned himself, refusing to let his mind drift to her, to all the exquisite details of her face.

The radiant smile.

The beautiful eyes.

The jet-black eyes of Barnaby!

Bermuda shook the thought, a quick flash of the piercing, burning holes that sat in the skull of the most dangerous Other he had come across. He could still see the smirking face, lined by the three scars that marked him as a traitor.

Barnaby had nearly destroyed all life in this world.

Somewhere in Glasgow, in the wet, dark concrete jungle surrounding him, another force of evil was threatening humanity. It had happened before, Bermuda recalled. The news clippings from the Nexus had revealed that a series of murders that matched his case had happened years ago.

This Absent Man had been here before.

Bermuda ducked into a Cafe Nero, queueing patiently before stepping back out into the busy high street of Glasgow, his hands wrapped around a piping-hot flat white. The caffeine was warm and welcome, following the path well-worn by ale and Tic Tacs to his stomach. His eyes flickered around the town. The premature colours of the Christmas lights lined the gothic buildings, the festive season being forced upon the city earlier every year.

The Christmas Square, marred by a tragic driving incident a few years previously, was bright and busy, the memory of those who had lost their lives that year being honoured by the celebration of family and fun. He strolled through the square, watching as kids battled the cold to ride the cheap, fun-fair rides while their parents partook in watered-down alcohol from the pop-up bars.

The smell of hotdogs wafted through the rain from a small van that looked like a health code violation on wheels.

The main event, the ice rink, encompassed most of the square, with couples and children flying by, all trying their best to outdo gravity. A few kids collided, one of them bursting into tears as panicked parents tried their best to keep their feet.

An overweight man took a corner too quick and slammed into the barricade. A video would likely be on

YouTube within minutes. Bermuda scorned the world they lived in now, where instead of reaching to the man, who looked in considerable pain, the audience reached for their phones.

Randomly, an Other skittered through the crowd, coasting along the ice with the grace of a majestic swan. It sauntered through, its movements fluid before it cast its one jet-black eye on Bermuda and abruptly stopped.

Bermuda nodded, as if to grant permission. He turned and headed to the exit as the Other continued its rather bizarre passion for skating.

After a few more moments, Bermuda exited the square and turned right, heading back down a parade of shops. With Christmas less than six weeks away, every shop was bursting with colour, signs tacked all across their large, floor-to-ceiling windows that beckoned consumers in with promises of tremendous discounts. Shoppers danced around each other with less grace than the Otherside's answer to Torvill. Bermuda passed a number of clothing outlets before he stepped out on the road.

The deep blast of a horn rocked his body and caused him to leap back. The tram, a hulking metal people-carrier, glided past, sticking rigidly to the tracks that were indented into the pavement. The sides were littered with advertising boards, again, promises of severe discounts and seasonal delights.

Bermuda's hand shook as he finished his coffee.

He took a moment to compose himself and then began laughing loudly. He had spent too long being called crazy to be concerned with people glaring at him with concern. As the laughter echoed out of his chest, he thought how he had been chased only a week before by a monster bigger than a bus. How six months earlier he had fought Barnaby to the death with the fate of the world on his shoulders.

How over three years before, his fuzzy memory of the

Otherside had seen him narrowly escape the deep red eyes and the screams.

He had survived all that.

It would be just his luck that he would get killed by a tram.

While his laughter died down to a chuckle, his hand still shook. A flash had danced across his eyes before stepping back, images of beautiful faces he knew he couldn't see. With a grumble he turned on his heel, facing the rain, and headed back to the hotel.

The dark eyes of the two hooded figures, watching from separate sides of the street, had witnessed his near-death experience.

The streetlights bounced off their white masks as they stared at Bermuda.

---

ARGYLE STOOD outside the Premier Inn, his hands behind his back with one resting in the other. His broad chest, plated with armour, stood puffed out, the stance of a proud soldier. His grey eyes flickered up and down the street.

He scorned himself for his lack of vigilance earlier.

Argyle prided himself on his ability to sense Others, but also his strict attention. He should have seen McAllister barge into the house, but he had been distracted. He had been staring at the alleyway.

Were they there?

Had they finally come for him?

Argyle shuffled uncomfortably on the spot, readjusting his stance and ensuring he stepped back as close to the wall of the hotel as possible. The last thing he wanted to do was scare a human. Being an invisible wall tended to upset people.

The rain was relentless, smashing against the concrete city with a fury that Argyle found beautiful. At least it meant fewer people would be out.

Perhaps it would keep the heart-stealer indoors.

Argyle knew better. Whoever they were hunting, he knew that there would be no stopping. The only outcome was for them to find this Other.

Bermuda could find it. Argyle knew it.

Taking a deep breath, Argyle felt a small tinge of sorrow for his partner, who had been trying earnestly to rebuild a relationship with his child, one that had been brutalised by his gift. While Bermuda could see a different world, it blinded him from the one he wanted to build. It was a heartbreaking sacrifice, and one that he had punished himself for. His body bore the scars, physically and emotionally, be it from a needle and ink or the claws of a violent beast.

But Bermuda never gave up.

They would fight together until the bitter end. Argyle knew that, had witnessed it atop the grand clock tower that overlooked their city when they had felled Barnaby.

When they had witnessed a fellow agent die in the line of duty, despite his appalling attitude.

When the stunning woman had walked away from Bermuda.

They still fought.

Over the wonderful echoes of the pounding rain, Argyle could hear a raised voice, an inaudible rant from a voice rife with intoxication. He glared through the heavy downpour to the homeless man from the evening before. The group of kids who had terrorised him were nowhere to be seen, safe and warm in their homes that they held over this unfortunate human.

He was clearly influenced by some substance, which

made him as criminal as it did pathetic in the eyes of the powerful soldier who stood before him.

The homeless man yelled and yelled at the other passers-by, for them to look in the direction he was wildly pointing.

For them to look at the hotel.

To look at the armour-plated soldier who stood valiantly by the front door, clear as day.

# FIFTEEN

THE BLOOD WAS WARM, a thick stream of it sliding down his arm as he held it aloft. In his hand, the heart had come to a stop, the final beats petering out like a song as it quietens to its finish.

The heart had belonged to Rosie Seeley, a young blond student who had been enamoured by his charm.

She lay across the back of the sofa, her hands reaching for the front door to her modest studio apartment. Her tears were still wet down her face as she had struggled. Unlike the others, who had simply cried, frozen, or wet themselves when he 'turned', this one had fought back.

A swift knee to his groin and a dash to the door.

It had been admirable.

Pointless. But admirable.

After shaking off the shock of her battle for self-preservation, Kevin Parker had stomped after her, wrenching her short blond hair and snapping her head back before hurling her away from her freedom. She had collided hard with the coffee table, the modest furnishing collapsing under her weight and shooting a jagged piece of wood into her thigh.

She had screamed, but the sounds were choked from her by his powerful hand, the fingers wrapping around her throat and squeezing like a boa constrictor. She could feel the life leaving her, his eyes, now black and embedded in a monstrously distorted face, bored into her, searching.

Not for her.

For someone else.

As he had lifted her petite frame from the ground, he had gazed at her, contemplating. She had no idea; all she had known was a warm stream of urine began to trickle down her legs, dripping gently onto the wooden floor. In an instant, she had been slammed facedown onto the hard wooden ridge that ran along the back of the sofa.

Moments later, she had felt the skin of her back being punctured. The pain had been breathtaking as she felt his knuckles slam against her spinal cord, the vertebrae cracking as she had lost all feeling in her body.

Shock had washed over her as she lay motionless.

The last thing she had felt was his fingers on her heart before her consciousness, like her life, was literally snatched from her.

Now, in the shoddy light cascading from the cheap bulb above, Kevin admired the life source. It gleamed; a thick layer of blood coated it like a toffee apple.

This one should be enough.

It had to be.

Silently, he stepped away from the motionless body of the young lady. She had told him things about her life – things of little consequence. He had been stood in her store, a quaint florist on the outskirts of the city, staring intently at the roses when she had approached. He had charmed her.

Selected her.

With his fingers grasping the very essence of life, Kevin Park stepped through the blood which was pooling across the floor, and had turned the back of the sofa are darker shade of blue.

Rosie's eyes were wide open but saw nothing.

Her final moments had been spent in terror.

As had hers, he told himself. The one that he demanded from them. The one that they needed to return to him.

Careful not the use his fingers, Kevin slid his hand back into his sleeve and unlatched the door. A concerned neighbour cowered behind his own door as the classically handsome man left the flat where he had heard the commotion.

The screaming.

His right arm, from the elbow to the fingertip, was coated in scarlet.

His fingers encased a young woman's heart like a makeshift rib cage.

With measured steps, he exited the building to make his delivery, leaving behind a body that had been ripped open and a discovery that would rip many lives apart.

---

BERMUDA SAT in his hotel room, his bare legs stretched across the bed. The television screen was alive with colour, with some program about rich people looking to invest money humming annoyingly in the background. He had hoped it would take his mind off of the case – the two dead women and the likely discovery of another this evening. The evidence suggesting this had happened before.

The growing list of employees of the Glasgow Police Service that hated his guts.

He sighed, sliding off the bed and heading across the purple-and-white identikit Premier Inn room. The rain clattered against the window of his sixth-floor room. The desk before him was littered with local leaflets, all offering authentic Scottish experiences and cuisine. To the left of them, the shards of glass from the night before.

His mind flashed to McAllister, the two run-ins he had had with her that day as well as the terrible sexual encounter the night before.

The unsexy cherry on a very shitty cake.

His eyes ran past the cheap, hotel-provided hairdryer affixed to the wall and caught a glimpse of himself in the mirror. As soon as he had returned to the hotel, he had been greeted by Argyle, who had seemed on edge. While he had checked in with his partner, he had noticed the grey, pupilless eyes flicking from street to street as if he was expecting someone.

Or something.

The drunk homeless man had returned, screaming about guardian angels and medieval knights of some description. Of large men in suits of armour. Of hooded warriors that stalked the alleyways. Of bright, white masks.

Bermuda had dismissed it as inebriation.

Sweet, sweet inebriation.

As soon as he had entered the hotel room he had stripped off, his drenched clothes being strategically balled up and tossed into the corner of the room. He had stood in the shower for over twenty minutes, the water hitting him at a surprisingly powerful rate. Bermuda's mind raced to the day he had had, leaping from moment to moment. Arriving at the crime scene, the venture to the Necropolis. Tobias and his creepy loose skin. The BTCO Scotland Office and its bizarre inhabitant. The run-in with Strachan.

A hell of a day.

Most confusing of all, that while the near entirety of it had been spent being pummelled by water, Bermuda had stepped in and willingly stood under more.

Now he stood glaring at his ink-covered body in the mirror. Through various sources and his own research, he had spent thousands of pounds on his ink work. The symbols and incantations, many written in the criss-cross scrawl that he had seen in the archives under Vincent's watchful eye, kept him safe.

Physically or mentally.

Either way, he looked at them, agreeing that in the eyes of Angela, he must have seemed mental. No wonder she had taken his daughter from him and run from their marriage.

No wonder Sophie had left as well.

His brow furrowed in frustration, deploring himself for immortalising her as 'the one that got away.' His toned body had filled out slightly over the last six months, the result of quitting smoking and Argyle forcing at least some combat training.

Across his chest, the ink ruptured into three jagged scars.

A reminder of the violent beast upon the *Cutty Sark* and his trip through the roof of the boat.

And a further reminder of how only six months earlier, his body wasn't healing as it did now.

He had almost forgotten his condition, losing himself in the labyrinth of the case. His body was changing. He could feel it. It was that feeling you have when you have a trapped nerve, the sudden, uncontrollable jolt within your skin, like something blocking a vein.

Something dark and vulgar lurked within him.

He could feel it invading every part of his body.

Calling to him.

Demanding him.

A few days ago he had hurtled off of a thirty-foot bridge and shattered his ribs and his collarbone. His bones had healed completely. With a shudder, he rolled his shoulder, feeling zero effects of the drop that should have ended his life.

The Otherside wouldn't allow it.

It fixed him.

So at some point, it could claim him.

With a grunt, he threw on his jeans and a T-shirt. He pulled on another pair of Converse – red ones this time – and yanked a thick woollen jumper over his head. His still damp coat wrapped around him, protecting him from the elements and the dangers hidden in the shadows. The inside pocket shook with Tic Tacs against his e-cigarette.

'Let's go,' he told his reflection, as his wet beanie hat flattened his hair as he stomped through the door and out into the wet Glasgow night.

---

HIS CAB RUMBLED to a stop at the bottom of the hill, the Necropolis spanning the rise like a gothic painting. Bermuda paid the driver who had treated him to an impromptu talking tour of the city as they had coasted through the streets, his thick accent making his descriptions undecipherable. Bermuda had nodded politely, instead gazing out through the window and wondering which building the Absent Man would be in.

Who would be losing their heart this evening?

As the cab indicated and pulled away into the freezing night, Bermuda shuddered, wrapping his arms around his body and wishing he had an ale in his hand.

'You seem cold.' Argyle's words were the opposite.

'No shit,' Bermuda responded before turning and entering through the thick metal gate and ascending the twisted concrete path that slithered its way through the graveyard.

The tombstones shot out of the ground, each one a

dark pillar against the moonlight. They walked across the land of the dead, each step crunching on the fallen leaves that had given up for the winter.

They walked quietly for a few minutes, the slight gradient of the land growing steeper as they returned to the tomb where Bermuda had been earlier in the day. In the dark, the old brick looked on the verge of collapse, the door was a dark tunnel that led to oblivion.

The rain was relentless.

Bermuda sniffed, the stench of wet, rotten leaves filling his nose as he gazed around the entire grounds. Dead trees loomed over the entire graveyard like long, skinless arms with twisted fingers. Beyond, on the road that surrounded the Necropolis, he could make out two police cars. McAllister would have assigned them to keep watch, but with as easy as it was for Bermuda to enter the grounds, he didn't think their murderous friend would have any problem getting by either. He turned back to Argyle, who was also staring at the police cars.

'Do you think the officer I struck has recovered?' Argyle asked, his worry evident.

'I'm sure he will be okay. Hopefully he is pissing blood for a week or two, but he should be fine.'

'I have brought shame to you and the BTCO.' He spoke softly, his words wet with regret.

'I think you need to give yourself a break, Big Guy,' Bermuda offered softly. 'There are worse things you could have done than strike a policeman. I mean, you didn't reveal yourself, did you? The man probably just thought he was going into labour.'

'I did not reveal myself. To willingly expose an unseeing human to our world is a crime punishable by imprisonment.'

'Exactly. You didn't do that.'

'To expose this world to the uninitiated is a crime that

is second only to that of a killing a human,' Argyle stated, his eyes staring dead ahead. 'To kill a human is punishable by death.'

'Less of the death, Big Guy.' Bermuda patted his friend on his armour-clad shoulder. 'There's already plenty of that going around.'

Bermuda slowly stepped through the icy wind and approached the wall of the tomb, resting his hand across the wet stone, begging a touch of the Otherside to stroke his palm. The blood of Katie and Nicole had long since washed away. Leaving only a memory.

A third would likely arrive tonight.

Bermuda sighed, patting his coat until he located his e-cigarette, and brandished it under the bright moonlight. The blue bulb winked as he inhaled, and a burst of cherry-flavoured smoke instantly hitched itself to the wind.

'I'm going to see if Tobias is around.' Bermuda shrugged as Argyle kept whipping his head from side to side. 'Are you okay?'

'I am just alert.'

'Well stop it, will you? Usually you are so calm I struggle to believe you have a pulse. But the last few days, you seem on edge.'

Bermuda offered him a smile that struggled against the downpour before calmly walking around the corner of the tomb towards the door. Argyle stood tall, deciding not to tell his partner of the hooded figures from the shadow. The cloaked figures from the alleyways.

The danger that was slowly stalking them.

The cloaked figures had retreated for the evening, Argyle was sure of it. He could sense the presence of Others, could feel when they were near. He had never questioned the ability and could recall the hideous voice of his commander telling him it was a gift that made him what he was.

A killer.

Argyle shook the dark memory from his mind and reassured himself that they were not following tonight. The only death that followed them tonight was from the surrounding graves.

There were no Others near.

It was the final thought that ran through Argyle's head before a heavy stone clattered the back of his skull, a sharp pain shot to the back of his eyes, and everything went dark.

---

KEVIN PARKER HAD VENTURED through the backstreets, keeping his pace steady and his blood-soaked arm hidden. Eventually he approached the Necropolis, the wonderful, vast collection of death. The place where he would find her.

Where they would return her to him.

Steering clear of the police cars, he clambered over a fence and dropped down into the wet grass, the mud splattering up the leg of his grey suit. His brown leather shoes slipped slightly in the mud but he forced himself to balance. He walked through the dark, weaving in and out of the stone monuments that bore the names of the deceased.

Many a knee had been taken before them, all in the name of pointless grief.

For a moment he wondered if Rosie Seeley's family would be grieving, their daughter taken from them for a purpose that was inherently selfish. But necessary.

His suit clung to his tall frame as he walked, his eyes flashing from grave to grave as he ascended the hill towards the tomb, ready to deliver and make good on his challenge.

Ready to accept her back.

*'But the last few days, you seem on edge.'*

Kevin Parker stopped dead, his hands dropping to his sides. Blood dripped through the hand that clutched the heart like a baseball. He peered through the dark towards the crooked concrete building and saw the two men before him. One of them was clearly human; his body language omitted fear, even as he tried to walk bravely.

The human disappeared around the corner, presumably into the darkness.

To return her? Was he the voice in the dark?

Determined to confront him, Kevin Parker sized up the other figure. Over seven-foot tall with a metal torso that shimmered majestically in the moonlight. A blade was strapped to his back, a clear deterrent, and a man capable of killing him.

They would not get the chance.

His fingers clenched slightly. The chance to meet the one who had taken so much from him had arrived. Carefully he reached down, picking up a large stone from a collection a family had lovingly arranged around their departed's grave.

With careful, measured steps, he approached the warrior from behind, marvelling at the sheer size of the creature.

He swung.

The rock made a sickening crack as it collided with bone and the large warrior crashed to the earth, limp and lifeless. He could have been dead, but there was no time to make sure.

The rain poured down over both of them, the moonlight causing it to twinkle.

With a deep breath and determined to have her returned, Kevin Parker entered the tomb.

# SIXTEEN

BERMUDA NEVER THOUGHT STEPPING into a dark tomb would be so welcoming, but the icy rain ushered him inside quickly. As before, the walls felt thick and close, the space to breathe slowly evaporating by the claustrophobia. Water leaked through the cracks in the old brick, a thin sheen of moss stretched across it like body hair.

The tomb smelt damp.

Of death.

'Tobias?' Bermuda called out, his voice echoing off the wet walls. There was nothing, just the patter of rain and the crumbling of brick somewhere.

*Why here?* Bermuda thought, his mind racing back to earlier, when he had run his hand across the wall, hoping to feel something.

Anything.

'Tobias?' he called again, scorning himself for repeating himself. The creepy groundsman was clearly no longer there. Bermuda chuckled to himself at the thought of the man sleeping in the tomb; the large stone table that lay in the centre of the room, encompassed by shadow, was hardly a fitting bed. A shudder danced up his spine as he wondered what it could have been used for.

He reached into his pocket and pulled out his e-cig, pressing down on the button. A hiss accompanied the blue light that flashed forward, illuminating a small section of the wall. As the flavoured liquid substitute bubbled away, Bermuda slowly edged along the wall, running his hand across the stone.

'Give me something,' he muttered to himself, his voice reverberating gently back at him. He crouched down as his fingers felt the rough grooves that had been etched into the wall.

A quick jolt of the Otherside passed through his fingertips.

He could feel it, pulling at his fingerprints, trying to drag him through the very brick before him. He squatted back, resting on his ankles as he pulled his notepad from his pocket.

The crude drawing of the 'Gate-maker' still occupied a page, as did Sophie Summers's phone number.

Two memories that brought nothing but pain.

Clasping the e-cig in his mouth, he had to push it further down so his teeth could lock on the button, the smoking implement daring to touch the back of his throat. Fighting the urge to gag, Bermuda aimed the blue beam at the wall and began to sketch the markings down.

After a few strokes of the pen he dropped the notepad and swiped the e-cig from his mouth. A shiver ran through him as his mouth went dry, his stomach slowly knotting itself out of fear. He peered in closer at the marks, unsurprised that he had managed to feel the other world in their grooves.

They were not markings.

They were fingernail scratchings.

'What the fuck?' Bermuda questioned out loud as he guided the light further around the base of the wall, the stone slathered with the horrific scratches of a panicked hand. Someone had been in here.

Someone had been trying to get out.

Right on cue, a flash of lightning illuminated the shadowed tomb for a split second, followed by a roaring clap of thunder that shook the entire graveyard. Bermuda heard something shuffle behind him as the rain picked up its pace.

'Who are you?'

The voice caused Bermuda to spin on spot. He pushed himself so he was standing and took a cautionary step backwards. The words were cold, inquisitive but laced with menace. The creature before him was not a beast.

It was a man.

But not quite.

Bermuda's eyes had adjusted to the darkness of the stone enclosure and he looked at the 'man' before him. He instantly saw why the victims had been easily led. The man was strikingly handsome but in a way that reminded Bermuda of the olden days. His suit, damp and clinging to his sturdy frame, was splattered with the unmistakable colour of blood. It looked half a size too big for him.

The short brown hair was shimmering from the downpour, but was still slicked across his skull in a neat side parting.

His eyes were piercing and his strong jaw sat rigid, like an alligator ready to snap.

His hand was covered in blood, his powerful fingers wrapped around a fresh heart that had undoubtedly been ripped out from a young lady who would be discovered soon.

The Absent Man.

A cold-blooded killer.

Bermuda took another step back, trying his best to put the stone table between him and whatever it was posing as a man before him. As he slowly stepped back, he could feel the hate from the stare, the eyes ripping through him like he imagined the man's hand had to the poor victims.

Not man.

Something else.

As the silence sat as heavy as the damp between them, Bermuda held his hands out, as a sign of piece.

'What did you do to Argyle?' he asked, concerned that Argyle hadn't stopped his visitor.

'What's an Argyle?' The man's voice was calm, a slight bass to it. His eyes were unblinking.

'You know. Big guy, armour, sword, constant look of constipation. Argyle.'

The Absent Man stared at him, unmoved by the humour. Bermuda's eyes flashed to the doorway, hoping Argyle would race in at any moment. All that entered was the wind carrying the rain.

'He is outside. I am unsure if he is still alive.'

Bermuda felt his heart jump; the fear of losing Argyle hit him harder than he thought. His mind flashed back to that rainy night in Big Ben six months before when he had seen Argyle plummet to what he thought would be his death.

He had survived then.

Please let him survive now.

The Absent Man snapped him back to reality.

'Where is she?' His words were laced with venom.

'Who?' Bermuda asked, looking around with genuine bemusement.

'Where is she?' he repeated, taking a step closer. 'You promised.'

'I have no idea what you are talking about.'

'In the dark.' The Absent Man took a step closer, and Bermuda held his hands up again in a worthless display of surrender. 'You promised me her return.'

'Who are you?' Bermuda asked, stepping further around the stone structure between them, trying to edge towards the door.

'You know who I am. You kept me in the darkness. You took her from me and you demanded this.'

He tossed the heart onto the stone between them, blood and rain splattering across the surface like a Jackson Pollock painting. Bermuda felt a small rise of vomit clamber up his throat, but he controlled himself before it reached the surface.

The blood-soaked heart glistened like a rare jewel.

'Now where is she?' The words were harder, the patience thinning.

Bermuda reached into his pocket and pulled out the small leather wallet that house his badge. 'I am not who you think I am, and I am not the person you spoke to before.' He flicked it open, revealing his badge. 'My name is Franklyn Jones and I am an agent for the BTCO. I am trying to help.'

'Help?' The Absent Man twisted his handsome face into a crooked grin. 'There is no help. Just her.'

'Who?'

The Absent Man stared longingly towards the wall, his eyes resting on the thousands of scratch marks.

The years of pain.

The lifetime of darkness.

The memories.

'She was my everything.' His words slipped through quietly, drenched in sadness. 'She was my reason for being. My great love.'

'And that's why you are killing these women? For her?'

'For love.'

Bermuda ignored the obvious response and took another step nearer. The wind from the doorway shot past him, beckoning him to safety.

'What's your name?' Bermuda asked, trying to keep the momentum up. Begging for Argyle to enter.

'It is Caleb. No, Kevin.' The Absent Man shook his head, wrestling with a dark memory. 'Kevin Parker.'

A pin could drop as the two of them stared at each other. The heart of another deceased between them.

'Who told you to steal the hearts?' Bermuda asked.

Kevin's eyes flickered from side to side, resting on the heart and then on the scratching of the wall. A panic filtered through, his movements more frantic.

'Kevin!' Bermuda's voice rose. 'Who told you to steal the hearts?'

'They held me in the dark.' He spoke, as if to himself.

Bermuda took a few careful steps towards Kevin. Towards the entrance.

'Why here? Why do you bring the hearts here?'

'You lied to me,' Kevin whispered, the darkness of his pupils slowly filtering into his sclera, blending together with a smoky beauty. Bermuda could see him changing.

'Who did they take from you?' Bermuda's question was stern and he reached out towards Kevin, hoping beyond hope to restrain him. To stop him from hurting another person.

He was wrong.

'You lied to me!' Kevin roared, the final word distorting into a vicious roar beyond humanity. In a sudden burst of speed, Kevin shot towards Bermuda and swung his bloodied hand. The back of his powerful wrist caught Bermuda across the jaw and sent him over the stone altar.

The SOCOs would be pleased he cleared the entire table, missing the heart and the blood splatter.

His jaw and, after colliding with the wall, spine weren't so grateful.

Kevin grunted before turning and setting off through the door, racing at a freakish pace back down the hill, the rain crashing around him. Bermuda pulled himself to his feet, doing his best to block the fear and sense of self-preservation from his mind, and gave chase.

He burst out of the tomb and into the howling wind of the night, noticing the crumpled body of Argyle to the side of the building. The wound on the back of his skull was healing and Bermuda could feel him stirring. His eyes narrowed, trying to peer through the curtain of rain enveloping the grounds before him, the treacherous slope back towards civilisation.

A flash of lightning drew his gaze towards the gate just as Kevin Parker was reaching the metal barrier.

'Find me,' Bermuda said hopefully, leaving his partner and heading down the hill, weaving between the tombstones and racing across the fields of death beneath him.

For the first time in six months, Bermuda was glad he had quit smoking, his eyes fixated on Kevin Parker, who raced through the streetlights of the street ahead. Bermuda pushed through the gates and gave chase, his breaths getting deeper as his clothes got heavier.

His jaw ached and his spine roared in agony as he slowed, the feeling of failure fitting him like a bespoke suit as he watched Kevin Parker disappear around the corner.

Suddenly, the sound of bike tyres thrashing through the rain had him stepping into the road, causing the cyclist to almost crash as he squeezed the brakes.

'What the fuck are you doing?' The courier's voice was thick with Scottish fury.

Bermuda pointlessly flashed his badge. 'Sir, I need to commandeer this bicycle.'

'You can go fuck yoursel—'

Bermuda's punch landed right on the side of the man's jaw, rocking him gently on his feet before he fell into a spandex-covered pile on the floor.

He checked his knuckles – two of them had split on impact and a trickle of blood rushed through his fingers, like the blood of Kevin Parker's victims.

At the end of the street, the police assigned to the literal 'graveyard shift' flared up their sirens at the assault they had just witnessed.

Bermuda sighed. 'Ah shit.'

He hoisted the bike from the ground and swung a leg over, trying his level best to remember the last time he had ever cycled and hoped that the well-worn saying was true. His feet pedalled, and he flew up the street, taking the corner too fast and almost colliding with a parked car.

Halfway down the long road which led towards the city centre, Bermuda could make out the figure of Kevin Parker. The speed of the man matched his strength.

Not human.

Pushing the fear of the Otherside and an impending traffic collision from his mind, Bermuda continued pedalling, the wailing of the sirens behind him causing him to increase his efforts. After the last few run-ins with Glasgow's finest, he was sure they wouldn't go easy on him.

Strachan would see to that.

He whipped in and out of darkness, the streetlights passing at an increased rate as he flew up the street, the police car right on his tail. Kevin Parker turned at the next left. The hill would lead him back into town, towards a beehive of activity that would swallow him up. Bermuda instinctively turned left as well one street earlier, the wheels wobbling as he somehow maintained his balance and swerved, missing the car that emergency stopped.

The police car didn't.

The collision was shockingly loud, the shattering of glass and the slow death of the siren the last thing Bermuda heard as he eased up on the pedals and let the hill do the work. As the city centre rushed to meet him, he peered to the right and saw Kevin Parker heading towards the orange signage of the subway.

Bermuda turned sharply, hammering through the main square towards the steps that led down to the station. Weaving between a young family, Bermuda collided into Kevin Parker at the top of the stairs, the impact sending the bike crashing down them to the underground as the two of them hit the hard concrete. A few passers-by gasped in shock as Bermuda did his best to ignore the pain of the crash and restrain Kevin.

Thrashing wildly, Bermuda and Kevin Parker came face to face and, in the bright streetlight that hung above, Bermuda could see he wasn't human. His eyes were jet-black, the colour of death, and his mouth had distorted into a heinous snarl. The veins in his neck were straining against the skin, ripples of movement beneath his muscles that looked like he was infested with insects.

The Otherside trying to get out.

Kevin growled furiously and snapped backwards, sending Bermuda crashing to the pavement. With remarkable speed he spun around and stood, reaching down and grabbing Bermuda by the neck, his fingers pressing into his throat and slowly crushing his larynx. The crowd gasped and stepped back, and a sea of phones were revealed – some for the emergency services, most for the social media opportunity.

Somewhere behind them, Bermuda could hear the joyful chiming of the tram's bell.

Kevin Parker held Bermuda in front of his face, his black eyes boring into him, reminding Bermuda of Barnaby.

Reminding him of evil.

'I must have her.' Parker's words were soft, betraying the vicious, contorted scowl that rested upon his face. 'Don't try to stop me.'

And with that, he hurled Bermuda upwards. The bright lights of the city seemed to whip past Bermuda as gravity reached its reliable hand up and welcomed him to the hard concrete below. The wind raced out of his lungs on impact and the back of his skull hit stone, sending his vision and mind in different directions.

The crowd began screaming in terror as Bermuda slowly pushed himself to a seated position, something loud ringing in his ears.

A bright light shone in his eyes.

It took Bermuda a split second to realise that he wasn't being welcomed into heaven.

He was sat on the tram tracks that sliced their way through the town centre.

A few feet away, the tram hurtled towards him, blasting its shrill horn as the driver did his best to slam on the brakes.

The on-looking crowd screamed as it failed to stop.

---

RAINDROPS WELCOMED Argyle back to consciousness, the water splattering his face as his grey eyes blinked themselves open. He gently rolled onto his front, the feeling of his body returning to him. The back of his head throbbed, the sure sign of an assault that he didn't expect.

Couldn't sense.

Perplexed by his hidden assailant, he pressed his big

hands into the sloppy mud beneath him and pushed himself to his knees. The wind whistled past, the force shaking the sword that clung to his spine. With a gentle wobble he pulled himself to his feet, resting a hand on a monument to the dead for support.

What had attacked him?

Where was Bermuda?

He had a vague recollection of his partner being next to him, a bizarre request to 'find him'.

Where?

Argyle slowly scanned his surroundings, trying his best to align his thoughts that had been shattered like a windowpane by his attacker.

Suddenly, the night sky was awash with flashing blue lights and sirens. He turned his head to the roads at the base of the hill, watching as one of the police cars burst into life and moved towards the street. Narrowing his eyes, he watched as small figure boarded a two-wheeled vehicle and then uncomfortably began to steer it.

Bermuda.

Without hesitation Argyle set off, whipping in and out of the tombstones and respectfully refusing to step on the graves of those long gone.

There was honour in death.

Honour he would always respect.

As he got nearer the bottom of the hill, Argyle used the elements to his advantage, leaning his body weight into the decline and sliding down the gradient. Nearing the bottom, he pushed off with his powerful legs, soaring through the air and clearing the fence to the Necropolis in one mighty bound.

He landed down on one knee, his hands pressed on the concrete before he burst forward like an Olympic sprinter, racing through the centre of the road.

He overtook a car, its inhabitants unaware of the armoured warrior passing.

A mighty crash could be heard up ahead and he could see the police car had collided with another earth-destroying machine, the occupant showing little respect for the uniform that the officer wore. Argyle questioned if it was all humans who disrespected nobility and a uniform, not just Bermuda.

With his mind refocused, Argyle approached the arguing policeman and his aggrieved civilian, smoke filtering between them from the crumpled bonnet of the modest vehicle. Argyle whipped past them, leaping and sliding across the roof of the police car and maintaining his speed out the other end.

As he approached the bottom of the hill, Argyle heard the crash of a bike, the screams of people that began to huddle around the entrance to Queen Street Station. As he neared, he saw Bermuda fly through the air, colliding with the concrete with a vicious thud.

A tram rushed past Argyle, catching him by surprise, the shrill ringing of its bells breaking Argyle's concentration. He shook the noise away and followed the tram's trajectory.

The metal tracks.

The prone body of Bermuda that lay across them thirty feet away.

In an instant, Argyle raised his right arm, the spike of the Retriever shooting off, followed by the unbreakable chain that clung to it. It weaved beyond the civilians and ripped into the metal panel of the driver's carriage. Instantly, Argyle reversed the retrieval, launching himself forward towards the spike and the front of the vehicle.

Bermuda woozily pushed himself up.

The tram hurtled towards him.

Cutting through the rain, Argyle caught up to the front

of the unstoppable vehicle and reversed the retrieval again. As more chain shot out he pushed himself away from the tram with one foot, he swung around the front of the tram and reached for Bermuda.

Everyone gasped.

Argyle hauled him out of the tram's way a split second from death.

As the two partners rolled across the concrete, the world witnessed only Bermuda sprawled in the rain.

Unable to remove the Retriever in time, Argyle felt the chain tightened followed by the wrenching of his right arm, dislodging itself from its socket.

The tram wobbled, the sudden jolt freeing it from its set tracks and causing the driver's carriage to jack-knife slightly, shooting into the wet, Christmassy air in a burst of sparks like a pyrotechnic show. The rest of the tram followed, with the civilians screaming and running in a wild panic as the entire tram flipped onto its side, its occupants rattling inside as the metal slid to a stop on the wet concrete.

The power lines above were wrenched downwards, cables snapping and electric wires flickering with imminent danger.

After a few moments the entire square was quiet, the public gathering around as the emergency services rushed onto the scene, a few police officers pushing the public back as a few people rushed to the upturned carts of the tram to help those inside.

The city of Glasgow was in chaos.

Bermuda sat up, his head, jaw, and spine all competing for his attention. With a grimace, he turned and looked at the carnage. The backlash from Strachan would be like hellfire.

From Montgomery Black, brimstone.

With a deep sigh, he reached up to the outstretched left

hand of his friend and saviour, the right arm hanging loosely from the armour. Argyle helped him to his feet, and the two nodded to each other through the rain.

Bermuda watched as his partner scanned the destruction with horror.

'Bet you a fiver that Monty is gonna be pissed.'

Before Argyle could respond, a police officer roughly wrenched Bermuda towards a police car and to what would inevitably be one hell of an arse-kicking.

# SEVENTEEN

THE HUM of the halogen bulb gnawed into the back of Bermuda's skull like a woodpecker, adding to the throbbing pain from his collision with concrete. He sat at the empty metal table with a cold bag of peas pressed against his head and the glaring eyes of Detective McAllister burning through him.

For all its noise, the bulb was doing a poor job of illuminating the room, the corners draped in curtain-like shadows. Beyond the door to the room, the walls were blank besides the 'mirror' that sat adjacent to where they sat. Bermuda was pretty sure that Nicola Strachan was pressed against the other side, salivating at the idea of ending Bermuda's career.

After Argyle had saved his life, two police officers had roughly pulled him away from the crash scene, slapping the metal cuffs roughly around his wrists and then manhandling him into the back of a car. The tram carriages had zig-zagged across the street, sprawled randomly like a child's playset. The passengers had been helped out, some of them requiring medical attention.

From what Bermuda had heard, there were no deaths,

which he took as a tick in the win column. The resulting damage to public property and general panic were not. As he sat dabbing at his skull, he felt the pain dance along his jawbone from the crushing blow that Kevin Parker had delivered, the quickly appearing bruise at the base of his spine the proof of the wall that had caught him.

He could already feel his body healing itself.

The Otherside taking over.

Shuddering to himself, he slowly turned on his seat and faced McAllister, her glare tightening around him like a boa constrictor.

'Do you have any idea how irritating you are?' Her words were firm, laced with menace.

'I have a fairly good idea, yeah.'

His response only enticed a larger snarl.

'Look, we have some bastard out there killing innocent women. We had another call come in last night and—'

'Whoa, wait. Last night?' Bermuda interrupted, slamming the ice pack on the table and realising his hands were no longer cuffed.

'Yes. Last night. Her name was Rosie Seeley.' McAllister's voice softened with sadness at the name.

'How long was I out for?'

'You sustained quite a blow to the back of the skull. You lost consciousness in the back of the car and have been asleep for over sixteen hours. It's now two p.m. Tuesday.'

'Fuck.' Bermuda sighed, slumping back in his chair.

'What were you doing at the Necropolis?' McAllister's voice was firm and authoritative, as if this was any other interview.

'Jesus Christ, you're not going to read me the riot act again, are you?' Bermuda shuffled slightly, but she just stared at him. 'I was doing my goddamn job.'

'Your job?' Her tone was mocking. She shifted the

paper in front of her, Bermuda realising he hadn't noticed it beforehand. 'Your job is to, and I'm only reading what has been provided by eye witnesses, assault cyclists and steal their bikes, ignore a direct order to pull over, cause a traffic collision by dangerous driving, cause widespread panic with erratic driving, and then, of all things, and we still don't know how, derail a tram?'

McAllister raised her eyes to Bermuda, a smug look on her face.

'Have I missed anything else?'

'You forgot to mention shit in bed,' Bermuda joked, smirking. The glare he got in return told him it wasn't appreciated.

'Look, Jones. I'm not going to refer to you as an agent because I don't think you are one. But we have real police work to do. I don't have the time or the resource to chase after you. Now somehow, your little phone call you made when you got here has got you off all charges and we have to release you. I don't like it. Strachan, she is fucking furious about it. But can you do me a favour? Just stay the fuck out of this?'

Bermuda shook his head, the small prick of pain slowly evaporating like a single line of smoke from a candle.

'I can't do that,' he uttered quietly.

'I'm asking you nicely. We have a killer who is targeting women at random and butchering them. We have no leads. A few witnesses have stated they saw the victim and this gentleman every evening of the murders. Although we have CCTV footage, we are unable to match it to anyone on our databases. We have no information, no name, no prints, no nothing. And the last thing I need is you destroying the public transport system, understand?'

'Am I free to go?' Bermuda asked, ignoring her question.

With a heavy sigh laced with hatred, McAllister nodded. 'Yes.'

'Good.' Bermuda pushed himself up slowly, feeling every single one of his vertebrae click together like snapping pieces of Lego. 'Oh, and by the way, I found a print.'

'Bollocks,' McAllister snapped, pushing her metal chair back, causing the legs to shriek against the hard floor.

'It's true. I'll get it sent over from the lab when we've done our analysis.' Bermuda walked towards the door, stopping before he gripped the handle. 'Oh and another thing: it may be worth widening your database. Despite what your little report says, I spoke face to face with the man responsible for this, and I'll tell you right now, he isn't from here.'

'Glasgow?' McAllister queried, her hand scrawling notes on the paper that fanned out over the desk.

'No. Our time. Wherever he is from, he's a long way from home.' Bermuda frowned, reliving the troubling words Kevin Parker spoke. 'He's looking for someone and he's done it before. Back in the eighties.'

'The eighties?'

'Yeah. Have someone go through your archives and pull up any murders from those times. There was a small burst of them where the victims were found heartless.'

McAllister noted it down again but then stopped. She turned a sceptical eye towards Bermuda as he flung open the door.

'How the hell do you know this, anyway?' she asked, her accent thick with annoyance.

'Like I said, I'm just doing my job.'

Bermuda flashed a handsome grin before turning towards the one-way glass that adorned the wall. With great relish, he raised a middle finger, the thought of Strachan going redder than a tomato with fury filling him with joy. He stepped out into the corridor of the police station, the outside chill inviting itself in. He walked past a few police officers who grunted in his direction, undoubtedly wanting to rub the smile that he wore off his face.

He wore it all the way to the front door before pushing them both open and stepping out into the freezing cold winter's day.

---

BACK IN THE INTERVIEW ROOM, McAllister gathered her notes and stormed back towards her desk, her anger outweighing her confusion. A few officers nodded their respect towards her as she marched through the open office, a few of her colleagues were glued to their desks, phones to their ears as they worked their cases.

McAllister reached her desk and dumped the folder on top of the rest. Each folder encased details of the departed, the unfortunate women who had lost their hearts.

Literally.

She sat down in the uncomfortable chair and rummaged through the messy drawers that sat next to her desk. It had been four years since she had passed her detective's exam; the certificates were pinned to the wall before her, surrounded by cheap plastic frames. It was all she had ever wanted to be from a young age – to be able to help people and solve cases.

Make the world a safer place.

The stack of files next to her made a mockery of that. Three women dead in three evenings. All three with their hearts removed, all three hearts delivered to the Necropolis. Not only that, some annoying agent from some secret organisation had been assigned to the case and was really getting under her skin.

She regretted sleeping with him.

It only added to the annoyance which made her head pound.

Under some paperwork pertaining to a driving offence she would never get round to investigating, she found some paracetamol. The previous evening's hangover had wrapped its fingers around her skull and was slowly squeezing her brain like it was trying to make fresh orange juice.

She popped the pills into mouth and sent them sloshing down her throat with a gulp of water.

She really should stop drinking.

Get things back on track.

Her heart spasmed in her chest and her green eyes fell upon the picture on her desk. The handsome smile belonged to David, his powerful arms wrapped around her in a photo that captured a pleasant, love-filled memory.

A memory long since passed.

Her heart had taken control of her body and her hand reached for the phone on her desk, her ears longing to hear his voice. She just needed to hear it once more.

Her head took control, and she slammed the phone back down.

Angrily, she turned the photo of her husband down onto the desk with such force that it sent a crack through the glass between them.

Just like everything else had.

McAllister pushed the seat back and stood up, massaging her temples. The hangover would go, slowly but surely, but that wasn't the issue. It was Agent Jones. As annoying as he was handsome, she scolded herself for letting him get under her skin. Their one-night stand, as drunken as it may have been, was ill advised and was only adding to the fact that he was possibly the most irritating man she had ever met.

There was something not right about him.

He didn't think the killer human? It was something else?

Not from our time?

As she angrily ran through the vague comments he had made, her sometimes-partner DC Greg Butler tapped her on the shoulder, causing her to jolt and spin.

'Woah, easy, guv.' He opened his palms in surrender. 'You okay?'

'Aye.' She looked around the room, losing herself in the hustle and bustle. 'I'm grand.'

'Do you need anything?' he offered, his admiration for the dedication and toughness of his colleague apparent.

'Yes actually, I do.' She shook her head in disbelief. 'Bring me any files we have from the archive room for murders in Glasgow in the 1980s that involve any damage or removal to the heart of the victims.'

'Aye.' Butler made the note in his book. 'A hunch, guv?'

'Yeah, sort of.' She shook her head. 'A really annoying hunch.'

---

AFTER RETURNING to the Premier Inn for a shower and a change of clothes, Bermuda sat on the edge of his bed, phone in hand. The screen was smiling at him, his daughter's beautiful face etched across the glass. His thumb hovered over the button. He chuckled to himself as his body was gripped by fear. He had come face to face with many monsters, been hurled through the roof of a boat, willingly driven off the edge of the Hammersmith flyover, and even fought the most dangerous creature in two worlds to the death at the top of Big Ben.

Yet nothing scared him more than calling his ex-wife.

He pressed the call button. It only took a few rings.

'Franklyn.' The voice was deeper than usual.

'Angela. You sound different.'

'It's Ian.' Angela's husband and Chloe's stepdad. Although he wasn't a laugh riot, Bermuda respected the man for being everything he wasn't. He was a good husband, and regrettably, a wonderful role model for his daughter.

'Hey, Ian. Is my daughter there?' Bermuda asked, pinching the bridge of his nose and trying hard not think of the life he could have had.

'Let me check with Angela.'

'I don't need permission,' Bermuda snapped. 'Sorry, mate.'

'It's fine.' Ian's voice was soft and reassuring. 'I'd just rather leave this between the two of you.'

'It's my daughter's birthday, for crying out loud. Let me talk to her.'

The words registered with no one as Ian had obviously passed the phone across. A stern cough, like a head teacher ready to dress down a naughty student, echoed down the line.

'Franklyn. What do you want?' Yep. She was pissed.

'Hey, Ange. Can I speak to our daughter please?'

'Why?' Angela sounded angrier than usual. 'She's upset as it is.'

'I know, but she knew I couldn't make it to her party. We spoke before I left.'

'But you couldn't call her first thing? Like you promised.'

The pain in the back of Bermuda's head returned, stabbing at the top of his spinal cord and at his heart at the same time. He was pretty sure it was guilt.

'Ah fuck.'

'Yeah, fuck, Franklyn!' She angrily continued. 'Why do you make promises to her that you *never* keep?'

'Look, about this morning, I was—'

'Drunk? Hungover? Fighting monsters? Which of your wonderful list of character defects do you want to select?'

The words cut through him like a knife through butter. Not because they were harsh. Because they were true.

'I was unconscious.'

'Brilliant.' Angela applauded sarcastically, the faint sound of clapping echoing around her voice. 'Why this time?'

'Would you believe me if I told you I derailed a tram?'

The phone went dead. Bermuda sat still for a few moments, the dial tone echoing in his ear like a life support flatlining. A symbol of his relationship with his daughter.

A single tear slid up and over his eyelid and cascaded down his stubbled cheek.

He had done so much over the past six months, from the moment Angela and his best friend, Brett Archer, had duped him into 'fixing her car'. That moment, outside his local watering hole the Royal Oak, seemed so long ago. He met his daughter properly for the first time, falling in love with her as she accepted him as her father.

Since then, Angela had been begrudgingly indulging him and his 'curse', agreeing to let Bermuda and Chloe meet in secret, out of the eyesight of the world.

It wasn't our world he was worried about.

Knowing that the Otherside both craved him and hated him in equal measure, Bermuda had pushed his family away to protect them, especially since he had escaped the mental institute and joined the BTCO. With enemies in both worlds, the last thing Bermuda wanted to give them was leverage. He would never forgive himself if anything, from this side or the other, hurt his Chloe.

But the need to be her father had led them down a path where Angela let them speak, even spend the odd day together.

He finally had a daughter.

But now, as the rain slammed against the window of his lonely hotel room, his bloodshot eyes met his own reflection, and in a snap of pure self-loathing he launched his phone at his own face. The mirror cracked, and a few small pieces of glass clattered on the small dressing table. His phone burst into a number of pieces, random segments of technology joining the shards of glass and inevitable hotel bill.

His daughter had been heartbroken.

He had done the one thing he promised he wouldn't.

He had hurt her.

Bermuda's teeth gritted together and his fists clenched, the angry tension tunnelling through his muscles until he erupted in a furious roar that almost shook the room. After a few moments he stopped to catch his breath as angry tears rolled down his cheeks and splattered the carpet below. Calming himself with deep, long breaths, Bermuda wiped his eyes with the back of his sleeve.

'I need a drink,' he said to no one.

And at that moment, for the first time he could remember, fate conspired in his favour as the hotel phone rang.

# EIGHTEEN

'THIS TOWN IS A SHIT-HOLE.'

Bermuda chuckled as he tipped his head back, allowing the last remnants of his Doom Bar to bubble in his throat. Brett Archer, his best friend, did likewise. The busy pub, the one where he had met McAllister two nights previously, was rammed with the locals, the noise levels consistently rising as everyone got a little drunker, and ergo everyone spoke louder.

They both put their empty pint glasses down on the table between them at the same time, the force shaking the menu holder and the promise of cheap, barely edible food.

'Another?' Bermuda offered.

'Another.' Brett smiled.

Reciprocating, Bermuda pushed himself up from the table and ambled through the Scottish crowd, making his way to the long bar, the draught pumps sticking up like a rib cage. Each one was adorned with a logo, the latest ales and craft beers which would eventually be filtered out by the usual suspects. Carlsberg, Fosters, Peroni. And of course, as he rested his forearms directly in front of it, Doom Bar.

The barmaid, pretty and overworked, flashed him a warm smile, holding up three fingers to indicate his place in the queue. She glanced at his forearms, the black ink that peeked out from under the rolled-up sleeves of his black shirt.

As the noise enveloped him, Bermuda cast his mind back to the previous afternoon. The searing pain needling its way into the back of his skull had subsided, but he wasn't sure if that was due to the two pints already consumed or the other-worldly power that coursed through his veins.

He had a feeling that McAllister may have believed him when he had left the awkward meeting in the interview room, but he had been more concerned with flipping Strachan the bird. From there he had ventured back to his Premier Inn room, the manmade 'comfort' welcoming him like a fart in an elevator.

Then there was the heartbreak of breaking his promise.

Chloe.

He shook the pain away, annoyed that he hadn't fully confronted it. Yes, he had let her down, but it was the job. He was making the world safe.

After that he had grabbed a coffee from one of the many outlets that were rubbing shoulders on the high street, this time settling on a Costa. With that in hand, he had strode across the town centre to the BTCO HQ, pressing his hand on the metal letter box and marvelling as the symmetrical lines began to form in the wooden panel.

A key he never knew he had.

Once he had ascended the steep steps, he was welcomed into the rundown office by Kelly, who once again wore a goofy smile and overly large woollen jumper. Her eyes, magnified by her huge glasses, locked on him and never left.

She had led him to a stairwell which went further underground, to a set of doors which hid agent housing. Behind door number one, like some bizarre game show, he found Argyle, sat quietly, cross-legged on the floor, his mighty blade resting on the unit before him.

Apologising for breaking his meditation, Bermuda checked his partner was okay. The wound on the back of his head had completely healed.

His arm and shoulder were successfully reattached.

The only thing broken was his pride.

Bermuda told him to rest up, and that they were banned from the Necropolis for now, which Argyle noted probably wouldn't stop Bermuda due to his lack of respect for any type of authority. Bermuda agreed, but thought they had earned a day off.

While he was there, Kelly, amongst her continuous offers of cups of tea, told him that Montgomery Black had called three times and had demanded that Bermuda contact him instantly. Something about 'doing the complete opposite to what was ordered'.

Bermuda gave it a miss.

As he departed, Kelly slapped an envelope into his hand, telling him that Malcolm had completed the print, but as yet could find no match within the last fifty years. Surprised, Bermuda offered to thank the elusive technician, only to find he was nowhere to be found, again. With a strict instruction for them to widen the year range, Bermuda left with the print safely tucked in his jacket pocket.

Which now sat over the chair opposite his best friend. It had been a mere moment after he had smashed his phone into his own reflection that Bermuda received a call from the hotel reception, telling him he had a guest. Expecting a furious 'Monty' or a grizzled Glaswegian police officer cracking his knuckles in anticipation,

Bermuda was shocked as his best friend Brett had emerged from the waiting room.

They had arranged for drinks that evening, and as the pretty barmaid held the card machine steady, Bermuda tapped his card, paid contactlessly, and then returned to their table, fingers clasped around fresh pints.

'Cheers,' Brett exclaimed as they tapped their glasses together.

Brett had been Bermuda's best friend since they went to Derby University and fully believed everything about 'the Knack'. In fact, Bermuda sometimes got the impression Brett wished he could see the Otherside too.

'Cheers, buddy.' Bermuda took a swig. 'So why the hell are you here again?'

'We organised a drink.' Brett also partook. 'I thought you were a detective or some shit.'

'No. I meant why are you here in Glasgow?'

'Oh, right. Well, I had a few days free before we go on tour. We are hitting up a few nights in Warsaw, Budapest, and Sofia. It's going to be messy. But figured before I left I should come up here and see Elaine.'

Bermuda nearly spat his drink out. 'Elaine?' He wiped his mouth. 'Shit man, it's serious then.'

Brett rolled his eyes. As the lead singer of the thrash metal band Frozen Death Cull, Brett had always thought monogamy was a sort of wood. But during Bermuda's quest to stop Barnaby six months previously, Brett had met a beautiful nurse named Elaine. Despite being Scottish, which Brett never let go, he seemed fairly taken with her. He nervously tucked his long brown hair behind his ear and stroked the thick brown beard that hung from his chin like a sloth.

'Shut up.' A measured response.

'Nah, cheers to you.' Bermuda offered his glass. 'It's about time you found a bonny lass.'

'Eurgh, thanks for reminding me about the Scottishness, BJ.'

Bermuda hated the nickname – it was too sexually recognisable for his liking. Within the next few moments, the glasses were empty, and Brett was at the bar, heartily chatting with a burly Scotsman and drawing a deep, booming laugh from him. Bermuda was happy for the company. Everyone he had met so far had been too keen, wanted to smash his face in, sexually aggressive, or creepy and dangerous.

Pretty much like back home.

Brett settled down opposite him again, passing him another pint of beer and disregarding any notion that they may have a problem.

'Hey, here's a question.' His words were slightly jumbled, the beginning effects of the ale. 'Is Argyle here?'

'In Glasgow?' Bermuda hiccupped.

'No, here. Now. I miss our beers together!'

'You've never spoken one word to him,' Bermuda stated.

'Yeah, but I have through you. I know, I know, he's not allowed to reveal himself to me and like you say, the guy has a stick shoved so far up his arse it wraps around his tongue, but I like it when he is here.'

'Really? Why?'

'I don't know. I guess I feel safer with a sword-wielding warrior at our table.'

'Hear, hear.' They tapped glasses. 'To answer, no, he is back at our base in town.'

'The BTCO has a base in Glasgow?'

Bermuda smiled at Brett's knowledge and interest. It made him feel less crazy. 'Yeah, apparently. Am trying to find one in Tenerife next.'

Brett chuckled and took a big gulp of his ale. Someone slotted a coin into the jukebox and coaxed it to life, but then let the entire pub down by selecting an Abba song. Bermuda shook his head, storing the Swedish mega-band into his own personal room 101. The grimace on Brett's face told Bermuda that his friend agreed.

'So, what you doing here in Glasgow then? It clearly isn't for the ladies.'

'Your girlfriend is from here – you know that, right?'

'Yeah, but she is unique,' Brett retorted, saving his skin.

'Something weird, man. Something is killing one woman per night at complete random and then removing their heart.'

'Like a game of Operation?' Brett offered, his fingers wrestling a packet of tobacco from his pocket and instantly reigniting Bermuda's cravings.

'No. More like a test of strength. It's ripping them out with its bare hands.'

Brett made a disgusted face.

'The thing is, I think it has a reason for doing it. I met it last night, and it seemed human. But there is something underneath. It kept talking about being trapped in the dark, how whatever held it prisoner had taken someone from it and had requested the heart of these women.'

'Wait, if you met it last night, why didn't you arrest it?' Brett asked, running his tongue down the cigarette and clasping it shut.

'Because it seems human. Like, it's a human body and called itself Kevin Parker. Also, it nearly broke my jaw and pushed me in front of a tram. I'd have died last night if once again Argyle hadn't saved my life.'

Brett nodded and sipped his beer. Bermuda could almost see the lightbulb ping above his head.

'Wait, a tram? Did Argyle derail that tram last night? It was all over the news.'

Bermuda sighed and nodded his head, lifting his glass again.

'Man. Argyle is a fucking boss.'

'Yeah, well instead of a get well soon card, apparently Monty back home is after my ass for destroying more public property. I guess he has a point. I should probably be a little more discreet.'

'Yeah,' Brett chimed in. 'Blowing up Big Ben and derailing trams hardly emanates secret organisation. So, what you going to do?'

'About?'

'About this heart-stealer? This Kevin Parker.'

'Find him. Catch him. Send him back to the Otherside.' Bermuda took a final swig and emptied the glass. 'Simple.'

Brett patted him on the shoulder as he stood, popping outside to the heated smoking area to quench his nicotine addiction. Bermuda watched on enviously before pulling out his e-cig and taking a long, thoughtful puff. A cloud of berry-filled smoke bellowed out, encasing him like a game show prize reveal.

He staggered to the bar slightly, requesting their fifth pint of the evening. The pretty barmaid began pulling them and he looked around the room. Everyone seemed in high spirits, groups of lads sharing banter while a clutch of girls surrounded two tables and watched on in a mixture of attraction and disappointment. They could do a lot worse than take one of them home.

They could end up with him.

Furiously, he scolded himself for his self-pity. Sure, the job had pulled him further away from his daughter again, but he would make his way back to her. He always would.

He was away. Not gone.

Just as he was pulling his mind away from the fracture of his relationship with his daughter, his mind flickered to Sophie Summers. Brett had met her that spring, even secretly texting her to bring the two of them closer together. He was thankful that his friend hadn't brought her up or made any jokes.

He still missed her.

She had rightly decided she was better off without him, but now, sat drinking with his best friend, his mind went back to that London evening, where they had shared wine and thoughts about both worlds.

Where she finally believed him.

A thick Scottish accent caught him by surprise.

'Disaronno and Coke. Double.'

Bermuda turned, and his drunken eyes slowly returned to clarity. DC McAllister stood before him, dressed in a nice black top and a well-fitted pair of jeans that hugged her slim frame. Her hair, usually a bird's nest in a blender, was slightly curled and cascaded down her sharp face like a waterfall.

'What the hell do you want?' Bermuda sneered, clearly at his most charming.

'Look, I think we need to clear the air between us. I mean, we probably couldn't have got off on a worse foot, and if we are going to work together, then I think maybe we should bury the hatchet?'

Bermuda sized her up for a moment as the barmaid placed the two beers next him. McAllister offered an awkward smile.

'Can I have a double Disaronno and Coke as well, please?'

McAllister nodded her thanks and then pointed to the table.

'Yeah, I'll bring it over. My friend is outside but will be back in a minute.'

'You have friends?' she smiled.

'Shocking, isn't it?' Bermuda tapped his card on the machine that was presented to him. It beeped with success. 'You?'

'Sort of. It's a long story.'

'Well, we aren't planning on leaving until they kick us out, so feel free to share.'

The two of them left the bar and headed to the table, the group of girls and guys and smashed together like a bizarre cocktail and one of them nearly knocked the drinks from Bermuda's grip. A harsh scowl drew a whimper of an apology and Bermuda settled back down at the table, McAllister sliding herself into the chair next to Brett on the opposite side.

They sat in silence for a few moments; the notion of being civil to each other was completely alien. Bermuda took the first step.

'So, What's up?'

'First off, I wanted to apologise for the whole sex thing.'

'Wow, you sound like me after my school prom.' Bermuda sipped his ale through his smile.

'I mean, I know we were drunk, but I shouldn't have acted like that and—'

'Forget it. Water under the bridge.' Bermuda waved his hand, dismissing it entirely.

'Thanks. And I know I haven't made life easy for you since you got here. I was angry about what happened, but also that higher-ups have sent you here. It feels like they don't believe I can catch this bastard. I've spent a long time on the force, Jones, and believe me, I've dealt with a fair share of shit and my fair share of discrimination. I wasn't going to give up this case if my life depended on it.'

Bermuda took a careful sip of his Doom Bar, letting the bitter taste accompany her words. She continued.

'But you were right. As much as it pains me to say it.'

'Sorry, I was what?'

'Right.' McAllister sipped her own drink. The red nail polish on her fingers was recent.

'I've been called many things in this world, but *right*

usually isn't one of them.' Bermuda took a triumphant swig. 'By the way, what was I right about?'

'The murders. It's happened before. I had a fellow DC, a good guy, hunt through some archives for me. I've spent the whole afternoon reading through some chicken scratch reports from the eighties of a murdering bastard ripping hearts from the victims. They even labelled him the Heart Snatcher.'

'Sounds like a crap rom-com novel,' Bermuda chortled, refusing to share that he had nicknamed Kevin 'the Absent Man'. He fished into his pocket and tossed an envelope across the table which slid to a stop before McAllister. 'Here.'

'What's this?' she asked, her eager fingers ripping the top open.

'It's that print. It was lifted off of a photo from Nicola Miller's flat.'

'How did my guys miss this?' McAllister muttered to herself.

'Because the guy you are looking for looks human, thinks it's human, and even calls itself a human name.' Bermuda shook his head. 'But it isn't human. It's something else, something so fucked-up it would make your head spin. When that fucked-up shit happens, that's when they send for me.'

McAllister's hand shook slightly as she knocked back the last of her drink, the ice shaking gently as she dropped it back down. Her eyes were wide, a cocktail of fear and amazement, when suddenly the blustering wind flew through the pub, a sea of groans and complaints turning the freezing air even colder.

Brett approached the table with confusion plastered across his wet face.

'Hello.' He offered a hand to McAllister, who half stood to greet him. 'I'm Brett.'

'Sam.' She shook, firmly.

'It's a pleasure to meet you.' He turned to Bermuda and winked.

'It's not like that. I mean, we did sleep together, but it was sort of an accident.' Bermuda looked to McAllister, who had suddenly become the poster child for 'if looks could kill'. 'Anyway, Detective McAllister here is working the case with me.'

'Oh, you're a detective?' Brett took a massive gulp of his ale, quickly playing catch-up. 'I won't hold it against you.'

McAllister chuckled, a pretty smile spreading across a face that Bermuda had pinpointed as looking predominantly sad – that despite all of her bravado, something dark and upsetting simmered just below like underlay on a fresh new carpet.

'So What's BJ done?' Brett asked, jabbing a thumb in Bermuda's direction.

'Umm ... it may sound crazy, but I think we may be dealing with something more than human?' McAllister offered, throwing a hopeful glance in Bermuda's direction.

Bermuda shuffled on his seat, offering her a comforting smile.

Brett lifted his pint glass and downed the rest of his pint, winking at them both before leaping to his feet and snatching his coat up. Before he left, he smiled at McAllister.

'Believe me, if you think it is completely batshit crazy and there is no way it can be true ... if they called Bermuda in ... then it's true.'

Brett offered them both a smile before dramatically bowing before them. He flung open the door and ventured out into the freezing darkness, with the night's wind dancing back through the pub and running a chill down everyone's spine as if a herd of Others had just run through the building.

After a few awkward moments of silence, McAllister lifted her head, looking Bermuda dead in the eye. 'What the hell is going on?'

Bermuda finished his pint and set the glass down firmly. 'Oh, we're going to need another drink.'

# NINETEEN

THE PIERCING SCREAM that ripped out of Emma Mitchell's throat was haunting, like a wolf howling at the moon.

Her bare feet slapped the concrete that led her to the end of her front garden. The gate was rocking furiously in the wind and collecting whirling leaves. The rain was relentless, almost as frenzied as the creature back in the house. Tears ran from her eyes, merging with the rain and completely drenched her cheeks. Half of her clothes were on the floor of the living room, her underwear-clad body shaking in the cold of the night.

That didn't matter.

It had Mark.

That creature.

She scolded herself as she fumbled with the wooden gate, screaming for help at the top of her voice.

A light flicked on in the neighbouring house, a curtain twitched across the road. No one raced from their homes. The only knight in shining armour she knew was being dismantled by Kevin Parker in the living room of their family home.

A home they had built together.

One she had destroyed with a single act of infidelity.

She had been out after work with the usual drinking crew, all of them working round the clock as part of a marketing team for a high-end insurance broker – nothing too fancy, but it paid well and had a good social crowd. Within their usual watering hole, weaving in and out of all the suits and after-work conversations, she had met Kevin Parker.

She had been blown away.

Foolishly, after a few hours of more drinking and overly flirtatious conversation, she had decided to heed her colleague's advice and take advantage of her husband's work trip.

When the cat's away, etc.

But her husband had surprised her with an early train back, to stumble into the house just as Kevin Parker's eyes had changed to black. When the monster that coursed under his skin like a wolf in sheep's clothing leapt to the surface.

He had meant to kill her, she knew that.

As she ran from the house, she had seen Parker's hand rip through the flesh of her husband's throat, the love of her life gurgling blood as fear overtook him, his bladder emptying down his leg as the blood poured over Parker's hand.

She was already up the garden path, racing through the cold rain as he wrenched her husband's head from his shoulders and discarded both parts of him like yesterday's trash.

With a snarl and the need for another heart causing him to shake, he set off after her.

Emma screamed helplessly again, her voice struggling against the downpour as she raced up the middle of the road, praying for a set of headlights to approach her. Her throat burnt with soreness, her vocal cords straining as she roared for a saviour.

Footsteps clattered behind her, and suddenly she felt the full force of Kevin's hand on the back of her neck – and with the flick of a powerful arm, he sent her flying to her right, her hip snapping as it collided with the bonnet of a parked Mercedes.

The alarm began its usual song, a bright orange glow illuminating the pained face of Emma in intermittent flashes.

She mumbled quietly to herself, begging for her life. As he approached, her eyes fell to his hand; the blood that covered it confirmed what she knew. Mark, her loving husband, was dead.

All for nothing more than a cheap fuck with a handsome stranger.

She didn't even resist as he wrenched her up from the ground, his phenomenal strength hoisting her high above his head like a makeshift umbrella. The rain washed away the urine that trickled down the inside of her thigh.

Her pleas were barely a whisper.

Kevin Parker pulled her closer to him, his face twisted, the teeth gritted together in fury. The eyes burnt through her, searching her soul for answers she would never have.

'I must find her.'

His words were laced with malice and she muttered a feeble plea for her life.

A few neighbours watched in shock from their doors. Some spoke to the authorities. Others hid in fear. Somewhere in the distance, sirens wailed, announcing the arrival of police officers who would find nothing but a massacre.

Still holding her up to the starlit sky, Kevin Parker launched his right arm forward, the blood-soaked hand taking another bathing as it ripped through her skin and shattered her ribs, the bones ripping out of her chest like an overstuffed grocery bag.

His fingers latched around her heart.

Her eyes flashed in agony before rolling back into her skull.

He let her slide down his arm into a crumpled mess on the floor at his feet.

Slowly, Kevin Parker lifted his right hand and felt the final beat leave her heart. Then, as the panic levels rose in the surrounding houses and the shrill call of the sirens ripped through the night sky, he turned and lost himself in the shadows.

---

ON THE OTHER side of Glasgow, two sets of feet were also stepping across rain-soaked pavement. Bermuda and Sam McAllister walked quietly, their hands stuffed in their pockets and their chins pressed against their chests, shielding their eyes from the bitter bite of the rain.

It had actually been a relatively peaceful evening.

Almost enjoyable.

After Brett had made his exit, the two of them had shared a few more drinks, burying the hatchet the last two days had created. They even joked about the shoddy sexual encounter they had shared, unbeknownst to them both that they'd be hunting a vicious serial killer together just hours later.

Bermuda had cracked that it was better than most second dates.

As the evening progressed, the drinking slowed, and while both of them realised that the original attraction between them had been exacerbated by alcohol, they were both fighting on the same side. Bermuda was certain that what was killing these women wasn't human, and when he began to relay this point to McAllister, he could see the scepticism in her eyes.

He had seen it a million times from hundreds of people.

After a few more drinks, McAllister had been more open-minded, the wine unlocking the sensibility and setting it free from her mind. She had asked for proof beyond a fingerprint she would have to investigate – that, according to the report, belonged to a hand that was last logged on record over eighty years ago. Despite his protests, she had struggled to believe a monster was quantum leaping through time to steal hearts.

It just wasn't possible.

They marched in silence, both of them lost in the case, the feeling of helplessness at knowing that somewhere this evening, another woman would be found dead. The press were cottoning on now, with a story about to hit the morning papers it would bring even more pressure down on both of them. Bermuda weighed up who he would rather be facing, Montgomery Black or DCI Strachan, and decided that either one would be as enjoyable as sticking his bollocks in a blender.

McAllister stopped, the wind rushing through the hair that poked out from under her woolly hat so it sprayed out like tentacles.

'This is me.' Hands stuffed deep in her pockets, she motioned with a nod.

The house was quaint, slightly bigger than the one Bermuda had broken into with the help of Argyle on their first night in Scotland. The home that Nicola Miller was murdered in.

'Okay. Cool.' Bermuda offered a Doom Bar-infused smile. 'It was good to clear the air.'

'Do you want a tea or coffee or something?'

'Umm, I'm not sure that's a good idea.' Bermuda shuffled uncomfortably in the rain, and the lamppost above them shone down like a spotlight. Bermuda looked over his shoulder, almost positive that he could see something in the alleyway.

Something watching them.

'Jesus, I'm not going to try to jump your bones, if that's what you're worried about.' She rolled her eyes.

'I'm sorry. I'd love one.' He smiled again, trying to dispel the nervousness that was brewing.

Something was out there.

She strode through the gate, past the recycling bins that lined her front garden. Bermuda noted the number of empty wine bottles. McAllister had kept up with him throughout the evening, but the bottles were a sure sign that she didn't just like the occasional glass of red with dinner.

The warmth of the house was welcoming, the nicely decorated hallway minimal but stylish. McAllister dumped her keys on a small wooden hallway table that was strewn with unopened letters and a dead plant. She whipped off her hat, releasing a nest of flat, wet hair. Staring into the mirror, she tried to fluff it up, but gave up with a shrug before tossing her coat over the bannister.

'I'll put the kettle on.' Five of the most comforting words a human can say.

Bermuda shook himself out his coat before placing it over hers and ventured through the door to the dark living room. A flick of the switch and the room illuminated, again a simple but fashionable look. A grey corner sofa rested across the far wall, with a large metal clock pinned above it. Opposite sat a modest TV on a stylish unit, surrounded by dead plants. A bookcase rested beside it, the shelves and books all wearing a thick coat of dust.

Bermuda looked over the photos that sat on the shelves – photos of McAllister as a child, presumably with a sibling. The standard picture of her with proud parents, the smart uniform suggesting it was the day she had marched out as a police officer. Next to the photo of her smiling folks, a photo frame lay face down. By the surrounding layer of dust, it had been for a while.

Bermuda flashed a quick glance over his shoulder. The faint clattering of crockery emanated from the kitchen and he quickly lifted the frame.

It was McAllister and a man kissing. On their wedding day.

Bermuda quickly placed it back and felt a tinge of guilt. McAllister hadn't mentioned a husband, and he was almost positive she wasn't wearing a ring. Knowing the full weight of a dysfunctional personal life, he turned towards the sofa just as McAllister entered with a tray.

It had two cups of steaming hot tea and a bottle of vodka, along with two shot glasses.

Bermuda flashed her a look with raised eyebrows.

'The night is still young.' She smirked, placing the tray down on the white rectangular coffee table in front of them. She poured out two shots, knocking hers back instantly and hissing through her teeth as it burnt.

'When in Rome,' Bermuda muttered, whipping the shot back and letting the vodka burn the back of his throat. He coughed slightly before reaching for his tea. 'You have a nice house.'

'It's okay.' McAllister looked around with a look of disdain. Empty bottles lined the side of the sofa, and random items of clothing were dotted about.

Bermuda lowered himself down, gently pushing a work shirt over the arm of the chair. 'You live alone?' He was prying – the photo had piqued his interest.

'Yup.' The answer was stern enough to end that line of questioning. 'What about you?'

'What about me?' Bermuda sipped the tea, hesitant to comment on the overbearing amount of milk.

'You have a partner?' She sipped hers without a problem. 'Besides your imaginary friend.'

'Argyle isn't imaginary.'

'No?' She smirked. 'Everyone has an invisible warrior, we just don't like telling people.'

'Fuck you.' They both giggled. 'No. I have an ex-wife who thinks I'm batshit crazy and a daughter whose heart I keep breaking. But beyond that, I'm pretty much a family man.'

She scoffed, her eyes focused on a random space in the carpet. Bermuda wanted to ask about the photo, but the tension had ramped up slightly. She twiddled a finger through her dark, knotted hair.

'So, What's the next move?' He cut the silence.

'No idea. We will run your print, see what comes up. Beyond that, there are no links between the victims, no witnesses to any of the attacks. The only difference we have seen is that it looked like Rosie tried to fight back – there were signs of a struggle with her. All that got her was a slightly more painful death.'

Bermuda grimaced inwards. The vision of the young woman having her heart wrenched through her spine would haunt him.

McAllister let out a deep sigh. 'Beyond that, nothing. Our officers didn't see the guy you were chasing, but a few witnesses did confirm he was by the station and threw you in front of the tram. None of them, however, made any sort of notion towards him being a ... what do you call your shadow monsters?'

'Others.' Bermuda sighed. 'And they are not shadow monsters. They are creatures that seek refuge from the Otherside.'

'Right.' McAllister didn't even bother hiding the

sarcasm in her tone. 'Before we even touch on how you derailed a whole fucking tram, I need to take a leak.'

Bermuda chuckled. Sometimes a woman could really catch you off guard. McAllister was tough, he knew that. She had clearly been a prodigy in the police due to being a lead detective on a serial killer case at such a young age. Bermuda had guessed she was early thirties, but wouldn't have been surprised if she was younger. The booze clearly didn't help, and the confrontational behaviour married with the drinking told him there was a darkness there.

He knew, because he had lived it.

Her abrupt end to a conversation about having a partner told him that whoever had watched her walk down that aisle whenever that photo had been taken wouldn't be waiting if she did it again. A flush echoed from upstairs, followed by hurried footsteps as McAllister bounded back into the room.

Bermuda stood up, pointing upwards. 'Toilet upstairs?'

'Yeah, to the left.' She added extra emphasis with a hand gesture.

Bermuda nodded appreciatively before leaving as McAllister poured out another shot. He ventured up the cream carpeted stairs, past another few photos as well as vacant picture hooks. A logical guess would be they once proudly displayed the husband.

Empty bottles of wine greeted him on the landing floor. The bathroom door on the left-hand side was slightly open, the white and black lino covered by a fluffy, dirty, white bath mat. Two doors opposite him were closed completely, but the door to the right was slightly ajar. Bermuda glanced at the gap for a split second but was instantly drawn to the paper that scaled the wall.

It was of teddy bears.

Confusion gripped him, and like a tractor beam he was drawn to the door, pushing it open with measured care. It opened silently, the light from the landing gushing in like lowering a dam.

An empty cot stood before him, the blanket neatly tucked down the sides, a row of teddy bears propped against the wooden bars. Their warm, comforting smiles and cuddly bodies were shrouded in darkness. A changing table was pushed to the far end of the room beneath the window; the brightly coloured curtains were drawn tight.

The wardrobe was open, with a number of outfits all neatly ironed and hanging from their hangers like an up market boutique. Except every item of clothing was for a newborn baby.

To the left of the cupboard was a chest of drawers, with more tiny clothes neatly folded, along with unopened packets of nappies and baby wipes – the essentials any new parent would need. As he ventured into the room, a memory crashed against him like a wave: the image of his Chloe, as delicate and tiny as a snowflake, crying in her cot as he came in to comfort her.

Her knight in shining armour.

His fist clenched involuntarily. The rage of being so far from what he treasured most was soul destroying, but this entire room was heartbreaking. He took one last look at the feeding chair in the corner, the cushions as crisp and plump as the day it was bought – a sure sign it had never been used.

This wasn't a nursery.

It was a shrine.

Bermuda turned to exit and came face to face with McAllister, her face twisted in fury while tears poured from her eyes. She wobbled slightly, undoubtedly from countless hits of vodka. He had no idea how long he had been in the room, but she had eventually come looking. And now, as she shook with venomous anger, he had never seen someone look so devastated.

'What the fuck are you doing in here?' Her words bubbled with menace.

'I'm so sorry.'

'I said the door on the fucking left.' Her fists clenched till the knuckles turned white. Her nails punctured her hand, and a trickle of blood oozed through her bony fingers.

'What happened?'

'GET OUT!' she screamed at him and lashed out, her open palm slapping hard against the side of his face.

Bermuda hunched his shoulders up, raising a forearm too as the drunken detective rained a few more desperate slaps in his direction, directing him to the stairs. With a shove, she followed him down while Bermuda quickly whipped the coat from the bannister before he got to the bottom.

'Sam, I am so sorry,' he tried to offer. He received another strike to the arm. Her face gleamed from the tears, the agony resting on her like a horrific Halloween mask.

'Just get out.' Her words were quieter; the will to stay angry was submitting to the sheer pain that was crippling her. She leant against the wall and howled one pain-filled scream before sobbing wildly.

Bermuda watched without a clue – a crying woman was not exactly his forte.

Especially one that was clearly in mourning.

'I'm going to go.' Bermuda's words were weak. He felt pathetic.

McAllister didn't respond, she just cried silently, hunched down on the bottom step. She was drunk, but he had trespassed somewhere sacred.

He had caused her this pain tonight.

Guilt pressed down on his mind like a weight, and he reached for the door. Only as he began to turn the handle did he notice the blue lights flashing from the other side of the glass. As Bermuda pulled the door open, a police officer had his fist raised, ready to knock.

It was DC Greg Butler.

Both men looked shocked, with Butler instantly taking a stance that told Bermuda he was trained.

McAllister stood up, wiping her eyes with the backs of her sleeves. She pushed Bermuda roughly to the side. 'Butler.'

'McAllister.' He shifted his glance to Bermuda, pushing out his broad chest as a sign of strength. 'Everything okay?'

She nodded. All three of them didn't believe her.

'What's going on?' Bermuda asked.

'Police business,' Butler snapped.

'Something tells me you didn't turn up here because you boys are out of doughnuts.'

Before Butler could react, McAllister slid her sleeves into her coat.

'Take me to her.' She stepped out into the rain, followed by Butler as they shuffled quickly to the car. Bermuda closed the door and followed. Another woman had been killed – that much was obvious. As he marched to keep up, he heard the faint words of Butler mention that the husband had been killed too.

Two dead?

Reluctantly Butler let Bermuda hop in the back of the car, and they sped off into the rain with the tension in the vehicle more volatile than the elements around them.

Bermuda shut his eyes as they left the street, wondering what the hell had happened.

One thing he had been right about was the eyes that stared from the dark alleyway as the hooded creature watched with intent before disappearing into the dark.

## TWENTY

HALF of the street had been cordoned off, and a few unfortunate officers stood by the police tape, hands firmly being their backs. Despite the raincoats and the small plastic shower caps over their hats, they were defenceless against the rain.

The journalists had arrived, a crowd of them snapping their cameras and shoving a microphone under anyone's chin, eager for any scraps from the table.

A few feet from them, Emma Mitchell lay slumped on the concrete, half-naked and heartless. The blood that had pooled around her had been washed away by the night. Only a faint tint of red remained, like lipstick on a collar. There was a sizeable dent in the car – the shattered bones of her hip would connect the two together.

SOCOs littered the area, dressed in their white boiler suits. Bermuda was pretty sure they wouldn't get much – the elements would see to that. Cause of death was obvious too. Emma lay hunched over on her front, her body being slightly propped up by the open rib cage that had pierced the skin. Kevin Parker had ripped her heart from her body and she had felt every moment of it. Now she had been dropped on the street like a piece of litter, with a chest looking like the welcoming mouth of a Venus fly trap.

Beyond the hustle and bustle of the busy street, more SOCOs swarmed over what Bermuda assumed was the family home like an army of highly trained ants. Her husband, Mark Mitchell, had apparently returned home early and wished he had caught his wife with another man. What he interrupted instead had cost him his life, his head removed from his body after having his throat ripped out.

Again, by Parker's bare hands.

The very idea sent a chill down Bermuda's spine, as did the raindrop that slyly fell behind the collar of his dark shirt. He wrapped his arms around his chest and shivered, nodding respectfully at a few SOCOs who looked at him in wonderment.

A hulking presence loomed next to him.

'This is a sad night.'

Argyle's words were apt as he glanced up and down the crime scene. His grey eyes flickered over the movement, absorbing every minute detail and committing it to an alcohol abused memory. Bermuda watched him in awe, the dedication to his duty and the pain he felt when he saw what his own kind were capable of.

'It sure is, Big Guy,' Bermuda agreed.

Just outside the front door to the house, McAllister stood, deep in discussion with the head SOCO, Mullen, and DC Butler. It annoyed Bermuda to think that DCI Strachan was probably sat in the back of her warm car while her underlings ran the crime scene in the freezing rain.

That and the fact that Strachan was a first-class bitch.

Bermuda took a puff on his e-cig, coughing as he came to the end of the liquid and tasted nothing but burning. McAllister slowly made her way across the crime scene, carefully dodging past a few forensics specialists as they carefully scanned the pavement for anything of use.

They'd find nothing.

Argyle leaned down to Bermuda, his breath warm but odourless. 'Is she the one you mated with?'

'Argyle.' Bermuda spoke from the side of his mouth as not to draw attention. 'Not now.'

Argyle stood silently and obediently as McAllister approached. Bermuda wished beyond anything she would notice the hulking protector beside him, but it would do no good. He had met eyes with her a few times as they had scanned the crime scene. Wisely, he had stayed away from her. After half hour or so, she had offered him half a smile, a pitiful flick of the mouth to build a bridge.

Now she stood before him, her arms wrapped around her thin frame, struggling for warmth. Or to keep the anger in.

'I think I owe you an apology.' Her words struggled to find their way from her mouth.

'No worries.' Bermuda looked around dismissively. 'We both drank too much, and I stuck my nose where it wasn't wanted or invited.'

'I shouldn't have … I mean I …' McAllister trailed off.

Bermuda sighed. 'Look, we all got shit. I get it. But right now that woman right there is dead.' He pointed at the crumpled, mutilated body of Emma Mitchell as a paramedic slowly placed a white sheet over her. 'Kevin Parker is still out there, and we need to find him. So whatever shit we do have, or whatever problems we have, we need to put it to the side.'

'Agreed.' She nodded purposefully, her words picking up strength.

'Good. Look, run that print and see what you can find. I'm going to head back to my office, see what I can dig up my end.'

She looked at him in surprise at the mention of an office.

'I'll meet up with you again tomorrow?'

'Okay.' She smiled, the first time it seemed genuine.

Just as Bermuda was about to turn and leave, DC Butler strode over, his suit soaked through and stuck to his impressive frame. He was built like a boxer and Bermuda was pretty sure he fought like one too. Training with Argyle aside, Bermuda didn't fancy having his arse kicked.

He was too cold and too tired.

'Everything all right, guv?' Butler spoke to McAllister but stared at Bermuda, who couldn't help but smile.

'Just fine,' she replied. 'Jones was just about to leave.'

'Aye, leave it to the real police, eh?' Butler chortled.

Bermuda stopped and turned back, smiling. 'Yeah. Keep an eye out, they'll be here soon.'

Bermuda turned and walked off, triumphant, while McAllister smirked. Butler's face went even redder, the anger joining the cold to flush his cheeks. The rain clattered both of them as they watched Bermuda walk away.

The other eyes that peered from the shadow belonging to two hooded creatures watched Bermuda and Argyle.

As they passed a group of reporters that Bermuda ignored, Argyle looked back to the crime scene, noticing Butler still staring angrily in their direction before being summoned away by McAllister. He turned back to his partner, confused.

'That DC does not like you, does he?'

'Not a lot of people do.' Bermuda shrugged, popping two wet Tic Tacs into his mouth as he yawned, his body craving the apparent comfort of a Premier Inn bed.

'He doesn't wear a uniform like the other officers.'

'That's because he isn't a police officer.'

Argyle looked back one final time. 'Then what is he?'

Bermuda smirked. 'A cunt.'

KEVIN PARKER HAD STOOD at a distance, the shadows cast down from the houses either side enveloping him and kept him hidden. The usual pathway through the tombstones was blocked. The entire Necropolis was swarming with humans, all of them in their thick vests, flashing their torches as they swept the area in pairs.

They were there for him.

He could feel his grip on the heart tightening, pressuring the muscle to bursting point.

He had to get through them. He could see the vehicles that had been carefully driven up the slanted graveyard to the tomb, the pinnacle of his journey. He needed to deliver this tonight. This would be the one.

They would return her.

He felt a twinge of pain course through his body, a horrible reminder of her face as they led her from him, trying desperately to look back over his shoulder as they chained him to the wall.

To the darkness.

His skin was crawling; the feeling it didn't quite fit him was too familiar. This was his body.

He was Kevin Parker.

He looked around the quiet street, noticing a lot of passers-by staring up through the large iron gates that surrounded the land. The flashing blue lights were rhythmic, almost soothing.

On and off.

Blue then dark.

Ahead, he could hear a thudding noise repeating itself, a helicopter that hovered above them.

All of this for him.

They were trying to stop him.

Like that agent. The man who had been waiting in the

tomb for him, the one who claimed not to be the voice in the dark. He was a man who wanted to stop him. Keep him from her yet again.

Jones.

Again, he felt the muscles in his arm tighten, the sensation travelling like an electric current to his fingers.

He felt hatred for that man.

Agent Jones.

The creature that had been guarding the door, he was not human. The broad shoulders, the shining armour. The giant blade that swung from his back like a pendulum in a grandfather clock. When he had smashed the rock over its skull, it had crumpled. Possibly died.

Caleb squeezed the heart again.

No, not Caleb. Kevin.

Kevin Parker.

A light burst down from the helicopter, illuminating random tombstones, basking them in an undeserved spotlight.

This was meant to be a quiet place.

A place where he gave them what they wanted, and they returned her to him.

These men were here now because of Agent Jones, who interfered. Who was trying to stop him from collecting the hearts that he needed to find her once more?

Slowly he edged his way from the darkness, ducking behind a few parked cars that were littered with raindrops. His hand was red, the dried blood of Emma Mitchell crusted to his arm like a cheap tattoo.

He tried his best to feel remorse for the death of both her and her husband.

He felt none.

With a watchful eye, he waited until the gate was completely clear and laid the heart at the threshold, hoping that it would still be enough. That they would still collect.

In an instant, he was back in the shadows, hoping beyond hope that this would be the one. That she would be returned. Then, with a crooked snarl across his handsome face, he made a silent promise regarding Agent Jones.

That he would kill him.

---

DESPITE THE BITTERNESS OF WINTER, the sun decided to make its unwelcome return three hours into Bermuda's slumber. The beams cut through the curtains he had roughly drawn when he had stumbled in and slashed across his face. His head pounded slightly from the alcohol, the heaviness of the evening keeping him firmly against the pillow as he blinked himself awake.

What had been a nice evening with his friend had turned into a decent drink with a colleague. Eventually, it had descended into emotional breakdowns with a side of violent outbursts.

Oh, and a double murder.

Without looking, he slapped his hands slapped across the bedside table, clattering his phone and watch to the floor before he clasped the plastic bottle. The water was room temperature and populated with bubbles, but he drained it like a vampire.

Slowly, he pushed himself to a seated position, his heavily inked body hunched over as he stared at the floor. It had been three days that he had been in Glasgow, but it felt like a lifetime. As he puffed his e-cig, which had been topped up with a fresh apricot flavour, he recounted the trials of his trip so far.

One count of breaking and entering, along with scarring a police officer for life. One horrifying sexual experience with the lead detective of the case. Several dead bodies, a confrontation with the killer (who also tried to kill him), and also the destruction of an entire public transport method.

'Not bad,' he muttered to himself as he hauled himself to his feet, stretching his back as he walked across the room. The pain from colliding with the wall and the concrete had subsided. So had the ache in his jaw. He showered quickly, the soap sliding across the scars that he wore on his chest, a painful reminder of the dangers he faced.

Of the Otherside.

It was easy to forget sometimes just how thin the ice was that the truce sat upon. While Neithers such as Argyle, Denham, and Vincent were allies – even friends in some cases – it was easy to overlook the world they came from. The giant beast that had chased him through London wasn't interested in being friends. Nor was the behemoth that had sent Bermuda crashing through a poop deck.

Barnaby had tried to end the world.

Kevin Parker was murdering women.

The Otherside was dangerous, and what terrified Bermuda the most was he could feel it coursing through his veins like a drug. When he ran his fingers across the nail scratches on the Necropolis walls, he could feel it calling to him, trying to lure him back across the doorway.

He marched out of the room once he was dressed. The traffic was roaring and echoing off the overarching buildings that lined the streets on either side. As impatient Glaswegians honked and hurled obscenities, Bermuda tucked his headphones under his hat and clicked play on his phone; the guitar riff for 'Back in Black' by AC/DC accompanied his footsteps.

The sunshine was still painting itself across Glasgow, but the temperature was just above zero. His breath puffed out of his mouth like a cheap imitation of his electric cigarette. He strode past the homeless man who patrolled the street outside his hotel, the music drowning out the muffled yells and pointing.

The man was trying to say something, but Bermuda didn't have time this morning. He followed the cheap Christmas decorations that snaked around the lampposts, the trail of muted festive cheer leading all the way into the centre of town where he, for the third day running, stood in awe as the door revealed itself in the cardboard. A dark corridor and steep concrete steps later, and he was in the small, overly stuffed office of the BTCO. He could hear the clicking of Kelly's nails on the keyboard, but couldn't see which cubicle she was at.

'Hello?' he called out, sliding his hat from his head and pushing his hair off his skull.

She shot up from behind a stack of papers, her eyes magnified by her thick glasses.

'Bermuda!' she exclaimed, scurrying out from the cubicle, a horrendous homemade Christmas jumper wrapped around her plump frame. 'Welcome back. You have a message.'

'Is it from Argyle?' he asked, suddenly concerned for his friend's whereabouts.

'Oh no. Argyle is fine. He is resting in his quarters.'

Bermuda chortled to himself at the idea of Argyle laid back on a bed, arms behind his head and listening to the soothing sounds of Enya.

'No, you have a message from the London office.' Kelly returned to her desk. 'You can use the communications device in the conference room.'

Before Bermuda could ask for directions she was gone again, her fingers clattering against the keys once more. He rolled his eyes and slowly wandered through the office until he found a modern-looking room with a screen attached to the wall. Making a logical guess, he entered, shutting the door behind him.

An oval oak table sat in the centre of the room, with six high-backed leather chairs around it. They looked unused, which Bermuda wasn't entirely shocked by, considering he was more likely to see a tumbleweed than another agent.

Beside the screen was a small panel, a few buttons, and a flashing red light next to it. Beneath was a card reader, which Bermuda slipped his agent badge into. The scanner beeped his ID like a self-service check out.

The screen burst to life and began dialling. On the third ring, Vincent appeared on the screen, turning in bewilderment like Nosferatu. His pale skin looked almost transparent, like it was stretched across his sharp, featureless face.

'Jones.' His greeting wasn't the most exciting.

'Hey, Vinnie. You rang?'

'No, that would be Montgomery Black. He is currently indisposed, but he wanted to discuss the incident with you. According to him, you haven't been careful.'

'He said that?' Bermuda asked, a trail of apricot smoke filtering from his lips.

'His wording was slightly more … colourful.'

Bermuda smiled.

'I needed to speak to you to tell you some bad news.'

'Don't you dare tell me I am being reassigned up here full time, Vinnie.' Bermuda scowled. 'I swear, I will kill you all.'

'No.' Again, very matter of fact. Suddenly, a sadness fell across Vincent's face, which caught Bermuda off guard. 'It is Mr Ottoway.'

Bermuda, sat on the table cross-legged, looked up, concern hauling his eyebrows upward. 'What about him?'

'Jones, it is with great sadness that I inform you that Mr Ottoway has been battling cancer for a few years. He didn't want it to be public knowledge due to the moral of the organisation.' Vincent paused. 'He has been taken into hospital.'

'Fuck.' Bermuda gasped.

'We need you to continue the case. The Oracles have relayed worrying information that this Other may be more dangerous than we thought.'

'Yeah, no shit,' Bermuda responded, his mind flicking back to the moment Parker had introduced him to a stone wall.

'I know how much Ottoway means to you, Jones.'

Bermuda smiled to hide his anger, nodding gently as he pushed himself off the table. 'I need some help.'

'Anything.' Vincent's words were earnest and true.

'I uploaded a print through the technician here in the Glasgow office – which, by the way, is horrible.'

'Ah, Malcolm is one of our top technicians.'

'How does everyone know Malcolm?' Bermuda shrugged. 'Anyway, run the print past the Oracles. Also, have them look for Kevin Parker. It's a pretty common name, but go back like eighty years. Whoever this Other thinks he is, he isn't from our time.'

Vincent nodded firmly. 'Consider it done.'

'Also, I get this feeling that something is wrong. Argyle seems nervous. He wasn't able to detect Kevin Parker, which is odd considering he is an Other. But there's more.'

'More?'

'Yeah, I keep feeling I'm being watched. I don't know.'

'Hmmm.' Vincent took a moment. 'There has been an increased level of Other detection within your area. More so than what yourself and Argyle would bring.'

Bermuda shuddered at the reminder of his condition. Vincent realised but didn't apologise.

'I shall have the Oracles focus in and try to decipher why. Anything else?'

'Yeah, pass on my best to Ottoway. Tell him I'll be back soon.'

'Just focus on the case, Jones. Remember, two worlds—'

'One peace,' Bermuda interrupted. 'Yeah, I get it.'

'You seem to have recovered well,' Vincent offered.

Bermuda shrugged, the memory of falling from the Hammersmith flyover was still fresh in his mind. 'Well, I have a slight advantage don't I?'

Suddenly, the door behind Vincent burst open and in stormed the irate figure of Montgomery Black. His glasses sat at the end of his hooked nose like an angry headmaster's, his thinning white hair giving up the comb-over and flapping like a flag in the wind.

'There you are!' Black pointed a furious finger at the screen. 'Do you have any idea just how much damage your little stunt on the high street has caused?'

Bermuda began to make a crackling noise. 'Oh no … crrrrkkk … you're breaking up.'

'Jones! Are you even listening to me?' Black's face was turning red, a vein becoming worryingly visible.

'I'm losing … crrrrkkk … you.' Bermuda hopped off the table and approached the screen. 'I'm going through a … crrrrkkk … tunnel.'

'Jones!' A fist thumped a desk in London. 'This is a video call. I can see you.'

'Sorry … crrrrkkk … horrible signal.'

With that, Bermuda ended the call. He let out a deep sigh, knowing that poking a bees' nest was usually a good way to get stung. Running up and booting it full pelt probably wouldn't end any better.

Nervously, he reached for his Tic Tacs, popping two into his mouth and making a hasty exit. Kelly offered a goodbye, but Bermuda had already stormed through the large iron door that separated the crazed woman from the real world. He stomped through the dark, taking each step in his stride.

He thought about Ottoway, the man who had shown unwavering belief in him. He was dying and Bermuda knew there was a good chance he wasn't going to see him before he made it back.

The man had been the father figure Bermuda had never had, his own dad disappearing when he was younger and never coming back. From the stories of drink and drugs, Bermuda saw it as good riddance. But Ottoway would leave another hole in his life.

Another glaring hole that he would never be able to fill.

As the door revealed itself and presented the cold streets of Glasgow, Bermuda stepped out, feeling more alone than ever.

# TWENTY-ONE

MCALLISTER SPUN ON HER CHAIR, immediately regretting it as the room whizzed by. She felt the effects of the hard drinking rumbling up her from her stomach and caught herself before she vomited over her desk.

DC Butler had left a coffee on the side of her desk and she devoured it gratefully, the caffeine burning on its way down. It would bring her back from her hangover. She popped a few paracetamols into her mouth and dry-swallowed them, frantically searching her drawers for a bottle of water.

'Everything okay, guv?' Butler asked, taking his seat in the adjacent cubicle.

They had been partnered for a few years now; he was aware of her heartache. A few years older than McAllister, Butler was as open about his failed boxing career as he was about his homosexuality.

No one gave him any stick for it though. Not because the Glasgow Police Service was a beacon of equal opportunities, but more for the very real possibility that Butler would systematically smash your face in.

Without even waiting for McAllister to answer, he

tossed his bottle of Evian across the office. She caught it and knocked it back.

'Rough night?' His question was clearly rhetorical.

'Yup. Two dead.'

'That wasn't what I was asking.' The silence hung between them for a few intense moments. Butler shuffled forward slightly on his wheeled chair, his voice just above a whisper. 'You can't keep doing this to yourself, Sam.'

'Doing what?' Her green eyes lit up with fury.

'Drinking yourself to death.' Butler opened his hands and shrugged. 'And maybe don't keep fucking every random guy you meet.'

'Pot. Kettle. Black.'

He glared at her. She knew that was out of line. Butler had been in a committed relationship with Kieran for over ten years. That had come to an abrupt end when Butler had had an affair with a young officer who no longer worked in Glasgow.

Temptation had taken everything from him.

She wasn't giving in to temptation. She was just surrendering to self-destruction.

They both turned back to their desks, neither one even moving. After a few, guilt-ridden moments, McAllister turned again.

'Greg, I'm sorry. That was uncalled for.'

'Aye. I'm tougher than most. I'm just more concerned about your liver and the fact that you're spending more time shagging that arrogant prick than communicating with Ethan.'

'Ethan and I are through.' The words came out broken.

'Well, you will be if you keep straying.' Butler shook his head. 'I should know.'

'I'm not screwing Jones.' She sighed.

'Then why the hell was he at your house last night

when we turned up?' Butler turned and face her, his eyebrows raised as if he had just solved a riddle.

McAllister felt her hangover tap dance across her brain. 'We were clearing the air. Look, we have a serial killer on the loose and not one lead. Despite how much of a prick he can be, Jones is here to help, and he at least has some theories on what is happening.'

Butler sternly crossed his arms. If McAllister had to guess, she would have said he was jealous that she was listening to Bermuda over him.

'Like what?'

'He thinks that this could be linked to a creature from a separate world to ours – one that his organisation monitors. That is why he is here.'

Silence for a few seconds. Then Butler burst out into a deep, hearty laugh. McAllister sat unimpressed as her partner hunched forward, hands clasped to his muscular stomach as he roared at the implausible theory. A few colleagues looked over the office partitions that separated the desks, and after a few moments Butler began to reclaim his breath.

'Ah, thanks for that, Sam. I needed that.' He turned back to his desk, still chuckling at the idea put forward by his partner.

McAllister tutted, pushing herself out of her chair and through the doorway next to their desks. The incident room was empty, the few chairs and desks unfilled as the team were out trying to solve the case. A huge whiteboard sat on the nearside, covered in photos of the victims. She could see the smiling face of Nicola Miller, the beautiful blue eyes of Rosie Seeley. These were mixed in with photos of the open chest cavity of Katie Steingold as well as the brutal slaying of Emma Mitchell and her husband Mark.

A wall of death, staring back at her and mocking her inability to stop it.

It was inhumane.

As her eyes fixated on the sheer brutality that ended these women's lives, she wondered if Bermuda Jones's theory was that insane after all.

---

BERMUDA TOOK advantage of the random sunshine to enjoy his coffee on a bench, the heart of Glasgow passing by. As he sat in the city centre, he watched as a construction crew got to work on the decimated tram tracks; the project to undo his and Argyle's handiwork was well underway. A few Others slithered by, their movements ghostly as they filtered around the side of a building before disappearing into the alleyways.

Bermuda kept checking the surrounding streets that wrapped around the shops, his paranoia telling him he was being watched.

He had been sure he had seen a hooded figure.

As he sunk the last of the caffeine into his body he pushed himself up, walking back past the station where he had confronted Kevin Parker and nearly lost his life. The whole memory flooded back, and he felt a shiver race through his body. If Argyle hadn't been there yet again, Bermuda would have been killed.

It was getting to a point where a simple thank you just wasn't enough, yet Bermuda didn't peg Argyle as the hamper basket type.

Making his way back through the city centre, he saw a Santas of different heights, girths, and skin colour which was sure to confuse those children who still believed. A smile spread across his face as he mocked the notion of jolly old St Nick when he spent his life hunting monsters with a warrior from another world.

Maybe he should leave out some carrots and milk.

As his mind raced with possible theories of Kevin Parker's motives, Bermuda's autopilot brought him back onto the street of the Premier Inn. Without realising, he was approaching the concrete steps that led to the automatic doors. Sat beside them was the same homeless man as always, his possessions bursting out of a few plastic bags that sat scruffily beside him.

Despite the sunshine, the wind carried a chill that nipped like a teething puppy. Bermuda stopped in front of the homeless man, who was mumbling under his breath as he played with the frayed threading of his tatty blazer.

'Hello, mate.' Bermuda spoke, aware of how cockney he sounded. 'Can I get you a coffee?'

The man looked up. His wiry hair looked like he had been recently electrocuted. His beard was wispy and greasy and clung to a thin, gaunt face.

'Where's the other one?' He looked back at his blanket.

'Other one?' Bermuda questioned, before reasoning that the man spent most of his time inebriated. Having spent many evenings drowning his sorrows at the Royal Oak under the watchful eye of Paul back in Bushey, Bermuda was more than familiar with double vision.

Now, as the day slipped seamlessly from morning to afternoon, Bermuda politely smiled and turned, ready to leave the man to his sobriety. As he took two steps away, the man spoke again.

'The one with the sword.'

Bermuda froze. Slowly, he turned back, meeting the keen eyes of the homeless man. 'Excuse me?' he spluttered.

'The one with the sword.' The man gestured. 'And the armour. He stands there, by the stairs, and keeps a vigil.'

'Argyle?' Bermuda asked, completely flabbergasted.

'If that's his name. Is he not here?'

'You can see him?' Bermuda ignored the original question. He knew people had 'the Knack', but never in his near four years as an agent had he met someone that he didn't know about.

'Aye.' The man slowly scrambled to his feet. 'My name is Gordon Foster. And yes, I do see monsters.'

He offered a grubby hand which Bermuda, still speechless, shook instantly. The sun shone down, casting both their shadows high against the wall behind them. Bermuda slowly began to come round and stumbled over a few words. Gordon smiled a row of faintly yellow teeth.

'I think we should have that coffee now.'

---

THE WAITER at Costa looked at Gordon with unease as he approached the table. The idea of a homeless man sat in their store obviously wasn't what their 'all welcome' sign on the front window was intended for. Bermuda glared at the waiter as he plonked two large coffees down as well as a toasted panini.

Gordon didn't bat an eye as he began shovelling the hot bread into his mouth, long strands of cheese latching to his beard like spider's web. Tatty plastic bags sat on the other chair at the table which was surrounded by empty tables as the public backed away from them.

'Thanks, lad.' Gordon spoke, breadcrumbs crashing to the table. 'This is bloody delicious.'

'My pleasure.'

They sat in silence as Gordon demolished the hot snack, even taking the time to pick the crumbs off the tray and pop them into his mouth, like the final sock into a full washing machine. Once it had been swallowed, he reached his freshly washed hands around the mug and drew the coffee in.

'Smells good.' He smiled. 'Not like that shite from Starbucks.'

Bermuda chuckled, as he was sure all the high street coffee shops tasted exactly the same. 'Tell me about yourself, Gordon.'

Gordon took a few more sips of his coffee and then placed it down carefully. He sat back, the buttons on his tatty shirt opening slightly, showing thick spools of chest hair.

'I wasn't always a gross mess.' He smiled with self-deprecation. 'Aye, I had a family once. A wife, beautiful lady named Linda. We were married for, oh it must have been twenty years. University sweethearts. You know how it goes.'

Bermuda nodded but refused to interrupt. He gently sipped his coffee as the eccentric man continued.

'We tried but couldn't have kids, so we focused on our work. She was a scientist and worked for University here in town. I worked for the *Herald*.'

'The paper?' Bermuda interjected, the logo of the paper appearing in his mind's eye.

'The very same. Usual puff pieces for a few years, but then I started getting meatier stories. Some real investigative journalism. That was when I really had to confront my problem.'

'Your *Knack*?'

'My what?' Gordon sipped his coffee with confusion spread across his face thicker than his messy beard.

'Sorry, the *Knack*. The ability to see the Otherside.'

Gordon's eyes were blank.

'Creatures and beasts, usually confined to the shadows. Creatures like Argyle.'

'Aye, you boys call it 'the Knack'?'

'I work for an organisation that monitors that world and their impact here. We get advances in medicines and science, et cetera, and they get to escape their world. It's a shaky truce, but it exists for now.'

'For now? You don't like it?'

'I think it's very dangerous. Six months ago, an Other nearly brought this world to its knees. I watched him kill a colleague of mine like he was swatting a fly. Eventually we managed to stop him, but he was pure evil – an evil that I don't think is worth keeping the door open for.'

Gordon polished off his coffee and looked at Bermuda with pleading eyes. Bermuda smiled and motioned to the young waiter for another. Despite the man scrunching up his face, the bistro machine roared into life.

'Like this bastard killing those women.'

'You know about that?' Bermuda sat forward on his chair, needlessly lowering his voice.

'I am homeless, Bermuda. Not crazy.' Gordon suddenly shuffled in agitation. 'Linda told me I was crazy. Told me that science dictated that there were no monsters in the dark. That the creature that lived in our back garden couldn't exist due to its nutritional needs not being met. No matter what I told her, or my boss, they just labelled me crazy. One by one, they turned their backs on me.'

Bermuda felt sympathy rattle through him like a lightning bolt. He could relate to this man. One wrong turn and he could have been looking in a mirror.

'But I'm not crazy. I know I'm not and you have confirmed it.'

The waiter, with a slightly friendlier demeanour, placed another coffee down in front of Gordon, and a few extra dipping biscuits. He collected the tray and left. Neither of them even registered it.

'So, what do you know about the killings?' Bermuda spoke in hushed tones.

'He's been here before. About thirty years ago. I didn't cover it then, I was still relatively new, but I had access to the stories. It was fascinating. Every one of them had their heart removed.'

'Yeah, sounds like our guy.'

'But it isn't a guy. It's one of those … what do you call them?'

'Others,' Bermuda stated with a tinge of hatred.

'That's it.' Gordon turned and started rummaging through one of his bags. 'Look at this.'

He removed a large folder, a thin, worn string holding it together as papers hung out of the side like an overstuffed sandwich. It slapped down on the table, shaking both cups of coffee, before Gordon rummaged through its contents.

'I did some digging. Despite them telling me that I was crazy and it couldn't be possible, I tried to find further proof – further evidence that it wasn't human.'

Gordon was frenzied, flicking page after page of scrambled notes over, so indecipherable they reminded Bermuda of the books back in the archives. Eventually he stopped and slapped a newspaper article in front of Bermuda.

It was dated July 12, 1926. The grainy paper had withered – a gentle rub and it would smudge like a moth. The ink on most of the article itself had run, pooling together like that blood from Emma Mitchell's chest. The photo and the headline were still, all things considered, in decent condition.

The article was from the *New York Post*.

The headline announced the opening of a new nightclub, one of many to hit the famous city during the well-documented 'boom' period, where flapper girls and mob bosses ran roughshod over the country and every bank was setting the economy up for the biggest crash since Nicholas Cage's career.

The photo was grainy but sure enough, a host of scantily clad women stood in a row, ready for the can-can theme to kick in. The apparent owner, fat and well-groomed, stood with a beaming smile as he shook hands.

With Kevin Parker.

Bermuda sat upright, like he had just sat on a pin. Parker's face, this time twisted into a happy grin, was clear as day. The suit looked the same, just without the extra trimming of blood. On his arm was a beautiful woman, her dark skin only highlighting her beauty. She clung lovingly to his side as his arm protectively ran around her waist, clutching her floral dress.

Was that the one? The one he must find?

The spoons on the table began gently rattling the saucers, and it was only then that he realised he was shaking.

'That's him,' he finally managed to gasp.

'Yup.' Gordon nodded firmly. 'That right there is the man you are after.'

'I have to go.' Bermuda fished into his pockets and pulled out his wallet. He removed the final few notes, a measly twenty-five pounds, but he slapped it down on the table.

'I don't need your money, Franklyn. Your time has been enough.'

Bermuda refused to collect it. He gently folded the picture and slipped it into the inside of his pocket. He then leant forward, his palms against the table. 'Gordon, don't go too far, okay? When all this is done, I will come back for you.'

'Aye. I am hardly likely to go jet-setting, am I?' he motioned to his body and mishmash of loose possessions.

Bermuda smiled. 'I will come back for you. I promise.'

Bermuda pushed himself back up and made for the door. McAllister already had images of Parker from CCTV. But now, with this piece of evidence, she might finally believe him that Parker wasn't what they thought. That the man killing those women wasn't a man after all.

He was something else.

Bermuda gripped the handle of the door and pulled it open when Gordon called after him.

'Just catch this bastard.'

Bermuda stepped out through the door and into the rapidly fading sun, determined to do just that.

## TWENTY-TWO

MCALLISTER SAT at the desk opposite the incident board, her head planted firmly against the wooden table and the will to live dripping away like a leaky tap. The photos of smiling women were pinned symmetrically across the wall like trophies. Below them, photos of their nightmarish ends.

The desk before her was a makeshift pillow of paperwork and hard wood and she squeezed her eyelids harder together, willing herself to come up with the answer.

Strachan had already read her the riot act; her disdain for Agent Jones was apparent, and the fact he was still actively investigating the case was clearly pissing her off. McAllister had reported in to Strachan for over two years now and knew full well the wrath of her superior. If Jones was to solve the case before them, she was pretty sure Strachan would have a heart attack.

What she gathered from the monumental roasting from her boss was that she needed to start coming up with viable leads quickly as staking out the Necropolis and waiting for another woman to die were not good enough. The press had smelt a story and Detective Chief Inspector Alex

Fowler wasn't one for shying from the cameras. Strachan had her orders, and with gravity usually the deciding factor in which way the shit travelled, her anger was taken out on McAllister.

She sighed deeply, slowly rising up from the desk. A sheet of randomly scrawled notes and messy doodles flopped from her forehead, the sweat sticking to the paper. McAllister peeled it off and dropped it onto the rest of the paperwork, none of it making any sense or pointing in any direction.

The entire case was like a constantly spinning compass.

DC Butler had gone to follow up a potential eye witness to the murder of Emma Mitchell. A fifteen-year-old girl had watched in horror from behind the curtains of her bedroom as this killing machine had brutally removed the woman's heart in front of her.

Two other neighbours, whose craving for the spotlight far outweighed their bravery, also spoke about the murder to the local news team.

Both had said the killer had removed her heart with his bare hand.

Both had been scared shitless by McAllister when they were sat across from her in the interview room.

Slumping back in the chair, her body ached for a glass of wine. McAllister knew it was becoming a problem but refused to acknowledge it. There were more important things to worry about right now than her ever-increasing reliance on several bottles of wine. Or her need to confront anyone who possibly rubbed her up the wrong way. Or to seduce and screw random men at a second's notice.

She snapped back to the room, locking her long list of character defects away along with the reasons for them.

Focus on the now.

Focus on finding this bastard.

After what felt like a few more hours of staring blindly

at the wall and seeing nothing, she looked around the office. A sea of blank screens and empty chairs. The team had slowly filtered out and home to their lives, all of them with something or someone to care about.

There was nothing waiting for her except several glasses of wine and another evening under the overarching wing of failure. Rubbing her temples, she sighed again, pushing herself up from the uncomfortable chair and slipping her arms into her blazer.

She was doing no good to anyone sitting here.

With a heavy heart, she walked out of the incident room, clicking off the light and accepting the failure of the day.

Another day where they had failed to catch Kevin Parker.

Another night of murder awaited them.

It was just after eight o'clock. That would mean there was roughly three to four hours before another innocent woman was ripped from this world, and all McAllister could offer was an apology and a toast from her wine glass.

It was days like to today when she questioned whether she was the detective her superiors thought she was. Maybe she had been once – before everything that happened. When she had had Ethan in her corner and an entire future riding on her. But now, her job was just a place that surrounded her with horrors while she waited to drink them all away again.

She had no hope of catching Kevin Parker. She was just too scared to admit it.

Resigning herself to failure and taking on the responsibility of the deaths still to come, she strode through the doors to the police station and stopped at the top of the concrete steps. A couple of officers walked out from behind her, sending her an unreciprocated greeting as they marched towards their beat and another freezing night watching over the city of Glasgow.

She slowly descended the steps, unsure of how to greet the handsome smile that welcomed her at the bottom of the stairs. McAllister shrugged it off, pulling on her armour and taking purposeful steps towards Bermuda Jones.

'Very brave of you. Coming here.'

'I have something you need to see.'

His response had her intrigued, and she followed him as he turned and walked off, heading towards the one place they both knew as sanctuary.

---

MCALLISTER SETTLED into the booth at the back of the bar. The red leather seat that lined the wall had seen better days. The table, old and scratched, wobbled gently, a number of folded coasters stuffed beneath it. Two chairs, both on their last legs, sat opposite her. She watched as Bermuda walked over, his fingers clutching a pint of Doom Bar and a glass of wine along with a manila envelope.

There was something about him that was different.

A spring in his step.

He set the glasses down and removed his jacket, draping it over the back of one of the chairs before lowering himself into the other. She noticed the flashes of ink that lined the bottom of his neck and the cuffs of his sleeves. She had a blurry flashback to their night of misguided passion, remembering the tattoos that covered his body.

And were there scars too?

'Cheers.' Bermuda broke her concentration, gently tapping her glass.

'Aye.' She took a deep sip, the frustration of the day

disappearing as quickly as the wine. 'What's got you all excited then?'

Bermuda tapped the envelope.

Curiously, she gently eased it open and slid out the tatty paper clipping. She scanned the article, some nonsense about a new bar opening in New York, when suddenly her eyes bulged.

It was him. The same man from the CCTV.

Kevin Parker.

McAllister's eyes flashed to Bermuda, who raised his eyebrows and nodded. He calmly sipped his pint as she stared in amazement. A fruit machine somewhere behind them sprang to life, followed by a few cheers as money fell from it. A lucky punter scraped it out, promising his supporters a free drink as McAllister slowly lowered the photo, her hand shaking slightly.

A few more moments of disbelief passed in silence.

'How?' she finally managed.

'Remember how I told you that there is more going on than what you can see. And how I told you that I work for an agency that monitors and maintains a truce between our world and another.'

She nodded slowly.

'I wasn't lying.'

'But ... but ...' McAllister stared at the paper.

'Yeah, I know. It's like that moment all over again when you find out Santa isn't real. Everything I told you was true.'

'But it can't be.' McAllister spoke, more to herself.

'This isn't the only world,' Bermuda offered. 'And it certainly isn't the most dangerous one. There are creatures and things I have seen from the Otherside that would haunt your dreams.'

'The Otherside?'

'That's what we call it. It has some official name, but I

leave that to the higher-ups. The creatures that come from it, they are all clumped together and known as Others – except Neithers.' He had lost her, causing him to sigh. 'Basically, this guy right here, he looks and acts human. But he isn't. Not by a long shot.'

McAllister necked the rest of her wine and rocked back on her seat, the beaten leather providing little comfort for her back. She ran her fingers through her matted hair and stared in disbelief. Her eyes watered; the realisation that her reality had been shattered by a single photo was beginning to overwhelm her. She placed a hand on the table to steady herself, trying her best to breathe heavily. Bermuda's fingers slid over her hand and she grasped it tight.

'It's okay.' His words were calm.

She breathed deeply and wiped away the tears with her other hand before shaking her head and returning to him. His handsome face greeted her with a warm smile and he stood, striding across the empty pub to the bar and getting them another drink. She gratefully clutched it upon his return, the glass shaking as she battled the fear and excitement of having her mind blown. A few more moments passed in silence when she finally looked up at him.

'Please explain.'

'What do you want to know?' Bermuda took a big swig from his glass, wiping the foam moustache that optimistically clung to his lip.

'Everything.'

Bermuda nodded and started from the very beginning, telling her how for his whole life he had seen monsters. How he had told his alcoholic mother, who had just dismissed him and blamed it on his deadbeat drug addict father that he had never met. How he had tried to hide from them, that he had seen monsters sitting on the end of his bed, their eyes shiny and grey.

The years spent as an outcast until he met Angela,

their whirlwind love and marriage, the birth of his beautiful daughter – which he noticed caused her to fidget on her seat. How his wife had slowly turned on him, worrying that his behaviour and beliefs were putting their daughter in danger, and the soul-crushing sound of a padded cell being shut with him on the wrong of it.

The months spent in a cell protesting his sanity that he could see the truth that encompassed this world and that everyone else was blind. The realisation that all he was doing was pushing his family away and vindicating their diagnosis.

The divorce.

Before he could continue, Bermuda felt a tear trickle down his cheek. The painful trip down this heartbreaking road had caused him to finish his drink.

McAllister slid out from the booth and returned moments later with a fresh drink for them both. She settled back in, her face and eyes filled with wonderment, as if listening to a ghost story around a campfire.

Bermuda wet his whistle and continued, telling her about the doorway which had opened in his cell and beckoned him through, the dark, ashen world that had flickered to him like a grainy TV with a dodgy aerial. The eyes that had latched onto him, the moment he had realised he was going to die. Everything had still been fuzzy, but he had felt himself being carried back to the light, and he had crossed the divide once more and was in a small town in Morocco.

The BTCO had come then, instantly locating him, expunging his medical records and putting him to work tracking down people and dealing with crimes that our world could never comprehend. As he spoke about his job, McAllister cut in.

'What's an Argyle?'

'Argyle is my partner.' Bermuda smirked. 'He has been at every crime scene with me.'

'Wait. Has he? I can't see him, can I?' Her words came out slowly, as she remembered the rules to the world.

'No, because you don't have the Knack. Also, you would have remembered him. The guy isn't exactly the most inconspicuous.'

'Well none of us can see him. So he ain't too bad!'

They clinked their glasses together.

'Touché.' Bermuda took a sip. 'I owe Argyle my life so many times over it's become almost redundant. If he hadn't have been there the other night that tram would have killed me. If he hadn't have helped me stop Barnaby, I would have died in Big Ben.'

'He's like your guardian angel.' McAllister smirked, sipping her wine.

'No, he's my best friend.'

Silence sat between them for a short while as McAllister dealt with the discovery of another world. She scolded herself a few times, convinced that Bermuda must be a charlatan of some sort, a con man with an ulterior motive. But she found herself leaning towards him.

She wasn't sure if she fully believed him.

She did know that she wanted to.

It had been a long time since she had felt she could trust someone. Her heart was yearning for Ethan but she immediately shut it away, refocusing on the chilling truth of another world and the case in front of them.

'So Kevin Parker is an Other.' McAllister returned to the picture. 'Why is he doing this?'

'I haven't the foggiest. He asked me if I was the voice in the dark.' Bermuda frowned, remembering the painful night. 'He wanted to know where "she" was.'

'Who is she?' McAllister's tone was all detective.

'Beats me. All I know if that whatever Parker is, he isn't going to stop until we find him.'

They sat in silence, the gravity of their task pulling

them downwards. Bermuda felt tired, the pain of the last week or so hanging from his neck like a weight. McAllister quietly sipped her drink and placed the empty glass back down, her entire body screaming for another.

Bermuda cast a curious eye in her direction, watching as her finger gently caressed the stem of the glass.

Addiction had never been so blatant.

'You know, Bermuda isn't my real name.'

She turned and faced him as he spoke.

'It's actually Franklyn.'

'Oh.' McAllister's eyes fell back to the empty wine glass.

'I was nicknamed Bermuda after a few of my first cases. I found missing people.' He looked at her, seeing if she got the reference.

'Well we are not dealing with missing people. These women have been murdered.'

McAllister's words were curt and Bermuda leant back in his chair, his toned arms folded tightly across his chest.

'I wasn't talking about them.' He braced himself. 'I'm talking about you.'

Suddenly McAllister's head snapped up, and the fury he had seen during their drunken tryst and the anger that had exploded within her the night before gleamed from her eyes.

Bermuda refused to break her stare. 'You are lost, Sam.'

'Fuck you.'

'Look, you keep telling me I'm not a detective. But I don't have to be one to see the signs. The bottles of wine. The anger. The nursery. The downturned pictures of your husband that litter your house.'

Her head dropped.

'Whatever it is, it's pulling you deeper and deeper underground.'

She lifted her head, her eyes glistening with fresh tears that began to barrel down her cheeks.

Bermuda, despite the guilt, maintained his gaze.

'I don't know what to do.' Her words were hopeless.

'What happened?' Bermuda finally leant forward, placing a hand on top of hers. 'What did this to you?'

Sam took deep breaths, the pain and torment rising up and crashing inside her like a tidal wave. After a few composing exhales, she gritted her teeth and shot Bermuda a bloodshot look.

'Ethan and I got married two years ago. He's a really good guy – too good for me and this job.' She sniffed a few times, trying her best to pull back the tears. 'All he wanted was to love me. And our little girl.'

Her voice cracked, but she breathed through, Bermuda watching silently.

She needed to speak it.

Confront it.

'We were going to call her Emily.' McAllister swallowed her sadness. 'We picked out her nursery together one Saturday. Ethan was so sure it would be a girl, and so he bought everything before we even knew. Then a week later we had our sonogram, and they said he was right. He squeezed my hand so tight …'

She broke off, the memory calling to her and causing a fresh batch of tears to rise up.

Bermuda watched, his heart slowly breaking for her. After a few more moments and some sharp breaths, McAllister turned back to him with a measure of calm.

'When I was just over seven months, I woke up one morning and I felt wrong. Worse, I felt alone. I couldn't feel her.'

Bermuda raised a hand to his mouth, the horror of her story causing his stomach to turn.

'When I got to the hospital, she was already gone.'

Silent tears lined her face once more. 'There was nothing they could do. She just didn't make it. My poor, sweet Emily.'

'Sam, I'm so sorry.'

McAllister lifted a hand. She hadn't finished.

She needed to finish.

'I had to carry her for four more weeks, and then they removed her from me. They took away my baby girl. She was so tiny, Jones. She was so delicate, and for some goddamn reason I will never know, she never got to feel the air in her lungs. Or feel my heart beat next to hers.'

McAllister sobbed a few times. A few other customers peered over at the emotional outburst and quickly decided to look away.

'She never got to hear me say, I love you.' She took a deep breath, the pain finally leaving her and a sense of relief bursting through. 'After that, Ethan and I spent six months trying to pick up the pieces of our shattered lives, but I just couldn't do it. I couldn't stand to look at him and see how damn devastated he was every time our eyes met. So I started drinking, we started arguing, and eventually I told him to leave.'

'Did you want him to go?' Bermuda asked, his own eyes shiny from sadness.

'Of course not.' McAllister shook her head. 'But it was easier to push him away than deal with the pain. Soon we lost contact, and I just started doing whatever I could to punish myself. Drink, men, whatever. None of it matters.'

'Bullshit.' Bermuda's words cut through the air with precision.

'Excuse me?'

'I've spent my whole life pushing the people I care most about away from me for reasons that are out of my control. I spent so long hating myself and fucking everything up. It took me a long time to realise that some things just can't be controlled. Sometimes, shit really does happen.'

McAllister stared at the table, sullen.

Bermuda stood up, slipping his arms into his jacket. 'What I'm trying to say, Sam, is don't do what I did. I spent six years pushing my daughter away. I'm doing my best to fix that now.'

Bermuda walked around the table and squatted down slightly, his eyes meeting hers and projecting warmth into the pain.

'Don't let the things you can't control destroy the things you can.' He smiled warmly and squeezed her shoulder. 'Your husband is out there, wishing you were too.'

Slowly, and with an ache skiing down his spine, Bermuda stood and turned, heading towards the door and the bitter world awaiting him. After a few steps, McAllister's voice followed him.

'Thank you, Jones.'

He turned back to her grateful face.

'You're not so bad after all.'

Bermuda flashed her a gentle smile. 'Don't tell anyone.'

They nodded, a friendship forged and cemented. Bermuda headed to the door, knowing full well that a killer of two worlds was most likely ready to strike again. He pushed through the doors to the whipping cold of the Glasgow night, a freezing rain dancing on the cusp of the wind. He pulled his hat down lower over his ears and his collar up, cocooning as much of his face as possible. Through squinted eyes he looked up.

And saw a hooded figure in the alleyway ahead.

It stood, monstrously tall and broad, with a hood casting a shadow that cut its white mask in half. The streetlight cast a shine across the two buildings, with the edge splitting the creature into part light and part darkness.

It didn't move.

'HEY!' Bermuda yelled, dashing across the road and barely missing a cab hurtling through the downpour, a cocktail of car horns and expletives filling the air. Bermuda held up a hand in apology before continuing. He looked again.

The alleyway was empty.

The rain clattered the pavement where the figure had stood, and Bermuda could feel the eyes on him still. The Otherside was nearby, and it was slowly stalking him.

Stuffing his hands into his pockets, he dipped his head and headed back towards his hotel, knowing that the Otherside was watching every single step.

## TWENTY-THREE

ARGYLE STOOD on top of the Premier Inn, casting his eye out over the city of Scotland. In the building beneath him, his partner had retired to his quarters, sleeping a tortured sleep that would undoubtedly shake him to his core. He worried for Bermuda, a man who had so much pain trapped in his body but the heart of a warrior.

A man who would surely die protecting the world.

As noble a death as that would be, and one that Argyle would accept with glee, it was his job to ensure it wouldn't happen. He had sworn an oath, not just to the BTCO but to Ottoway himself, that he would protect Bermuda. They both knew that he would the moment he had crossed the divide and joined Earth when he had looked Ottoway in the eyes and their silent agreement was made.

He would stand between Bermuda and the Otherside.

Even if it meant death.

The wind circled him, spinning raindrops into his shiny armour. He didn't move; he stood, stoic and proud, as his eyes scowled at the city below. Somewhere in the darkness, a creature that he had more in common with was killing innocent women and destroying the lives of countless others.

Somewhere in the darkness, death was waiting.

But something didn't sit correctly within. Argyle was one of the greatest warriors the Otherside had ever produced, despite the lifetime of abuse and hatred from his own kind. Despite being beaten and despised, he had become a soldier of extreme capability, and the sword which clung to his spine had ended many a battle.

But this Kevin Parker, they knew he wasn't human.

He was an Other.

Yet Argyle could not sense him. Ever since he had crossed to the human world, Argyle could sense when another creature of his world was nearby, a voice whispering in his ear to notify him of their presence. Usually, a firm stare from his grey eyes was enough to let them know the consequences if they were to leave the shadows.

His mighty blade had delivered them to those who dared.

But Kevin Parker had walked up directly behind him and left him bloodied and beaten. A mighty hand reached up and rubbed the back of his skull, the wound healed but the skin felt scarred and rigid. In time it would fade, like every other wound. Yet the memory of it wouldn't. It wasn't the pain or the surprise that would stay with him.

It was the fear.

A feeling as alien to Argyle as he was to this world, he had been brought up through the barracks of his world to face it head-on. To wrestle his fear to the ground and execute it without hesitation.

Argyle hadn't even seen him coming.

Knowing that protocol was for him to return to the BTCO HQ and rest, Argyle kept vigil. His eyes fixated on the city below, the small orange squares of car windows whipping by. Shadows of humans moved between the windows on the surrounding buildings. Creatures that humans wouldn't even concoct in their nightmares slithered through the shadows.

Argyle watched.

Kevin Parker was out there somewhere. Another sundown had come, which meant another woman would die.

They would find her.

They would not be able to save her.

With a solemn shake of the head, Argyle returned his gaze to the city, doing his best to sense Parker. To sense anything that could stop him that would alleviate the fear.

All he sensed was that he and Bermuda were in serious trouble.

---

BERMUDA SHOT up from his dream in a cold sweat. The image of the Otherside ripping his daughter to pieces had become all too familiar. After a few deep breaths he muttered a curse or two before swinging his legs round and pushing himself out of the bed. He tapped his phone, the screen bursting up like a spotlight in the dark room.

It was quarter past five, which meant he knew that McAllister was probably at a crime scene.

He sent her a quick message which simply said, '*where?*' A quick blast under the shower and Bermuda was raring to go, running the toothbrush back and forth across his teeth as he checked the cupboard for what clothes he had left. The 'system' in the corner of the room, which consisted of his previously worn clothes, was yet another mess he was keen to avoid.

A check shirt and jeans, along with his beanie and coat, would suffice, and Bermuda turned as his phone rumbled. Within minutes he was in a taxi, hurtling down the dimly lit wet streets of Glasgow as the rest of the city was still safely in bed.

As the taxi rumbled on, Bermuda watched the dark streets as they passed. The city was a labyrinth, thin dark streets lined by tall gothic buildings. Each alleyway was crawling with Others, the darkness that enveloped most of the city was alive.

Kevin Parker was in that darkness, reaching out and taking these women.

Bermuda had to stop him.

They turned onto the street and instantly stopped. The flashing blue lights of two police cars signalled the way, and Bermuda paid the man and then stepped out into the cold. The taxi slowly reversed and left him to it. A cordon had been set up, a few early risers trying their best to get a peek of the action. Bermuda could see DC Butler, his wet shirt clinging to the muscular arms that would choke him out in a heartbeat. He stood by the door, his face like thunder as he spoke angrily to a SOCO. McAllister appeared through the doorway, ushering Butler away from the house and talking quietly to him as they headed towards a tented area.

Partners looked out for each other.

As if on cue, Bermuda felt an invisible shadow cast over him.

'Morning, Argyle.'

'It is indeed,' Argyle said sternly. 'Another human has been murdered.'

'Yep. This is what happens when we make no fucking progress,' Bermuda said, angry at himself.

He marched towards the cordon, lifting the police tape and entering the crime scene. A police officer moved to stop him but Bermuda flashed him his badge for a second and continued through, shocked at how much easier it was to get this far in with such little resistance. Back in London, he had to jump through more hoops than a basketball just to even see the police tape.

Argyle gracefully entered the crime scene too, doing his best to avoid an invisible collision. Bermuda ducked into the tent, almost causing his own head-on smash with two SOCOs, one of whom muttered something inaudibly Scottish.

'Jones.' Butler's voice was as welcoming as a red-hot poker to the genitals.

'All right, mate.' Bermuda flashed him a grin before turning to McAllister. 'What's the story?'

Before McAllister could speak, Butler stepped forward, his nose a few inches from Bermuda's.

'The story is you getting the fuck out of here and leaving this to the real police.' He smirked. 'Sam's already told me about your ghosts and goblins. Why don't you fuck off back to your comics and leave us to work, aye?'

Bermuda sighed and looked past Butler to McAllister, who offered an apologetic shrug.

'Can you tighten his leash?' Bermuda asked, instantly feeling the full force of Butler as he shoved him in the chest. Bermuda stumbled back a few feet before quickly regaining his balance.

'DC BUTLER!' McAllister yelled.

'Don't do that,' Bermuda warned, his mind racing back to the moment Hugo LaPone had shoved him in the brightly lit corridors of the BTCO HQ in London. A sudden twinge of guilt hooked his heart like an expert fisherman.

'I swear to God, if he utters one more word to me, I'm gonna smash his teeth down his fucking throat,' Butler said to McAllister, loud enough for Bermuda to register the threat. Never had Bermuda heard truer words spoken. With a grunt, Butler stormed out of the tent and into the mayhem of the crime scene.

McAllister slowly walked up to Bermuda, who went to call after him.

'Just don't, Jones,' McAllister suggested. 'He is aching for a reason to go all Mike Tyson on you.'

'What, speak with a lisp?'

McAllister rolled her eyes and approached the small refreshments table. A large, metallic cylinder was surrounded by a few jugs of room temperature milk. She pressed down on the black lid, syphoning the tepid coffee out of the container and into a plastic cup.

Bermuda shuddered, as the Glaswegian Police Department were hardly going to erect a pop-up Starbucks at every crime scene. McAllister forced the coffee down before transforming into detective mode.

'The woman is a young foreign exchange student named Mika Hayagashi. Only nineteen years old. We are trying our best to contact her parents, who live back in Tokyo.'

Bermuda nodded, realising he hadn't noted any of it down and immediately couldn't be bothered.

'Same as before. Heart ripped clean out. Her left wrist is broken, which indicates a small struggle, but again, the force in which the bone has been snapped indicates…'

'That Parker isn't human.'

Both of them stood silent in the tent, the crime scene alive with activity beyond the flapping tarpaulin door.

After some careful consideration, McAllister spoke. 'Butler spoke to Strachan about your theories and, well, suffice to say she wasn't too keen on them.'

'Shocking.' Bermuda's tone was heavy with sarcasm.

'I've been ordered to abandon all investigation into Parker not being human and dedicate all my time to other leads.'

'Oh come on. You know I'm right.'

'Franklyn, I'm sorry.' McAllister looked beaten. 'Maybe

I was just so upset about everything that I wanted to believe you, I don't know. But I can't go hunting ghosts with you.'

'Really? You're going to deny the fingerprint, the photo, everything?'

'I've been instructed to have you removed from all crime scenes going forward. Strachan says she has spoken to a Mr Black at your organisation and has agreed to your dismissal from the case and your leaving the city.'

Bermuda stood quietly, the failure of his case almost outweighing the betrayal he felt from McAllister. They had shared some heated moments, but had opened up to each other when no one would listen.

She had been one person who hadn't turned her back on him.

Until now.

A few more moments of silence passed.

'I'm sorry,' she offered meekly.

Bermuda forced a smile and retrieved his hat from his pocket, slicking his damp hair back against his head and then slipping the wool over his skull.

'All the best, Sam.' He held out a hand. 'I hope you find what you're looking for.'

She clasped his hand and squeezed, the two of them nodding before Bermuda turned and threw open the tent door and strode back across the crime scene. A few police officers looked on with intrigue. Paramedics carefully wheeled a table out of the gate towards the ambulance, the blood-drenched blanket failing to keep Mika's death a secret. SOCOs stood silently in respect as the dead was transferred to the vehicle, Butler one of the few stood in silence with his head dropped.

Bermuda kept his head up and his eyes focused as he passed, only for Butler to step out behind him, his thick Scottish voice travelling through the rain.

'Good riddance to ya.'

Bermuda stopped. He muttered to himself not to turn around and instantly ignored his own advice. Butler, sensing the impending confrontation, cracked his neck slightly and rolled his shoulders. Bermuda stepped up to him, but then to his shock, extended a hand.

'All the best,' Bermuda offered.

Butler sneered and slapped it away. 'Fuck you,' he spat. 'Why don't you piss off back to London and go back to chasing your tail?'

Bermuda smirked. 'I could do that. However, due to the complete incompetence of Glasgow's finest, I'm actually going to stay and stop a serial killer.'

Butler's eyes widened with rage.

'Feel free to stay the fuck out of my way.'

Butler swung, but instinct overtook Bermuda with surprise. He ducked and instantly raised his knee into Butler's solid stomach. The detective arched over, the air leaving his body, and Bermuda stepped back, watching as Butler fell to his knee.

Two police officers raced forward, each grabbing him by the arm and dragging him through the crowd of onlookers towards the tape.

McAllister rushed out of the tent and stopped by her partner, helping him to his feet only to be shoved away. Butler was tough, but even he could have his pride hurt. McAllister sent a sad glance towards Bermuda, who shrugged as the two officer threw him under the tape. He hit the hard concrete and rolled slightly, his body covered in dirt and rainwater. A civilian offered him a hand up, muttering something about police brutality that Bermuda ignored.

He straightened his coat by its lapels and stormed up the road, determined more than ever to catch Parker.

'You handled yourself well and applied your training,'

Argyle complimented, walking powerfully beside him. 'I am impressed.'

'Thanks, Big Guy,' Bermuda responded, ignoring the pain of his scratched hand. 'He had it coming.'

'Because he is a cunt?'

Bermuda stopped dead and tried not to laugh. A sadness swept through him which he wouldn't know due to his absence, but it must have been the feeling a parent gets when their child swears. The word seemed so harmless and innocent coming out of Argyle's mouth. It struck Bermuda dumb how something so large, powerful, and deadly could be the personification of innocence.

'Don't use that word, Argyle. Trust me.'

Argyle nodded, never questioning a direct order.

They continued their march towards the BTCO office, with Bermuda affording himself a wry smile. McAllister may have abandoned their case, but beside him, he knew Argyle would be there until the bitter end.

Whenever that might come.

---

KEVIN PARKER SAT on the stone floor, his legs crossed. Some rain had infiltrated the brickwork of the tomb, and a faint sound of water splashing against concrete could be heard in the darkness. On the stone wall before him, he could see a smudge of dried blood, undoubtedly from where that human had collided with the wall two nights ago.

The one they called Bermuda.

The one he wanted to kill.

As the shadows of the tomb encompassed him, he reached his hand outwards, his fingers gently caressing the scratched markings on the stone.

The very markings he had made when held here,

locked in this stone prison. The only solace he had was that one day he would see her again. That he would hold her, let her know that he loved her.

They would return her to him.

As fury filled up inside him, he heard the slow, purposeful footsteps behind him as his handler entered the cage. Parker knew the rules; he was never allowed to turn. To lay eyes on his captor would result in her death.

He remembered when they had brought him two of her fingers, the blood still fresh from where the bone had been severed.

Parker closed his black eyes and held his breath. A hand gently landed upon his shoulder.

'You have done well, my child.' The voice was seasoned and well spoken as each word sent a chill down Parker's spine.

He slowly turned his face, resting his cheek on the hand like a loyal guard dog. 'Can I have her now? Have I done enough?'

The hope in his words bordered on pathetic, and he refused to turn to face the voice in the dark. It clearly didn't belong to Bermuda, whose interference might now impact her return. He had made a sworn promise that the moment he saw Bermuda again, he would tear him apart.

'Not yet.' The voice broke his concentration, the pain returning. The hand gently soothed his face. 'We are so close.'

'But I did what you asked.' He looked to the altar that sat in the middle of the tomb, the bloodstained heart of Mika resting in the centre. 'I brought you the heart. Same as before.'

The voice soothed him, gently shushing away his concerns. 'One more.' The voice was almost pure, gentle and soft. 'For tonight, we will take him. My men have followed his every move, and tonight we will manoeuvre him to where we need him. He will kneel before me, right where you are now, and will surrender.'

'Who?' Parker's voice rose with worry, his understanding of the agreement slowly disappearing like a sandcastle in a rising tide.

'The one who walks in both worlds.' The words slithered through gritted teeth, laced with menace.

Parker nodded, pretending to understand. All he needed was to see her again. He didn't care why.

'How many more do you desire?' he asked the shadows, the hand tightening its grip on his shoulder. He felt the darkness of another world pulling him back; the name *Caleb* filtered through his mind and was instantly dismissed.

He thought of her.

Only her.

'One more.' The response made him sit up straight. 'Bring me one more and let that be the end of it. Either we will return what was taken or end it completely.'

'You promised.' His words were feeble.

He felt the face of his captor drop down to his ear level.

'We will see, after I have spilt the blood of the one we have come for.'

And with that, the fingers left his shoulder, and within moments Parker was surrounded by nothing but cold concrete and curtains of shadow. The rain hammered the outside of the tomb, echoing through the stone structure like chattering teeth. Tonight, one more woman would have to die.

One more heart would have to be stolen.

He slowly closed his eyes, dreaming fondly of what they would do when they took what they came for.

The death of Bermuda Jones.

For the first time in decades, Kevin Parker slept soundly, knowing it was time for his final collection.

## TWENTY-FOUR

BERMUDA SAT at a small table at the back of Costa, watching as the first few customer filtered in, all of them yawning and with heavy bags under their eyes – the price to pay for having intense jobs. As he sipped his latte, he waited impatiently for McAllister to message him back.

The very thought of her caused him to tense up with frustration. She believed him, he knew she did. But obviously toeing the line was more important than the truth, and he found himself respecting her less. She had been through hell outside of the police force, so she was always going to look for the easier path at work.

But she knew the truth.

Ignoring it would just lead to more hearts being ripped out and more women being killed.

Bermuda knocked back the last of his coffee, his body screaming for the caffeine after his half-five start. The world was still enveloped in darkness, the sun a long way off from waking. Bermuda left the coffee shop and headed back out into the cold, the wind whistling through the narrow streets. Luckily the rain had died down, but the temperature still clung to him like a frozen koala.

Argyle had headed straight to the BTCO HQ, which was where Bermuda was headed to now. Furious after McAllister's rejection and his confrontation with Butler, Bermuda had needed to be alone. To gather his thoughts and to grab a coffee. Without question, Argyle had stepped away, as loyal as ever.

What would Bermuda do without him?

With his hands stuffed in his pockets, Bermuda walked down the high street, the streetlights reflecting off the shutters that covered the front of every shop. A few early birds wondered through, wearing expensive suits that their long-houred, highly paid jobs dictated they wore. A few homeless people lay huddled in the front doorway of a River Island, straining for warmth and begging for a better tomorrow.

An Other strolled past on the other side of the street, refusing to allow its black eyes to meet Bermuda's.

They all knew who he was.

The Other broke into a faster stride as soon as it passed Bermuda before joining a shadow and merging with it.

Bermuda was only interested in one creature.

Kevin Parker.

As he approached the damp boards that acted as the front door to his office, he thought back to that night. The loathing in Parker's voice.

The desperation.

Bermuda descended the large steps, going deeper underground and into the secrecy of the BTCO, consumed with the thought of finding Parker and catching him.

Of saving the next young woman who he would slaughter.

The office was dark and empty as he walked in, the old school desk lifeless and covered in dust. He slid his hat off his head, his hair spiking up like a pineapple. Argyle would undoubtedly be in his chambers; Bermuda smirked at the idea of him sleeping upside down like some sort of vampire bat. He closed his eyes, appreciating the warmth and the silence of the BTCO office. The isolation was welcoming, the loneliness for once sliding around him like a loving hug.

He opened his eyes and saw the bespectacled eyes of Kelly McDonald staring back at him.

He jumped back, cursing under his breath. She smiled a smile of pure adulation.

'Hello, Bermuda.' Her words were thick and Glaswegian. 'Can I get you a cup of tea?'

'Yeah, sure.' He wrestled his heartbeat back to normal. 'Why are you here so early?'

'Someone has to water the plants.'

Bermuda shook his head in amazement as the small, tweed-wearing ball of chaos disappeared amongst the desks, not a plant in sight. He found a quiet corner of the office and checked the PCs on the surrounding desks; the bulky white machines were a decade out of time. He blew away the dust and booted one to life, the components within screaming in pain as they were called to action for the first time in eternity.

The heavy screen burst into life, the Windows Vista logo proudly displayed despite its expiration. Bermuda almost felt guilty for the state of the office compared to the one underneath the Shard, with technology only seen in a Philip K Dick novel. However, for all the advanced computers and nude blue creatures tracking other monsters, the BTCO HQ back in London didn't have a tornado of tweed jackets, woollen jumpers, and nailed-on spinsterhood quite like Kelly McDonald.

Bermuda provided her with a knee-weakening smile as she placed a cup of tea down, her hero-worshipping causing her to walk away backwards to maintain eye contact. When she had finally disappeared, he logged into his terminal and was instantly confronted by a demand from the one thing the BTCO HQ in London did have.

Montgomery Black.

A barrage of emails flooded Bermuda's inbox, all of them finding new and colourful ways to tell him he had ruined the case and was relieved of duty. The final one, a video recording of the furious Scotsman, demanded Bermuda return to London immediately, and that he was more than likely going to be relieved of his duty, especially now that Ottoway looked unlikely to resume control.

That hit Bermuda hard.

Throughout the years as a BTCO agent and through the acceptance of his curse, Bermuda had two people he had relied upon. One of them strapped a sword to his spine and followed him into the darkness.

The other sat back in the office, defending his actions and fighting his corner after every indiscretion and every broken landmark.

Ottoway had put an arm around him when the world had turned their backs.

Now he was dying. Laid up in a hospital bed with more tubes than the London Underground. Bermuda felt a sadness swell in his chest, the thought of losing one of the few people left in his life filling him with sadness.

Six months ago, Sophie Summer had walked away, her fear of his life far outweighing their growing attraction. Chloe had been broken by his failure to be there at her birthday. Not calling her had just added a dot to the already painful exclamation point.

Ottoway was the closest thing he had had to a father figure, his own father nothing more than a rejected footnote that never had an input in his life.

As the thoughts swirled in his head like a vintage wine, he realised he had shed a tear. Embarrassed, he wiped it away and unlocked his phone. He thumbed through the bizarre names that formed his address book before selecting the direct line to Ottoway, hoping beyond hope that the voice at the end of the line was the welcoming one.

'Hello.' It was.

'Vincent.' Bermuda exhaled with relief. 'It's Bermuda.'

'Ah, Agent Jones. We have been trying to get hold of you.'

'I can see.' Bermuda rolled his eyes. 'Has Monty ever heard of spam?'

'Spam?'

'Never mind.' Bermuda leant back in his chair, sipping the tea that was basically hot milk. 'How's Ottoway?'

'Lord Felix is comfortable.' Vincent's sadness betrayed the calmness of his voice. 'We are in the final stages of a potential cure.'

'For cancer?' Bermuda sat up straight. The idea of vanquishing one of the world's greatest evils was remarkable.

'We can but try,' Vincent said, dampening the optimism. 'As you know, the breakthroughs in science we have provided for your race have been substantial. Yet cancer is a different beast entirely.'

'Speaking of beasts,' Bermuda started dryly. 'This Kevin Parker chap, he isn't a normal Other.'

'The information we are gathering from the Oracles seems to correlate this. Due to his heightened strength, ability to be seen by the human world, and Argyle's lack of detection, they are categorising him as an Exceptional.'

Bermuda laughed. The new labelling system was too scattergun for him – he wanted to label all of them a threat and close the goddamn doorway. Yet with Ottoway laid up in bed, his life slowly being eaten by something worse than any Other, Bermuda knew why they kept it open. The

Otherside would one day kill him, he knew that. Kill him and claim him.

It had already started.

But it was still Ottoway's best chance of survival.

'Agent Jones.' Vincent refocused him. 'Did you hear me?'

'Yeah, yeah. An Exceptional or whatever it is you are calling your new project.'

'That is exactly what we are calling it.' Vincent spoke almost as matter-of-factly as Argyle. 'You are to return to London immediately under orders of Montgomery Black, and in no way are you to engage with Kevin Parker until we can develop a greater understanding of his powers.'

Suddenly, a door slammed on the other end of the phone and Bermuda could hear a rustling sound, like somebody wrapping the phone in a paper bag. After a while, the volume of the call got louder. Another voice told him he was now on speaker phone.

And in a hell of a lot of trouble.

'Jones, you are to come back to London right now, do you hear me!' Bermuda could almost hear the veins straining against Black's forehead.

'Hello, Monty.'

'Shut up.' Venom spat from his lips. 'You just shut your mouth. Not only have you disobeyed direct orders from your acting commander, but you have also brought the entire investigation into disarray. In fact, I've had Detective Chief Inspector Fowler, someone I admire very much, call me and demand I remove you from the goddamn case.'

'Based on what I have seen so far, I wouldn't go on any decision made by a member of Glaswegian Police Service.'

'Just shut up!' Black snapped. 'You assaulted a detective at a crime scene.'

'To be fair, he swung at me first.'

Vincent interjected. 'Argyle has corroborated that fact,

and Jones is a trained agent. Self-defence is necessary.'

'So you could say I was just doing as trained, right?' Bermuda cursed himself for antagonising.

'Trained? What you have done, Jones, is discuss the Otherside with a detective who has pushed the idea higher. Not only has it been laughed out of the door and put her career in jeopardy, you have actively gone against one of the fundamental rules that we abide by here at the BTCO.'

'Oh, fuck your rules.'

A collective gasp echoed down the phone. Kelly McDonald rose from behind a partition, her mouth wide open, a look of pure horror across her face. Bermuda felt every muscle in his body tense. Silence.

'How dare you speak to me like that?' Black finally uttered, astounded by the offence.

'You know what? In case you haven't realised, this thing is killing. Every day. Without fail. Innocent women are dying. Now we know what the fuck is going on, but that doesn't mean we keep it to ourselves. Now if I get laughed out of every damn room, if I get swung at by every fucking inept detective, then so be it. I am not going to stop hunting this bastard until I bring him to his fucking knees.

'So you can fire me, you can threaten me, whatever. I'm not leaving. I'm not going anywhere until I stop Kevin Parker.' Bermuda stood, his hand on his hip. 'You got a problem with that, Monty, then you know where I am.'

Bermuda ended the call amidst Black's threats of coming to Glasgow immediately and tossed the phone down onto the desk. He looked at Kelly, who slowly slunk into her seat, her fears of meeting her hero clearly solidified. With a deep sigh, he slid his hand to his back pocket and retrieved the small leather wallet, his BTCO Agency card securely fastened behind the clear plastic.

He placed it on the table alongside his phone.

The gentle clicking of a keyboard was the only sound

in the room and Bermuda decided against an awkward goodbye. With purposeful steps, he strode through the giant steel doors and up the steep, dark stairwell for the final time. As he emerged through the reality-shattering door, the rain hit him hard.

The next few words hit him harder.

'I don't want you to go.'

Bermuda's mouth pulled into a thin line and he turned, shielding his face from the hard downfall. Argyle stood to the side of the door, his arms folded across the armour plate. His eyes, piercing and pupilless, stared at Bermuda with hope.

'I'm sorry, Big Guy.' Bermuda shrugged. 'But I can't just turn my back on this and go home. It's not an option.'

'We have strict orders …' Argyle began.

'To hell with the orders,' Bermuda interrupted, immediately regretting it. 'Look, Argyle, I know you are a soldier and you were drilled from whatever age to be this well-oiled machine. But there are times when the orders shouldn't be followed.'

Argyle's brow furrowed. 'I don't understand.'

'I wouldn't expect you to, buddy.' Bermuda let out a deep sigh, the pain of the goodbye coiling around his heart like an anaconda. 'My whole life, I have been scared of this other world and what was waiting for me in the shadows. I have hated this curse, no matter how many times I have tried to accept it. It has brought me nothing but pain. Except you.'

'I was assigned to you by Lord Ottoway,' Argyle said with the clarity of a football commentator.

'I know. You have been the best friend I could have asked for, and you have saved my arse more times than I care to remember. But I can't walk away from this, Argyle. I just can't. I have to stop him.'

Argyle stood silently, casting his eyes back to the

entrance of the BTCO Headquarters and the only life he had ever known on this side of the divide.

'It has been an honour to serve by your side.' Argyle stood proudly, resting his fist across his chest in a sign of respect. 'And a pleasure to call you my friend.'

Bermuda felt tears slowly welling behind his eyes, but puffed his chest out and offered the same salute to his partner. They nodded their final respect.

'Take care of yourself.'

Bermuda's final words hung in the following silence, the rain clattering the short distance between the two of them. As the conversation ended, Bermuda turned and headed back towards the town, his hands stuffed into the pockets of his coat. Argyle watched his partner walk away, a pathway he could not follow.

They had their orders.

Argyle turned slowly and headed back to the secret office below the bustling city, trying his best to maintain his formidable composure. A sadness swept through his body, a feeling that was both overpowering and alien. The BTCO had been his saviour, pulling him from the Otherside and protecting him from all the horrors that would surely await him should he ever return. Bermuda had been assigned to him after what had happened.

Argyle had saved him more than he knew.

But the sadness Argyle felt was for the fading essence of Bermuda in his senses. He knew Bermuda was connected to his world, and like his own kind, he could sense his partner.

That feeling was fading.

The case, like their partnership, had come to an end, and he was to return alone.

There was no essence of Otherside on the street anymore. Only the rain.

Bermuda had gone.

## TWENTY-FIVE

THE AFTERNOON WAS BRISK, with a dark cloud painting itself across the skyline. The darkness it cast loomed heavy over the Necropolis as Bermuda felt the mud squelch beneath his Converse. Whatever colour they were before, they were mud brown from now on. Inching his way between gravestones, he ascended to the top of the hill, the broken stone of the tomb the cherry on a depressing, muddy cake.

It was empty.

Frustrated at his lack of availability, Bermuda called for Tobias, his words dancing their way to oblivion on the howling wind. Leaves spun up off the ground, swirling through the dark graveyard and clattering the monuments to the dead. Bermuda entered the tomb, shuddering as he looked at the wall that Kevin Parker had sent him crashing into.

The large platform in the centre of the room smelt damp, with flecks of dried blood scattered across the surface. The edges of the wall still showed the finger scrapings of a madman.

Or a captive?

Bermuda called out to Tobias again, immediately scorning himself for thinking he was hidden in one of the small coves within. Maybe he should have brought Argyle with him. The posh old groundsman was keen to meet his partner. Bermuda slid his notepad out and flipped it open, fanning the pages of crude notes until the day he met Tobias.

*Argyle?*

Bermuda scoffed; the senile old gatekeeper was certainly as bizarre as Monty had made out. It had probably been a long time since he had met a Neither, especially one with the reputation of Argyle. Bermuda said Argyle's name a few times in the overly posh tones of Tobias, then stopped suddenly, checking the corners of the tomb in case he was there.

The shadows offered nothing but cold silence. Rain dropped through a crack in the wall, splattering against the back of Bermuda's neck. Wiping it away as he turned, Bermuda noticed the broken stones of one of the walls, the brick a shaky foundation on borrowed time.

Everything here was dying.

With a sudden chill tunnelling through his body like a starving termite, Bermuda wrapped his arms around his body and stepped back out into the world. Carefully treading through the slippery graveyard, Bermuda turned as he approached the gate, casting an eye back up to the tomb. The shadows of the Necropolis loomed from every angle, like thousands of ghastly fingers all reaching in from the edges of our world.

He stepped through the gate and back onto the pavement, only then realising that he had been holding his breath.

The entire walk back to his hotel was spent running through the case in his mind, trying his best to figure out how Kevin was selecting his victims and who he was looking for. He had spoken of a voice in the darkness, promising her return. They needed to know who *her* was.

After a while the rain failed to register with him, his body soaked through to the core. He dipped into a coffee shop, stepping out a few moments later with a hot cup in his hand and a fresh stream of caffeine trickling down his throat. Checking his phone, Bermuda immediately ignored the fifty-seven missed calls that he assumed were from Montgomery Black, the impending bollocking and likely sacking the furthest thing from his mind.

Veering into the town centre, Bermuda was surprised at the volume of the footfall, the downpour doing little to discourage shoppers from buying into the Christmas spirit. Trying his best to remember what day it was, Bermuda walked towards the dismantled tramline, his heart racing as he revisited yet another near-death experience.

Another life owed to Argyle.

Bermuda frowned, the amicable breakup with his partner still a very raw wound that he knew the Otherside couldn't heal. Without his partner, Bermuda felt every shadow slowly stalking him, knowing that the Otherside could sense his vulnerability.

Occasionally, he had spun his head quickly and thought he had seen a hooded figure in a dark alley. Or a featureless, white face watching from a building above.

He was alone.

Finishing the last of his coffee and dumping the disposable paper cup in the nearest bin, Bermuda scanned his eyes across the dislodged tram track. He recalled the venom in Parker's eyes as he had held him close, the sheer desperation to get away. A desperate creature was a dangerous one – even he knew that.

But why?

Bermuda sighed, time slipping through his fingers like raindrops. The streetlights that lined the high street burst into life, casting bright orange glows amongst the grey. Shop fronts lit up, showing a library of discount posters, all of them offering the best deals in a hope of attracting customers.

A busker wrapped in a thick coat strumming a guitar with frozen fingers, grateful for any coin that was tossed into his bag, suddenly found himself under a spotlight. A few passers-by watched as he strummed another Ed Sheeran rent-a-song.

The lights bore down on parked cars, families strolling through the town, and on the other side of the road the streetlight cast a shine across a pop-up florist. The portly gentleman grinned as he wrapped a bouquet up in a few sheets of paper before handing them over to an overly ambitious young man.

Flowers either meant an anniversary or a fuckup.

Bermuda never remembered either.

The new brightness brought a beautiful burst of colour to the otherwise dreary street, with Bermuda's brain forcing him to look. The tulips. The daisies.

The roses.

Slowly, Bermuda began walking towards them, his mind trying its best to decipher a message at the back of his mind. Slowly, dots began to land on a canvas, with lines connecting them, an image gradually becoming clearer and clearer. Like a page in a child's dot-to-dot, Bermuda connected them, his eyes widening in realisation.

'Can I help you, lad?' The florist offered a big, boorish smile.

Bermuda stared at him, the answer dropping on him like an anvil.

Without answering, he slowly backed away before turning on his heels and running off into the gloomy Glasgow evening.

'HOW'S IT GOING, GREG?'

McAllister leant against Butler's desk, one arm folded across her stomach and the other lifting a warm cup of coffee to her mouth.

She wished it was something stronger.

'Aye, can't complain.' Butler didn't look up from the mountain of paper before him, different sheets laid out in no obvious system. It drove McAllister mad how messily Butler worked, but then she shrank under the blanket of hypocrisy when she thought of her own life.

'What's our play?' She took another sip as he dropped his pen and looked up.

'We don't have one.'

'We need one.'

'Aye,' he agreed. 'We also need a fuck-tonne more funding and a pay rise for putting up with all of this shit, but it ain't coming anytime soon. At least that prick has been sent back to London.'

McAllister frowned at the thought of Bermuda leaving even though she agreed his theory was bizarre. As a dedicated detective, she had scolded herself many times over for entertaining his wild stories of other worlds and a scorned monster who was killing for the return of a woman.

But what else did they have?

Glancing beyond Butler's desk, she saw Strachan stood in the incident room, pointing to the pictures of the deceased and their brutal murder scenes, the whiteboard covered in different-coloured inks that all pointed to a massive question mark.

No one had a clue how to catch Kevin Parker.

All the proof they had, besides the bodies, was a fingerprint from decades ago and a photo that proved he was alive almost a hundred years ago.

All of it came from Bermuda.

And none of it made any sense.

Realising Butler had returned to his work, McAllister gently rubbed the bridge of her nose, annoyed at the unravelling of her career. She had lost Ethan after the devastation that had fallen upon them. The loss of their child had broken their marriage and her resolve, and she now relied upon bottle after bottle of wine. But her career was different. She had always been at the front of the line, fast-tracking to detective and proving herself to be one of the brightest minds in the service. Strachan had already earmarked her for the sergeant's chair.

Putting forward theories of the boogie man was not going to help her cause.

Throughout it all, Butler had been her rock. He knew the shattered life she kept hidden away, the devastating self-hatred that led to such destructive behaviour. On more than one occasion, he had covered for her with Strachan or collected her, drunk and disorderly, from a bar where she had overstayed her welcome.

He had been her friend.

Yet now, after the altercations with Bermuda and her propensity to believe his wild theories, she could feel him pushing her away.

She was alone.

Suddenly, a wave of sadness rose inside her like an elevator and she pushed herself off of her partner's desk and headed to the bathroom. Keeping her head down to hide the tears building in her eyes, she passed the other cubicles and the incident room – where her superiors were undoubtedly discussing her failings – until she hit the corridor. Throwing open the door, she entered the bathroom and quickly shut it, leaning against the door for a few moments as she struggled to catch her breath.

McAllister leant down, checking under the doors, and was relieved to see no evidence of any occupants. Splashing some lukewarm water onto her face, she angrily scowled at her reflection: deep sunken eyes on a sleep-deprived face, with a mess of thick hair perched on top.

She looked like hell.

As the water droplets slithered down her pale skin, McAllister let out a deep breath. She felt calmer, the numbing feeling of isolation slowly rising from her like steam. She hated second-guessing herself. Having built a career as a strong detective, her conviction had always been heavily praised by DCI Fowler and above.

She had laughed off Bermuda's original theories. Her life as a detective was surrounded by hard evidence and pure fact, not wild speculation and proof of existence beyond our world. Yet the nagging doubt hung from her brain like a sloth, pulling her back to the idea.

Kevin Parker was not of this world.

The evidence and the facts that she lived by backed that theory. Bermuda had been removed from the case and admonished, sent back to London to face the superiors of his secret organisation which, if Bermuda's descriptions of the other world were correct, would be a horrifying experience.

What if he was right?

McAllister rolled her eyes and reached for her phone, her loneliness taking control of her hands, her head and heart wrestling for control. Neither won as she began typing, repeating Bermuda's words in her head like a mantra.

*'Don't let the things you can't control destroy the things you can.'*

Slowly, with tears falling between her eyelashes, her unpainted nails clattered the bright screen of her phone.

McAllister took a deep breath as she dabbed at her eyes with the back of her hand and read the message.

*ETHAN. I miss you. Xx*

GUILT AND PAIN combined in her chest, shaking her body like an earthquake. The world had moved them in different directions; the devastating loss of their child had brutally ruptured their life together. God knew what he had been doing.

She had been self-destructing.

And then some.

McAllister scowled in the mirror. The once proud, tough female detective she had built herself to be was nowhere to be seen. She looked frail and beaten.

She looked alone.

Determined to be that woman again and get her life back, she pressed send. Instantly, she slammed the phone facedown on the sink, splashing tepid water over her face and running some through her matted hair. She pulled it into a ponytail before straightening her jacket.

She was going to take her life back.

And catch Kevin Parker.

As her mind raced to think of a new angle to take on the case, a vibration echoed through the bathroom. McAllister stopped dead.

Slowly, she turned the phone.

It was Ethan.

*MISS YOU TOO. Xx*

. . .

MCALLISTER LET OUT A SMALL SIGH. Just the idea of hearing from him brought back a joyful feeling she had long since forgotten. Almost instantly, the gaping hole she had been trying to fill with drink and random men began to shrink.

They had a lot to talk about.

None of it would be nice.

With a steely determination, McAllister pulled the door open and marched back towards her office, phone in hand. She would organise a time to meet Ethan, then she would bring Kevin Parker to justice. As she pushed through into the office, her entire concentration was broken by the huge commotion at the other end, the clattering of bodies as paper flew through the air and everyone watched open-mouthed.

McAllister's eyebrows raised with surprise as the person wrestled Butler out of the way and made a march towards her.

It was Bermuda.

## TWENTY-SIX

'MCALLISTER!' Bermuda called out as DC Butler manhandled him to the wall, slamming his face against the plasterboard with a sickening thud.

The detective was certainly strong, and from the roughness of his actions, Bermuda ascertained he was champing at the bit to meet him again. Butler, with years of training, roughly pulled Bermuda's arms behind his back, clutching his wrists before slamming his face against the wall again.

'This is a police station, you little prick.' His words oozed with Glaswegian menace. 'You know, where the real police work.'

'Look, mate, I know you can't stand me, but I need to talk to McAllister.'

'What? More stories of ghosts?'

The surrounding group of officers laughed, all of them clearly behind Butler. Bermuda was used to resistance from the police, but not to the point of tasting the paint of the walls.

'I know how to find him!' Bermuda spoke, his cheek pushed against his teeth and the taste of blood filling his mouth.

'Look, pal, you got more chance of finding Santa.' Butler shook him again, rubbing his face against the rough wall. 'Just as fucking make-believe as your monsters.'

'Let him go.'

Butler turned in surprise but made no effort to stop the pressure against Bermuda's neck. Bermuda, unable to turn his head, rolled his eyes.

He could recognise the voice of DI Nicola Strachan anywhere.

'Ma'am?' Butler asked. His upset at not being able to take Bermuda apart was evident.

'Take him to the incident room. DCI Fowler wants to speak to him.' She turned sharply, her fierce eyes latching onto McAllister and digging in. 'You are not to speak to this man under any circumstance. That is a direct order.'

'Yes, Ma'am,' McAllister spoke, her feet planted and her words directed to them. The rest of the office slowly returned to normal as Strachan, with a sneer across her sharp face, turned back to Butler, allowing him a few more moments of retribution.

'DC Butler,' she eventually ordered. 'Incident room.'

She turned on her heels, which clapped against the lino covered floor as she headed to the room.

'There's a good dog,' Bermuda needlessly added, ensuring another painful slam against the wall and a twisting of his wrists.

Butler manhandled him through the door and shoved him angrily into a desk. The wood clipped Bermuda in the thigh and he hunched over, gently massaging his wrists.

'Prick,' Butler muttered before offering a respectful salute to the two other officers.

Bermuda slowly stood straight, his wrists burning. The shutters covering the large window were pulled to, blocking out the rest of the office. Three rows of desks sat in neat rows, usually full of detectives and officers getting the latest details of a case. The incident board behind him was three whiteboards pressed together, all of them decorated with smiling photos of the brutally slain, and the evidence of the slaughter below them.

Random scribblings of useless facts surrounded them, all of them leading to the name KEVIN PARKER in the centre of the board. Next to it were the CCTV footage and the photo he had provided, along with the fingerprint.

Bermuda smiled, knowing he had provided their only hard evidence, despite their constant reminders of his lack of police training.

A gentle cough caught his attention and his focus turned to the tall man clearing his throat.

'Let me guess – Alex Fowler, right?'

'That's Detective Chief Inspector Fowler to you.' Fowler's voice was as authoritative as it was calm. His greying hair sat like a cloud atop his cleanly shaven face. He stood proudly, his tunic immaculate and his hat resting neatly under his arm.

'No it's not.' Bermuda slammed his last Tic Tacs into his mouth. 'Your boy out there keeps telling me I'm not a real detective.'

'You're not,' Strachan interjected with disgust in her voice.

'She has a point,' Fowler interjected before Bermuda could respond. 'You are not technically supposed to be here. Now before you go waving your little badge at me, I will stop you. I have never heard of your organisation, and believe me, I've heard of everything in my nineteen years.'

'Have you heard her laugh?' Bermuda chucked a thumb in Strachan's furious direction.

'Very funny.' Fowler's voice was cold. 'Now you have already been informed by McAllister that we have requested your removal from the case, and I spoke with a Montgomery Black, who agreed this would happen. I don't know how things work in your little ghost-hunters club, but here in the GPS we respect the chain of command.'

'I do. Just not when it's wrong.'

'An answer for everything,' Fowler uttered under his breath. 'Well, considering your blatant disregard for the order and your trespassing here today, I have no choice but to raise a formal complaint with the London Metropolitan Police Service.'

'For what?' Bermuda stepped forward, his patience finally thinning.

Fowler, not to lose authority, stepped forward too. 'For assaulting my officer.'

'Fuck off.' Bermuda chuckled.

'I will not. We have a number of witnesses swearing that you kneed him in the stomach in retaliation to being asked to leave the crime scene this morning.'

Bermuda shook his head at the obvious lie. The smirk on Strachan's face, mirrored by Fowler, told him that he couldn't undo this one.

After a few moments, Strachan leant forward. 'Maybe you should run along now?'

'Agreed.' Fowler spoke, his stare unwavering.

After a few more moments, a smile cracked across Bermuda's face, splitting his stubble. He shrugged, turning to the door as Fowler sent a victorious nod in Strachan's direction. As he passed the whiteboard, Bermuda picked up a black marker pen and flicked the cap off. As it clattered to the floor, he stopped near a poster on the wall of a body lying face down on the floor, a message about 'good crime scene etiquette' framing it.

Quick as a flash, he wrote the letter *E* on the elbow and an *A* on the buttocks. He tossed the pen back across the room to a bewildered Strachan. Fowler stepped forward, scratching his head.

'What on earth is that for?'

'*E* is for elbow. *A* is for arsehole,' Bermuda said, opening the door. 'For the next time you guys realise you haven't got a fucking clue.'

Slamming the door and trapping any response, Bermuda strode with purpose back towards the entrance. Butler instantly pushed his chair back, the legs screeching against the floor.

Bermuda held out a calming hand. 'Down boy.'

Butler raised a middle finger in response, to Bermuda's amusement. As he rounded the corner that led to the corridor, he almost collided with McAllister, pressed against the wall.

'Bermuda.' She shook her head at the nickname. 'What the hell did you come here for? Do you know how much trouble you are in?'

Bermuda peered around the corner again, noticing the partitions of the blinds flickering. 'Oh yeah. I'm knee-deep in shit.'

'I told you that this was over.' McAllister spoke softly, Bermuda detecting her sadness at the situation.

'Sam, I know how to find him.'

She perked up.

'What? How?' She scrambled inside her blazer jacket, looking for her notebook. As she did, Butler rounded the corner, soon followed by Strachan. Bermuda could take the hint and pulled open the door to the corridor.

'The roses, Sam.' Bermuda offered her his warmest smile in a way of goodbye. 'It's the roses.'

McAllister looked on in disbelief as Bermuda disappeared into the corridor, sliding his hat over his head and pulling the collar of his coat up. He reached the front door and without even turning, threw out a hand to wave goodbye. McAllister found herself waving back as Butler and Strachan instantly reprimanded her.

She didn't listen to a word of it.

AS BERMUDA WALKED through the town centre, every fibre of his being told him to hail a cab or check to see how Uber was getting on in Glasgow. He ignored his own weakness, braving the elements as a freezing drizzle swept the dark Glasgow evening clean. The Christmas lights were beaming down from the buildings, the late-evening shopping in full force as he weaved his way through endless mobs of consumerism. He spotted a few Others fighting over what looked like an old violin in an alleyway. Knowing his tenure as a BTCO agent was probably at an end, he opted not to check to see the validity of their latch stones.

Did Kevin Parker have a latch stone?

Bermuda threw his mind back to their meeting a few nights prior, the monstrous human gently stalking him around the tomb. While he spoke of his desired and the voice in the darkness, Bermuda couldn't see the stone.

Was he human?

Argyle hadn't been able to sense him like he usually could. Not an Other got by Argyle without him at least knowing it was in the vicinity. But Parker was too strong, moved too fast.

Bermuda had seen the darkness in his eyes.

The Otherside.

Convincing himself that Parker was just another creature to go back across the divide, Bermuda felt the phone in his pocket begin to vibrate. As the chilling grip of the night wrapped its fingers around him, he hoped it was his daughter, offering her forgiveness and mending his heart back together.

Or perhaps his sister Charlotte, just calling, because unlike his deceased dad or deadbeat mum, she was one of the few people in the world who gave a damn about him.

He prayed it was Sophie, realising theirs was a love that she couldn't be without.

With a deep sigh, he answered the unknown number, praying his hope wasn't misguided.

It was.

'Jones.' Montgomery Black's voice bellowed down the phone, the audible squeal of an airplane in the background. 'What the hell do you think you're playing at?'

'Are you at an airport?' Bermuda asked, surprised more than anything that Black wasn't bluffing.

'You're damn right I am.' Black was breathing heavily, telling Bermuda he was walking somewhere. 'I just touched down in the motherland, and what do I receive? A call from DCI Fowler saying that you practically broke into the police station?'

'Technically I didn't break in.'

'For Christ's sake, do you actively try to piss me off?' Black continued before a smart response came. 'Go to your damn hotel room and wait there. Vincent and I will be with you within the hour.'

'Great,' Bermuda said dryly, turning the corner, the Premier Inn appearing at the end of the road in all its purple majesty.

'Don't get smart with me, Jones,' Black warned with venom. 'Do you know how much damage you have caused? Not just to the investigation or the great city of Glasgow, but to the whole organisation? No, of course you don't. Because you don't care. Because you think you are above the rules and regulations that we need to abide by to keep the truce steady.'

'No offence, Monty, but I couldn't give a shit. I know how to find this guy and I'm going to stop him. You're welcome to wait in the bar until I get back.'

Bermuda climbed the steps of the Premier Inn and entered through the automatic door to the empty reception, so engrossed in his phone call that he failed to notice the row of hooded figures that lined the other side of the street, all of them burning a hole in him with their jet-black eyes.

Eight white masks all turned in his direction.

He failed to notice them advance towards the hotel.

Bermuda pushed open the door to the stairs and began his ascent, ignoring the tirade of abuse like a school child who didn't care about detention.

'You're finished, Jones. Do you hear me?'

'Tell me something I don't know.'

Bermuda heard the sound of car doors closing and an engine roaring to life. They were on their way.

'Well, you are on your own now. Unlike you, Argyle knows how to follow orders. He is a soldier. He was until you corrupted him.'

'Argyle is a good man. Leave him out of this,' Bermuda pleaded angrily. He pushed open the door to his floor, his thighs and calves burning.

'Did he enjoy his reunion?' Black asked, his words calmer, as if arguing had taken a physical toll on him. Bermuda thought about Black's age, and for a second actually felt a twinge of sympathy.

'Who?'

'Argyle.'

'Reunion?' Bermuda stopped in the hallway. It was eerily quiet. 'What the hell are you going on about?'

'Argyle and Tobias.' Black spoke with an irritated tone.

Bermuda stopped, nothing made sense. 'What? Tobias kept asking to meet him. He said he had heard things about Argyle.' Bermuda tried to force it all to make sense. 'He was really keen, in fact.'

Black chuckled as if he had heard a terrible joke. 'The silly old fool. They've met before.'

Black sighed while Bermuda tried to place it all. There was something that didn't sit right with him.

Something about Tobias.

Black suddenly shattered his concentration. 'Above everything Jones, I'm actually surprised you understood a word the man said.'

'What do you mean?' Bermuda asked, unease coursing through him like a pulse. 'Apart from talking like he belonged on Downton Abbey.'

'What the hell are you talking about? The man has thicker Glaswegian accent than I do!'

With that, Bermuda froze. There had been something the entire time – something nagging him about the way Tobias spoke. The way his skin sat on his body, like he had withered and it hung loose.

The way he knew more than he should.

Tobias.

At that moment, the corridor became entrenched in darkness. Every light cut instantly, painting the entire hotel in shadow. Bermuda looked at the screen of his phone, and a warning saying his battery was low greeted him. The screen, refusing to light up to preserve battery, projected nothing but a pathetic, faded imitation of his daughter's face.

Pocketing his phone, Bermuda walked slowly into the darkness, his fingers wrapping around his e-cig. Bringing it to eye level, he pressed down on the button and a small blue light burst out, illuminating a few feet before him like a torch. The e-liquid bubbled as he burnt through it. He took a few steps forward before pressing again, the blue light guiding him down a few feet further before it dipped and faded.

He heard footsteps behind him.

Bermuda swivelled, holding the e-cig like a weapon. The only damage it provided was to the tobacco industry.

He pressed the button again in the direction of the shuffled footsteps, but the blueness provided nothing.

Slowly, he turned with his finger down on the button.

A pure white mask greeted him.

The hooded figures moved so quickly that Bermuda was unconscious within moments, the e-cig clattering to the floor and switching off.

The creature uttered a crude grunt before more of his kind emerged from the shadows, surrounding the motionless body of Bermuda.

They were the Legion.

They had claimed him.

With no piercing blue bulb to light the way, Bermuda was dragged into the darkness.

## TWENTY-SEVEN

ARGYLE BLAMED HIMSELF.

Stood at the entrance of Bermuda's temporary quarters, Argyle watched as the rain fell down upon the glorious city before him. The high, gothic towers that lined the roads reminded him of home, each one a monument to endurance and sacrifice. All of them built by hand, all of them a shadow that threatened to move.

He should have seen it coming.

Ever since they had arrived in the city, he had sensed it. From the very moment he accompanied Bermuda from the train station, he could feel the eyes upon them. Every movement, every moment.

They had been waiting.

Outside Steingold's residence, Argyle had seen them in the alleyway. Vincent had even spoken of a rise in the Other activity in the city. The signs were there, every alarm was ringing, but Argyle had failed his primary objective.

Protect Bermuda at all costs.

It was Ottoway himself who had decreed it, and their last interaction on the viewing platform of the Shard six months prior had reiterated it. Then, with Bermuda hunting Barnaby, the importance of his life was stressed heavily.

Now, with Ottoway on his final journey, Argyle had let that objective slip.

He had followed his orders.

But he had failed.

Vincent had contacted the BTCO HQ when they arrived in Glasgow, asking Argyle to meet them at Bermuda's hotel. They were to relieve him of his duty and Vincent had permitted Argyle the opportunity of a farewell. Argyle had already made peace with their split, but assumed Montgomery Black wanted to hurt Bermuda further.

Soldiers follow orders.

Argyle watched as a few police officers waited at the bottom of the steps, their bright jackets reflecting off the flashing blue lights of their vehicles. Argyle scoffed at the memory of him lifting one, causing panic amongst the humans. If only they knew what surrounded their world. What lurked in the shadows.

Inside, Vincent and Black were combing through Bermuda's chambers, looking for any sort of clue. Argyle knew they would find none. All they found was his e-cigarette in the hall, a few doors down from his own.

They had taken him far from here.

Argyle felt restless, his command to stay and watch the entrance felt needless. Whatever had taken Bermuda wouldn't be back. They should have been combing every alleyway of the city, searching through the darkness like Argyle had all those years ago.

When he had found Bermuda on the Otherside.

As Argyle began to replay the memory in his mind, a voice behind broke his concentration.

'Bad night, eh?'

Argyle turned his neck slightly to see the homeless man

they had seen on a number of occasions. The man was soaked through, his filthy clothes glued to his wiry frame. His hair, plastered to his head, ran in uneven clumps, framing a face that needed a wash and a shave.

He was a disgrace.

Argyle eyed him up and down, convinced the man was speaking to the police officers, and returned his gaze to the downpour ahead.

'Hey. Big man.' The voice grew. 'You with the sword.'

Argyle instantly spun round, his blade finely slicing a number of raindrops as they hurtled to the ground. The tramp stumbled backwards, steadying himself before falling.

'Are you addressing me?' Argyle's shadow, cast by the light hanging above him, completely enveloped the man.

'I'm sorry, I thought you were with that guy, Bermuda.' The man held his hands up in surrender.

'I apologise,' Argyle offered, bowing his head. Being seen as a monster was something he truly hated. 'I, of course, mean you no harm.'

'Aye. Good to know.' The man flashed a toothless grin. 'The name's Gordon.'

Argyle grunted a response and turned his attention back to the front door.

Back to his orders.

A gentle cough behind him caused him to turn back.

'I saw them. The shadow people.' Gordon rustled in his bag, pulling out a surprisingly clean apple. He sunk his remaining rotting teeth into it, drawing a loud crunch which alerted the officers.

'The shadow people?' Argyle questioned.

'You know. Your kind. The kind normal folks can't see.' He took another bite, bits of apple falling into his beard. 'Aye, there were a number of them.'

'How many?' Argyle turned, towering over the informant.

'Seven. Maybe eight.' Gordon gestured to the street, indicating where they went. 'All of 'em had big hoods on, you know? But they weren't human.'

Argyle's face tightened, the fury bubbling within him. Despite the BTCO taking him in when he had betrayed the Otherside, Bermuda had been his friend. His orders may have come from them, but his loyalty was with Bermuda. The man may have had zero respect for authority, but Argyle had never met a human with a clearer understanding of right and wrong.

Above all else he was his partner.

His friend.

Gordon took a step forward, standing beside the rain-soaked giant. 'Argyle, isn't it?'

The eye contact told him he was correct. The grey, pupilless eyes sent a shudder down his spine.

'I don't think they were taking him anywhere nice.'

'Why do you care?' Argyle spoke through gritted teeth, his inner turmoil wrestling inside him.

'I sit on these streets every day telling this world I ain't crazy.' Gordon chuckled. 'For years, no one has listened. Except your pal. Now I can't do much for anyone. But you can.'

Argyle exhaled before standing up straight. The blade gently swung from its latch, the smooth, polished steel grazing the back of his legs. He reached out his rough hand and placed it on his new acquaintance's shoulder. Argyle knew with enough focus he could track Bermuda. He did whenever they needed to travel long distances, a skill that always surprised his partner. He had done it a hundred times, but was about to do one thing he had never entertained.

Defy his orders.

'Thank you.'

Gordon looked up at him in awe, slowly chomping another lump out of the apple. Argyle burst forward with such power that he almost collided with the police officers, who wobbled slightly as he dashed past. They glared at the homeless mess before them, infuriated when all he offered them was a hopeless shrug. Gordon smirked as Argyle raced across the road, whipping between two cars before disappearing into shadows.

At that moment, an old man stormed out of the Premier Inn, his glasses almost slipping from his large nose. He wore a smart, three-piece suit and walked with an air of arrogance that immediately identified him as the one in charge.

'Argyle?' Montgomery Black's accent was thick and welcoming. He looked around vacantly.

'The big guy with the sword?' Gordon offered, scraping the scraps from the apple core.

Black hobbled down the steps and approached him with a scowl on his face. 'Who the hell are you?'

'Just a handsome stranger.' Gordon tossed the core back into one of his bags.

The rain began to hammer an agitated Black before a noble-looking creature with a large head and long, thin fingers genuinely floated across with an umbrella.

Gordon nodded at Vincent, who returned with a warm smile.

'What did you do?' Black demanded.

'Me, nothing.' Gordon turned to walk away. A few taxis slowly veered down the street, a fresh spray of water lifting from their tyres.

Black grabbed Gordon and turned him back. 'Where is he? What is Argyle doing?'

'Judging by the look of him…' Gordon removed

Black's hand and looked at both man and monster. 'What he does best.'

---

THE DAMP SMELL of concrete and moss greeted Bermuda as he slowly regained consciousness, his head beating like a marching band. His eyes blinked a few times, all the dingy colours of his surroundings gradually coming into focus like someone was tuning an old television. He was lying on his front, and the ground beneath him was cold and solid, the concrete stretching all the way to crumbling walls.

Light danced across the room; a few torches had been lit and lodged in the gaps of the brickwork. Six shadows were hazily cast against the wall, and the hooded figures stood still and straight. As Bermuda pushed himself to his knees, he pressed a hand to the back of his skull, the warm claret he retrieved evidence of a head wound.

It hurt like hell.

As he looked around the room, he saw the six hulking creatures, their hoods pulled forward, their entire faces bathed in shadow. Outside, two more stood guard. In the centre of the room, the large stone table stood, the bloodstains still splattered across it. Bermuda knew where he was.

He was in the tomb at the top of the Necropolis.

And he was in deep shit.

'It's nice to see you again.'

The voice echoed from behind him, heavy footsteps soon following. He recognised the voice instantly.

Tobias.

'Yeah, well I wish it was mutual.' Bermuda did his best to keep the trembling from his voice. He didn't succeed.

'It's okay to be afraid, Agent Jones.' Tobias walked

slowly, his hands clasped behind his back. The skin hung slightly from his fingers. 'In fact, I would expect you to be.'

Bermuda took stock of his situation, knowing full well with his imminent concussion and the eight hooded bouncers that he had no chance of running.

All he could do was keep Tobias talking.

And hope.

'Who are you?'

'Ah, not the best disguise, was it?' Tobias stopped in front of Bermuda, his offset face twisted in a horrific grin. The skin dropped slightly beneath one eye, a darker grey skin evident. Behind the human teeth, a few sharper, greyer ones revealed themselves. 'It is a little tight.'

Bermuda watched in horror as Tobias reached a crooked hand to the back of his own head, and like a zip on the back of a dress, he pulled open his own skin. Like a peeled banana, the skin flopped over and dropped onto the floor like Bermuda's discarded laundry. The inside was a dark red, the remnants of Tobias's blood.

Human blood.

Bermuda's mind raced back to his first case, and he shuddered at the brutality of these creatures. Fear dragged him back to his reality. The creature before him was terrifying, his razor teeth pressed together in a vicious smile.

'I am General Mandrake. Commander of the Eight Warriors of the Legion. I have come to claim he who walks in both worlds.'

Mandrake's voice echoed powerfully, spoken with the poise of a high-ranking soldier. His face was a dirt grey, cracked with scales. The tip of his skull veered to a point and his eyes were like two yin-yang symbols pinned to the sides of his skull.

While not as tall as Argyle, Mandrake looked just as powerful, his thick arms surrounded by impressive metal that was clearly not of Earth. His metal breast plate shimmered in the firelight, with years of war plastered across it with dents and scuffs. At his side a circular blade hung, the handle embedded within the metal to ensure the entire circumference was used.

This was a creature of death.

Bermuda suddenly didn't feel like talking. Knowing that his final grains of sand were falling through the hourglass, his eyes searched the tomb, wanting to look anywhere but at the general before him. Mandrake noticed it and suddenly stood to attention, stomping his right foot on the floor.

'Legion. Recognise your commander.'

With military precision, all six creatures slid their hoods back and Bermuda's anxiety leapt forward. The two guarding the door slid back their hoods too, the rain gently rattling against their white masks. The flames illuminated their featureless faces, their lack of detail causing the hairs on Bermuda's neck to stand.

With precision movements, they reached up and one by one they removed their masks. Bermuda saw them, the creatures, for the first time. Their skin, a faded grey, had the sheen of marble. Their eyes, jet-black, stared at him unblinking. A horrible gurgling sound emanated from one of them, through a vertical slit where its mouth was.

These were clearly once feral.

Conditioned to be soldiers, willingly or otherwise.

Bermuda could sense the lust for his blood in the air; the piercing stare of twelve eyes shot through him and out the other side. All of them stood taller than Argyle, clad in all-black armour, a hood slung over one shoulder. All of them had the same rounded blade on their hip, a few had visible swords hanging off the other.

All of them would slay him in a heartbeat.

Bermuda swallowed hard, thinking of his daughter and the ever-decreasing likelihood that he would see her again.

Now that their masks were removed, Mandrake slowly walked a lap of the tomb, the rain sneaking in through the cracks in the walls and splattering against the Legion.

None of them even flinched.

As their commander inspected them, they remained focused on Bermuda, who slowly started to push himself up.

'I wouldn't stand,' Mandrake warned without turning. 'Never interrupt the inspection. They would take it as a sign of hostility and would remove your head without thinking.'

'Well, I'm feeling pretty fucking hostile right now.'

'Of course.' Mandrake returned to the centre of the tomb, a beam of moonlight shone through the rain and illuminated one side of his face, casting his monstrous shadow over Bermuda. He swung his foot forward planting it firmly against Bermuda's chest and sending him crashing back into the stone altar.

Bermuda groaned as he collided with the solid brick, his blood joining the collection.

One of the Legion gurgled, the saliva in his throat rotating like a washing machine. Mandrake shook his head. Bermuda looked up at him in confusion.

'He asked if he can have the honour of killing you when all this is done,' Mandrake said dismissively. 'I denied him.'

'Why's that then?' Bermuda sat up, his throbbing head trying its best to give in to gravity. 'One human enough for you?'

'Tobias was regrettable. It was quick, however.'

'Doesn't matter. It's still punishable by death.'

'Ah yes.' Mandrake's words were slightly stunted, like a tourist searching for the next word in a second language. 'These laws that have helped govern our worlds. Let me tell you, I have lived through over a century of the BTCO and your governance. What amazes me is that you do not know the name of my world, do you? You refer to it as "the Otherside". You don't know the name of my kind. You label us Others.' Mandrake squatted down, his bright eyes hooking onto Bermuda. 'You don't know how to deal with traitors. You hire them and call them Neithers. Never has a species been more arrogant than the species of man.'

'Is that what this is all about?' Bermuda asked, his eyes darting from one soldier to the other. 'Your hate for humanity? No offence, buddy, but I've already done this dance with Barnaby.'

Mandrake struck Bermuda with the back of his hand so fast that Bermuda was trying to figure out what hit him. The material of his glove was as coarse as sandpaper and Bermuda felt the skin ripped from his lip.

'Don't you dare speak his name,' Mandrake hissed. 'That creature was a treacherous disgrace who slaughtered a number of my soldiers. We spit on his memory. No, this is about taking matters into our own hands and fixing a mistake that your organisation has allowed to go on for too long.'

Bermuda slowly pushed himself back to his knees, his eyes resting on the engravings in the stone. 'Kevin Parker?'

Mandrake's laughed told him he was off. 'His name is not Kevin Parker. His name is Caleb. And how can he be a mistake when I was the one who let him free?'

'What?' The revelation hit Bermuda like a sledgehammer to the stomach.

'Caleb was imprisoned here in this very tomb. He was guarded by Tobias. It was a simple job – the restraints we placed on him were unbreakable, forged within the walls of my city. Your beloved BTCO allowed us to stash him here. Shackled in the dark. He was simply too dangerous to keep in our world.'

'Due to him looking human?' Bermuda asked, battling the striking pain in his skull for concentration.

'Due to him possessing one,' Mandrake explained. 'Caleb was a unique creature. When he first came to this world, he carried with him a latch stone. He was soon struck by a carriage, and as he lay dying, he discovered his ability to transfer himself to a human body. A gift, unique, and one never recorded before in the history between both worlds.

'Over time he learnt to control it, making the possession less destructive to the internal workings of you humans, and began to live as one of you. He killed a number of humans, but each one was a necessary step to perfecting the merge between two species. Years passed, and he became impossible to trace, your organisation failing to act. You didn't have your precious Oracles then. Eventually he possessed a gentleman called Kevin Parker from the land of America.'

Mandrake shook his head and stood straight again.

Bermuda wiped a trickle of blood that ran from his busted lip. 'Then what happened?'

'He did what you humans do. He fell in love. Her name was Cynthia Blaine. She was a dancer at an establishment he frequented. No one of consequence. Not then. They eventually became companions, and he lost himself to humanity. As time went by, he began to believe he existed as one of you. He was Caleb no more. They wished to begin a family, which required our interference. We took her from him.'

'You killed her,' Bermuda stated coldly. 'You killed her and locked him up and now he is fighting back.'

'Not quite. We couldn't bring him to our world, and as this was a decommissioned BTCO gateway, we negotiated an imprisonment. When he begged me for her return, I told him he would need to bring me the heart of every woman before he would get to hers again.' Mandrake's hideous grin appeared again. 'It was merely a threat. After nearly a century in the dark, I guess he ended up taking it literally. Confinement for that length of time could send even the strongest creature insane. Eventually he began to plead with me, begging me to release him so he could bring me the hearts of humans. It's quite sad when you think about it.'

Bermuda shook his head in disgust. 'So you let him off the leash?' He glared at the demon before him. 'Why?'

'We needed you here.' Mandrake's eyes glistened. 'We needed to put right the mistakes that your organisation failed to act upon. So I led my squadron to your world through the decommissioned gate and killed Tobias before he could report it. But I needed a reason for them to send you to me. Therefore I released Caleb, and one request to a dear friend later, here you are.'

Bermuda leant forward, challenging Mandrake to meet him at eye level. He accepted gleefully.

'Innocent women have died because of you. Because of the monster you created and because you set him free,' Bermuda snarled. 'You deserve the death that they will sentence you to.'

'We will end Caleb when we have finished our mission,' Mandrake stated. 'The blood of those women is on the hands of the BTCO and their failure to correct the mistake that will be corrected tonight.'

'What fucking mistake?' Bermuda yelled, angry as Mandrake turned his back to him.

'We cannot have one who walks in both worlds.'

'All of this is for me? To correct me? Well here I fucking am.'

Mandrake turned, his eyes alive with anger. 'Who said we were here for you?'

Suddenly it fell into place. Bermuda fell back on his

knees and stared into nothingness. He tried to recollect all the moments he had spent with Argyle, and was sure he had seen a latch stone – that Argyle needed assistance to serve in our world. As he ran through the archives of his mind, Mandrake stepped towards him, reaching down and lifting his head with a finger under the chin. His gloved touch was ice cold.

'Argyle betrayed us all when he took you through that gateway.'

Bermuda's brow furrowed with confusion.

'But we will have him back with us.'

'What do you mean?' Bermuda's brain darted in several directions, each one a different rail of thought. All he had were questions. 'Back through the gateway? With me? What the hell are you talking about?'

'Argyle was my second in command. He himself led this Legion to battle. Many have died by his watch. Whatever you see in him, whatever hero he is made out to be, there is a darkness that reached beyond any shadow of this world. Argyle is a soldier through to the core. He will have his orders from the BTCO to wait for our demands. We will trade your life for his, and once that mistake has been corrected, I will take my punishment with honour.'

Bermuda's head dropped in defeat. Surrounded by nine trained creatures of extreme power, he knew there was no escape. The inevitable would be a trade which would see his best friend undoubtedly murdered. The two worlds would keep spinning, with the loose ends tied up, and the truce would be one crack closer to breaking point.

Argyle would die in his place.

What hurt Bermuda the most was that he knew Argyle would do it willingly.

As the rain clattered around them, the high-pitched sound of metal piercing the air grew. Suddenly a metal chain shot through the dark opening of the tomb, a brutal spike attached to the end of it. It ripped through the neck of the Legion soldier nearest to the door, bursting out of the other side and splattering its neighbour in black blood. The spike split into four and then hooked into the skin. The life drained from the soldier's eyes.

In an instant, the Retriever hauled the soldier out of the tomb and into a dark, wet death.

The rest of the Legion turned, refitting their masks to their faces and drawing their weapons. Mandrake, experiencing fear for the first time, took two steps back, ensuring he was protected.

Bermuda, with blood dripping from his mouth, smirked.

'Oh, you boys are in trouble now.'

# TWENTY-EIGHT

THE MUSIC THUMPED out of the speakers, drowning out any notion of conversation, as more people squeezed into Waxy O'Connor's, a popular bar just round the corner from Queen Street Station. Six bars spread out over three floors, it was a regular drinking spot for many of Glasgow's police officers. However, tonight, as she sat near the bar, McAllister failed to register a single recognisable face.

Taking her spot on the quieter floor of the establishment, she marvelled at the grand building's gothic design, the interior fitting in seamlessly with the other large, demonic structures that framed the city. With bars and balconies made of carved oak, it truly was an impressive place to drink.

Judging by the sheer number of people downing shots and shouting over the music, she wasn't the only one who thought so. Finishing her glass of wine, she anxiously looked at her phone. Ethan had responded, yet she still wasn't sure how to take the first step.

A bridge needed building; she just didn't know how to lay the first foundation.

With Bermuda's words echoing in her ear, she refused the offer of a refill, instead ordering a soda water and lime. Besides, she was meant to be working. As the bartender sorted her drink, she caught a glimpse of herself in the mirror that ran around the back wall of the bar. Hidden between the reflections of the many bottles of different mixers, her face poked through. With her hair straightened and a bit of makeup on, she was impressed with how well she scrubbed up.

The rose-patterned dress she wore felt uncomfortable but clung nicely to her athletic frame.

Bermuda's other words also hung heavy in her mind, as he had marched out of the police station earlier that evening.

The roses.

Sure enough, once Fowler and Strachan had retired to his office, undoubtedly for an undeserved drink and a back slap, and Butler had calmed and left for the evening, McAllister had snuck into the incident room. Every victim had a link to a rose of some description. Nicole had worn a rose on her hair clip whereas Katie Steingold had met Parker while wearing a rose-covered shirt. Rosie Seeley had been a florist and CCTV had captured Kevin Parker in her store the day of her murder, admiring the very flower. Emma Mitchell, despite being butchered half-naked in the street, had been relieved of a rose-patterned dress in her living room. Lastly, Mika, the poor foreign exchange student, had a rose-covered and blood-splattered rucksack.

As she had run through the case files, she had sat back in amazement. Staring at the picture of Kevin Parker from the nineteen twenties, she had zeroed in on the stunning woman beside him.

She too, wore a dress adorned with roses.

None of it made sense, but she knew that Bermuda was

right. The man who had been kicked off the case for interfering had done what none of her team could.

He had found a link.

She had to admit, it was a loose one, but with another woman sure to be found dead in the morning, there were no better options. Pushing the folders aside, she had rushed home, rounded up all the empty wine bottles and binned them, and then told herself it was time to change.

It was time to control what she could.

Then, after a quick shower, she had got ready, easing her slender frame into the dress she had worn to Ethan's sister's wedding three years before.

Ethan.

She shook her estranged husband from her mind, promising herself she would take that step the moment she put Parker behind bars. She was still slightly unsure what he was, wanting to look beyond reason and science to admit to this other world. She wanted to believe.

One thing she knew: she trusted Bermuda.

Despite his propensity to irritate, she felt a genuine bond with him. Usually, two broken pieces tend to fit together somehow.

As the music thumped from the floor beneath, McAllister felt her chair rise with the beat. As she gently sipped her non-alcoholic drink, her eyes lit up. Quickly she grabbed her phone, flicking through it quickly and pressing dial.

Her gaze locked on.

Kevin Parker was sat across the bar.

After several rings, she tutted as Bermuda's bored voicemail message piped through. Staring at a violent murderer, she waited for the beep.

'Hey, it's McAllister. I reviewed the files and all of our victims were either drinking here at Waxy's or nearby. Rosie's flower shop is also on a surrounding street.' She looked up; Parker hadn't noticed her. Yet. 'Anyway, I am at Waxy's. Roses on. Parker is here. I am going to distract him. Get here as soon as possible.'

McAllister stopped speaking as Parker turned and their eyes locked. She froze, captured by the genuine beauty of his face and also the terror. His eyes were dark and drilled holes through her skull as if looking right through her.

She hung up the phone, sliding it into her bag. She looked back, and he offered her a warm smile, one she admitted would be hard to resist.

As the music shook the building, Kevin Parker lifted himself from his stool and walked across the bar towards her, a confidence to his walk and a hidden, murderous menace that only she knew of.

She pulled her dress down, ironing out the creases and quickly fluffing her hair. Nerves pulsed through her as if she was experiencing her first kiss all over again.

As the murderous creature from another world took the seat next to her, she wished upon a god she had long since given up on that Bermuda checked his phone soon.

---

WITH THE INCREASING force of the rainfall, the wind howled through the tombstones of the Necropolis. Slowly, each member of the Legion filtered out of the tomb in single file, their hands to their weapons. They walked with regimented precision, splitting into equal paths that fanned out around the structure and were slowly enveloped in the darkness. One of the creatures standing guard at the door joined as six separate entities entered the darkness of the Necropolis.

One remained guarding the door, its weapon drawn and its eyes wide and searching. Inside, Mandrake stood calmly, hands behind his back as he waited for Argyle to be defeated swiftly.

None of the creatures had even acknowledged the death of their own. Bermuda shivered in the cold as he struggled to his feet, the chill of the night biting at him with razor teeth. His skull trembled with pain as he reached for the top of the altar, trying to lift himself silently.

Argyle was out there somewhere, outnumbered but willing to fight to save Bermuda's life. Bermuda, much to his own surprise, found himself willing to fight for Argyle's life too.

Willing to die for his friend.

Mandrake took a few steps towards the tomb wall, the bricks stacked precariously as they lost their fight with Father Time. The wind whistled through the cracks as he slowly slid his hand from its armoured glove. With an uncovered finger, he dabbed at the blood of his soldier that painted the wall.

Bermuda pulled himself to his feet.

'I would stay down if I were you.' Mandrake didn't turn. 'I will turn you over alive, but I said nothing about mobile.'

Bermuda froze.

Mandrake turned, a horrifying grin across his scaled face.

'Argyle will kill them. You know that, right?'

'I think it's entirely possible,' Mandrake agreed, his hands returning behind his straight back. 'Yet I know Argyle better than you and it's his appreciation for life that will kill him. The Legion are many. They do not cry for a fallen comrade. They will surround him and he will kneel by their swords.'

'Or they will die by his,' Bermuda countered.

'Time will tell. However, you should be worried,

Bermuda. Argyle has broken his rank and defied his orders. Without a negotiation, your life now holds little value.'

With the threat looming, Bermuda suddenly made a dash for the doorway. In an instant, he felt the cold grip of Mandrake lock onto his arm like a clamp. Without his glove, the Otherside pulsed from Bermuda's body into his fingertips. Mandrake's eyes widened with fury.

'You are infected,' he uttered. 'You belong to my world.'

'Get off me.'

Before Bermuda could continue, he found himself hurled across the tomb and colliding with the wall for the second time that week. His spine cracked against the hard stone, the wind fleeing his body rapidly.

Mandrake slowly eased the glove back over his hand, his face a mask of disgust, as if he had just used it to unclog a toilet. 'Like Argyle you walk in both worlds, and like Argyle you shall be executed.'

Mandrake took a few measured steps towards Bermuda as he writhed on the floor, his hand pressed against the small of his back. Mandrake smirked at the pathetic human before him. While his squadron hunted one mistake and sent him to the afterlife, he would do the same with another.

He stepped forward again.

Bermuda leapt forward.

Catching Mandrake off balance, Bermuda launched his entire body weight into the murderous general, his shoulder catching him in the stomach below the breast-plate. Mandrake stumbled back, growling like a rabid dog, but his mighty frame collided with the fragile stone wall. It collapsed, the thick bricks falling on top of him, slamming him to the hard ground. He roared in pain as the heavy stone toppled, the weight growing and crushing his legs to dust. Bermuda scurried back on his hands and feet, just out of arm's length as Mandrake reached and clawed for him, his fangs gnashing wildly.

After a few moments, the noise stopped. Bermuda sat a few feet from the trapped soldier, their eyes locked. The flames from the torch fizzled out as the rain burst through the gaping hole of the tomb. It sizzled gently, and a thin line of smoke washed away into the darkness.

Mandrake went to speak, but was instantly shut down by the full force of Bermuda's foot to the face.

'Fuck you,' Bermuda spat angrily before slowly easing himself to his feet. The base of his spine felt like it was on fire and he limped to the exit, stumbling over the threshold and onto the thick mud.

Instantly the guard turned, its face a sheet of white, and it marched towards him, drawing its sword from the sheath that swung from its belt.

Bermuda tried to push himself from his knees, but the mud had engulfed his legs like thick, gooey fingers holding him in place.

He heard the blade freed from its holster, the moon bouncing from its clean steel like a floodlight.

The deathly pale face stayed locked on him as the blade was risen.

The soldier brought it down with full force.

Argyle's blade deflected the blow before Argyle launched a kick to the soldier's chest, sending him back a few steps. The creature growled beneath its mask before lunging forward, swinging its sword with deathly precision. Argyle leant back, the blade swinging just above his chest, before he spun on his foot and flicked his own blade across the calf of his opponent.

A spray of black shot up like a fountain, and the creature barked in pain as it dropped to one knee. Before another sound came from its gruesome mouth, Argyle spun his sword expertly before driving it down two-handed into the creature's neck, severing its spinal cord and killing it instantly.

Bermuda watched wide-eyed, having never seen Argyle kill with such brutality before. Without flinching, his partner drew his blade up with one hand, letting his former comrade slump lifelessly into the mud. As the sword swung from his powerful mitt, Argyle turned to Bermuda and offered him his other.

'Are you hurt?'

'I'm fine, Big Guy.' Bermuda smiled as he took the offer, his partner helping him to his feet and once again saving his life. 'It's good to see you.'

'You too.'

They shared a smile. Bermuda then looked past Argyle to the dead creature that was slowly being surrounded by a puddle of black blood. It was as if Argyle had struck oil.

Bermuda pointed at the body. 'By the way, that was awesome.'

Suddenly, the sound of twirling metal picked up in volume and Argyle dove forward, dragging Bermuda to the ground with him. As they fell to the ground, a razor disc cut through the air a foot above them.

It would have decapitated Bermuda.

As they hit the ground, Argyle ushered his scared partner to move, the two of them scrambling to their feet and shuffling through the shadows and into the darkness of the graveyard. As they passed a few rows of tombstones, they heard footsteps approach the dead body. A loud roar echoed through the grounds, shaking the trees. They reached a small yet sharp drop of about six feet, with Argyle helping his partner down. They leant back against the muddy wall, cloaking themselves in darkness. Mandrake's voice bellowed from the broken building at the top of the hill, his words lost to Bermuda.

Not to Argyle.

'He is demanding our heads,' Argyle translated as Bermuda fished his phone from his pocket.

'I figured.'

He had several messages and missed calls, the majority from Montgomery Black and all of them the same message just at various stages of anger. With the battery clinging valiantly to life, Bermuda raised his phone to his ear as he listened to his voicemail.

It was McAllister.

*'Hey, it's McAllister. I reviewed the files and all of our victims were either drinking here at Waxy's or nearby. Rosie's flower shop is also on a surrounding street. Anyway, I am at Waxy's. Roses on. Parker is here. I am going to distract him. Get here as soon as possible.'*

'Fuck!'

'Fuck?' Argyle echoed.

'It's Sam.'

Argyle looked blank.

'Detective McAllister. She called me an hour ago. She's with Parker.'

'I will distract them. You go to her.' Argyle drew his sword again.

Bermuda shoved him angrily. 'No. Come with me.'

'I must stay.'

'But you will die, Argyle.' Bermuda felt a lump growing in his throat. 'You have to come with me.'

'This is my fight, Bermuda. I will not run from it. These creatures have killed humans to face me. Those deaths will not be for nothing.'

Bermuda raised both hands to his head, interlocking his fingers amongst his wet hair. He had to go – McAllister was in serious danger.

Argyle reached out his hand and placed it on Bermuda's shoulder. 'I bet you ten pounds I will see you again.'

Bermuda smirked, Argyle turning his own joke against him and once again proving to him that he was more than a monster. Whatever he was, Bermuda knew he was the best man he knew.

His best friend.

'I will gladly pay you when I do.'

Argyle placed a fist on his chest as a sign of respect and Bermuda nodded. Argyle lifted his sword and in one leap cleared the six-foot back onto the tier above and, keeping low to the ground, moved swiftly through the cold. A moment later he spun the Legion soldier around, and with one swift slice of his sword, slit its throat clean open.

Mandrake yelled another order and suddenly all the attention was back to the top of the hill. Argyle raced into the darkness, knowing he would be hunted by the five remaining Others who knew nothing but to kill.

With the coast clear, Bermuda began descending the hill as quickly as he could, navigating through the fields of death, knowing they were about to be sprinkled with even more.

As Argyle charged into the darkness to battle monsters, Bermuda made his way through the gate, covered in mud and hoping he wasn't too late to stop a different monster entirely.

# TWENTY-NINE

ARGYLE RESTED ON HIS HAUNCHES, his blade held steadily over his shoulder. Ducked behind a large tombstone, he used the monument of death to plot another. The decades of training at the hand of Mandrake were flooding back to him, the perfection he expected from his soldiers. Argyle knew what was expected of them, each member of the Legion.

They were not an army.

They were a death squad.

Argyle knew – he had led them to slaughter many, and he regretted every life that fell at his command. Mandrake, with his lust for blood, never batted an eyelid. The remaining five of those stalking him had seen horrors that would give even those of his world nightmares. They had trekked the dark fields for decades, eventually landing at the gates of his city.

They were as feral as the Other Argyle had slain on that momentous land ship in London.

Mandrake had weaponised them.

Their loyalty was as fierce as their combat. There was

no regard for life, be it their opposition's or their own. They were the perfect squadron.

They were the eight.

Now reduced to five.

Argyle held his breath, allowing the rain to run down his dark face and drip onto his blade, the water joining the black blood that ran up the steel like a tribal tattoo. As Argyle drew inwards, the sound of each drop bouncing off his sword echoed through his skull. The wind howled like a wolf on a full moon.

The crunch of grass underfoot drew his attention.

Zeroing in, he estimated the distance and time he had before the soldier was within reach.

After slitting the throat of the soldier to draw them back to the top of the Necropolis, he had rushed in the direction of the fallen, knowing the soldiers' flanking patterns. They would have regrouped at the corpse and would slice the Necropolis into four equal quarters and sweep the entire ground looking for him. One of them would guard Mandrake. From the glimpse Argyle had taken when executing the guard, the general was incapacitated and seriously wounded.

He would wait.

Another crunch as the soldier approached, its white-clad face slowly sweeping from left to right, looking for any sign of life. In both hands it clasped the circular blades, ready to end Argyle's life without hesitation.

One more step.

Argyle spun and rolled over the tombstones, thrusting a heavy foot forward and catching the Other by surprise with a clubbing boot to the chest. It stumbled back two steps before drawing its fists up, the razor wrap shimmering in the moonlight. Argyle drew his sword and the two soldiers took a moment to acknowledge their duel.

To the death.

The creature swung fists like a champion boxer, the blades slicing the falling raindrops and narrowly missing Argyle as he ducked and weaved. Argyle ducked a fast right, but failed to spin in time as the left hook sent the blade into his arm, slicing the skin across his bicep. Without flinching he spun back, blocking the next blow with the solid band that wrapped his wrist. Deflecting the strike, Argyle swung his sword, the blade slicing through the flesh and bone of the soldier's wrist like it was hot butter.

The creature gurgled as a stream of thick, black blood chased after its severed hand before it tried to swing its remaining fist.

But it too was severed from its arm.

A sickening dark spray splattered its white mask, but before it could muster another noise, Argyle drew the sword back and lunged, plunging the steel through the armour and into the creature's chest. Twisting the blade, he yanked it back, watching the creature drop to its knees, its life rapidly leaving it.

Now reduced to four.

Argyle, a few tiers down and hundreds of tombstones from the tomb, bent down and pulled the severed hand from one of the round blades, impressed by the craftsmanship. The edge was dangerously sharp – the blood oozing down his arm would testify to that. Hunching down to keep low, Argyle ran quickly through the mud, the pelting rain, and the darkness. He circled the vast, towered grounds that housed centuries of death.

His steps were silent.

Ahead and to the left, another faceless member of the Legion stalked the graveyard, a sense of death in the air. Without breaking stride, Argyle whipped the circular blade through the air, the metal spinning like a propeller as it sliced through the night sky before bedding into the soldier's neck. Severing an artery, the soldier's jet-black blood pumped down its chest like a shadow.

As he approached, Argyle spun his blade from his back, and in one swift motion disembowelled the soldier. He moved on, not witnessing its innards fall to the ground but hearing the squelch as its intestines hit the mud.

The body followed swiftly after.

Another Legion fallen.

Now reduced to three.

As he rounded another corner, Argyle stopped behind a large tree. The leaves had long since deserted and the jagged branches reached for the sky like broken fingers. Argyle scouted the area. The faint outline of his next adversary was shuffling slowly between the protruding stones. Argyle was trained for combat, he knew that this was what he was trained to be.

But the feeling in his chest wasn't adrenaline or the thrill of the battle, the feelings he was ordered to feel to be a true soldier.

What he felt was hate.

Hate for the Legion.

Hate for the vile commander who lay prone in his broken fortress.

Hate for what they had forced him to be all those years.

Suddenly, a searing pain overpowered his mind, and a burning roared from his side as the jagged blade sliced through his armour. The masked soldier pulled it back harshly, ripping through Argyle's muscles and skin, the pain causing Argyle to stumble forward, his hands grasping at the gaping hole in his hip. The creature stepped forward, wielding its sword with both hands and slashing diagonally for Argyle, who dove and rolled just beyond its reach.

With another lunge, the soldier thrust its blade downwards, missing Argyle as he spun away, its blade plunging into the deep mud. Wrenching at the handle like a demonic King Arthur, the soldier reached for its side blade in vain. Argyle had already launched his blade with as much power as he could muster, hurling it through the air like a spear. Covering the short distance between them in no time, his sword ripped through the chest of the Other, the propulsion sending it blasting through its spine and bedding into the mud behind it.

Argyle could see the tomb through the gaping chasm in the creature's chest as it fell forward, collapsing on its own blade and bleeding out within seconds.

Argyle could feel his own blood pouring down his leg.

It would hinder him.

But it would heal.

Now reduced to two.

Yanking his sword from the mud with one forceful wrench, Argyle slowly limped up the slight incline, the broken walls of the tomb in his sight. At the door to the fallen building, the guard had been joined by his final comrade, the two soldiers putting on one final, united stand.

It was to the death.

Argyle knew that there was a good chance he would die at the top of this hill, overlooking acres of death. But he would face it like a true soldier, with pride in his heart and death on his mind.

He would fight to the end.

Whatever the end was.

As he approached the final row of tombstones before the entrance, he scouted the two soldiers. Both of them towered over him, their broad frames wrapped in armour. Their white masks hid their dark eyes, but Argyle knew they were watching.

Waiting.

Argyle pressed a hand to his hip; it returned dripping with blood.

Like Parker holding a heart.

Argyle's mind immediately jumped to Bermuda, his partner who had run willingly towards that murderous creature. The one that had left him for dead on this very hill.

Parker would kill Bermuda.

That much was certain.

With his partner's safety now fresh in his mind, Argyle took one deep breath, closing his eyes and pushing all the anger and pain from his body. He thought of his partner, his only friend in the world.

Bermuda needed him.

Ottoway's voice filtered into his mind, reminding him of his primary objective.

Protect Bermuda at all costs.

Argyle's eyes shot open. His stare was of pure focus. Every raindrop that struck the earth clapped loudly like thunder. Every slight twitch of the Legion soldiers rumbled through the air like sonar as his senses heightened.

His mind cleared of everything except death.

Argyle moved.

Whipping round the final tombstone, he instantly shot his Retriever, the blade snaking through the cold air and shattering the shin of the nearest soldier. The chain tightened as the blade imbedded into the bone, and Argyle wrenched it back like a fisherman with a prize catch. With its other foot planted in the mud, the soldier slid forward like a struggling gymnast, its legs split open. Its sword was still in its hand, and Argyle ran and swiftly kicked the handle, the blade flipping into the air, while he simultaneously swung his own blade at waist height.

The blade cleanly took off the soldier's head, the white mask falling from its face as it bounced onto the mud.

Now reduced to one.

Catching the other sword in the air, Argyle spun under the swinging blade of the final guard before planting the sword in its chest. He quickly followed it with his own blade, the two swords stacked atop one another and sticking out of the dying soldier's chest like a terrifying dartboard. Grabbing both handles, Argyle let out a roar of anger as he swiftly pulled them outwards, slicing the soldier open, its head and shoulders falling backwards as its body flopped to the ground.

They were the Legion.

They were no more.

Stood in the rain with the two swords held down by his side, Argyle took a moment to catch his breath. Killing his own kind had always weighed heavy on his mind; the banishments he recited as he collected their essences and sent them back to his world were always trying.

This was different.

He would not honour any of those fallen.

Both worlds were better with them gone.

The blood pumped out of the hole in his side and the slice across his arm. The rest of his armour was splattered with the blood of the deceased.

All eight of them.

The sound of brick colliding with brick brought him back and Argyle dropped the second blade, returning his own to his back holster with an expert spin. With careful, measured steps, he approached the doorway to the tomb like an avenging angel of death.

Mandrake, trying his best to remove the collapsed wall from his body, looked up with the resignation Argyle had seen at many an execution.

His former commander had removed some of the bricks, but Argyle could see the damage. His legs had been flattened, the bone to dust, the muscle to paste.

Mandrake would never walk again.

The two soldiers looked at each other for a moment before Mandrake's face turned into a hideous snarl.

'Do it!' he demanded, tilting his head back and presenting his neck.

'Your men are dead.' Argyle spoke softly. 'You are relieved of your command. You will be tried for your crimes against both human and Other, and you will be held to your punishment.'

'Other?' Mandrake spat at Argyle. 'They even have you saying it? You truly are a disgrace.'

Argyle ignored him and continued. 'For your mutiny of your council, you will be tried for treason. For your murder of Tobias Hendry, you will be tried for murdering a human. Punishable by death.'

'Kill me then.' Mandrake again tilted his head. 'Go on, do it. Kill me, you coward.'

Argyle drew his blade and held it to Mandrake's face. The crippled commander tensed, ready for the eternal blackness. The blade sliced into the scales on his cheek, three vertical lines that bore the legacy of treachery.

The very scar that Barnaby had worn.

'You will wear that mark for our kind to know what you did,' Argyle said, slowly returning the sword to his spine. 'You will be put to death, but not by me. It is not my duty and you are not mine to kill.'

Argyle turned and headed for the door.

'But you killed a human too,' Mandrake snapped after him.

Argyle stopped and turned. 'Your lies will not save you, Mandrake.' Argyle dropped the rank. 'I am sworn to protect these humans, and I will do so with my life.'

'You killed her. You may not have held the sword, but it was because of you that we had to.' Mandrake spoke with a sickening pleasure. 'We didn't think you would survive.'

'Survive what?' Argyle dropped to one knee, grabbing his former commander by the neck of his armour. 'Who did you kill?'

'Cynthia.' Mandrake smirked. 'Cynthia Blaine.'

'Cynthia Blaine? Who is she?'

The entire Necropolis froze.

'Your mother.'

Argyle released Mandrake and stood, staring at the brick wall but seeing nothing. Raised in the dark barracks of Healund, he knew nothing of his lineage. Only that his appearance and very existence was despised by the other soldiers.

By every Other he had ever come across. Mandrake could see him trying to connect the dots and spoke with eagerness.

'Your mother was human, Argyle. She is the one that Caleb seeks. We took her when she fell pregnant – the first ever human to be impregnated by one of our own. He may have been wearing a human body, but what he put inside her was not. His seed was of our world. Our kind.'

'No,' Argyle uttered under his breath, his world slowly dissolving, the drab colours of his surroundings merging into one.

'We couldn't allow a hybrid to be born,' Mandrake continued. 'A cross-species would lead to a revolution, the chance to merge both worlds that some have taken to extremes. Like Barnaby. There would be several more like him, believing that the worlds could be combined. We took Cynthia through the threshold, back to Healund. Our atmosphere turned her to ash within seconds. But you survived. From the ashes, you were born.'

'You let my mother die?' Argyle spoke through gritted teeth.

'We had to protect our species. What would you know? You fight for just the humans. We took you and decided to train you, to see what you would become, if we could harness your unique structure. You look more human than any of us. You fought with the ferocity of our fathers. But you could do what none of us could. You could walk in both worlds. You didn't need one of these.'

Mandrake ripped the dark green emerald from his armour and threw the latch stone at Argyle. It bounced off his breast plate and clattered in a dark corner.

'You were our greatest soldier, Argyle. But you turned on us. You sided with the humans without knowing what you truly were.' Mandrake shook his head in sorrow. 'So for that, I am glad I killed your mother.'

Argyle swung a boot, the metal plating knocking out three of Mandrake's teeth.

The defeated former general chuckled. 'As for your father, he never got over it. I kept him chained in here like an animal. His mind left a long time ago, Argyle. The idea grew like a seed into a tree of obsession. He will not stop. He will kill again and again. All of your precious humans. Just like your mother.'

Another vicious kick to the face, and this time a spray of blood shot from Mandrake's mouth. He sloshed some of it round before spitting it at Argyle.

'He will kill your friend, then as many as you let him. Your father, the murderer. Your mother, the human whore.' Mandrake sneered. 'The shame that will hang from you will be heavy.'

Argyle leant down, a mere few inches from his fallen foe's face. 'I will send them to collect you and will watch with joy when they put you to death.'

Mandrake's cockiness fell.

'You raised me to kill, to be a weapon that I will no longer be. Whatever fate awaits me, I will face it with the conviction that a soldier carries. But I will stop him.'

Argyle stood, towering over the entire Legion, their

blood and limbs littering the famous graveyard. Argyle turned, heading for the door and back to the town, to find and protect Bermuda and bring his own father to justice.

As he stepped through the door, he stopped one final time as Mandrake's voice echoed after him.

'There is only one way to stop him. You know that as well as I do.'

Argyle grimaced, the thought of agreeing with the vulgar creature sickening him. He marched through the anarchy of his battle, the severed corpses of the Legion littering his path to the streets below.

The entire way to the gate, Argyle gritted his teeth with frustration, ignoring his handiwork as he battled the thought that burrowed into his skull like a ravenous termite.

Mandrake was right.

There was only one way for this to end.

# THIRTY

WHEN BERMUDA REACHED the gates of the Necropolis, he stopped. Casting a glance back towards the dark hill, he heard the clanging of metal. Argyle was fighting a heavily trained army to the death.

For him.

For humanity.

Fighting every urge to turn back and run headlong into a brutal slaying, he pushed through the wet metal bars and felt the hard surface beneath his feet. The Necropolis had been churned up by the downpour, the mud welcoming each step and the ground doing its level best to swallow him.

He looked like he had dived into a mud bath. The thick, wet earth clung to his clothes. It dotted his face and thick clumps had engulfed his hair. Turning towards the city, he ran without caring. A few passers-by stepped carefully aside as this crazed, mud-covered man sprinted past. Bermuda focused ahead once again commending himself for giving up smoking.

He still wished for a cyclist to approach like the previous evening, but he carried on. As he dashed through the rain, the bright lights of the gothic city soon emerged, beckoning him to the case's conclusion.

It would end tonight.

Bermuda hoped Argyle was okay, refusing to accept that they had experienced their final goodbye. He turned down the hill where the cars had crashed that fateful night. There was no traffic and Bermuda ran in the middle of the road, pushing through the pain barrier.

His lip had stopped bleeding, but the dirt had caused it to swell.

His spine shook, the bones bruised after colliding with the wall again.

He would heal, he told himself.

He always healed.

Turning onto High Street, Bermuda pushed forward. Soon he would be on George Street, which would lead him straight to the city centre. Someone would know where the bar was. As his breathing became heavier, Bermuda hoped to God he wasn't too late.

After almost a mile, he stopped outside the front of Queen Street Station, hunched over with hands on his knees. Doing his best to reclaim his breath, he felt the bitterness of the night nip at his skin like a playful puppy. He looked around, reminded of the confrontation he had had with Parker in this very spot.

The hard crack of the concrete on his skull.

The moment he thought he would die.

Argyle saving him at the last second.

As he controlled his breathing, Bermuda asked a young couple walking by where Waxy O'Connor's was. Understandably cautious due to his appearance, the girl stepped away. The young man pointed over his shoulder and Bermuda offered a half-hearted thanks before he pushed himself forward again, racing as fast as he could to save McAllister's life.

MCALLISTER HAD SAT SMILING for the entire evening, listening to the soothing voice of Kevin Parker. The more she studied him, the more alien he appeared. He seemed slightly off beat as if his movements were too sharp. His words were a struggle at times, overlapping each other as he struggled for cohesion.

He was not human.

McAllister had played along, smiling beautifully and chuckling at his attempts at humour. Every second felt like an hour, the company of a killer causing her spine to tingle like it was her own personal ski slope. When he placed his cold fingers on her arm, every hair stood to attention.

Her stomach turned, and she was almost sick.

Parker didn't seem to notice, his dark eyes locking onto hers. His gaze was almost hypnotic and McAllister understood the attraction the women felt. As he ordered another drink, she checked her phone.

Nothing from Bermuda.

She was in the process of texting Butler when Parker turned back to her, his eyes flicking to her phone.

'Who are you contacting?' His voice was calm, yet oozed menace. McAllister suddenly wished they were in the noisier bar.

'No one.'

Unconvinced, Parker snatched the phone and read the screen. The plea to Butler was half written, her request for him to bring backup causing Parker's jaw to tighten. Closing his eyes, he took a deep breath.

He squeezed.

The phone shattered in his hand, causing McAllister to jump and a few neighbours to turn with interest. Through gritted teeth, he spoke.

'You will leave with me right now.' Parker met her terrified gaze with his own. 'Or I will butcher these people.'

'Look. Just come with me. I can help you.'

Parker laughed, stepping off his stool and suddenly seeming a lot more imposing. 'You know who I am and what I must do.'

He looked to the door where a bouncer had noticed his intimidation. The burly man, wearing an ill-fitting black shirt, bounded across the bar, the lights reflecting off his shiny bald head. As he approached, he ignored McAllister's shake of the head.

'I think you should be leaving, pal.' The bouncer spoke threateningly, his mouth a few inches from Parker's ear. Parker moved so fast he was a blur.

Reaching the back of the man's skull, he drew it down ferociously, shattering the man's jaw against the bar. The customers gasped and screamed, all of them leaping from their seats and backing away. The bouncer dropped to the floor, a collection of his teeth falling into the pool of blood. Parker gently rested his foot on the back of his head.

'I will not ask you again.'

McAllister held her hands up to placate him, slowly rising from her stool. Parker's eyes never left her as she stood, collecting her bag and slowly heading towards the exit. Two more bouncers rushed through the door to the bar, but stopped as they saw their damaged colleague. Parker stared at them, the two men allowing them to leave and following a few steps behind to ensure the offender left the premises.

Then he would be the city's problem.

They stepped out into the street, the cold wrapping itself around McAllister's bare shoulders and shaking her to her core. Parker pressed his palm on the small of her back, ushering her to the left, towards a dark, secluded street. A few patrons of Waxy's stood in the roped-off area, clouds of smoke surrounding their curious gaze. The sound of her heels echoed as they marched past a closed Starbucks, the chairs all upturned and shrouded in darkness. They turned left at the NatWest, onto a small road that was framed by Forbidden Planet and the back gates of many establishments. Parker stopped, his hand clasping on her shoulder and spinning her to him.

His eye spilled into the iris, turning it black.

'You shall be the final one.' He tilted his head slightly. 'They promised me.'

'Who promised you?' she managed, her voice escaping her through fear.

'The darkness. The voice.' Parker's mind had been shredded – years of the stone walls and one repeated promise. 'You will bring her back for me.'

McAllister tried to call for help, but the dark street offered the perfect cover. The rain had sent the majority of the public home to their warm homes and rich lives. McAllister felt the cold touch of loneliness; the first steps to mending her life with Ethan would be in vain. Parker shoved her against the wall, pinning her by the shoulder under his powerful hand.

'SAM?!' echoed through the night sky.

McAllister and Parker both turned, the voice echoing up the street in the direction from which they had just walked. With the distant thumping of Waxy's behind him, Bermuda burst onto the street, his cheeks red, his lungs clutching at as much breath as possible.

'Bermuda!' she screamed, only for Parker to slam her harder against the stone, driving the air from her and then wrapping his hand over her mouth.

'Bermuda,' Parker repeated, remembering his promise. Bermuda would die.

Taking calm and measured steps, Bermuda slowly approached, his hand out as a sign of submission.

'Caleb,' Bermuda said carefully. 'Caleb – that is your name.'

Parker/Caleb shook his head as if wrestling with a painful memory, the confusion spreading across his face like a virus. His hand pressed harder against McAllister's face, slowly crushing her head to the wall. Her eyes screamed for help as he restricted her throat.

'Caleb, let her go,' Bermuda demanded, another cautious step closer.

'My name is Kevin. It's Kevin. It's Kevin,' Caleb said, staring into the rain-soaked reflection of the nearest car mirror. 'I must take her.'

'Let her go, Caleb. It's over.'

'One more. I was promised.'

'There is no promise. There is no return.' Despite all the slain, innocent women, Bermuda felt a small speck of sympathy for the confused creature. 'You have been gone a long time, Caleb. It's time to stop and go home.'

Parker drew his lips back, his teeth grinding together in agony. His eyes were alive with fury, the confusion wrapping around him like a turban.

'I will kill you, Bermuda.' He then turned back to McAllister, blood slowly trickling from the side of her head. 'But after I take what I need.'

Every muscle in Bermuda's body tensed, knowing that the following assault was going to push his pain threshold beyond anything he had ever experienced.

But maybe, with the added essence of the Otherside pumping through his veins, he might stand a chance at survival.

Parker reached back his hand, primed and ready to snatch McAllister's still-beating life from her chest.

Bermuda called out through the rain. 'Cynthia is dead.'

Parker instantly let go of McAllister and turned, his

suit clinging to his body. The wet hair fanned across his forehead as his brow furrowed. He marched towards Bermuda. 'She will be returned to me.'

'She is dead, Caleb. She has been this whole time.'

'Liar!' Parker furiously swung his arm, the back of his hand crashing into Bermuda's jaw and rocking him sideways. Bermuda stumbled back and instantly Parker lunged, driving a knee into his gut before ramming the same knee into Bermuda's nose. Blood burst out of both nostrils as he shattered the bridge before grabbing the back of Bermuda's coat and ramming him into the nearest car. Bermuda's head shattered the glass window, the shards clattering to the wet pavement along with him. Bermuda coughed harshly, drew up, and then spat blood that was instantly washed away by the downpour. Bermuda pulled himself forward on his forearms, then slowly began to push himself to his knees.

Parker connected with a vicious kick to the side, lifting Bermuda off the ground and slamming his spine into the same car, the alarm screeching in time with its orange flashing light. Parker hauled Bermuda up by the lapels of his coat before casually tossing him across the bonnet, watching with glee as the interfering man clattered across the metal and collapsed hard on the concrete.

Parker would beat him to death.

And he would enjoy every moment of it.

McAllister had regained her composure on the side of the street and dashed back towards any sign of life, bumping into a few drunken friends who at first offered her nothing but an inappropriate comment. When the two men saw the bleeding, followed by her police badge, they handed her their phone.

She called for backup.

Then for an ambulance.

In the street, a few passers-by watched in horror as a

blood-soaked Bermuda was thrown across the street and landed on the windscreen of a parked car. It screeched to life, its alarm singing wildly into the night sky. The screen burst, flaring out into a thousand cracks as Bermuda rolled over and collapsed onto the hard pavement. His tried to crawl, hearing the approaching click of Parker's shoes.

Parker stepped in front of him, Bermuda trying to best to peer through his swollen eyes that pulsated around his blood-drenched face.

'You will die tonight.'

Parker then stamped with all his might, the heel of his expensive shoe crushing every bone in Bermuda's left hand. Bermuda yelled in pain before receiving another firm kick to the mouth.

As he rolled onto his front, his left hand flopped like a bag of loose pencil shavings. The pain caused all energy to leave him.

This was over.

With his last moments arriving, he swivelled his head and shot a glance through the downpour to confirm that McAllister had gone.

She had.

In the distance, he could hear the wailing of sirens, their welcome sound just a little too late. Parker placed the sole of his shoe onto the back of Bermuda's head, holding him in place. With the fight beaten out of him, Bermuda felt his head being gently pressed to the floor. With his bones broken and blood sprayed all over the street, Bermuda closed his eyes.

A vision of Chloe flashed before him.

He closed his eyes.

Parker slammed his foot down.

The sound of metal piercing flesh and a roar of agony above caused Bermuda's eyes to flash open. As he did, he saw the spike of the Retriever shunted out of the side of

Parker's leg before he was hoisted away. Parker stumbled to the ground, the bone shattering as the chain retracted, dragging him like a plough across the harsh concrete. The Retriever ripped back through the leg, its chain snaking back across the wet floor until it leapt up and took its rightful place on the golden slate that adorned Argyle's arm.

Bermuda's vision was blurred, a cocktail of bruising, blood, and rainwater all stifling his view, the images burning and stinging with no clarity.

Parker pushed himself to his knees, kneeling in the rain. Argyle marched towards him, the sudden arrival of Montgomery Black and Vincent doing little to slow him down.

A burst of blue light filled the street, two police cars blocking off either entrance as the officers bundled out and took their positions. McAllister ran to the front of them, her dress soaked through and tears running down her face.

Bermuda lay broken and motionless.

Parker knelt a mere ten feet away from him.

Black yelled for Argyle to stop, the crowd regarding him as insane. The words echoed down the street; Bermuda heard them ringing but saw them ignored.

Argyle marched across the urban battlefield, splashing the blood that pooled from both men. Ignoring the fallen killer, Argyle dropped to one knee beside his partner, reaching out a caring hand and placing it gently on his shoulder.

'You owe me ten pounds,' he said softly.

Bermuda smiled, but instantly groaned in pain.

'Sadly, this is goodbye.'

Bermuda fought for words, but the blood in his throat choked him. He watched through his heartbreak as Argyle stood and slowly walked back towards Parker, his hand raised and clutching the handle to his murderous blade.

Bermuda tried to reach out a hand, anything to stop Argyle from what he had to do.

The finality of the coming execution.

Argyle circled round, ignoring the wild calls from Black and now Vincent for him to stand down, to obey his orders. As the rain clattered against his mighty frame, he glared at the harbinger of death before him.

The Absent Man.

His father.

'Is she gone?' Parker's words were drenched in defeat.

'I'm afraid so.' Argyle felt his heart ache for his mother. 'Goodbye.'

With a swing of his blade, the entire crowd gasped in horror. The man before them slunk backwards, his throat opening in a large gash and blood spraying out like a crimson firework. Parker fell back against the pavement, the blood gurgling in his throat.

After a few moments, the sickening noises ceased.

Kevin Parker was dead.

## THIRTY-ONE

BERMUDA LIFTED off the floor as the paramedics placed him onto the gurney, the comforting mattress a welcome change from the ice cold concrete. The flashing lights of the ambulance danced with the police cars for authority, the watching faces of the crowd a mixture of flashing blue and red.

A paramedic held a massive umbrella over them as they wheel him towards the ambulance, Bermuda trying this best to see beyond them.

After Argyle had watched Parker bleed out, he had slowly lowered himself to his knees and laid his sword out before him. Unclasping the Retriever, he had placed it alongside his other weapon and then placed his hands behind his back in a show of surrender.

Parker, despite his possession, had been a human.

Argyle had murdered him in full view of the BTCO.

Bermuda had passed out through the pain as a few other agents flooded the scene, hoisting Bermuda away with only he and Black witnessing.

DC Butler berated a few officers, screaming at them to clear the path for the paramedics, demanding Bermuda get the attention he needed. Despite their animosity, Butler knew that Bermuda had sacrificed himself for his partner. He needed to be treated.

He deserved his respect.

As the paramedics had tended to him, he heard a number of horrifying injuries being listed out.

'A fractured eye socket …'

'Several cracks to the collarbone …'

'Deep lacerations to the skull …'

'Crushed left hand, possible amputation …'

None of it hurt as much as the pain of watching Argyle be marched away as a prisoner. Refusing to think of the outcome, Bermuda knew their partnership was over. Parker had been obsessed, but Argyle clearly had reason to end his life. His partner was the most caring creature spanning two worlds.

He was not a murderer.

The wheel of the trolley squeaked as they led him to the ambulance, the buzz of the crime scene humming all around him. A sheet had been thrown over the lifeless body of Kevin Parker, a senior officer taking pictures of the entire area.

Any forensics would be lost to the rain.

Before Bermuda was loaded onto the ambulance, an authoritative voice dismissed the two paramedics. As they left, along with the protection from the rain, Bermuda's headache grew as DCI Fowler loomed over him.

'Don't think this clears anything, Jones,' he threatened, enjoying Bermuda's clear anguish. 'You will be facing every inch of my wrath.'

'Mrs Fowler sounds like a lucky lady,' Bermuda muttered through his blood-soaked, broken smile.

'They will charge you, Jones. I have friends who will ensure the charges stick and you will soon be on the all-meat diet in Pentonville.'

'No he won't.'

Both men looked up with surprise as the deep voice of Montgomery Black cut the tension between them. Marching with the authority that Bermuda constantly undercut, he approached the gurney, stepping between Fowler and his injured agent.

'How dare you?'

'I dare, lad. This man, despite himself, has just done what your entire police department couldn't. He managed to figure out how to track that monster and he brought him to justice.'

'That man is dead.'

'Justice is justice.' Black spoke through gritted teeth. 'I understand he also saved the life of your detective.'

'So she says.'

'Well let me make it clearer to you. I have your superior by the balls, aye. I want to squeeze them, so he makes you disappear, I'll bloody squeeze them.' He clenched his fist to emphasise. 'Now you drop the charges against this man and fuck off.'

Fowler stood straight, his jaw pushed out in frustration. He looked deep into the unrelenting stare of Black before trading a few glances with the battered Bermuda. Sighing, he turned and walked off into the rain, barking his frustration at DI Strachan as she followed like an obedient lapdog.

'What a horrible man,' Black uttered, watching the DCI depart with disgust.

'Thanks, Monty.' Bermuda tried to lift his right thumb, the left probably gone forever.

'Well, despite everything, Jones, the usual breed of chaos, you did manage to stop Parker and save a young lady's life.' Black removed the glasses from his hooked nose, wiping them on his shirt. 'That at least deserves to be respected.'

Bermuda nodded his thanks, coughing roughly and feeling a sharp pain in his chest. Did the paramedics mention a punctured lung? Probably.

'As you know, Jones, I don't really like you. Not at all.'

'Charming,' Bermuda managed, drawing a dry smile from his superior.

'But Ottoway was right about you. You can be the balance that we need, the man who can step in both worlds and keep them both turning. With Ottoway's regrettable condition, I have been elected to perform his role in the interim. I have therefore dismissed the notion put forward by the Committee to have you removed from the agency.'

'Didn't you put that notion through, sir?' Vincent interjected, with the usual perfect timing.

Bermuda smirked.

'That is neither here nor there.' Black waved a hand dismissively. He straightened his tie before looking at Bermuda without the usual malic. 'Good job, Jones.'

Bermuda watched him trundle off, the enigma of a man doing his best to ward the demons knocking at Bermuda's door.

Vincent cast a caring eye over the crumpled mess before him. 'You don't look good, Jones.'

'Funnily enough, I don't feel that great either.'

'Quite.' Vincent's eyes scanned him. 'Several breaks, a number of of internal bleeds. You will heal but it will be painful for a few days.'

'Days,' Bermuda scoffed quietly, reminded once again of his condition. The world that had just tried to beat him to death was alive and kicking inside him. 'How did you guys find me, anyway?'

'The Oracles can track the activity of our world. After the overload at the Necropolis, we went there first. A number of soldiers slaughtered. We counted eight dead.'

Bermuda raised his eyebrows, impressed at Argyle's kill count.

Vincent continued. 'General Mandrake was found, incapacitated and ready to surrender. He has been taken back to the BTCO to be transferred back to his world for his sentence.'

'His death,' Bermuda corrected.

'His sentence.'

After a few moments of silence Bermuda turned to Vincent, his eyes slightly watering. 'What will happen to Argyle?'

Vincent paused. 'It is out of our hands now.'

'Vincent,' Bermuda snapped, a tear rolling down his cheek. 'Will they kill him?'

'I am sorry, Jones.'

Vincent turned and walked away from the growing confrontation, leaving Bermuda to drop his head back to the pillow. His left arm had been tied tightly across his chest in a sling, a bag of ice had been forced into the crushed remnants of his left hand.

'Vincent,' he called out, the senior Neither turning. 'Do right by Gordon, okay? He needs something to reach out to him.'

Vincent nodded. The homeless man who had spoken to them earlier in the evening had already been accompanied back to the BTCO HQ. They would afford him a shower and a change of clothes. Anyone who was aware of the world that enveloped humanity was an asset.

They would look after Gordon Foster.

He was one of their own.

As Vincent disappeared into the crowd, Bermuda felt the bed shift slightly before being lifted into the back of the ambulance. The paramedic, a petite lady with mousy brown hair and a cute smile, spoke calmly to Bermuda, assuring him that he was going to be okay.

He ignored her, already aware of his body piecing itself back together. Suddenly, a knock rattled the inside of the door.

'Can I have a moment?'

The young paramedic looked to Bermuda, who nodded his approval. With a smile she left the ambulance, allowing McAllister to climb up into the vehicle and take a seat next to him. Her dress, clinging to her slim body, was soaked through, but she held a towel in her hand and had evidently dried her hair slightly.

She offered him a warm smile, looking with shock at the extent of his injuries.

The sheer brutality of the beating he had taken.

For her.

Silently, a few tears ran down her cheeks.

'Bermuda, I have to say that what you did this evening was the most …' she struggled as another tear raced down after the others.

'Heroic thing ever? Brave?' Bermuda flashed his cracked grin.

She laughed, shaking her head. '*Idiotic* was the word.' She squeezed the only hand still intact. 'But you saved my life.' She leant forward and gently kissed him on the cheek.

'You're welcome.'

'I just wanted you to know that you were right. There are things I can't control in this world. What happened to my little Emily will always stay with me. But it can't dictate the rest of my life.'

'It can't,' Bermuda agreed, nodding slowly.

'I've spoken to Ethan. We have agreed to meet this weekend for dinner. Cards on the table. Get everything out.' McAllister's eyes filled with hopeful tears. 'I just want my husband back.'

Bermuda lifted his free arm and beckoned her in for a hug. She leant in, squeezing his broken body. Bermuda ignored the pain, squeezing with as much energy as he could muster before she slowly pulled away.

'Look after yourself, Bermuda.'

'You too, Sam.' He smiled. 'You too.'

She waved delicately before stepping back out into the rain, lifting the towel over her head. Butler approached her, nodding his goodbye to Bermuda, who returned in kind. The paramedic returned, closing the door, and the engine roared to life. As the ambulance pulled away, Bermuda closed his eyes.

Images of his bizarre life danced through his mind: The scarring first case he ever worked, being chased through the Cutty Sark by that dangerous creature. The jet-black eyes of Barnaby, his own fingers gripping the edges of a doorway at the top of Big Ben. He thought of Kevin Parker, the various dead women he had encountered this past week. Slowly his thoughts faded to the real world, to having a beer with Brett, discussing all things inappropriate. A flash of Sophie Summers made his heart ache.

A discussion with Angela, her voice berating him for being a lousy father to Chloe, that his delusions were dangerous. His mind raced to Ottoway, the father he never had and the inevitable journey he would soon take to the afterlife.

He thought of Argyle, his partner and loyal friend, who had once again saved his life on numerous occasions. Who had gone to war with eight of the most dangerous creatures on either side of the divide and walked away victorious.

Who had protected him at all costs.

Bermuda's one working hand clenched into a fist at the images of that sinister world welcoming Argyle home to an undoubtedly horrible fate.

Then Bermuda thought of Chloe.

His beloved daughter.

Her breathtaking smile that shone underneath her silky blond hair. Her tears when she had realised her dad hadn't called on her birthday.

The continuous strain his life had on their relationship.

As the ambulance roared through the wet Glasgow streets, Bermuda thought of his daughter and the pain slowly filtered away. The mind-numbing agony of his broken body dissolved at the very idea of her.

With the image of his daughter firmly in his mind, he slowly closed his eyes to rest.

The case was over.

He'd be with her soon.

# EPILOGUE

THE AFTERNOON SKY had already begun to darken, the wintery night doing its level best to dominate the remainder of the day. It was only ten past four, but the dark fingers of the night were creeping in through the large floor-to-ceiling windows of Ottoway's hospital room.

His bed was pressed to the far wall, poking out into the centre of the sparse room. He lay under the white quilt, his eyes firmly closed as he drifted in a medically induced sleep. Plastic tubes scattered out of him in different directions, hooking him up to a number of different machines, ready to be shocked like Frankenstein's monster.

The beeping of his heart monitor synchronised with the heaving of his breathing apparatus.

All of this just to keep him alive.

The cancer eating away at him, winning the battle against Western medicine.

Bermuda stood in the doorway in jeans and a white shirt, leant against the frame with a sullen look on his face. His fractured eye socket had healed, his eye now framed by a deep purple bruise and a smattering of cuts.

His collarbone, for the second time that month, had

healed, the bone fusing itself back together and allowing him movement. The rib that had punctured his lung had been reattached, the lung itself blocking the gap and keeping him alive.

His left arm was still strapped to his chest, his hand tightly wired to a metal cast. There was only so much they could do with a bag of dust. But they were confident that, given time, his hand would at least reform, but the muscle fibres and nerves might never recover.

Still, as Bermuda watched the closest thing he had to a father clinging desperately to life, he realised his situation wasn't so bad. It had been a week since he had been flown back from Glasgow, treated by the BTCO in their secret medical facility on one of the Shard's upper floors. With a view spanning the length and width of London, Bermuda was reminded of Ottoway once more.

The elegant chairman had always enjoyed the view, spending most of his days literally watching over the city from the viewing platform.

The city and the organisation was Ottoway's life.

A life that was slowly fading.

Bermuda cursed the world for the way it worked, allowing good people to suffer such pain while the worst got to live healthy, full lives of sin and debauchery. He was a fine one to talk, the number of beers and loose women that had passed his lips.

Things would change.

He would change.

He had already met with Brett at their local watering hole, the Royal Oak, in Bushey, the quaint pub set back from the street and surrounded by the well-maintained green and expensive houses. Sat inside the snug, rustic property, Bermuda ordered a diet Coke to the shock of the landlord, Paul.

Brett was livid.

But after a thorough explanation of what had happened, including a detailed account of Argyle's heroics for Brett's benefit, his best friend understood.

Bermuda was changing his life.

The only thing he wanted was to spend some time with his daughter. Seeing the heartbreaking pain of Sam McAllister when he had discovered her empty nursery had been a wake-up call.

He had the daughter that she was denied.

And he wasn't doing enough.

McAllister had sent him a message the day before, excitedly telling him that she and Ethan were going to make a second go of things. The marriage and family they had always planned for was back on, and she thanked him for being the worst mistake she ever made.

He replied with a middle finger emoji and congratulations.

When he had called Angela, she had instantly dismissed his notion of change. But as he had discussed his plan with her, she had slowly come around. Although their love had long since left, he admired how protective she was of their daughter.

He had to mean it.

And he had to prove it.

Starting with dinner that evening

As he stood in the doorway, offering his silent goodbye to Ottoway, he turned and almost collided with Vincent. He startled loudly before resting a hand on his chest.

'Christ, Vinny. You almost gave me a heart attack.'

'An exaggeration, I'm sure.' Vincent glided past Bermuda towards Ottoway, the man he had partnered with for sixty years.

'How is he?' Bermuda asked.

'So-so.' Vincent spoke sadly. 'We are trying our own

ways to treat him. The results are sporadic. I fear he doesn't have much time.'

'He's a great man. We all know that.'

Vincent nodded, his eyes not leaving Ottoway. 'He would respect your decision.'

'I know,' Bermuda replied, the guilt of his decision to quit the BTCO clawing at him like a scared animal.

'Is it because of Argyle?' Vincent asked, turning to face him. 'His crime is one that we cannot overlook. I assure you we have tried, but the law dictates he return to our world.'

Bermuda nodded, refusing to respond. While Argyle would face the death penalty, it was the fate he would face before then that worried Bermuda.

The Otherside despised Argyle.

The BTCO was doing nothing.

'I'm going to go, Vinny. I am going to go and spend time with my daughter.'

'Very well.' Vincent extended a thin, bony hand.

Bermuda looked at it, slapped it away, and drew him in for a hug. Taken aback, Vincent eventually patted Bermuda on the spine which no longer twisted in pain.

'Look after him, yeah?'

'Of course.' Vincent released him. 'What will you do now?'

'I don't know.' Bermuda shrugged. 'Tram driver?'

Vincent looked at him blankly. 'You know where we are.'

'Yeah.' Bermuda patted him on the arm. 'You guys still owe me a new car.'

Vincent smiled, a rarity that caught Bermuda unaware, like when a dog winks.

'I'm sure Mr Black will be thrilled.' Vincent nodded knowingly. 'Remember, Jones. Two worlds.'

'One peace.'

With that, Bermuda turned and left the medical centre, riding the fastest lift in London down to the ground floor before navigating his way through the gift shop. He stepped out into the cold, wrapping his coat around his body and walking away from the BTCO HQ.

He stepped into London Bridge Station, ignoring the Other that sat in the cold, dark corner of the platform.

Venturing deeper and deeper underground, he eventually appeared on the Northern Line platform, hopping onto a train that was just about to depart.

It would take him to Euston where he would get the over ground to Bushey. The train grunted to life and disappeared into the darkness.

A smile cracked on Bermuda's scarred face.

He was heading home.

# BERMUDA JONES CASEFILES

*DOORWAYS*

*THE ABSENT MAN*

## SAM POPE NOVELS

Did you know I also have another series? The Sam Pope books have hit No.1 in several charts in several countries. If you like non-stop, high octane action, then Sam Pope is the man for you!

*THE NIGHT SHIFT*

*THE TAKERS*

*LONG ROAD HOME*

*TOO FAR GONE*

*THE FINAL MILE*

## ABOUT THE AUTHOR

Robert lives in Buckinghamshire with his family, writing books and dreaming of getting a dog.

For more information:
www.robertenright.co.uk
robert@robertenright.co.uk

You can also connect with Robert on Social Media:

facebook.com/robenrightauthor
twitter.com/REnright_Author
instagram.com/robenrightauthor

# THE POWER OF REVIEWS

As a self-published author, I am in charge of all my own marketing and promoting. One of the most powerful tools are reviews, which not only help other readers to buy my books, but can also help me gain more visibility with Amazon and get them to advertise my books for me.

If you enjoyed THE ABSENT MAN, please could you consider leaving me a review wherever you purchased the book.

Thanks for reading and your support!

COPYRIGHT © ROBERT ENRIGHT, 2018

All rights reserved. No part of this publication may be reproduced, stored in a retrieval system, or transmitted in any form or by any means, electronic, photocopying, mechanical, recording, or otherwise, without the prior permission of the copyright owner.

All characters in this book are fictitious and any resemblance to actual persons living or dead is purely coincidental.

Cover by The Cover Collection

Edited by Amy Jackson

Printed in Great Britain
by Amazon